LEGACY OF THE REANIMATOR

Also from Chaosium

Lovecraftian Fiction

The Antarktos Cycle

Arkham Tales

Atomic Age Cthulhu (Coming Soon)

The Book of Eibon

Cthulhu's Dark Cults

Eldritch Chrome

Frontier Cthulhu

The Hastur Cycle

The Innsmouth Cycle

The Ithaqua Cycle

The Klarkash-Ton Cycle

Madness on the Orient Express (New)

The Necronomicon

The Nyarlathotep Cycle

Steampunk Cthulhu

The Strange Cases of Rudolph Pearson by William Jones

Tales out of Innsmouth

The Tsathoggua Cycle

Twice Upon an Apocalypse (Coming Soon)

The Xothic Legend Cycle

The Yith Cycle

Weird Fiction Collections

The Complete Pegana by Lord Dunsany

Eldritch Evolutions by Lois Gresh

Mysteries of the Worm by Robert Bloch

The Terror & Other Stories by Arthur Machen

The Three Impostors & Other Stories by Arthur Machen

The White People & Other Stories by Arthur Machen

The Yellow Sign and Other Stories by Robert W. Chambers

Science Fiction

A Long Way Home

Extreme Planets

Horror

Edge of Sundown (Coming Soon)

Once Upon an Apocalypse

Undead & Unbound

Occult Texts

The Book of Dyzan

LEGACY OF THE REANIMATOR

EDITED BY

PETER RAWLIK

&

BRIAN M. SAMMONS

Legacy of the Reanimator
Edited by Peter Rawlik & Brian M. Sammons.
Legacy of the Reanimator is published by Chaosium Inc.

Cover and Interior Design by Nicholas Nacario

www.chaosium.com.

Contents

Introduction

That Tow-Headed Fiend

I never set out to be Herbert West's biographer. It wasn't my plan. I just needed him, used him as a McGuffin to motivate my own character Doctor Stuart Hartwell in my novel, *Reanimators.* I needed West to have an enemy and an equal, someone who would have all his abilities when it came to the reanimation of the dead, but none of his storyline. You see at the time I was writing *Reanimators*, Doctor Herbert West had a seriously complicated storyline. I mean at one point he's working for the Nazis.

You knew that right?

No?

Let me explain.

Herbert West didn't die. Well yes he did. The problem is he didn't stay dead. He was brought back in two round robins edited by Robert m. Price. The first was *Herbert West-Reanimated* followed by *Herbert West—Reincarnated.* These were published in old issues of Crypt of Cthulhu, and are terribly hard to get a hold of. I being the obsessive collector had copies and used the events contained in these stories as gospel while I was writing *Reanimators.* I thought I was being clever. I made sure that my novel stayed faithful to events in "Herbert West-Reanimator", "The Dunwich Horror", "The Shadow Over Innsmouth", "The Dreams in the Witch House", and these two round-robin sequels. That last part didn't matter much because I hadn't realized how rare, how legendary, these stories actually were.

After *Reanimators* came out I got branded as the Reanimator guru. I knew a lot about West, not because I was a fan of the character, but because I'm a fan of continuity and understanding how things fit together, to me timelines matter. That didn't make a bit of difference people pegged me as the expert on Herbert West. Not that I regretted it. But I should have kept my mouth shut at this point.

But there I was reminiscing about high school and how I once stole my grandmother's Buick Skylark to go see a movie. And then I realized that the move was *Re-Animator*, and the year was 1985, and soon the Thirtieth Anniversary would be upon us, and wouldn't it be cool to do a tribute anthology. I said that on Facebook.

I had my first volunteer in 18 minutes. By the end of the hour I had an email from a publisher asking me to pitch the idea.

My wife used the words WHAT HAVE YOU DONE!

Thankfully my friend and frequent editor, Brian M. Sammons, was there to pull my fat out of the fire and set me on a track to get this thing out of my head and into the real world.

At one point I said "Let's gather up all the existing Herbert West fiction into one volume publish it, after all, how much could there be." I thought I knew. The truth is I knew so little.

One of our priorities was to get the round robins all in one volume. Getting in contact with the authors and their estates was no easy task. Then of course we had to include Lovecraft's original story. We also wanted to include Molly Tanzer's subversive prequel, "Herbert West in Love", and one of Tim Curran's Herbert West stories, "Charnel House", though his longer piece "Morbid Anatomy" is equally as good and is worth seeking out. We also excluded Robert M. Price's "The Thing from the Trenches" as he was already represented in the book three times, and was included in his collection *Blasphemies and Revelations*. From the episodic novel by Ron Shiflet and Glynn Owen Barrass *Two Against Darkness*, which has several appearances by the mad doctor, we took the story, "A Man Called West."

We also, for practical reasons, had to exclude novels, most notably CJ Henderson's excellent *An Eternity of Self* (currently out of print), which is a direct sequel to the round robins. Also of note are the novels by Audrey Driscoll entitled *The Friendship of Mortals, Islands of the Gulf* and *Hunting the Phoenix* which can be viewed as stories about Herbert West in an alternate universe with very different characters.

Finally, items not included here were works of my own, including "The Issue of Doctor Jekyll" and "Pickman's Marble", both of which I plan to include in my forthcoming novel concerning the life and death of Megan Halsey, *Reanimatrix*. I would hope that you buy that book, and never want to be accused of double dipping (too often) on a story.

To offset these losses, Brian and I went to our colleagues and sought out new tales of the good doctor to thrill you with. Christine Morgan provides "Thought He Was a Goner" a rather touching tale of schoolyard life (and death) that shows us how West may have got his start. Fantasist Richard Lee Byers tackles the tough question about why the unnamed narrator never seems to stray in "The Horror on the Freighter." Dave Bernard mixes fiction with fact in a rather gruesome little episode that could only have happened in "The Crypt in Key West." The erudite Rick Lai digs deep into the mysterious Orient and forges links to obscure Lovecraftian lore in "Cruel Heaven." Finally, Edward Morris merges Herbert West's methods with the outsider teen and gives us the quintessential "Blood and Guts in High School."

Here is Herbert West fleshed out, and far beyond the madman that HP Lovecraft portrayed him as. Thanks to the authors of this book I know more about Herbert West than I did, but with every mystery and character quirk explored, new ones are raised, and there are still things about the doctor that I would like to explore. Maybe someday soon I'll have that opportunity.

Until then we will always have *The Legacy of the Reanimator.*

After all, death is just the beginning.

— Pete Rawlik

Thought He Was a Goner

Christine Morgan

"Go on." Mary Norris gave Sarah a nudge. "Go talk to him."

Sarah took a half-step, then hesitated. "Do you really think I ought to?"

"Well, I wouldn't." Rolling her eyes, Mary affected the worldly manner of their teacher, Miss Phelps. "But, since you fancy him, you might as well."

"Mary fancies Tommy Lowgate," Cecily confided to Peg and Meg, without glancing up from the hopscotch she'd almost finished drawing.

"I do not!" cried Mary, blushing the bright hue of a hothouse rose.

It might have been becoming on another girl. On sunny-blonde Cecily, perhaps. Or Sarah herself, whose curls were as black and shiny and glossy as fresh ink. On carrot-topped Mary, with her freckly cheese-curd complexion, the effect was fevered and blotchy.

Peg and Meg, twins, cupped their hands over their mouths and tittered. Mary blushed brighter than ever. She threw a quick look in the direction of the other girls, but the older ones were chatting beside the lunch-room with the older boys, and the younger ones from Mrs. Daunley's class had a jumping-rope and sang that new song about the man with the cat he couldn't get rid of no matter how hard he tried.

"... but the cat came back ... the very next day ..."

Sarah, twirling a ringlet, gazed over at the boy who sat reading in the shade of the big spreading oak.

"... yes, the cat came back ..."

The new boy.

Herbie West.

Beyond him, on a grassy sward, his classmates ran and shouted and kicked a ball back and forth. The smaller boys, armed with sticks, played war.

"... they thought he was a goner ..."

At lunch, Herbie West never threw crusts or spat cherry pips. During study-hour, he didn't draw rude sketches, pull girls' pigtails, make faces, or whisper when the headmaster stepped into the hall for a nip of what he called 'the revivifying,' from the flask he kept in his coat.

"... but the cat came back ..."

No, Herbie West sat just as he sat now, by himself. Sat by himself and read.

"... he just wouldn't stay away!"

Quiet. Polite and soft-spoken, as Sarah's mother would have said.

And smart, too. Sarah had overheard Mr. Pym telling Miss Phelps that the West boy was "sharp as a tack, smart as a whip, cleverest student I've ever had ... but insolent ... you wouldn't know it to look at him, meek as he is, but twice now he's corrected me in front of the entire class."

Sarah thought this was especially brave. Much braver and much cleverer than most boys, whose idea of wit was to make fake flatulence-noises and blame them on each other.

"But she's right," Cecily said. "Recess won't last much longer. Go talk to him. Don't be a ninny."

"Do I look nice?" Sarah asked.

"Yes," grumbled Mary.

The twins vigorously agreed.

She considered skipping, but decided against it and went at an idle-seeming stroll instead, as if she were simply going for a walk around the schoolyard that happened to bring her course near the big spreading oak.

As she approached, she let herself steal several peeks at him, though always ready to quickly pretend not to be, just in case he noticed.

Herbie West wasn't a tall boy. He was thin, and quite pale, with fine hair the color of buttermilk. His eyes, behind spectacles, were a very light blue. They remained fixed intently on his book, a great heavy thick thing unlike their school readers and primers. Sarah saw that the pages were covered with dense printing, big words in small letters, blocks of it broken only by diagrams and illustrations.

Feeling suddenly both giddy and shy, she stopped just within the patch of cool shade. She twisted her toe against the grass, turning her ankle this way and that.

"Hello, Herbie," she said.

He twitched as if she'd startled him, and shut the book with a musty kind of thump. His light blue eyes were wide through the lenses.

"Hello," she said again, smiling.

"I prefer to be addressed as Herbert," he said. He had such a soft voice, she had to lean forward to hear. "Or West, if you rather."

"Oh … sorry … Herbert." She bolstered her smile, which tried to falter, and resumed twirling the long black ringlet that dangled beside her cheek. "I'm Sarah. Sarah Grantham."

Herbert West nodded. There followed a slight, awkward pause.

"What are you reading?" Sarah asked brightly.

"Nothing of interest to you." He placed a hand on the cover. "A medical book."

"Medical? You mean, doctoring?"

"Sort of."

"Sort of? How so?"

"It's to do with …" Herbert took a breath. "It's to do with anatomy and dissections."

"With what and what?" She frowned, but made sure it was her pretty frown, not the sulky one her mother said made her look like a bulldog deprived its bone.

"Anatomy is the study of human physiology. Dissection is the more practical method of determining form and function through surgical exploration—"

Sarah tilted her head. "Cutting up dead people?"

He winced ever-so-slightly, one eye narrowing and the corner of his mouth on that side tucking into a tight line. "Dissecting cadavers."

"Have you done that?"

"No." The wince deepened into a brief scowl, then smoothed. "But I will, one day. I'm going to attend the medical school at Miskatonic University. Soon. Headmaster Abelton says I'll be an excellent candidate for early admission."

Most of that made scant sense to Sarah, but she didn't let on. She skipped up next to him and sat down, smoothing her skirt over her knees. "My grandfather died last winter," she said.

This, she reasoned, would give them something in common – rumor had it that his parents had both recently died, which was why he'd been sent here to live with his two maiden aunties.

Herbert West, however, did not seem inclined to commiserate over shared losses. "Did you see him?"

"No! He died in the hospital."

"I meant, after that. For a funeral."

"Oh," said Sarah. "Oh, yes. We had him laid out in the parlor for a few days, so that everyone could pay their respects while waiting for my uncle and his family to come from Chicago."

"So, you did see him. What was it like?"

She tilted her head the other way. "Not like he was sleeping. That's what they all said, how peaceful he looked, like he was sleeping, but I didn't think so."

"What did you think?"

"He looked … dead," she said. "He was all grey, his lips blue. Sunken-looking. Stiff and cold. His skin felt—" She caught herself with a guilty squirm.

But Herbert hadn't missed her slip. "You touched him?"

"My cousins and I, we dared each other," Sarah admitted. "I touched his hand. Where it was, you know, folded like this on his chest."

His nod this time was encouraging. "How did it feel?"

"Stiff and cold, like I said, but also … I don't really know."

"Waxy? Like a candle, or a cake of soap?"

"Yes! Yes, just like that! Not quite greasy, but somehow kind of …"

"Clammy and slick?"

"Yes!" she cried again, and clapped with delight. "You are the smartest boy in school, aren't you?"

"At this school, there's hardly much competition," he muttered.

"Well, I think you're the most smart and clever boy ever!" She attempted a winsome fluttering of her eyelashes. "And the handsomest."

He seemed not to know at all what to make of that, and certainly didn't rally back with a compliment for her beauty. Boys were so hopeless sometimes, honestly they were. Not that grown men were much different; Sarah often witnessed her own father needing pointed prompts to remark on Mother's new dress or hair style.

Before Herbert could decide what – if anything – to say, a giggling whirlwind of girls rushed to surround them. Not only her friends, but the younger girls from Mrs. Daunley's class – the ones who'd been jumping-rope while singing the cat song – and a few of the older ones as well.

Mary, of course, led the chant. "Herbie and Sarah, sittin' in a tree—"

"K-I-S-S-I-N-G!" the rest joined in.

"Stop!" squealed Sarah, giggling herself. And, she suspected, blushing her own shade of hothouse pink.

"First comes love," the girls chanted on, undaunted, "then comes marriage ... then comes Herbie with the baby carriage!"

"I prefer," he repeated, "to be addressed as Herbert."

The other boys, distracted from their game, had turned to look. Among them was Sebastian Crewe, who'd made no secret of fancying Sarah, while she in turn made no secret of not fancying him. Seeing her there with Herbert West, as the silly-chanting girls capered, he glowered. He threw down the ball with such a hard bounce that it soared over Tommy's head and rolled all the way to the schoolyard fence. Sebastian stomped after it with his face like a thundercloud.

At the main door, Miss Phelps rang the bell. Everyone began dispersing, gathering their things, getting ready to go back in. Herbert got to his feet, clutching his medical book.

"May I sit and talk with you again at recess tomorrow?" she asked, also rising, demurely brushing grass from her skirt.

He shrugged in a fitful, fidgety manner. "I suppose." His gaze strayed impatiently toward the school, where some of their classmates were already headed up the steps.

"Herbert?"

He looked at her, light blue eyes quizzical through his spectacles.

"You could, you know," she said. "If you like."

"Could what?"

She clasped her hands at the small of her back, bent forward, lifted her chin, and puckered her lips. Closed her eyes, too ... mostly ... peeking the teensiest bit to see his reaction ...

Recoiling with a look of alarm was not what she'd been hoping for.

"The bell," Herbert said. "Mr. Pym doesn't approve of tardiness."

With that, he was off, not at a run but at a pace almost brisk enough to be insulting. Sarah blew out a breath in an exasperated sigh.

Boys. They honestly were hopeless, weren't they?

Sarah could hardly wait until recess the next day. It was difficult going, too, what with a packet of licorice candy in her possession. But if she so much as ate one piece, the other girls would see and want to share, and she had to save them for later.

"You oughtn't go about with him," Sebastian Crewe told her at lunch-time, lagging behind the other boys while the girls helped clean up. "With West. He's peculiar."

"I think he's nice," said Sarah.

"Peculiar," Sebastian insisted. "Too smart for his own good, that's what Mr. Pym says. Always going on about dead things and brains and such. He told our whole class that if you stuck a wire into a frog's head, you could make it kick its legs."

"Eew."

"Eew's right, and that's not the half of it! So, you oughtn't go about with him."

"Who I go about with or not isn't your concern."

"Sure it is. You're my girl."

"Says who and since when?"

"Everyone knows!"

"I didn't!"

"Well, now you do."

"Fancy that!" Sarah cried, flinging her hands in the air. "You don't get to be telling me whose girl I am!"

"I only meant—"

Miss Phelps came in then, ending the conversation with a stern look that sent Sebastian hurrying on his way as Sarah busied herself dutifully with cleaning.

The nerve of him … saying she was his girl, telling her who she could talk to! Hmf!

When the recess bell finally rang, Sarah made no secret of her destination. She went bold-as-brass right over to the oak tree, and sat there with the packet of candies in her lap, waiting for Herbert West.

He arrived a bit late, clothes rumpled and spectacles askew, a cigar box tucked under one arm.

"What happened to you?" Sarah asked, though she already half had an idea, as if she couldn't guess.

"Nothing. Someone bumped me in the hallway, almost knocked me down."

"Sebastian?"

Herbert sat on the shady grass, straightening his spectacles. "He swears it was an accident."

"Oh, yes."

"But he also tried to trip me, so pardon me if I have my doubts."

"Herbert, I'm so sorry."

"Why? You weren't there. The other boys often pull pranks. They don't like that I'm good at lessons, and they make fun of me for living with my aunts."

She decided there was no need to explain. Why waste their recess on that? Besides, she noticed the cigar box and couldn't help but wonder what was in it. She'd brought licorice candies, after all … perhaps he'd brought cookies or toffees or some other sweets.

"No book today?" she inquired, twirling her ringlet.

"I didn't want to leave this in my desk."

"What's in it?" She started to reach for the lid and Herbert drew the box toward his knee.

"Mice," he said.

"Mice?" Sarah snatched her hand back. "Why do you have mice in a box?"

"Aunt Gertrude keeps them as pets. Aunt Ludmilla keeps budgies, but the mice are better. Not as good as rabbits, but, better."

"Mice?" she said again.

"Not ordinary mice," he said. "Not common field mice. These are fancy mice. They're becoming quite popular in London. Aunt Gertrude has a friend there, Mr. Maxey, who raises them. Breeds them."

"May I see?"

"I don't think you want to."

"Herbert West, I am not some kind of silly, skittish girl who cries eek at the sight of a mouse!"

"Well --"

"Show me!"

He sighed and opened the box. Sarah steeled herself to look. She wasn't sure how a 'fancy' mouse might differ from the ordinary kind, but –

But she certainly had never seen mice like these before. Not … not tacked out on a board with all four little pink paws pinned and the furry belly sliced open … not bobbing in a jam-jar of murky liquid with the top of the head missing …

That the mice were also, in fact, fluffy and cream-colored with pretty markings … was rather of far secondary importance.

"They're dead," she said.

"Of course. I brought them to show the class, for my report on biological studies."

"Why are they cut up that way?"

"I'm interested in the mechanics of life. It is my belief and theory that, somewhere, perhaps in the brain or central nervous system, is the key to what animates us, what makes us live. And that if those secrets can be unlocked, we'll have mastered the mystery of immortality."

She gazed at him with admiration as he made this fervent speech, the most she'd ever heard him say at once and by far the most impassioned. His light blue eyes fair to shone with excitement.

He, however, must have mistaken her expression for confusion, because he sagged somewhat. "You wouldn't understand."

"No, I do. You want to bring them back to life. Like my cousin's goldie-fishie, or the cat in the song."

"What?"

"My cousin," said Sarah, lowering the lid to conceal the sad sight of the splayed-open mouse, "has a goldie-fishie that she keeps in a bowl on her dresser. One day, she found it there … you know … floating. She was terribly sad, cried and cried. So, her father, my uncle, told her to say extra prayers that night at bedtime, and perhaps God would bring it back. When she woke in the morning, there the fishie was, swimming around good as new."

Herbert tucked down the corner of his mouth in a rather dubious sort of way.

"It's true!" she said. "My cousin says it's exactly the same as ever, except for one white spot just on its head, where the angels kissed it alive again."

He removed his spectacles long enough to rub his closed eyes and pinch the bridge of his nose, the way Sarah's mother did when she had one of her headaches. "And the cat?"

"In that new song. The little girls were singing it just yesterday while they jumped rope."

"I wasn't listening."

"It's about a man who can't get rid of his cat. No matter what he does, the cat keeps coming back. He sends it away on a boat, and the boat sinks but the cat comes back. Then he tries a train, but the train goes off the rails and the cat comes back. He even tries dynamite."

"That's absurd," said Herbert.

"That's how the song goes." She cleared her throat, daintily, and sang. "Ole Mr. Johnson had troubles of his own … he had a yellow cat that wouldn't leave his home … he tried and he tried to give the cat away … but the cat came back the very next day! Yes, the cat came back … they thought he was a goner but … the cat came back … he just wouldn't stay away!"

"No, I meant, I believe you that's how the song goes," he said. "But you can't think it's true."

"Why not? Cats do have nine lives, after all." She giggled.

"If you're going to tease and make fun of me, too—"

"I'm not, honestly!" She held out the paper packet. "Would you like a licorice candy?"

He studied her a moment longer, wary, then relented just when she thought he was going to pick up his cigar box and go. "Yes, please."

So they sat, and shared the candies. She did most of the talking, not quite chattering like a magpie. It did not escape her attention that Sebastian glared at them throughout the rest of recess.

Nor did it escape her attention that, after school, instead of taking his usual route home, Sebastian – with a furtive air – went by way of the winding lane through Owl's Green. Following Herbert West, whose aunties lived in a ramshackle old house on the other side.

Sarah caught up with them on the wooded hill above the creek. She heard them before she saw them, too … or, rather, heard Sebastian.

"… my girl!"

There must have been some scuffling already; Herbert's shirt was untucked and his spectacles hung on crooked by an earpiece. His eyes burned pale gas-flame blue with anger. Their book-satchels, and the box of dead mice, had been dropped on the path.

"I didn't do anything," Herbert said, smacking away the accusing finger Sebastian jabbed at his face. "Point that at me again, and I'll break it, see if I don't."

"I'd like to see you try --"

"Sebastian!" she cried, rushing toward the boys. "Stop it!"

"Go away, Sarah!"

"I said, stop it! Leave him be!"

She hadn't known she could push so hard.

Sebastian yelled, arms pinwheeling, as he stumbled backward. Chunks of dark, crumbly soil gave way under his heels. Roots tore like little threads. Herbert grabbed for him but missed. And Sebastian plunged over the edge.

He landed headfirst on the rocks, with an awful crunching thud. His body went all loose, flopping into the mud and muck.

"Ooh, we'll be in trouble!" fretted Sarah as she and Herbert scrambled down the embankment. "Is he dead? Do you think he's dead?"

"He must be, after such a fall."

"Well, do something!"

"Me? You're the one who pushed him."

"You're the one who's supposed to be such an excellent candidate for early admission to medical school at Miskatonic University!"

He blinked, then puffed up a bit, as if impressed she remembered. What a time for him to not be quite so hopeless after all!

They reached the bottom without falling themselves. The creek was low. Sebastian sprawled face up on the bank, feet in the mud, a hand in the rippling water, surrounded by the loose earth he'd taken down with him

One eye was shut, the other open with the white part gone reddish. Darker red trickles ran from his nose and mouth. Herbert crouched over him, first pressing his fingers to Sebastian's neck, then bending to set his ear to the other boy's chest.

Sarah felt sick, as if she were going to vomit up her lunch – not to mention all those licorice candies. Or if she might faint, the way ladies did, with a gasp and lifting her wrist to her brow.

Yet she also felt strangely curious, interested. Distant from everything, somehow, the way she felt about stories in the newspaper that took place far away, but were still exciting to read.

It was Sebastian there, Sebastian Crewe; she knew it was.

Or was it?

His face didn't look the same. Parts of it looked lumpy, pushed out of place. And his eyes, of course, his eyes definitely didn't look the same. His body lay limp, disjointed.

The longer she stared at him, the more it really did begin to seem it wasn't Sebastian at all. More as if someone had made a fairly cunning likeness, a scarecrow or boy-sized rag doll, and dressed it in Sebastian's clothes and a wig.

But it was Sebastian, it was!

Wasn't it?

"If he is," she said, "if he's dead, I mean, you can fix it, can't you? You can bring him back. Like the cat in the song, and my cousin's goldie-fishie. Or, wait, I know! The headmaster!"

"What are you yammering about?"

"That flask he keeps in his coat! The revivifying, he calls it. We asked Miss Phelps once and she said it means something to liven a person up … then she whispered something to Mrs. Daunley about how the old goat hardly needed it. But it might help, mightn't it? If we could get Sebastian to drink some?"

Herbert gave her an impatient, scornful look. "It's only gin, or whiskey, in that flask. You'd need something far stronger and more chemically complex to …" He trailed off, his expression becoming thoughtful. "… hmm, though I do wonder …"

"Never mind it then!" said Sarah. "What about Sebastian?"

"His skull's fractured in several places," Herbert said, probing at the hairy, bloody mess that was the back of Sebastian's head. "The dura is torn … look … you can even see his brain …"

Sarah wrung her hands. "Is he going to be all right?"

Fascinated, Herbert ignored her question. He took a slim wooden pencil from his pocket and poked around with it. He wiggled the pencil. He twisted it like a corkscrew, working it deeper. It made ghastly scraping and squishing noises.

Suddenly, Sebastian's arms and legs jerked, wild spasmodic jerks like a puppet with tangled strings.

"He moved!" Sarah squealed, skittering a step back.

"Reflex," said Herbert, almost absently, wiping his fingers on his shirt to take a better grip on the pencil. "Involuntary. Nerve impulses responding to stimulation of the motor cortex—"

"Yes, fine. But it's helping! He's moving! Do it again!"

"All right." He turned Sebastian's head to the side.

Sarah tried not to grimace at the sounds of the pencil digging around in the broken skull. It grated against bone, which was bad. And squelched in brains, which was worse. The juicy squelching reminded her of Sunday suppers as her father carved a nice fat roasted chicken.

Sebastian's whole body bucked and lurched. His back arched up from the ground. His hands beat the air as if swatting invisible flies. His left leg drummed madly, the way a dog's might during a vigorous rib-scratching. He thumped down again with a gurgling groan.

"You did it!" Sarah cried. She hopped up and down, clapping. "Whew, and good thing too. I thought he was a goner!"

"Oh, he is." Herbert prodded some more. A strange, cold grin curved his lips as he watched Sebastian's fingers twitch.

"But, he moved," she said.

"That was me," Herbert said. "Manipulating the pencil within his brain triggers muscle movement."

"You did that? You made his legs move and his fingers twitch?"

"Yes."

She clapped again. "What else can you make him do?"

Herbert sat back on his heels and looked at her then, a long and rather odd look. Not the warm and admiring kind of look a girl might hope for from a boy, but a cool, evaluating one. He absently pushed his spectacles further up his nose as he did so, leaving a reddish mark on his fair skin and the smudge of a thumbprint on one glass lens.

"What else can I make him do?" he repeated, askance.

Sarah nodded vigorously. "Can you make him sit up? Walk? Talk? Do a funny dance?"

"A funny dance? You do realize, he's dead."

"Are you sure?"

"Fairly."

"We killed him?"

"You killed him. You pushed him off."

"Well, you stuck a pencil in his brains."

"Only after the fall broke his skull."

"You still did. Besides, how can he be dead if he's moving?"

"I told you," Herbert said, with an impatient sigh.

"The pencil, nerves, motor cortex, fine-fine-fine-yes." She flapped her hand. "But if you can make him move, make him walk, then it's all right."

"Just how, exactly, is it all right?"

"We won't get in trouble. No one will have to know."

"His skull's smashed open."

"Then he can wear a cap! Honestly, Herbert West! Now, stand him up. Can you, or can't you?"

He set his jaw, showing that his pride had been stung. "Perhaps."

"Then get on with it." Sarah stepped daintily around to the other side of Sebastian and leaned over to peer into his lumpy, distorted face.

Funny, she no longer felt sick in the slightest. A momentary qualm from the licorice candies, no doubt. After all, while this was Sebastian, it really wasn't, was it? Not the Sebastian Crewe she'd known since forever, lively and bothersome.

His open eye, the one that had gone bloodshot, gazed past her toward the treetops with a blank, empty stare. She wondered, if she shined a light and peered very close into his dilated pupil, she might see the pencil's tip working around back there.

"This makes the fingers twitch ..." Herbert murmured as he fiddled and poked. "And this, the legs ..."

"Stand him up," Sarah urged. "What about his eye, can you open his other eye? He can't go home or around town with one eye shut. Someone will notice."

"I'm trying. And don't you think they'll notice if I'm walking behind him every step, wiggling a pencil in the back of his head?"

"Don't be silly."

Herbert hissed a breath through his teeth. He seemed on the verge of carrying on the argument, but at that moment a muffled sound like the crackle of gristle came from deep inside Sebastian's head and the pencil sank in another half-inch.

Sebastian's whole body lurched. The shut eyelid flew wide open – though that eye was, itself, canted off at an angle not the same as the other. His chest and stomach heaved. A choked, gurgling noise burst from his throat.

"Hhchhgluurk!" said Sebastian, or something like that.

His right arm flung suddenly upward in a clumsy arc. The back of his hand smacked Sarah on the hip, then slid down her leg, leaving a muddy blotch. His hooked fingers snag-tangled at her skirt.

She yelped, skipping back, snatching her skirt from his grip. His hand landed on her shoe. With another yelp, she kicked it away. It plopped into the creek again with a splash.

Sarah turned to Herbert, whose whole face was alight with excitement.

"Did you see—?" he began.

"That wasn't funny!" she cut in.

"What? But ... you told me to ..."

"Not to make him grab me. How rude!"

"I didn't try to make him grab you. It was involuntary, like I said."

"Well, it wasn't funny!"

His lips quirked, as if holding back a smile. It brought out a dimple, just one hidden lopsided dimple, on his cheek. If she truly had been very cross with him, she couldn't have stayed that way long. Not confronted with such an adorable dimple.

Doing her best to look cross nonetheless, she folded her arms with a huff, the way she'd often seen her mother do.

"But didn't you see?" cried Herbert, half in frustration, half in delighted exuberance. "He moved, he even vocalized!"

"Hmf," said Sarah.

Finally, he said, "Fine, fine; I'm sorry," in the by-rote tone they all used when lectured by a teacher. Then a devilish kind of sparkle lit his pale blue eyes. "And he's sorry, too. Tell Sarah you're sorry, Sebastian." He gave the pencil another corkscrew twist.

Instead, Sebastian's whole body lunged up from the ground. "Ggl-lyaaachhk!" He tottered in an unsteady, staggering circle. His arms waved. His fingers jerked in spasmodic, clutching fists.

"Yes! Look at him! He's up! That's independent, volitional motion! Not mere reflex!" Herbert nearly danced with glee, and Sarah thought that surely he must, in the spirit of exuberance, kiss her now.

She did the prim-and-pretty forward lean again, but all Herbert did was continue to babble about the motor cortex, staring at Sebastian lurching back and forth.

Then Sebastian made a blundering but decisive grab for Herbert. "Grahhhh!"

Herbert ducked away from the groping hands, uttering a yelp that sounded more excited than scared. "Did you see? He's attacking me!"

"He's trying to kill you!"

"Acting entirely on his own!"

"Sebastian!" Sarah shouted. "Stop it!"

Sebastian did not stop it. His ankles knocked together stupidly as he stumbled toward Herbert. Awful noises, grunting and groaning and gobbling noises, spewed from his mouth. So did bubbles of slobbering drool. It was quite, quite disgusting.

"Herbert, make him quit!"

"... doesn't seem able to speak, but ..."

A moment later, neither was Herbert, because Sebastian had him by the neck.

"Oh, honestly!" Sarah dashed up behind Sebastian and drove the heel of her hand hard against the end of the pencil, where it jutted out from his blood-matted dark hair.

The sensation of it was indescribably horrid, a sinking gelatinous but chunky squish, like sticking the handle of a wooden spoon into a mound of cold veal scraps encased in aspic jelly. Sebastian stiffened up on his tip-toes, quivering all over, and pitched headlong to collapse bonelessly face-down in the mud. Then he stopped moving altogether.

"Herbert? Are you all right?"

"What—" He coughed, rubbing his throat. "What did you do?"

"He was hurting you. I stopped him."

"You killed him."

"You said he was already a goner."

"Yes, but ..." Herbert knelt beside Sebastian, lifted a limp arm by the wrist, and let it drop. He heaved a sigh.

It was hardly the note of thanks she'd expected. She waited. She tapped her foot a little. But Herbert just kept peering and poking.

"Well, you're welcome," Sarah finally said, letting a sharp little hint of indignation show.

"Hm?" Adjusting his spectacles, he glanced up as if surprised to see her still standing there.

"I saved your life!"

"Oh. Mm-hmm." He pinched the end of the pencil and wiggled it. The only response was a thick dribble from the hole in the back of Sebastian's head. "Hand me that stick, would you?"

She bent and picked up a stick by her shoe. "This one?"

"Yes. And that rock ... no, the other, the flat one with the edge ..."

"Why?"

"I need to open his skull if I'm to get a better look at his brain. Once I pry up this piece, here ..."

"But he's dead."

"I know." That avid, excited sparkle had returned to his pale blue eyes. "He's dead now. He was dead before. But, for a while in between, he wasn't. All I have to do is figure out how."

Herbert West in Love

Molly Tanzer

It was the last day of the last week of the fall semester. Outside the smudged panes of the classroom's high rectangular windows snowflakes were slowly accumulating in the boughs and hollows of the trees; drifted down from the leaden sky to carpet the quad. Inside the classroom, most of the students dandled their pencils over their notebooks as they ignored the lecture, choosing instead to watch the slow transformation of the bland, institutional buildings of Miskatonic University into a Christmas picture-postcard.

Most, but not all.

A boy called West sat in the back row, hand aloft, arm quivering with tension. Behind his thick spectacles his eyes were firmly fixed upon the professor as the man scrawled "voluntas aegroti suprema lex" across the board. When the chalk squeaked halfway through suprema, West was the only student who did not flinch.

"I know we covered this fundamental of medical ethics—respecting the supremacy of the patient's will—in our very first unit," said Dr. Masheck Quinley, his tweed-swathed back still turned to the class, "but since you will be essaying on this idea as part of your final exam, I feel it would behoove us to review it." Without turning around, he sighed as he scraped the final hatch-mark of the x in lex and said, "Yes, Mr. West?"

The classroom momentarily transformed into a viper pit as sighs hissed out of many, many mouths. West, undeterred, lowered his hand, cleared his throat, and pushed his glasses up the bridge of his aquiline nose before speaking.

"Will we also be asked to essay on salus aegroti suprema lex?" he asked.

Dr. Quinley's voice was clipped and precise when he answered. "Of course, Mr. West. We covered 'beneficence,' or acting in our patients' best interest, in that same unit." He smiled unpleasantly. "Don't you remember? How surprising; all semester long we've heard so much about your amazing powers of recollection."

"It's not that I don't remember," snapped West, "it's that we never resolved how to negotiate the intersection of these, as you put it, fundamental concepts. I still don't understand why a patient's opinion is considered more important than his physician's! How can we, as doctors, possibly be expected to accept the idea that any random, uneducated person is more qualified to make decisions about his health than someone with an advanced degree in medicine? How could letting a patient make those decisions be acting in his best interest?"

"Don't let him get started, please," said a boy off to West's left. It was Reginald Gurganus, another first-year medical student. Physically the reverse of West, he was tall and placidly handsome, just the sort of fellow who would put a sick person at ease. West openly despised him, and the feeling had become mutual over the course of the semester. "He'll take over the whole class if you let him, and a bunch of us want to review that human experimentation case where—"

"I have the floor!" West's voice, never deeper than a tenor, rose into a girlish alto as he spoke over his colleague. "I shall not be interrupted by the likes of you, Gurganus. Your father might have donated enough to secure your acceptance to this university, but not all of us are so... lucky."

"What the hell are you saying, pencil-neck?" shouted Gurganus, his normally bovine appearance becoming bullish as he turned around in his chair to glare at West.

"I'm simply saying that unlike you, I cannot depend on hobnobbing my way into a position at a hospital. I will be forced to get one the old-fashioned way: earning it. Thus, I must pass this class—and I cannot do that if I am not properly acquainted with the material."

"Silence!" Dr. Quinley held up his hands. "I concede that the field of medical ethics can be tricky to navigate, Mr. West, but before you say another word, remember that your insistence that there is some irreconcilability between these ideas has already been noted during class-time."

"Noted, perhaps—but never addressed." West sneered as he spoke, no mean feat. "While I was able to discern what you obviously considered the 'correct' answers on the midterm, there's a difference between circling a number on a multiple-choice test and forcing one's hand to parrot those ideas at length in essay form."

Dr. Quinley's face was crimson with anger. "That is enough!" He withdrew a handkerchief from his breast pocket and dabbed at his forehead. "Mr. West, throughout the semester you have disrupted class with your pedantry and casuistic reasoning. I can see I hoped in vain that you would absorb some of the wisdom I believe can be found in the lectures and texts I have provided for your consideration."

West sniffed. "And I see Thomas Paine was right when he said that to argue with a person who has renounced the use of reason is like administering medicine to the dead."

Nary an eye lingered upon the winter afternoon beyond the windows; a boring review session had suddenly become a battle of wills. All through the classroom excited whispers slithered from ear to ear as incredulous looks were passed like notes.

West sat behind it all, above it all. He had the look of a man who knows he has won an argument... until Dr. Quinley recovered enough to clear his throat.

"You say you must pass this class if you wish to become a doctor," he said, so quietly that the classroom instantly followed suit. "Well, Mr. West," Dr. Quinley continued, his voice rising like the winter wind, "you shall not pass this class. As of now, you have failed it." West tried to protest, but Dr. Quinley shouted him down. "I shall be speaking to the dean about your performance, and advising him that you repeat this course in the spring. And if Dr. Halsey has any reservations about this course of action, why, there are plenty of witnesses to verify your statement that your answers on the exams in this class were mere parroting, not true learning. That alone should be sufficient to prove you have need of further instruction."

While West, shocked, opened and closed his mouth like a hooked fish gasping out his last, a pleasant voice came somewhere off to West's right.

It was Tristan Langbroek, a sweet-faced divinity student who had played peacemaker between West and Gurganus before, on the few occasions they'd really gotten into it during class. "Dr. Quinley," he said, "please, I'm sure Mr. West is simply overburdened by the strain of studying. The end of the semester puts enormous pressure on medical students, so I'm told, and—"

"I should have read my horoscope this morning," said Dr. Quinley. "There is no other way I could possibly have anticipated that today I would be insulted to my face by a student—something that has never happened to me in twenty years of teaching—and then be reprimanded, in my own classroom, by a member of the clergy." He mopped his brow again. "I suggest, Mr. Langbroek, that you close your mouth if you do not also wish to be failed."

The classroom went completely, utterly silent following Dr. Quinley's pronouncement. Tristan looked studiously down at his notebook, eyes shining with tears. West, on the other hand, sat up straight in his chair, his gaze fixed upon Dr. Quinley. He did not look like a reprimanded undergraduate. Chin held high, jaw set, shoulders back, he looked triumphant.

After a few more deep breaths, Dr. Quinley smiled. "My apologies to the rest of you for that momentary unpleasantness. Let us now continue to discuss the idea of respecting the will of one's patient. Mr. Gurganus," he said, startling the strapping stripling who'd been grinning at West, "you mentioned wishing to further discuss a case of human experimentation. I believe we covered two such incidents in depth this semester." Dr. Quinley then canted his head to the right, uttering an incredulous tchah when he noticed a hand raised aloft, hanging above the heads of the students like a crescent moon. "Mr. West, lower your hand—and remove yourself from my classroom. You are no longer a student, so you have no further right to disrupt our discussion."

"But—"

"But nothing! You have failed, and—"

"I have not failed!" West was on his feet, all ten fingertips tented on the desk in front of him. "You are the one who has failed! You have failed to consider any number of relevant ethical quandaries posed by your students, you have failed to acknowledge the possibility that—"

"Mr. Gurganus, will you please assist me by showing Mr. West the door?" interrupted Dr. Quinley.

West drew himself up. "I can see where it is," he said with dignity. "Unlike you, Dr. Quinley, I have a brain capable of processing the sensory input my eyes provide. I shall leave, but I assure you, I am not through with you."

"Indeed you are not," said Dr. Quinley sweetly, as he turned back to the chalkboard. "You shall be repeating this class next semester. Have a merry Christmas, Mr. West."

Tristan Langbroek felt just awful about what had happened in Dr. Quinley's class. Not that it had been his fault. Not entirely. He knew that, of course he did. West had made his own bed, had been making all semester, really. Yet he couldn't shake the feeling that his attempt to speak on West's behalf had further enraged the professor, causing Dr. Quinley to really dig in his heels. If only he'd kept his mouth shut! Then, perhaps, they might have settled things more amicably.

He sighed, and his breath steamed out of his mouth as he hurried carefully along the frozen sidewalk toward the cafeteria, head down against the light but persistent snowfall. Usually weather like this, at this time of year, raised his spirits. There really was nothing like a white Christmas to enkindle the spirit of love and charity in people.

But that afternoon, Tristan paid little heed to the weather or the season. He was preoccupied with thoughts about how his father had been right about him. There was no doubt about it, he was, as dear old Dad had always said, a busybody. And now his urge to be helpful had harmed someone.

Come to think of it, that was something his father had always said would happen, too.

The road to hell, thought Tristan, hugging his schoolbooks so tightly he could feel the buttons of his pea coat pressing into his chest. His intentions had been good, but what did that matter?

Maybe he shouldn't have signed up for that medical ethics seminar. He'd had reservations, but his advisor had strongly recommended it, for Tristan had wanted to become a hospital chaplain ever since the one at St. Mary's had refused to hear his mother's final confession on the grounds that she was Anglican. The injustice of a clergyman turning away someone who needed comfort had disturbed Tristan deeply at the time. More than it might an ordinary man, as Tristan had always felt God calling to him from an early age, telling him to go forth and help people understand Christ's eternal love. And now, when it was very nearly Christmas, he'd gone and injured a fellow man.

Tristan eyed the holly-wreath adorning the cafeteria door with despair as he pushed it open, but when the tip of his nose began to unthaw in the warm cafeteria, his spirits rose a little. Winter weather was always more enjoyable when you were warm and dry, and problems seemed less problematic, too. What he needed was to relax, get a bowl of soup and a cup of coffee, and watch the snow until it was time to don his Riverside Catering uniform so he could go serve champagne and hors d'oeuvres at the faculty Christmas party.

Then he spied West eating by himself in the darkest corner of the cafeteria. Tristan's spirits rose even more, and he thanked God for giving him the opportunity to apologize for his part in the disastrous review session. Best to do it sooner rather than later, so he padded over to where West was alternating between taking tidy little bites of his ham sandwich and wiping his nose with a handkerchief.

"Ah, hello, excuse me," Tristan mumbled, as he nervously shifted his weight from one foot to the other. West looked annoyed by the disturbance, which made Tristan self-conscious. "I just, I wanted to say I was sorry."

"For what?"

"For..."

West made an irritated sound in the back of his throat. "Say what you want, and then leave me be. I'm very busy."

"Busy eating a sandwich?"

West's spectacles glinted as he looked up. He seemed to see Tristan for the first time. Tristan felt something very like an electric shock when their eyes met, and found himself blushing.

"Oh, it's the preacher," said West, bringing Tristan back to himself. "No pamphlets, please. I hate seeing paper wasted."

"I'm not trying to give you a pamphlet," said Tristan. "I'm trying to apologize." He gripped his books tighter with his left arm as he extended his right hand to shake West's.

West made no move to return the handshake. "For what?"

"I further antagonized Dr. Quinley," said Tristan, awkwardly lowering his hand. "I only meant to help. You know that, don't you, West?"

West's smile unsettled Tristan, the way he pinched his lips together in the center and lifted only the corners of his mouth. "Herbert," he said, in a clipped but friendlier tone. "Sit down, will you? And don't trouble yourself further about Quinley. It was my fault. That ratfink's been looking for an opportunity to destroy me all semester; today, foolishly, I gave him one." He shrugged irritably. "You meant to help, and I've never believed all that rot about the road to hell being paved with good intentions."

It startled Tristan to hear his recent thoughts repeated by another. "No?" he asked, setting his books down and sitting across from West.

"No. It's not paved at all. It doesn't exist." West smiled that heinous smile again. "I believe neither in heaven nor hell, Mister…?"

"Langbroek. But call me Tristan."

"Well, Tristan, that's why I said your pamphlets would be wasted. To my mind, only what can be proved empirically is worthy of consideration. A boogeyman below the earth's crust and another above the clouds fighting over my soul, whatever that is… I have never seen any evidence of it." He looked Tristan right in the eye. "Does that shock you?"

Tristan shrugged. "Do you want it to?"

West shrugged back at him. "Not particularly, though I do enjoy seeing the various ways surprise manifests on the human face. Right now, all I want is to figure out how to persuade Quinley that I should be allowed to take the final and progress in my coursework. Spending another semester with that insufferable man is too much for anyone to endure."

Tristan had rather liked Dr. Quinley, but he decided against mentioning that. "Have you gone to his office and apologized?"

West chuckled with his lips closed. "I went to his office to reason with him. I owe him no apologies."

"And how did that go?"

"He wasn't there; I expect he's gone home for the day already." He snorted. "Tenure. Must be nice."

"I'm sure it's just he's gone home to dress for the faculty Christmas party tonight."

West looked at Tristan keenly. "Are you sure of that? How do you know?"

Tristan felt a chill at that moment, as if death had just kissed him upon the nape of his neck. He shivered, and turned around just to make sure no one was there. It reassured him to see the door to the cafeteria slamming shut; just a draft, of course.

"Tristan?"

"Oh," he said sheepishly. "Sorry. I—ah, what? Oh, the party. I work as a server for the catering company that's providing everything."

West looked thoughtful. "Indeed? Where's it being held?"

"The Pornelles Room, in Lemmington-Jekyll."

"Hmm. Good to know. Were I to crash the party, I could get Quinley alone and convince him that we actually agree on a very important matter."

"What's that?"

"That we'd rather see less of one another than more."

Tristan laughed. "It'll be hard. They always post a guard at the door."

"Why?"

"Free hooch," said Tristan. "Can't have the riff-raff drinking up all the wine. The professors would revolt if the sauce ran out before they did."

West considered this for a moment. "I bet you could help me, if you were willing."

"How? It's against the rules for us servers to talk to the guests about personal matters, and I can't risk losing my job. My scholarship barely covers tuition, much less books and—"

"You misunderstand me." West popped the last of his sandwich into his mouth, chewed it quickly, and swallowed. Tristan saw his Adam's apple bob as it went down his slender throat. "I'm proposing you take me along." He chuckled again. "You know, as your date."

Tristan blushed again, and he was just opening his lips to protest that servers obviously couldn't bring along dates when someone shouted "Faggots!"

The cafeteria went quiet. Tristan turned around, surprised and horrified to find Reginald Gurganus standing there behind him, looking mighty pleased with himself.

"Knew you faggots were faggots," he said smugly. "Going on a date? To a party? I'm not surprised you suck dick by choice, West, but you, Langbroek? You might actually get a girl to look at you! That is, if you weren't so busy sucking dick. By choice," he added, and then laughed loudly, hurr hurr hurr.

"Jealous, Gurganus?" said West. Tristan was amazed by his coolness under fire. "Funny, I thought your sort never tired of date-raping coeds. Well, they say you learn something new every day."

"Whatever, faggot," said Gurganus. "Never thought your sort ever left your dorm room. Too busy jerking it to pictures of Errol Flynn."

"Are you speaking from experience?" West took a sip of coffee. "Takes one to know one, Reggie. And anyways, you can have Tristan if you fancy him. I go for brains over brawn; when I jerk it to a picture, it's—"

But Tristan never found out who West jerked it too. Red-faced, he fled the cafeteria before West—or anyone else—spoke more of boys being aroused by boys.

He was halfway across the snowy quad before he realized he'd forgotten his books. What to do? He couldn't go back in there. He couldn't go anywhere, come to think of it. Oh, sure, boys like Gurganus threw around epithets like "faggot" and "queer" all the time, sometimes even as a term of endearment, but it always left him wondering, worrying really, if everyone could tell.

He sat down on a convenient bench, heedless of the snow chilling his bottom through his trousers, and hung his head. He knew it was always a possibility somebody—or many somebodies, for that matter—might guess his secret shame; figure out that it wasn't just a feeling of godliness that had prompted his wish to become a chaplain. Ministering was the sort of job where one could always put off marriage, being too busy with the flock and all that. Of course people would wonder, but he'd learned from an early age that people accepted uncomplicated answers. Or would pretend to, and gossip quietly elsewhere. He could live with that.

"Tristan."

Tristan looked up and saw West standing there, in a black overcoat a size or two too big for him. He was holding Tristan's abandoned books under his left arm, and when their eyes met, he reached out with his right hand to where Tristan slouched on his frozen bench.

"Get up, you'll catch your death," he said lightly.

"What do you care?"

"I need your help to get into that party tonight," said West. "At this point, you're my best shot at not having to repeat Medical Ethics 101 next semester. I'm sure Dean Halsey is going to this party, and he doesn't much care for me either, if you must know. If he and Quinley have a chance to drink wine and celebrate the prospect of hindering my academic progress, I'm done for. Thus, I need you alive." He shrugged and lowered his hand, shoving it into his pocket. "You can go ahead and freeze to death, feeling sorry for yourself because of whatever stupid reason, after you help me gate-crash."

Tristan discovered that, oddly enough, he appreciated West's frankness. He got to his feet and brushed the snow from his rear end before accepting his books.

"It's not a stupid reason," said Tristan, as they walked towards the dorms. "It's—"

"I don't care one bit," said West. "It doesn't matter to me if it was that lout Gurganus calling you a faggot who hurt your feelings, or if was my remark about preferring smarter fellows than you on the rare occasion that I allow my baser passions to take possession of my attention. Perhaps it was something else entirely. But I'm sure you have more important things to worry about than who you are, or what others think of you. And even if you don't, well, the first you cannot help, and the second is irrelevant. Don't let it bother you."

"You say that, but..."

"I say it because I mean it. You want to serve your god? Then devote yourself to serving him. Letting yourself become distracted by... irrelevancies... is the first step along the road to failure." West looked at Tristan keenly, his spectacles glinting. "If you're going to fret about roads paved with good intentions, my friend, that's the truly dangerous one."

Tristan was surprised that he found weird little Herbert West's pep-talk comforting, but he did. He smiled, and nodded, and the conversation moved on to just how they'd smuggle West into the faculty party.

By the time they finished planning out the details and West had left Tristan to prepare for work, Tristan felt positively chipper. He caught himself whistling as he drew his bath. His day may have begun badly, but it was ending well. And he owed it all to West. He was glad he could help West with his problems, after West had so generously helped him with his own.

It was only then, as Tristan shrugged on his white tuxedo jacket, that he realized that, come to think of it, he'd never actually agreed to help West. Well, no matter. He was happy enough to do it.

The Pornelles Room, where the faculty Christmas party was being held, ran the entire length of the top floor of the Lemmington-Jekyll Administration Building, which stood at the northeastern part of campus, near the intersection of Garrison and Lich. John Pornelles, one of Miskatonic's more recent benefactors, had several years prior earmarked quite a bit of money to convert the outdated faculty lounge and adjacent attics into a space for formal receptions.

This had required some architectural creativity, as there were kitchen facilities in Lemmington-Jekyll, but they were located in the basement. A large dumbwaiter, therefore, had been installed in a newly-constructed alcove along the northern wall. This worked well enough… except that the electrical light intended to alert kitchen-staff and servers to when dirty dishes needed to be taken down or hot food sent up had never worked right. Therefore, a system had been established where waves of food and drink would be sent up on the even tens (on the hour, twenty-past, and forty-past) and dishes sent down on the odds.

But given that the only stairs were in full view of the reception hall (it had been impossible for the architects to install a staff stairwell and keep the project under budget), the dumbwaiter was also—unofficially—used to transport staff in the middle of events, when they were on break, or needed to change out a soiled jacket for a fresh one, or whatever else.

Tristan had worked at several of these functions, Riverside Catering being the go-to for fancy college events. And, as the servers—most of them being strapping Miskatonic University lads—were often called upon to aid the catering staff with the heavy lifting, he was well acquainted with the kitchen, too. Not as recently renovated, it was dark and narrow and hot in there, and it tended to get loud in the thick of things, when cooks and back-of-house help were working hard to get food out and dishes washed. Tristan despised it when he had to go down there in the middle of an event, but he and West had agreed that the confusion would aid them in their plan.

The plan, however, was not confusing, thank goodness for that. All Tristan really had to do was dress, show up on time, and do his job until his first break, an hour into the party. Then he was supposed to leave by the dumbwaiter, pass through the kitchen, and cross over Lich Street to get to a florist's shop just out of sight of the kitchen exit. There, West would meet him, wearing Tristan's spare front-of-house jacket over his own. They would then both return via the kitchen, where the steam and ruckus and sheer mass of bodies would hopefully obscure the presence of an impostor. West would go up in the dumbwaiter, sending down his jacket quickly after reaching the party, so Tristan could stash it, and then go up himself.

"You're sure I can't just walk in?" West had asked, when Tristan initially proposed impinging on his dignity by cramming himself into a freight elevator.

"Do you think they'd spring for a doorman if they weren't serious about keeping out interlopers?" Tristan shook his head. "Trust me, this is the only option."

What West's plan was once he got into the party, Tristan didn't know—and he preferred it that way. Personally, he felt West was being a bit hasty and paranoid; having seen how professors tended to let loose during events, Tristan was pretty sure Dr. Quinley and Dean Halsey would be pouring so much wine down their throats they'd be hard-pressed to discuss anything. But West seemed resolved upon settling the matter as quickly as possible, and it was his neck on the line. So Tristan put the matter from his mind during the first hour of the party, except for noting when Dean Halsey appeared, and keeping an eye out for Dr. Quinley, who walked through the garland-bedecked door just as Tristan was beginning to despair of the professor arriving before he had to meet West.

"Ah, Mr. Langbroek," said Quinley, as he snatched a glass of champagne from a passing server's tray and a miniature quiche off of Tristan's platter of canapés. "Good to see you."

"You as well, sir," said Tristan, and then, unable to stop himself, blurted, "I know I shouldn't say anything, not now, but I must apologize for my part in the incident in class this afternoon."

"It is I who should apologize," said Quinley. "I was in the wrong to chastise you. You were acting in good faith, on behalf of a fellow student. West's behavior—well, we'll say no more about it. I'm here to go a-wassailing, if you catch my drift." He nodded at the four-piece band that was playing a jazz rendition of that very carol.

"Of course, sir."

"Better get some more of these quiches, I seem to have eaten the last of them. Will you make sure I get some? I'll be over there, in that corner. I have something I want to talk to Halsey about, do you see him? He's standing with Dr. Armitage. My goodness, have they commandeered an entire tray of bacon-wrapped shrimp between them?"

"Dean Halsey really loves those shrimp," said Tristan.

"Oh, I know," said Quinley. "I've watched him bolt down handfuls of them for decades. I don't know if you were at Miskatonic when there was that scandal over whether Halsey's secretly a Jew, but as I said at the time, anyone who believed such a rumor had never seen him at a faculty shindig."

"Enjoy yourself, sir, and merry Christmas," said Tristan, and noting how late it had become, he hurried off to get downstairs, through the kitchen, and outside.

West was waiting exactly where he said he'd be. He leaned casually against a lamppost, huddled in his coat, and was smoking a cigarette with short, almost mechanical inhalations. Ashes and butts littered the snow around his feet. He'd been there for a while. Well, West seemed like the sort who'd arrive early for something important even if it meant lingering outside in frigid weather.

He didn't immediately seem to notice Tristan's approach, so Tristan watched him for a moment, admiring the figure West cut in his black suit and black overcoat. It wasn't that he found West attractive; West wasn't handsome, not exactly, but the perpetual intensity of his eyes and facial expressions, paired with the delicacy of his features, made him… interesting to look at.

Well, that was all a bunch of hooey, mused Tristan, even as he shot a quick prayer skyward for thinking such sinful thoughts. He did find West attractive, damn it, and not for the first time he felt it unfair that he should have to hide his attraction, even from himself, just because Paul of Tarsus mouthed off about arsenokoitai being among those who would never inherit the kingdom of heaven. Tristan didn't want to inherit anything, he just wanted to live his life and preach charity and kindness as Christ did. Long ago he'd decided to become one of those "eunuchs by choice" mentioned in Matthew, but looking at West's lips contorting around his cigarette, the way the lamplight shone through his shell-delicate nostrils, how his coat hung on his slender shoulders, Tristan began to doubt his resolve. The way he moved, the sharpness of his profile highlighted by the lamplight… it made him want to brush the snowflakes from West's lapels, snake his hand around his waist and—

West checked his wristwatch, and Tristan, realizing he was wasting precious time, hurried over.

"Dr. Quinley's inside," he said, breath smoking like West's cigarette. "When I left, he was going over to speak with Drs. Halsey and Armitage."

"Rats," swore West, and stepped on his half-smoked cigarette. "Let's get inside, then. There's no time to lose." He shrugged out of his overcoat and stashed it behind some bushes. He was already wearing Tristan's spare jacket. It was far too large on him; Tristan hadn't realized just how slight he was.

"Are you sure you want to go through with this?" asked Tristan, hoping against hope that he could talk West out of the plan even at this late stage. "I just think—"

"Tristan." Tristan wasn't sure if it was West's tone or the breeze that made him shiver. "You can't back out now. I need you." West reached out and touched him on the shoulder, squeezing the muscle there ever so gently. "There's no way this will hurt you," he promised. "I don't even know you, all right? If anyone asks, I acted alone."

"I'm not worried about that," protested Tristan, though it occurred to him only now that perhaps he should be. "I'm worried about..." he trailed off, unable to say the word.

"Don't worry about me." West seemed to interpret his meaning just fine. "I can take care of myself."

Everything will be fine, Tristan told himself, as they elbowed their way through the crowded kitchen that smelled of melting cheese and human sweat. Breathe, he reminded himself, as West casually folded himself into a crouch inside the dumbwaiter as though he'd done it a thousand times. Don't worry, he repeated for the fiftieth time when his spare jacket was returned below a stack of trays and several dirty wineglasses.

It was with a not-insubstantial feeling of relief that Tristan, after tucking his jacket surreptitiously into a convenient cabinet, finally returned to the party. Studiously avoiding looking for West or Quinley, he offered around a platter of bite-sized mincemeat pies with more than his usual courtesy, and even hummed along with "I Saw Three Ships Come Sailing In" when the band struck up that lively tune.

"Massive turnout this year," commented another waiter, as they fumbled with the dumbwaiter door, attempting to send down another batch of dirty wineglasses. "Really keeping us running tonight."

"You're telling me," said Tristan, glancing at the clock. "We should suggest they do punch next year. Less work for us."

"Can you imagine?" replied the other boy. "It's only our human frailties that keep them from guzzling every ounce of the hard stuff within fifteen minutes of the doors opening. If they were pouring their own drinks..."

Tristan agreed with him absently. He hadn't realized it had been almost half an hour since he'd returned. Where was West? What was he doing? Had he left already? He and Tristan had agreed to meet afterwards at the Black Goat, a bar frequented by Miskatonic students that stayed open late, but that seemed an awfully long time to wait.

But Tristan had more pressing concerns, like the fact that Professor Wilmarth had actually slunk around the side of the server's alcove to enquire if there was more wine to be had. And as if that wasn't annoying enough, while babbling about needing more of the legendary ambrosia of the gods to keep young, he gesticulated suddenly, spilling the dregs of his pinot noir all over Tristan's jacket.

"It's all right," promised Tristan. Wilmarth looked close to tears over the mishap and wouldn't stop apologizing. "I have a spare, I just need to get it. Don't worry about anything, please—return to the party and go on enjoying yourself."

Wilmarth staggered off at last, and Tristan shed his soiled uniform so the red wine wouldn't soak onto his shirt. But just as he was thinking about how lucky he was to have a spare below, he heard, high and nasal above the party's dull roar of human voices, "You've made an enemy tonight, Dr. Quinley, mark my words!"

Tristan broke into a cold sweat. Poking his head around the edge of the alcove, he peeked through the gaps in a clump of poinsettias and caught sight of West striding away from a pissed-off looking Dr. Quinley. Dear God above.

Without thinking, Tristan hopped into the dumbwaiter and, reaching though the open panel in the ceiling, lowered himself quickly back down to the kitchens. "Sorry!" he said, brandishing the stained part of his jacket when one of the cooks jumped back upon seeing him bolt out of the elevator, very nearly spilling a tray of pieces of marzipan shaped like fruits. "These professors! Gotta change quick!"

But after grabbing his clean jacket out of the cabinet, instead of returning to his job, Tristan fled the kitchen and headed back outside. The only thing in his mind was catching West before he left. He had to know what had happened. One of the conditions of Tristan agreeing to aid West's gate-crashing had been him promising to be civil, and

Tristan didn't think West would go back on his word… at least, not without serious provocation.

"Herbert!" he cried, seeing the boy collecting his coat from behind the bushes in front of the florist's shop. "What happened?"

West whirled around, an ugly, furious expression contorting his dainty face. "What—oh, it's you, Tristan." He gained control of himself and smiled thinly. "What are you doing? I thought we were to meet up after you were finished? I wouldn't want you to jeopardize your job."

"It's all right," said Tristan, wondering if it was. "I just wanted to make sure you were okay?"

West cocked an eyebrow at Tristan. "Spare me the hysterics. I thought I told you I went for brainier sorts than you."

Tristan could not stop his lower lip from trembling. "Oh, I just," was all he could manage. But then he felt anger rising in him, hot, pricking resentment at being treated shabbily by West—teased about the thing he was most sensitive about—and after doing everything he could to help! "I'm going back inside!" he cried. "I've never in my life met such a horrible, ungrateful … I can't believe I helped you—I can't believe I thought you were cool! I hope you do fail that stupid class, and I hope—"

Tristan almost slipped on a patch of ice when West grabbed him by the hand and pulled him down into a kiss, right there in the snowy brightness under the lamppost, but West's grip was like iron, and it kept Tristan steady on his feet.

It wasn't the only thing hard about West, either; the pressure of his lips on Tristan's was so intense it was almost painful. Tristan didn't pull away. It was his first kiss, after all, and while it startled him to discover that West's tongue was as rough as a cat's, and his breath tasted strangely of formaldehyde, Tristan thought it was pretty wonderful to be kissing someone, God help him.

"You're brainy enough," whispered West, pulling away only enough to mouth the words under his breath. "I was just being mean because I was angry."

"S'alright." Tristan, eager for more, initiated the kiss this time, even if West's diminutive stature put a serious crick in his neck. Surely God, in His wisdom, wouldn't have made kissing another boy so fun, were it a sin? Because this was fun, innocently fun… well, except for the drum-like thrills shooting along the length of his stiffening cock. That wasn't so very innocent. Tristan was more aroused than he could ever remember feeling, things were getting almost painful down there. He dearly wished he could adjust himself, but feeling it would be indelicate, he let instinct take over and instead pressed his erection against West's belly with a moan. The pleasure definitely helped him bear the discomfort. He might be lost in Heaven without a map, but clearly his directional sense was decent enough.

"Well, well, well."

Tristan released West with a gasp and, horrified, turned around to see that Dr. Quinley had been standing behind him.

It was the worst possible thing. What could he possibly say to excuse what he'd been doing? There was no excuse for it. And all this after Dr. Quinley had been so nice to him… he felt a sudden pang over his betraying the professor. The man was all right.

Quinley, for his part, looked like Christmas had come early that year. Sick with nerves, Tristan turned back to West for guidance, but West had that weird, triumphal expression on his face again, the one he'd worn in class only a few short hours before. Was West insane? If Quinley spread the word about them, the consequences would be dire, likely beginning—and ending—with Tristan being summarily expelled from the divinity school. And as for West…

"Dr. Quinley," stammered Tristan, at last finding his voice, "I—what are you …"

"I was wondering how West managed to sneak into the party," said Quinley. "It seems he had inside help, hmm? What a shame, I'd thought better of you, Mr. Langbroek. Helping a misfit like West doesn't reflect well on your character, not at all. And that's without the sodomy."

"Sodomy!" West snorted, before Tristan could protest. "Oh come now, Dr. Quinley. Don't be melodramatic. Tristan didn't help me get into the party. I just walked in the door, and as for the other—"

"You didn't just walk in the door." A cold wind kicked up along the deserted side-street, and Quinley, shivering, popped the collar of his overcoat against the cutting breeze. "I asked the… door man, ticket-taker, whatever. He said the first time he saw you, you were storming off."

"Well, however you think I got in there, surely you'll accept it wasn't with Tristan's assistance. Look at him, he couldn't help assemble a ham sandwich."

"Nice boyfriend," remarked Quinley, looking piercingly at Tristan. Tristan flushed, but said nothing, his power of speech as frozen as the ground.

West began anew his attempt to dissuade Quinley that Tristan had been involved in his crashing the party or that they were romantically involved, even going so far as to claim Tristan had been whispering something to him; that Quinley's eyes had deceived him into thinking he'd seen a kiss. Tristan didn't try to help defend West—or himself. He watched his ruin unfold in silence, without emotion. Quinley and West's argument seemed to be happening somewhere very far away, like he was observing them through the wrong end of a telescope.

It was all just too terrible. Tristan took a step back, hoping to put even more distance between himself and the altercation, which was growing more heated as Quinley laughed away West's explanations. The less Tristan was involved the better. He wasn't like West, he would wait, go in early to try to catch Dr. Quinley in his office, apologize for his error and beg for mercy. Surely if he explained the situation Quinley would see reason. It didn't seem fair to punish him for such a momentary indiscretion as letting West gate-crash. And as for the other, this entire experience was enough to convince him that boys just weren't worth the trouble.

West, however, was moving in the opposite direction, advancing on Quinley so angrily that the professor was starting to look nervous. Though small, when he began shaking his finger and raising his voice, West was pretty scary. Quinley was casting about, clearly hoping to see someone else walking along the lonely stretch of sidewalk. But there was no one around, and the wind swallowed rather than blew away West's words, even when he shrieked, "I will make you see logic if you refuse to do so on your own!"

"West!" cried Tristan, the peril of being implicated in his companion's belligerent craziness too much to bear. He took a few, careful steps on the crusty, crunching ice toward where the quarrelers quarreled. "Stop this, let him go! There's no sense in this, you're going to—"

It happened so quickly Tristan wasn't sure what he saw. As ginger as his own steps had been, West was not being careful, nor was Quinley in his haste to put some distance between himself and the two boys. And walking backwards on slick concrete freckled with patches of black ice was hardly a good idea under any circumstances. So it wasn't that Tristan thought West had actually swiped out his foot under Quinley's own in some horrifying, deliberate attempt to trip the professor—not really. It was just an accident when Dr. Quinley slipped. The professor windmilled his arms in an attempt to regain his balance that proved futile. It wasn't that Tristan thought he saw West push him. He must have been trying to grab the man's tie, or shirtfront perhaps, in an attempt to keep him on his feet. Yes, that's what happened. An accident.

But an accident that resulted in them both kneeling over Dr. Quinley's prostrate figure.

He lay on the sidewalk like a corpse on a slab, an upsetting pool of steaming black blood spreading out from under the back of Quinley's head. Tristan, in something of a daze, reached out and touched the professor's brow.

It was still warm—and when he looked, he saw that a pulse yet beat at the man's throat.

"I think he's alive," said Tristan softly.

"And a good thing, too," said West, grinning ghoulishly. "We'd be in an awful lot of trouble if he died, don't you think?"

Tristan gawped at West. "What?"

"There's no time for stupid questions! We must, as he made the point in class earlier, act in our patient's best interest, and that means getting him to my dorm room. I can help him there." As Tristan wondered if this was truly what Quinley would want, West half-lay down on the sidewalk beside Quinley in his effort to get his arm around the professor's neck, slumping the body—no, Dr. Quinley—into half of a fireman's carry. "A little help, please? I can't carry him by myself. He's too heavy, the great oaf."

"Shouldn't we take him to the infirmary?"

"No! That's the worst thing we could do!" West sighed as if it was the most obvious fact in the world. "We need to reason with him once he wakes up. So he doesn't blab to the police."

"The police!"

"Obviously we know it was just an unfortunate accident, his fall, but who knows what he might say about us? Do you want to risk him spilling the proverbial beans? Over our kiss? Your helping me get into the party? What if he gets confused and wakes up believing I tried to trip him? We'd both be ruined!"

Tristan felt a yawing in his stomach, as if he might be sick. "Okay," he agreed. West was right, damn him. "How far is it to your dorm?"

"Not very." West grunted as they both heaved at once and got the distressingly-floppy Dr. Quinley on his feet. Quinley moaned weakly, and Tristan's stomach did a barrel roll. "If we see anyone, act intoxicated. Sing a Christmas carol loudly, shout, that kind of thing. That way they'll think Quinley's just drunk, too, and we're helping him home."

The walk back to West's dorm could not have taken fifteen minutes, but it felt like an eternity to Tristan. Quinley's body became increasingly burdensome as Tristan's arms began to shake with the effort of holding him, and his head lolled when one of them failed to support it properly. And despite Tristan's hopes, they did see a few people, but no one seemed to notice there was something strange happening, as West and Tristan pretended at making merry until any potential witnesses were out of sight.

Then there were the stairs. West's room was on the second floor, so there were clanging doors to worry about, and also the brighter light inside that better illuminated their misdeeds—and revealed that the damage to the back of Dr. Quinley's head was not so minor as Tristan had hoped. His skull looked almost caved in a little, though the man continued to breathe shallowly. Tristan hoped that meant he'd be okay.

"You're doing great," said West in soothing tones, when they finally reached his door. He pushed most of Quinley's deadweight onto Tristan as he fumbled for his key. "It's nice, having someone to help with this sort of thing—I'll have to keep that in mind. But now we're here, you can go home once we get him inside. I understand if medical matters make you nauseated."

Tristan's heart soared momentarily—the prospect of getting away from West, Quinley, and really everything about this night was a lovely one, a blessing—but then he realized he couldn't leave Dr. Quinley alone with West, and certainly not in such a helpless state. He would have to see this thing through to the end.

"There must be some way I can assist you," he said, trying to sound braver than he felt. "What are you planning to do?"

West turned the knob and his door swung open. "I have a few ideas," he said, as Tristan's jaw dropped.

The inside of West's room was filled with more microscopes, test tubes, Bunsen burners, pipettes, clamps, forceps, and wire brushes than a chemistry department's supply closet. Actually, given the labels on some of the items, perhaps the chemistry department's supply closet was a little less than full these days. Tristan's eyes began to water immediately, not just from the greenish steam or smoke produced by weird fluids bubbling away merrily in their beakers. He felt deeply creeped out, most of all because along with the scientific equipment, the place was absolutely decked out for Christmas. Garlands dripped from the ceiling, ornaments glistened everywhere, and there was even a tiny tree, listing slightly in its stand, on top of a stack of books with titles like Alternative Ideas On The Human Nervous System and Do I Not Bleed? A Concise History of Transfusion.

"What the ..." he said, catching himself before he swore. "West, what is all this?"

"My work," said West absently. "Let's get him settled, all right?"

As they finagled the limp Quinley into a metal chair beside a square table crowded with equipment, Tristan asked, "What sort of work?"

"Great work. Humanitarian work," answered West. He had left Dr. Quinley to Tristan's care, turning his attention to titrating some glowing greenish solution into a beaker. "Something that will change the world as we know it. I am on the brink of a great discovery, you see."

Dear Lord. "Should we perform first aid?" asked Tristan. As fascinating as West's discovery surely was, Dr. Quinley's face had lost all its color, and he didn't seem to be breathing any more.

"What for?"

Tristan made an incredulous noise in the back of his throat. "I think he's dying, Herbert!"

"Well yes, of course he is." West looked up from agitating whatever was in the beaker with a stirring rod. "He's well beyond ordinary medicine at this point, I'd say. But I am not an ordinary doctor."

"You're not a doctor at all!" Tristan cried, his horror mounting as it occurred to him that perhaps West had never intended to save Dr. Quinley.

"Not yet," West conceded. "But trust me, once I am able to publish my discoveries, the Nobel Prize shan't be far behind."

"I hope you enjoy it behind bars!" Tristan backed away from West, back towards the door. "He's going to die, and that makes you a murderer!"

West sighed. "Really, Tristan, you must learn to control these outbursts! He's not going to die. I'm going to save his life!"

"How?"

"With this—my reagent," he said. He set the beaker down carefully. "It restores life to those on the brink of death."

Tristan, despite himself, was impressed. He shouldn't have doubted West, West wasn't a psychopath or homicidal maniac, of course he wasn't. He was just a medical student, if one with more than his fair share of ego. "Thank God," he said with relief.

West smiled. "Get his coat off and roll up his sleeve while I prepare the syringe."

Once Tristan had Dr. Quinley's forearm free and bare, West swooped in like a falcon and jabbed the syringe into the professor's most prominent vein. Depressing the plunger, West whimpered a little, as if experiencing a jolt of pain—or pleasure—and then withdrew the needle.

Tristan imagined the result would be instantaneous, like Lazarus rising from the dead or some other famous miracle. Instead, Dr. Quinley continued to slouch in the chair as he had been, looking, well, corpselike.

West set down the syringe, folded his arms, and watched Quinley clinically. After perhaps a minute of this Tristan cleared his throat.

"Ah, should he ..."

West checked his watch. "Soon, if it works."

"If?"

"Well... this will be my first time using it on a human." West looked at Tristan in surprise when Tristan gasped. "What, do you think Miskatonic supplies its medical students—even its most brilliant ones—with an endless supply of near-death human specimens? I've had promising results with lab animals like rats and guinea pigs, but trust me, stealing anything with a more complex brain and circulatory system is nigh-impossible."

Tristan sank to his knees. Dr. Quinley had yet to show any signs of life. As a perturbed expression crept across West's face, Tristan began to doubt he would.

This was it for him. He might have been able to recover from a scandal like an illicit kiss, but murder? While God might forgive him, the legal system would surely require more penitence than a prayer. Perhaps if he demonstrated good behavior they'd let him work in the prison chapel...

"Damn it," muttered West, checking his watch once again. "Perhaps I miscalculated the dosage… it's possible Quinley's even fatter than I thought."

"Could we still get him to the infirmary?"

West raised both eyebrows. "If we get him anywhere it will be back to where he fell. That way we can make it look like an accident."

"It was an accident!"

"Oh, Tristan. If you're going to assist me in my work, you must dry off behind the ears!" West chuckled pityingly as he looked down at where Tristan yet knelt. "If what we learn from our failure with Quinley yields new insights that can help the sick, won't it have been worth it?"

"The end doesn't justi—"

"Oh, please. Come on, let's get him on the dissecting table, all right? The fresher he is, the more I'll be able to find out."

Tristan didn't move. He just shook his head and stared at the carpet. It was flecked with brownish stains.

"Well I can't let your attitude stand in the way of science," said West, with the air of a disappointed parent telling a child that no, they could not get ice cream, and it was all because he had cried while having a band-aid ripped off his skinned knee. "Get out of my way if you won't help."

Tristan's legs felt like they belonged to someone else; he couldn't make the muscles move. He heard West sigh again, somewhere above his head, and then West stepped over him, leaning down to pull open one of Quinley's eyes. He shone a light onto the glassy pupil.

"Hmm," he said.

Tristan didn't ask what was worthy of comment, which is perhaps why they both heard the low moan that came from neither of their throats.

"Was that…" asked Tristan, but West didn't answer, for Quinley's hand had shot straight out and grabbed him by the neck.

"Dr. Quinley!" cried Tristan, suddenly on his feet. What on earth was the man doing? Trying to murder his murderer?

But at least he was alive!

Tristan watched in terror as Quinley threw West across the room. His body hit the cement block wall with a thump, and Tristan cried out when West fell to the floor, which made Quinley turn his head and look at the divinity student with bleary eyes.

"Urnnngh," he said, and lurched toward Tristan.

"Dr. Quinley, I know you're disoriented," said Tristan, slowly backing away. What was wrong with the man? Why was he looking at him so queerly, like he wasn't really seeing him—or recognizing him? "Please, if you'll come with me, I'll get you to the clinic, or the hospital, you need help, you need ... Dr. Quinley? Dr. Quinley, can you hear me?"

West awoke to find Dr. Quinley choking Tristan, both hammy hands wrapped around the fair lad's neck. Tristan's head rolled from side to side as Quinley throttled him, moaning and groaning like a creature in a horror flick. West could tell at a glance that Tristan was not yet dead, but very close to that final state.

"Oh, Dr. Quinley," said West pityingly, as he retrieved a bottle of powerful muscle relaxant from his private supplies. "The pressures of academia seem to have finally gotten to you. What a shame. But you can't do that in here, no no no. You might get me in trouble, and then where would we be?"

Calmly, West drew an enormous dose of carisoprodol into the barrel of his syringe. Then, hands perfectly steady, he injected the whole of it into Dr. Quinley's neck.

Quinley cried out and then fell atop Tristan's prostrate form, the professor once again insensible if not now entirely dead. That could wait. What was important was Tristan being so close to death; West thought, after watching Quinley's reaction to his reagent, that he had gained some insight into the proper dosage.

He pushed Quinley's body off of Tristan's, humming "God Rest Ye Merry Gentleman" as he did so. May nothing you dismay, indeed—there was always something to keep one from idleness and despair. Tristan's lighter body would be fairly easy to get on the dissecting table, and West would strap him down in case he had the same rage-reaction to being called back from near-death. A resurrection more appropriate for Easter than Yuletide, West mused, but science follows no calendar but its own.

Herbert West Re-Animator

Howard Phillips Lovecraft

I. From the Dark

Of Herbert West, who was my friend in college and in after life, I can speak only with extreme terror. This terror is not due altogether to the sinister manner of his recent disappearance, but was engendered by the whole nature of his life-work, and first gained its acute form more than seventeen years ago, when we were in the third year of our course at the Miskatonic University Medical School in Arkham. While he was with me, the wonder and diabolism of his experiments fascinated me utterly, and I was his closest companion. Now that he is gone and the spell is broken, the actual fear is greater. Memories and possibilities are ever more hideous than realities.

The first horrible incident of our acquaintance was the greatest shock I ever experienced, and it is only with reluctance that I repeat it. As I have said, it happened when we were in the medical school where West had already made himself notorious through his wild theories on the nature of death and the possibility of overcoming it artificially. His views, which were widely ridiculed by the faculty and by his fellow-students, hinged on the essentially mechanistic nature of life; and concerned means for operating the organic machinery of mankind by calculated chemical action after the failure of natural processes. In his experiments with various animating solutions, he had killed and treated immense numbers of rabbits, guinea-pigs, cats, dogs, and monkeys, till he had become the prime nuisance of the college. Several times he had actually obtained signs of life in animals supposedly dead; in many cases violent signs; but he soon saw that the perfection of his process, if indeed possible, would necessarily involve a lifetime of research. It likewise became clear that, since the same solution never worked alike on different organic species, he would require human subjects for further and more specialised progress. It was here that he first came into conflict with the college authorities, and was debarred from future experiments by no less a dignitary than the dean of the medical school himself — the learned and benevolent Dr. Allan Halsey, whose work in behalf of the stricken is recalled by every old resident of Arkham.

I had always been exceptionally tolerant of West's pursuits, and we frequently discussed his theories, whose ramifications and corollaries were almost infinite. Holding with Haeckel that all life is a chemical and physical process, and that the so-called "soul" is a myth, my friend believed that artificial reanimation of the dead can depend only on the condition of the tissues; and that unless actual decomposition has set in, a corpse fully equipped with organs may with suitable measures be set going again in the peculiar fashion known as life. That the psychic or intellectual life might be impaired by the slight deterioration of sensitive brain-cells which even a short period of death would be apt to cause, West fully realised. It had at first been his hope to find a reagent which would restore vitality before the actual advent of death, and only repeated failures on animals had shewn him that the natural and artificial life-motions were incompatible. He then sought extreme freshness in his specimens, injecting his solutions into the blood immediately after the extinction of life. It was this circumstance which made the professors so carelessly sceptical, for they felt that true death had not occurred in any case. They did not stop to view the matter closely and reasoningly.

It was not long after the faculty had interdicted his work that West confided to me his resolution to get fresh human bodies in some manner, and continue in secret the experiments he could no longer perform openly. To hear him discussing ways and means was rather ghastly, for at the college we had never procured anatomical specimens ourselves.

Whenever the morgue proved inadequate, two local negroes attended to this matter, and they were seldom questioned. West was then a small, slender, spectacled youth with delicate features, yellow hair, pale blue eyes, and a soft voice, and it was uncanny to hear him dwelling on the relative merits of Christchurch Cemetery and the potter's field. We finally decided on the potter's field, because practically every body in Christchurch was embalmed; a thing of course ruinous to West's researches.

I was by this time his active and enthralled assistant, and helped him make all his decisions, not only concerning the source of bodies but concerning a suitable place for our loathsome work. It was I who thought of the deserted Chapman farmhouse beyond Meadow Hill, where we fitted up on the ground floor an operating room and a laboratory, each with dark curtains to conceal our midnight doings. The place was far from any road, and in sight of no other house, yet precautions were none the less necessary; since rumours of strange lights, started by chance nocturnal roamers, would soon bring disaster on our enterprise. It was agreed to call the whole thing a chemical laboratory if discovery should occur. Gradually we equipped our sinister haunt of science with materials either purchased in Boston or quietly borrowed from the college—materials carefully made unrecognisable save to expert eyes—and provided spades and picks for the many burials we should have to make in the cellar. At the college we used an incinerator, but the apparatus was too costly for our unauthorised laboratory. Bodies were always a nuisance—even the small guinea-pig bodies from the slight clandestine experiments in West's room at the boarding-house.

We followed the local death-notices like ghouls, for our specimens demanded particular qualities. What we wanted were corpses interred soon after death and without artificial preservation; preferably free from malforming disease, and certainly with all organs present. Accident victims were our best hope. Not for many weeks did we hear of anything suitable; though we talked with morgue and hospital authorities, ostensibly in the college's interest, as often as we could without exciting suspicion. We found that the college had first choice in every case, so that it might be necessary to remain in Arkham during the summer, when only the limited summer-school classes were held. In the end, though, luck favoured us; for one day we heard of an almost ideal case in the potter's field; a brawny young workman drowned only the morning before in Summer's Pond, and buried at the town's expense without delay or embalming. That afternoon we found the new grave, and determined to begin work soon after midnight.

It was a repulsive task that we undertook in the black small hours, even though we lacked at that time the special horror of graveyards which later experiences brought to us. We carried spades and oil dark lanterns, for although electric torches were then manufactured, they were not as satisfactory as the tungsten contrivances of today. The process of unearthing was slow and sordid—it might have been gruesomely poetical if we had been artists instead of scientists—and we were glad when our spades struck wood. When the pine box was fully uncovered, West scrambled down and removed the lid, dragging out and propping up the contents. I reached down and hauled the contents out of the grave, and then both toiled hard to restore the spot to its former appearance. The affair made us rather nervous, especially the stiff form and vacant face of our first trophy, but we managed to remove all traces of our visit. When we had patted down the last shovelful of earth, we put the specimen in a canvas sack and set out for the old Chapman place beyond Meadow Hill.

On an improvised dissecting-table in the old farmhouse, by the light of a powerful acetylene lamp, the specimen was not very spectral looking. It had been a sturdy and apparently unimaginative youth of wholesome plebeian type—large-framed, grey-eyed, and brown-haired—a sound animal without psychological subtleties, and probably having vital processes of the simplest and healthiest sort. Now, with the eyes closed, it looked more asleep than dead; though the expert test of my friend soon left no doubt on that score. We had at last what West had always longed for—a real dead man of the ideal kind, ready for the solution as prepared according to the most careful calculations and theories for human use. The tension on our part became very great. We knew that there was scarcely a chance for anything like complete success, and could not avoid hideous fears at possible grotesque results of partial animation. Especially were we apprehensive concerning the mind and impulses of the creature, since in the space following death some of the more delicate cerebral cells might well have suffered deterioration. I, myself, still held some curious notions about the traditional "soul" of man, and felt an awe at the secrets that might be told by one returning from the dead. I wondered what sights this placid youth might have seen in inaccessible spheres, and what he could relate if fully restored to life.

But my wonder was not overwhelming, since for the most part I shared the materialism of my friend. He was calmer than I as he forced a large quantity of his fluid into a vein of the body's arm, immediately binding the incision securely.

The waiting was gruesome, but West never faltered. Every now and then he applied his stethoscope to the specimen, and bore the negative results philosophically. After about three-quarters of an hour without the least sign of life he disappointedly pronounced the solution inadequate, but determined to make the most of his opportunity and try one change in the formula before disposing of his ghastly prize. We had that afternoon dug a grave in the cellar, and would have to fill it by dawn—for although we had fixed a lock on the house, we wished to shun even the remotest risk of a ghoulish discovery. Besides, the body would not be even approximately fresh the next night. So taking the solitary acetylene lamp into the adjacent laboratory, we left our silent guest on the slab in the dark, and bent every energy to the mixing of a new solution; the weighing and measuring supervised by West with an almost fanatical care.

The awful event was very sudden, and wholly unexpected. I was pouring something from one test-tube to another, and West was busy over the alcohol blast-lamp which had to answer for a Bunsen burner in this gasless edifice, when from the pitch-black room we had left there burst the most appalling and daemoniac succession of cries that either of us had ever heard. Not more unutterable could have been the chaos of hellish sound if the pit itself had opened to release the agony of the damned, for in one inconceivable cacophony was centered all the supernal terror and unnatural despair of animate nature. Human it could not have been—it is not in man to make such sounds—and without a thought of our late employment or its possible discovery, both West and I leaped to the nearest window like stricken animals; overturning tubes, lamp, and retorts, and vaulting madly into the starred abyss of the rural night. I think we screamed ourselves as we stumbled frantically toward the town, though as we reached the outskirts we put on a semblance of restraint—just enough to seem like belated revellers staggering home from a debauch.

We did not separate, but managed to get to West's room, where we whispered with the gas up until dawn. By then we had calmed ourselves a little with rational theories and plans for investigation, so that we could sleep through the day—classes being disregarded. But that evening two items in the paper, wholly unrelated, made it again impossible for us to sleep. The old deserted Chapman house had inexplicably burned to an amorphous heap of ashes; that we could understand because of the upset lamp. Also, an attempt had been made to disturb a new grave in the potter's field, as if by futile and spadeless clawing at the earth. That we could not understand, for we had patted down the mould very carefully.

And for seventeen years after that West would look frequently over his shoulder, and complain of fancied footsteps behind him. Now he has disappeared.

II. The Plague Demon

I shall never forget that hideous summer sixteen years ago, when like a noxious afrite from the halls of Eblis typhoid stalked leeringly through Arkham. It is by that satanic scourge that most recall the year, for truly terror brooded with bat-wings over the piles of coffins in the tombs of Christchurch Cemetery; yet for me there is a greater horror in that time—a horror known to me alone now that Herbert West has disappeared.

West and I were doing post-graduate work in summer classes at the medical school of Miskatonic University, and my friend had attained a wide notoriety because of his experiments leading toward the revivification of the dead. After the scientific slaughter of uncounted small animals the freakish work had ostensibly stopped by order of our sceptical dean, Dr. Allan Halsey; though West had continued to perform certain secret tests in his dingy boarding-house room, and had on one terrible and unforgettable occasion taken a human body from its grave in the potter's field to a deserted farmhouse beyond Meadow Hill.

I was with him on that odious occasion, and saw him inject into the still veins the elixir which he thought would to some extent restore life's chemical and physical processes. It had ended horribly—in a delirium of fear which we gradually came to attribute to our own overwrought nerves—and West had never afterward been able to shake off a maddening sensation of being haunted and hunted. The body had not been quite fresh enough; it is obvious that to restore normal mental attributes a body must be very fresh indeed; and the burning of the old house had prevented us from burying the thing. It would have been better if we could have known it was underground.

After that experience West had dropped his researches for some time; but as the zeal of the born scientist slowly returned, he again became importunate with the college faculty, pleading for the use of the dissecting-room and of fresh human specimens for the work he regarded as so overwhelmingly important. His pleas, however, were wholly in vain; for the decision of Dr. Halsey was inflexible, and the other professors all endorsed the verdict of their leader. In the radical theory of reanimation they saw nothing but the immature vagaries of a youthful enthusiast whose slight form, yellow hair, spectacled blue eyes, and soft voice gave no hint of the supernormal—almost diabolical—power of the cold brain within. I can see him now as he was then—and I shiver. He grew sterner of face, but never elderly. And now Sefton Asylum has had the mishap and West has vanished.

West clashed disagreeably with Dr. Halsey near the end of our last undergraduate term in a wordy dispute that did less credit to him than to the kindly dean in point of courtesy. He felt that he was needlessly and irrationally retarded in a supremely great work; a work which he could of course conduct to suit himself in later years, but which he wished to begin while still possessed of the exceptional facilities of the university. That the tradition-bound elders should ignore his singular results on animals, and persist in their denial of the possibility of re-animation, was inexpressibly disgusting and almost incomprehensible to a youth of West's logical temperament. Only greater maturity could help him understand the chronic mental limitations of the "professor-doctor" type—the product of generations of pathetic Puritanism; kindly, conscientious, and sometimes gentle and amiable, yet always narrow, intolerant, custom-ridden, and lacking in perspective. Age has more charity for these incomplete yet high-souled characters, whose worst real vice is timidity, and who are ultimately punished by general ridicule for their intellectual sins—sins like Ptolemaism, Calvinism, anti-Darwinism, anti-Nietzscheism, and every sort of Sabbatarianism and sumptuary legislation. West, young despite his marvellous scientific acquirements, had scant patience with good Dr. Halsey and his erudite colleagues; and nursed an increasing resentment, coupled with a desire to prove his theories to these obtuse worthies in some striking and dramatic fashion. Like most youths, he indulged in elaborate daydreams of revenge, triumph, and final magnanimous forgiveness.

And then had come the scourge, grinning and lethal, from the nightmare caverns of Tartarus. West and I had graduated about the time of its beginning, but had remained for additional work at the summer school, so that we were in Arkham when it broke with full daemoniac fury upon the town. Though not as yet licenced physicians, we now had our degrees, and were pressed frantically into public service as the numbers of the stricken grew. The situation was almost past management, and deaths ensued too frequently for the local undertakers fully to handle.

Burials without embalming were made in rapid succession, and even the Christchurch Cemetery receiving tomb was crammed with coffins of the unembalmed dead. This circumstance was not without effect on West, who thought often of the irony of the situation — so many fresh specimens, yet none for his persecuted researches! We were frightfully overworked, and the terrific mental and nervous strain made my friend brood morbidly.

But West's gentle enemies were no less harassed with prostrating duties. College had all but closed, and every doctor of the medical faculty was helping to fight the typhoid plague. Dr. Halsey in particular had distinguished himself in sacrificing service, applying his extreme skill with whole-hearted energy to cases which many others shunned because of danger or apparent hopelessness. Before a month was over the fearless dean had become a popular hero, though he seemed unconscious of his fame as he struggled to keep from collapsing with physical fatigue and nervous exhaustion. West could not withhold admiration for the fortitude of his foe, but because of this was even more determined to prove to him the truth of his amazing doctrines. Taking advantage of the disorganisation of both college work and municipal health regulations, he managed to get a recently deceased body smuggled into the university dissecting-room one night, and in my presence injected a new modification of his solution. The thing actually opened its eyes, but only stared at the ceiling with a look of soul-petrifying horror before collapsing into an inertness from which nothing could rouse it. West said it was not fresh enough—the hot summer air does not favour corpses. That time we were almost caught before we incinerated the thing, and West doubted the advisability of repeating his daring misuse of the college laboratory.

The peak of the epidemic was reached in August. West and I were almost dead, and Dr. Halsey did die on the 14th. The students all attended the hasty funeral on the 15th, and bought an impressive wreath, though the latter was quite overshadowed by the tributes sent by wealthy Arkham citizens and by the municipality itself. It was almost a public affair, for the dean had surely been a public benefactor. After the entombment we were all somewhat depressed, and spent the afternoon at the bar of the Commercial House; where West, though shaken by the death of his chief opponent, chilled the rest of us with references to his notorious theories. Most of the students went home, or to various duties, as the evening advanced; but West persuaded me to aid him in "making a night of it" West's landlady saw us arrive at his room about two in the morning, with a third man between us; and told her husband that we had all evidently dined and wined rather well.

Apparently this acidulous matron was right; for about 3 a.m. the whole house was aroused by cries coming from West's room, where when they broke down the door, they found the two of us unconscious on the blood-stained carpet, beaten, scratched, and mauled, and with the broken remnants of West's bottles and instruments around us. Only an open window told what had become of our assailant, and many wondered how he himself had fared after the terrific leap from the second story to the lawn which he must have made. There were some strange garments in the room, but West upon regaining consciousness said they did not belong to the stranger, but were specimens collected for bacteriological analysis in the course of investigations on the transmission of germ diseases. He ordered them burnt as soon as possible in the capacious fireplace. To the police we both declared ignorance of our late companion's identity. He was, West nervously said, a congenial stranger whom we had met at some downtown bar of uncertain location. We had all been rather jovial, and West and I did not wish to have our pugnacious companion hunted down.

That same night saw the beginning of the second Arkham horror—the horror that to me eclipsed the plague itself. Christ-church Cemetery was the scene of a terrible killing; a watchman having been clawed to death in a manner not only too hideous for description, but raising a doubt as to the human agency of the deed. The victim had been seen alive considerably after midnight—the dawn revealed the unutterable thing. The manager of a circus at the neighbouring town of Bolton was questioned, but he swore that no beast had at any time escaped from its cage. Those who found the body noted a trail of blood leading to the receiving tomb, where a small pool of red lay on the concrete just outside the gate. A fainter trail led away toward the woods, but it soon gave out.

The next night devils danced on the roofs of Arkham, and unnatural madness howled in the wind. Through the fevered town had crept a curse which some said was greater than the plague, and which some whispered was the embodied daemon-soul of the plague itself. Eight houses were entered by a nameless thing which strewed red death in its wake—in all, seventeen maimed and shapeless remnants of bodies were left behind by the voiceless, sadistic monster that crept abroad. A few persons had half seen it in the dark, and said it was white and like a malformed ape or anthropomorphic fiend. It had not left behind quite all that it had attacked, for sometimes it had been hungry. The number it had killed was fourteen; three of the bodies had been in stricken homes and had not been alive.

On the third night frantic bands of searchers, led by the police, captured it in a house on Crane Street near the Miskatonic campus. They had organised the quest with care, keeping in touch by means of volunteer telephone stations, and when someone in the college district had reported hearing a scratching at a shuttered window, the net was quickly spread. On account of the general alarm and precautions, there were only two more victims, and the capture was effected without major casualties. The thing was finally stopped by a bullet, though not a fatal one, and was rushed to the local hospital amidst universal excitement and loathing.

For it had been a man. This much was clear despite the nauseous eyes, the voiceless simianism, and the daemoniac savagery. They dressed its wound and carted it to the asylum at Sefton, where it beat its head against the walls of a padded cell for sixteen years—until the recent mishap, when it escaped under circumstances that few like to mention.

What had most disgusted the searchers of Arkham was the thing they noticed when the monster's face was cleaned—the mocking, unbelievable resemblance to a learned and self-sacrificing martyr who had been entombed but three days before—the late Dr. Allan Halsey, public benefactor and dean of the medical school of Miskatonic University.

To the vanished Herbert West and to me the disgust and horror were supreme. I shudder tonight as I think of it; shudder even more than I did that morning when West muttered through his bandages, "Damn it, it wasn't quite fresh enough!"

III. Six Shots by Moonlight

It is uncommon to fire all six shots of a revolver with great suddenness when one would probably be sufficient, but many things in the life of Herbert West were uncommon. It is, for instance, not often that a young physician leaving college is obliged to conceal the principles which guide his selection of a home and office, yet that was the case with Herbert West. When he and I obtained our degrees at the medical school of Miskatonic University, and sought to relieve our poverty by setting up as general practitioners, we took great care not to say that we chose our house because it was fairly well isolated, and as near as possible to the potter's field.

Reticence such as this is seldom without a cause, nor indeed was ours; for our requirements were those resulting from a life-work distinctly unpopular. Outwardly we were doctors only, but beneath the surface were aims of far greater and more terrible moment—for the essence of Herbert West's existence was a quest amid black and forbidden realms of the unknown, in which he hoped to uncover the secret of life and restore to perpetual animation the graveyard's cold clay. Such a quest demands strange materials, among them fresh human bodies; and in order to keep supplied with these indispensable things one must live quietly and not far from a place of informal interment.

West and I had met in college, and I had been the only one to sympathise with his hideous experiments. Gradually I had come to be his inseparable assistant, and now that we were out of college we had to keep together. It was not easy to find a good opening for two doctors in company, but finally the influence of the university secured us a practice in Bolton—a factory town near Arkham, the seat of the college. The Bolton Worsted Mills are the largest in the Miskatonic Valley, and their polyglot employees are never popular as patients with the local physicians. We chose our house with the greatest care, seizing at last on a rather run-down cottage near the end of Pond Street; five numbers from the closest neighbour, and separated from the local potter's field by only a stretch of meadow land, bisected by a narrow neck of the rather dense forest which lies to the north. The distance was greater than we wished, but we could get no nearer house without going on the other side of the field, wholly out of the factory district. We were not much displeased, however, since there were no people between us and our sinister source of supplies. The walk was a trifle long, but we could haul our silent specimens undisturbed.

Our practice was surprisingly large from the very first — large enough to please most young doctors, and large enough to prove a bore and a burden to students whose real interest lay elsewhere. The mill-hands were of somewhat turbulent inclinations; and besides their many natural needs, their frequent clashes and stabbing affrays gave us plenty to do. But what actually absorbed our minds was the secret laboratory we had fitted up in the cellar—the laboratory with the long table under the electric lights, where in the small hours of the morning we often injected West's various solutions into the veins of the things we dragged from the potter's field. West was experimenting madly to find something which would start man's vital motions anew after they had been stopped by the thing we call death, but had encountered the most ghastly obstacles. The solution had to be differently compounded for different types—what would serve for guinea-pigs would not serve for human beings, and different human specimens required large modifications.

The bodies had to be exceedingly fresh, or the slight decomposition of brain tissue would render perfect reanimation impossible. Indeed, the greatest problem was to get them fresh enough—West had had horrible experiences during his secret college researches with corpses of doubtful vintage. The results of partial or imperfect animation were much more hideous than were the total failures, and we both held fearsome recollections of such things. Ever since our first daemoniac session in the deserted farmhouse on Meadow Hill in Arkham, we had felt a brooding menace; and West, though a calm, blond, blue-eyed scientific automaton in most respects, often confessed to a shuddering sensation of stealthy pursuit. He half felt that he was followed—a psychological delusion of shaken nerves, enhanced by the undeniably disturbing fact that at least one of our reanimated specimens was still alive—a frightful carnivorous thing in a padded cell at Sefton. Then there was another—our first—whose exact fate we had never learned.

We had fair luck with specimens in Bolton—much better than in Arkham. We had not been settled a week before we got an accident victim on the very night of burial, and made it open its eyes with an amazingly rational expression before the solution failed. It had lost an arm—if it had been a perfect body we might have succeeded better.

Between then and the next January we secured three more; one total failure, one case of marked muscular motion, and one rather shivery thing—it rose of itself and uttered a sound. Then came a period when luck was poor; interments fell off, and those that did occur were of specimens either too diseased or too maimed for use. We kept track of all the deaths and their circumstances with systematic care.

One March night, however, we unexpectedly obtained a specimen which did not come from the potter's field. In Bolton the prevailing spirit of Puritanism had outlawed the sport of boxing—with the usual result. Surreptitious and ill-conducted bouts among the mill-workers were common, and occasionally professional talent of low grade was imported. This late winter night there had been such a match; evidently with disastrous results, since two timorous Poles had come to us with incoherently whispered entreaties to attend to a very secret and desperate case. We followed them to an abandoned barn, where the remnants of a crowd of frightened foreigners were watching a silent black form on the floor.

The match had been between Kid O'Brien—a lubberly and now quaking youth with a most un-Hibernian hooked nose—and Buck Robinson, "The Harlem Smoke." The negro had been knocked out, and a moment's examination shewed us that he would permanently remain so. He was a loathsome, gorilla-like thing, with abnormally long arms which I could not help calling fore legs, and a face that conjured up thoughts of unspeakable Congo secrets and tom-tom poundings under an eerie moon. The body must have looked even worse in life—but the world holds many ugly things. Fear was upon the whole pitiful crowd, for they did not know what the law would exact of them if the affair were not hushed up; and they were grateful when West, in spite of my involuntary shudders, offered to get rid of the thing quietly—for a purpose I knew too well.

There was bright moonlight over the snowless landscape, but we dressed the thing and carried it home between us through the deserted streets and meadows, as we had carried a similar thing one horrible night in Arkham. We approached the house from the field in the rear, took the specimen in the back door and down the cellar stairs, and prepared it for the usual experiment. Our fear of the police was absurdly great, though we had timed our trip to avoid the solitary patrolman of that section.

The result was wearily anticlimactic. Ghastly as our prize appeared, it was wholly unresponsive to every solution we injected in its black arm; solutions prepared from experience with white specimens only. So as the hour grew dangerously near to dawn, we did as we had done with the others—dragged the thing across the meadows to the neck of the woods near the potter's field, and buried it there in the best sort of grave the frozen ground would furnish. The grave was not very deep, but fully as good as that of the previous specimen—the thing which had risen of itself and uttered a sound. In the light of our dark lanterns we carefully covered it with leaves and dead vines, fairly certain that the police would never find it in a forest so dim and dense.

The next day I was increasingly apprehensive about the police, for a patient brought rumours of a suspected fight and death. West had still another source of worry, for he had been called in the afternoon to a case which ended very threateningly. An Italian woman had become hysterical over her missing child—a lad of five who had strayed off early in the morning and failed to appear for dinner—and had developed symptoms highly alarming in view of an always weak heart. It was a very foolish hysteria, for the boy had often run away before; but Italian peasants are exceedingly superstitious, and this woman seemed as much harassed by omens as by facts. About seven o'clock in the evening she had died, and her frantic husband had made a frightful scene in his efforts to kill West, whom he wildly blamed for not saving her life.

Friends had held him when he drew a stiletto, but West departed amidst his inhuman shrieks, curses and oaths of vengeance. In his latest affliction the fellow seemed to have forgotten his child, who was still missing as the night advanced. There was some talk of searching the woods, but most of the family's friends were busy with the dead woman and the screaming man. Altogether, the nervous strain upon West must have been tremendous. Thoughts of the police and of the mad Italian both weighed heavily.

We retired about eleven, but I did not sleep well. Bolton had a surprisingly good police force for so small a town, and I could not help fearing the mess which would ensue if the affair of the night before were ever tracked down. It might mean the end of all our local work—and perhaps prison for both West and me. I did not like those rumours of a fight which were floating about. After the clock had struck three the moon shone in my eyes, but I turned over without rising to pull down the shade. Then came the steady rattling at the back door. I lay still and somewhat dazed, but before long heard West's rap on my door. He was clad in dressing-gown and slippers, and had in his hands a revolver and an electric flashlight. From the revolver I knew that he was thinking more of the crazed Italian than of the police.

"We'd better both go," he whispered. "It wouldn't do not to answer it anyway, and it may be a patient—it would be like one of those fools to try the back door."

So we both went down the stairs on tiptoe, with a fear partly justified and partly that which comes only from the soul of the weird small hours. The rattling continued, growing somewhat louder. When we reached the door I cautiously unbolted it and threw it open, and as the moon streamed revealingly down on the form silhouetted there, West did a peculiar thing. Despite the obvious danger of attracting notice and bringing down on our heads the dreaded police investigation—a thing which after all was mercifully averted by the relative isolation of our cottage—my friend suddenly, excitedly, and unnecessarily emptied all six chambers of his revolver into the nocturnal visitor.

For that visitor was neither Italian nor policeman. Looming hideously against the spectral moon was a gigantic misshapen thing not to be imagined save in nightmares—a glassy-eyed, ink-black apparition nearly on all fours, covered with bits of mould, leaves, and vines, foul with caked blood, and having between its glistening teeth a snow-white, terrible, cylindrical object terminating in a tiny hand.

IV. The Scream of the Dead

The scream of a dead man gave to me that acute and added horror of Dr. Herbert West which harassed the latter years of our companionship. It is natural that such a thing as a dead man's scream should give horror, for it is obviously, not a pleasing or ordinary occurrence; but I was used to similar experiences, hence suffered on this occasion only because of a particular circumstance. And, as I have implied, it was not of the dead man himself that I became afraid.

Herbert West, whose associate and assistant I was, possessed scientific interests far beyond the usual routine of a village physician. That was why, when establishing his practice in Bolton, he had chosen an isolated house near the potter's field. Briefly and brutally stated, West's sole absorbing interest was a secret study of the phenomena of life and its cessation, leading toward the reanimation of the dead through injections of an excitant solution. For this ghastly experimenting it was necessary to have a constant supply of very fresh human bodies; very fresh because even the least decay hopelessly damaged the brain structure, and human because we found that the solution had to be compounded differently for different types of organisms. Scores of rabbits and guinea-pigs had been killed and treated, but their trail was a blind one. West had never fully succeeded because he had never been able to secure a corpse sufficiently fresh. What he wanted were bodies from which vitality had only just departed; bodies with every cell intact and capable of receiving again the impulse toward that mode of motion called life. There was hope that this second and artificial life might be made perpetual by repetitions of the injection, but we had learned that an ordinary natural life would not respond to the action. To establish the artificial motion, natural life must be extinct—the specimens must be very fresh, but genuinely dead.

The awesome quest had begun when West and I were students at the Miskatonic University Medical School in Arkham, vividly conscious for the first time of the thoroughly mechanical nature of life. That was seven years before, but West looked scarcely a day older now—he was small, blond, clean-shaven, soft-voiced, and spectacled, with only an occasional flash of a cold blue eye to tell of the hardening and growing fanaticism of his character under the pressure of his terrible investigations. Our experiences had often been hideous in the extreme; the results of defective reanimation, when lumps of graveyard clay had been galvanised into morbid, unnatural, and brainless motion by various modifications of the vital solution.

One thing had uttered a nerve-shattering scream; another had risen violently, beaten us both to unconsciousness, and run amuck in a shocking way before it could be placed behind asylum bars; still another, a loathsome African monstrosity, had clawed out of its shallow grave and done a deed—West had had to shoot that object. We could not get bodies fresh enough to shew any trace of reason when reanimated, so had perforce created nameless horrors. It was disturbing to think that one, perhaps two, of our monsters still lived—that thought haunted us shadowingly, till finally West disappeared under frightful circumstances. But at the time of the scream in the cellar laboratory of the isolated Bolton cottage, our fears were subordinate to our anxiety for extremely fresh specimens. West was more avid than I, so that it almost seemed to me that he looked half-covetously at any very healthy living physique.

It was in July, 1910, that the bad luck regarding specimens began to turn. I had been on a long visit to my parents in Illinois, and upon my return found West in a state of singular elation. He had, he told me excitedly, in all likelihood solved the problem of freshness through an approach from an entirely new angle—that of artificial preservation. I had known that he was working on a new and highly unusual embalming compound, and was not surprised that it had turned out well; but until he explained the details I was rather puzzled as to how such a compound could help in our work, since the objectionable staleness of the specimens was largely due to delay occurring before we secured them.

This, I now saw, West had clearly recognised; creating his embalming compound for future rather than immediate use, and trusting to fate to supply again some very recent and unburied corpse, as it had years before when we obtained the negro killed in the Bolton prize-fight. At last fate had been kind, so that on this occasion there lay in the secret cellar laboratory a corpse whose decay could not by any possibility have begun. What would happen on reanimation, and whether we could hope for a revival of mind and reason, West did not venture to predict. The experiment would be a landmark in our studies, and he had saved the new body for my return, so that both might share the spectacle in accustomed fashion.

West told me how he had obtained the specimen. It had been a vigorous man; a well-dressed stranger just off the train on his way to transact some business with the Bolton Worsted Mills. The walk through the town had been long, and by the time the traveller paused at our cottage to ask the way to the factories, his heart had become greatly overtaxed. He had refused a stimulant, and had suddenly dropped dead only a moment later. The body, as might be expected, seemed to West a heaven-sent gift. In his brief conversation the stranger had made it clear that he was unknown in Bolton, and a search of his pockets subsequently revealed him to be one Robert Leavitt of St. Louis, apparently without a family to make instant inquiries about his disappearance. If this man could not be restored to life, no one would know of our experiment.

We buried our materials in a dense strip of woods between the house and the potter's field. If, on the other hand, he could be restored, our fame would be brilliantly and perpetually established. So without delay West had injected into the body's wrist the compound which would hold it fresh for use after my arrival. The matter of the presumably weak heart, which to my mind imperilled the success of our experiment, did not appear to trouble West extensively. He hoped at last to obtain what he had never obtained before—a rekindled spark of reason and perhaps a normal, living creature.

So on the night of July 18, 1910, Herbert West and I stood in the cellar laboratory and gazed at a white, silent figure beneath the dazzling arc-light. The embalming compound had worked uncannily well, for as I stared fascinatedly at the sturdy frame which had lain two weeks without stiffening, I was moved to seek West's assurance that the thing was really dead. This assurance he gave readily enough; reminding me that the reanimating solution was never used without careful tests as to life, since it could have no effect if any of the original vitality were present.

As West proceeded to take preliminary steps, I was impressed by the vast intricacy of the new experiment; an intricacy so vast that he could trust no hand less delicate than his own. Forbidding me to touch the body, he first injected a drug in the wrist just beside the place his needle had punctured when injecting the embalming compound. This, he said, was to neutralise the compound and release the system to a normal relaxation so that the reanimating solution might freely work when injected. Slightly later, when a change and a gentle tremor seemed to affect the dead limbs; West stuffed a pillow-like object violently over the twitching face, not withdrawing it until the corpse appeared quiet and ready for our attempt at reanimation. The pale enthusiast now applied some last perfunctory tests for absolute lifelessness, withdrew satisfied, and finally injected into the left arm an accurately measured amount of the vital elixir, prepared during the afternoon with a greater care than we had used since college days, when our feats were new and groping. I cannot express the wild, breathless suspense with which we waited for results on this first really fresh specimen—the first we could reasonably expect to open its lips in rational speech, perhaps to tell of what it had seen beyond the unfathomable abyss.

West was a materialist, believing in no soul and attributing all the working of consciousness to bodily phenomena; consequently he looked for no revelation of hideous secrets from gulfs and caverns beyond death's barrier. I did not wholly disagree with him theoretically, yet held vague instinctive remnants of the primitive faith of my forefathers; so that I could not help eyeing the corpse with a certain amount of awe and terrible expectation. Besides—I could not extract from my memory that hideous, inhuman shriek we heard on the night we tried our first experiment in the deserted farmhouse at Arkham.

Very little time had elapsed before I saw the attempt was not to be a total failure. A touch of colour came to cheeks hitherto chalk-white, and spread out under the curiously ample stubble of sandy beard. West, who had his hand on the pulse of the left wrist, suddenly nodded significantly; and almost simultaneously a mist appeared on the mirror inclined above the body's mouth. There followed a few spasmodic muscular motions, and then an audible breathing and visible motion of the chest. I looked at the closed eyelids, and thought I detected a quivering.

Then the lids opened, shewing eyes which were grey, calm, and alive, but still unintelligent and not even curious.

In a moment of fantastic whim I whispered questions to the reddening ears; questions of other worlds of which the memory might still be present. Subsequent terror drove them from my mind, but I think the last one, which I repeated, was: "Where have you been?" I do not yet know whether I was answered or not, for no sound came from the well-shaped mouth; but I do know that at that moment I firmly thought the thin lips moved silently, forming syllables which I would have vocalised as "only now" if that phrase had possessed any sense or relevancy. At that moment, as I say, I was elated with the conviction that the one great goal had been attained; and that for the first time a reanimated corpse had uttered distinct words impelled by actual reason. In the next moment there was no doubt about the triumph; no doubt that the solution had truly accomplished, at least temporarily, its full mission of restoring rational and articulate life to the dead. But in that triumph there came to me the greatest of all horrors — not horror of the thing that spoke, but of the deed that I had witnessed and of the man with whom my professional fortunes were joined.

For that very fresh body, at last writhing into full and terrifying consciousness with eyes dilated at the memory of its last scene on earth, threw out its frantic hands in a life and death struggle with the air, and suddenly collapsing into a second and final dissolution from which there could be no return, screamed out the cry that will ring eternally in my aching brain:

"Help! Keep off, you cursed little tow-head fiend—keep that damned needle away from me!"

V. The Horror From the Shadows

Many men have related hideous things, not mentioned in print, which happened on the battlefields of the Great War. Some of these things have made me faint, others have convulsed me with devastating nausea, while still others have made me tremble and look behind me in the dark; yet despite the worst of them I believe I can myself relate the most hideous thing of all—the shocking, the unnatural, the unbelievable horror from the shadows.

In 1915 I was a physician with the rank of First Lieutenant in a Canadian regiment in Flanders, one of many Americans to precede the government itself into the gigantic struggle. I had not entered the army on my own initiative, but rather as a natural result of the enlistment of the man whose indispensable assistant I was—the celebrated Boston surgical specialist, Dr. Herbert West. Dr. West had been avid for a chance to serve as surgeon in a great war, and when the chance had come, he carried me with him almost against my will. There were reasons why I could have been glad to let the war separate us; reasons why I found the practice of medicine and the companionship of West more and more irritating; but when he had gone to Ottawa and through a colleague's influence secured a medical commission as Major, I could not resist the imperious persuasion of one determined that I should accompany him in my usual capacity.

When I say that Dr. West was avid to serve in battle, I do not mean to imply that he was either naturally warlike or anxious for the safety of civilisation. Always an ice-cold intellectual machine; slight, blond, blue eyed, and spectacled; I think he secretly sneered at my occasional martial enthusiasms and censures of supine neutrality. There was, however, something he wanted in embattled Flanders; and in order to secure it had had to assume a military exterior. What he wanted was not a thing which many persons want, but something connected with the peculiar branch of medical science which he had chosen quite clandestinely to follow, and in which he had achieved amazing and occasionally hideous results. It was, in fact, nothing more or less than an abundant supply of freshly killed men in every stage of dismemberment.

Herbert West needed fresh bodies because his life-work was the reanimation of the dead. This work was not known to the fashionable clientele who had so swiftly built up his fame after his arrival in Boston; but was only too well known to me, who had been his closest friend and sole assistant since the old days in Miskatonic University Medical School at Arkham. It was in those college days that he had begun his terrible experiments, first on small animals and then on human bodies shockingly obtained. There was a solution which he injected into the veins of dead things, and if they were fresh enough they responded in strange ways. He had had much trouble in discovering the proper formula, for each type of organism was found to need a stimulus especially adapted to it. Terror stalked him when he reflected on his partial failures; nameless things resulting from imperfect solutions or from bodies insufficiently fresh. A certain number of these failures had remained alive—one was in an asylum while others had vanished—and as he thought of conceivable yet virtually impossible eventualities he often shivered beneath his usual stolidity.

West had soon learned that absolute freshness was the prime requisite for useful specimens, and had accordingly resorted to frightful and unnatural expedients in body-snatching. In college, and during our early practice together in the factory town of Bolton, my attitude toward him had been largely one of fascinated admiration; but as his boldness in methods grew, I began to develop a gnawing fear. I did not like the way he looked at healthy living bodies; and then there came a nightmarish session in the cellar laboratory when I learned that a certain specimen had been a living body when he secured it. That was the first time he had ever been able to revive the quality of rational thought in a corpse; and his success, obtained at such a loathsome cost, had completely hardened him.

Of his methods in the intervening five years I dare not speak. I was held to him by sheer force of fear, and witnessed sights that no human tongue could repeat. Gradually I came to find Herbert West himself more horrible than anything he did — that was when it dawned on me that his once normal scientific zeal for prolonging life had subtly degenerated into a mere morbid and ghoulish curiosity and secret sense of charnel picturesqueness. His interest became a hellish and perverse addiction to the repellently and fiendishly abnormal; he gloated calmly over artificial monstrosities which would make most healthy men drop dead from fright and disgust; he became, behind his pallid intellectuality, a fastidious Baudelaire of physical experiment—a languid Elagabalus of the tombs.

Dangers he met unflinchingly; crimes he committed unmoved. I think the climax came when he had proved his point that rational life can be restored, and had sought new worlds to conquer by experimenting on the reanimation of detached parts of bodies. He had wild and original ideas on the independent vital properties of organic cells and nerve-tissue separated from natural physiological systems; and achieved some hideous preliminary results in the form of never-dying, artificially nourished tissue obtained from the nearly hatched eggs of an indescribably tropical reptile. Two biological points he was exceedingly anxious to settle—first, whether any amount of consciousness and rational action be possible without the brain, proceeding from the spinal cord and various nerve-centres; and second, whether any kind of ethereal, intangible relation distinct from the material cells may exist to link the surgically separated parts of what has previously been a single living organism. All this research work required a prodigious supply of freshly slaughtered human flesh—and that was why Herbert West had entered the Great War.

The phantasmal, unmentionable thing occurred one midnight late in March, 1915, in a field hospital behind the lines of St. Eloi. I wonder even now if it could have been other than a daemoniac dream of delirium. West had a private laboratory in an east room of the barn-like temporary edifice, assigned him on his plea that he was devising new and radical methods for the treatment of hitherto hopeless cases of maiming. There he worked like a butcher in the midst of his gory wares—I could never get used to the levity with which he handled and classified certain things. At times he actually did perform marvels of surgery for the soldiers; but his chief delights were of a less public and philanthropic kind, requiring many explanations of sounds which seemed peculiar even amidst that babel of the damned. Among these sounds were frequent revolver-shots—surely not uncommon on a battlefield, but distinctly uncommon in an hospital. Dr. West's reanimated specimens were not meant for long existence or a large audience. Besides human tissue, West employed much of the reptile embryo tissue which he had cultivated with such singular results. It was better than human material for maintaining life in organless fragments, and that was now my friend's chief activity. In a dark corner of the laboratory, over a queer incubating burner, he kept a large covered vat full of this reptilian cell-matter; which multiplied and grew puffily and hideously.

On the night of which I speak we had a splendid new specimen—a man at once physically powerful and of such high mentality that a sensitive nervous system was assured. It was rather ironic, for he was the officer who had helped West to his commission, and who was now to have been our associate. Moreover, he had in the past secretly studied the theory of reanimation to some extent under West. Major Sir Eric Moreland Clapham-Lee, D.S.O., was the greatest surgeon in our division, and had been hastily assigned to the St. Eloi sector when news of the heavy fighting reached headquarters. He had come in an aeroplane piloted by the intrepid Lieut. Ronald Hill, only to be shot down when directly over his destination. The fall had been spectacular and awful; Hill was unrecognisable afterward, but the wreck yielded up the great surgeon in a nearly decapitated but otherwise intact condition. West had greedily seized the lifeless thing which had once been his friend and fellow-scholar; and I shuddered when he finished severing the head, placed it in his hellish vat of pulpy reptile-tissue to preserve it for future experiments, and proceeded to treat the decapitated body .on the operating table. He injected new blood, joined certain veins, arteries, and nerves at the headless neck, and closed the ghastly aperture with engrafted skin from an unidentified specimen which had borne an officer's uniform. I knew what he wanted—to see if this highly organised body could exhibit, without its head, any of the signs of mental life which had distinguished Sir Eric Moreland Clapham-Lee. Once a student of reanimation, this silent trunk was now gruesomely called upon to exemplify it.

I can still see Herbert West under the sinister electric light as he injected his reanimating solution into the arm of the headless body. The scene I cannot describe—I should faint if I tried it, for there is madness in a room full of classified charnel things, with blood and lesser human debris almost ankle-deep on the slimy floor, and with hideous reptilian abnormalities sprouting, bubbling, and baking over a winking bluish-green spectre of dim flame in a far corner of black shadows.

The specimen, as West repeatedly observed, had a splendid nervous system. Much was expected of it; and as a few twitching motions began to appear, I could see the feverish interest on West's face. He was ready, I think, to see proof of his increasingly strong opinion that consciousness, reason, and personality can exist independently of the brain—that man has no central connective spirit, but is merely a machine of nervous matter, each section more or less complete in itself. In one triumphant demonstration West was about to relegate the mystery of life to the category of myth. The body now twitched more vigorously, and beneath our avid eyes commenced to heave in a frightful way. The arms stirred disquietingly, the legs drew up, and various muscles contracted in a repulsive kind of writhing. Then the headless thing threw out its arms in a gesture which was unmistakably one of desperation—an intelligent desperation apparently sufficient to prove every theory of Herbert West. Certainly, the nerves were recalling the man's last act in life; the struggle to get free of the falling aeroplane.

What followed, I shall never positively know. It may have been wholly an hallucination from the shock caused at that instant by the sudden and complete destruction of the building in a cataclysm of German shell-fire—who can gainsay it, since West and I were the only proved survivors? West liked to think that before his recent disappearance, but there were times when he could not; for it was queer that we both had the same hallucination. The hideous occurrence itself was very simple, notable only for what it implied.

The body on the table had risen with a blind and terrible groping, and we had heard a sound. I should not call that sound a voice, for it was too awful. And yet its timbre was not the most awful thing about it. Neither was its message—it had merely screamed, "Jump, Ronald, for God's sake, jump!" The awful thing was its source.

For it had come from the large covered vat in that ghoulish corner of crawling black shadows.

VI. The Tomb Legions

When Dr. Herbert West disappeared a year ago, the Boston police questioned me closely. They suspected that I was holding something back, and perhaps suspected graver things; but I could not tell them the truth because they would not have believed it. They knew, indeed, that West had been connected with activities beyond the credence of ordinary men; for his hideous experiments in the reanimation of dead bodies had long been too extensive to admit of perfect secrecy; but the final soul-shattering catastrophe held elements of daemoniac phantasy which make even me doubt the reality of what I saw.

I was West's closest friend and only confidential assistant. We had met years before, in medical school, and from the first I had shared his terrible researches. He had slowly tried to perfect a solution which, injected into the veins of the newly deceased, would restore life; a labour demanding an abundance of fresh corpses and therefore involving the most unnatural actions. Still more shocking were the products of some of the experiments—grisly masses of flesh that had been dead, but that

West waked to a blind, brainless, nauseous animation. These were the usual results, for in order to reawaken the mind it was necessary to have specimens so absolutely fresh that no decay could possibly affect the delicate brain-cells.

This need for very fresh corpses had been West's moral undoing.

They were hard to get, and one awful day he had secured his specimen while it was still alive and vigorous. A struggle, a needle, and a powerful alkaloid had transformed it to a very fresh corpse, and the experiment had succeeded for a brief and memorable moment; but West had emerged with a soul calloused and seared, and a hardened eye which sometimes glanced with a kind of hideous and calculating appraisal at men of especially sensitive brain and especially vigorous physique.

Toward the last I became acutely afraid of West, for he began to look at me that way. People did not seem to notice his glances, but they noticed my fear; and after his disappearance used that as a basis for some absurd suspicions.

West, in reality, was more afraid than I; for his abominable pursuits entailed a life of furtiveness and dread of every shadow. Partly it was the police he feared; but sometimes his nervousness was deeper and more nebulous, touching on certain indescribable things into which he had injected a morbid life, and from which he had not seen that life depart.

He usually finished his experiments with a revolver, but a few times he had not been quick enough. There was that first specimen on whose rifled grave marks of clawing were later seen. There was also that Arkham professor's body which had done cannibal things before it had been captured and thrust unidentified into a madhouse cell at Sefton, where it beat the walls for sixteen years. Most of the other possibly surviving results were things less easy to speak of—for in later years West's scientific zeal had degenerated to an unhealthy and fantastic mania, and he had spent his chief skill in vitalising not entire human bodies but isolated parts of bodies, or parts joined to organic matter other -than human. It had become fiendishly disgusting by the time he disappeared; many of the experiments could not even be hinted at in print. The Great War, through which both of us served as surgeons, had intensified this side of West.

In saying that West's fear of his specimens was nebulous, I have in mind particularly its complex nature. Part of it came merely from knowing of the existence of such nameless monsters, while another part arose from apprehension of the bodily harm they might under certain circumstances do him. Their disappearance added horror to the situation—of them all, West knew the whereabouts of only one, the pitiful asylum thing. Then there was a more subtle fear—a very fantastic sensation resulting from a curious experiment in the Canadian army in 1915. West, in the midst of a severe battle, had reanimated Major Sir Eric Moreland Clapham-Lee, D.S.O., a fellow-physician who knew about his experiments and could have duplicated them. The head had been removed, so that the possibilities of quasi-intelligent life in the trunk might be investigated. Just as the building was wiped out by a German shell, there had been a success. The trunk had moved intelligently; and, unbelievable to relate, we were both sickeningly sure that articulate sounds had come from the detached head as it lay in a shadowy corner of the laboratory. The shell had been merciful, in a way—but West could never feel as certain as he wished, that we two were the only survivors. He used to make shuddering conjectures about the possible actions of a headless physician with the power of reanimating the dead.

West's last quarters were in a venerable house of much elegance, overlooking one of the oldest burying-grounds in Boston. He had chosen the place for purely symbolic and fantastically aesthetic reasons, since most of the interments were of the colonial period and therefore of little use to a scientist seeking very fresh bodies. The laboratory was in a sub-cellar secretly constructed by imported workmen, and contained a huge incinerator for the quiet and complete disposal of such bodies, or fragments and synthetic mockeries of bodies, as might remain from the morbid experiments and unhallowed amusements of the owner. During the excavation of this cellar the workmen had struck some exceedingly ancient masonry; undoubtedly connected with the old burying-ground, yet far too deep to correspond with any known sepulchre therein. After a number of calculations West decided that it represented some secret chamber beneath the tomb of the Averills, where the last interment had been made in 1768. I was with him when he studied the nitrous, dripping walls laid bare by the spades and mattocks of the men, and was prepared for the gruesome thrill which would attend the uncovering of centuried grave-secrets; but for the first time West's new timidity conquered his natural curiosity, and he betrayed his degenerating fibre by ordering the masonry left intact and plastered over. Thus it remained till that final hellish night; part of the walls of the secret laboratory. I speak of West's decadence, but must add that it was a purely mental and intangible thing. Outwardly he was the same to the last—calm, cold, slight, and yellow-haired, with spectacled blue eyes and a general aspect of youth which years and fears seemed never to change. He seemed calm even when he thought of that clawed grave and looked over his shoulder; even when he thought of the carnivorous thing that gnawed and pawed at Sefton bars.

The end of Herbert West began one evening in our joint study when he was dividing his curious glance between the newspaper and me. A strange headline item had struck at him from the crumpled pages, and a nameless titan claw had seemed to reach down through sixteen years.

Something fearsome and incredible had happened at Sefton Asylum fifty miles away, stunning the neighbourhood and baffling the police. In the small hours of the morning a body of silent men had entered the grounds, and their leader had aroused the attendants. He was a menacing military figure who talked without moving his lips and whose voice seemed almost ventriloquially connected with an immense black case he carried. His expressionless face was handsome to the point of radiant beauty, but had shocked the superintendent when the hall light fell on it—for it was a wax face with eyes of painted glass. Some nameless accident had befallen this man. A larger man guided his steps; a repellent hulk whose bluish face seemed half eaten away by some unknown malady. The speaker had asked for the custody of the cannibal monster committed from Arkham sixteen years before; and upon being refused, gave a signal which precipitated a shocking riot. The fiends had beaten, trampled, and bitten every attendant who did not flee; killing four and finally succeeding in the liberation of the monster. Those victims who could recall the event without hysteria swore that the creatures had acted less like men than like unthinkable automata guided by the wax-faced leader. By the time help could be summoned, every trace of the men and of their mad charge had vanished.

From the hour of reading this item until midnight, West sat almost paralysed. At midnight the doorbell rang, startling him fearfully. All the servants were asleep in the attic, so I answered the bell. As I have told the police, there was no wagon in the street, but only a group of strange-looking figures bearing a large square box which they deposited in the hallway after one of them had grunted in a highly unnatural voice, "Express—prepaid." They filed out of the house with a jerky tread, and as I watched them go I had an odd idea that they were turning toward the ancient cemetery on which the back of the house abutted. When I slammed the door after them West came downstairs and looked at the box. It was about two feet square, and bore West's correct name and present address. It also bore the inscription, "From Eric Moreland Clapham-Lee, St. Eloi, Flanders." Six years before, in Flanders, a shelled hospital had fallen upon the headless reanimated trunk of Dr. Clapham-Lee, and upon the detached head which—perhaps—had uttered articulate sounds.

West was not even excited now. His condition was more ghastly. Quickly he said, "It's the finish—but let's incinerate—this." We carried the thing down to the laboratory—listening. I do not remember many particulars—you can imagine my state of mind—but it is a vicious lie to say it was Herbert West's body which I put into the incinerator.

We both inserted the whole unopened wooden box, closed the door, and started the electricity. Nor did any sound come from the box, after all.

It was West who first noticed the falling plaster on that part of the wall where the ancient tomb masonry had been covered up. I was going to run, but he stopped me. Then I saw a small black aperture, felt a ghoulish wind of ice, and smelled the charnel bowels of a putrescent earth. There was no sound, but just then the electric lights went out and I saw outlined against some phosphorescence of the nether world a horde of silent toiling things which only insanity—or worse—could create. Their outlines were human, semi-human, fractionally human, and not human at all—the horde was grotesquely heterogeneous. They were removing the stones quietly, one by one, from the centuried wall.

And then, as the breach became large enough, they came out into the laboratory in single file; led by a talking thing with a beautiful head made of wax. A sort of mad-eyed monstrosity behind the leader seized on Herbert West. West did not resist or utter a sound. Then they all sprang at him and tore him to pieces before my eyes, bearing the fragments away into that subterranean vault of fabulous abominations. West's head was carried off by the wax-headed leader, who wore a Canadian officer's uniform. As it disappeared I saw that the blue eyes behind the spectacles were hideously blazing with their first touch of frantic, visible emotion.

Servants found me unconscious in the morning. West was gone. The incinerator contained only unidentifiable ashes. Detectives have questioned me, but what can I say? The Sefton tragedy they will not connect with West; not that, nor the men with the box, whose existence they deny. I told them of the vault, and they pointed to the unbroken plaster wall and laughed. So I told them no more. They imply that I am either a madman or a murderer—probably I am mad. But I might not be mad if those accursed tomb-legions had not been so silent.

The Horror on the Freighter

Richard Lee Byers

In an attempt at self-purgation, I have already written one account of the crimes of Dr. Herbert West and my complicity therein. Should anyone ever read that document, and that document only, he will, quite properly, come away condemning us both.

But he won't see us as the same sort of man. He will loathe West for the fiend he was and despise me for a worm, because my previous confession suggests that while I came to recognize the abominable nature of my associate's experiments, I never once tried to stop them.

Until recently, I myself believed that to be true. But, torn to pieces by the terrible, pitiful creatures he reanimated, West has been dead a year, and over time, the knowledge of his destruction has apparently loosened a knot inside my mind. I now remember what was lost to me before.

Such being the case, I am appending this codicil to my original chronicle. I am not fool enough to imagine the new information mitigates my guilt. Nothing can ever do that. Still, I would have the record show that, appearances to the contrary, I was not after all an utter coward.

Dazzled by West's genius and what seemed the promise of his work, I functioned as his loyal assistant for several years. But I came to my senses when he murdered a traveler named Robert Leavitt to obtain the freshest possible subject for his next attempt at reanimation.

It was by no means the first death in which we were culpable. Two of our previous experiments had embarked on homicidal rampages. But I told myself those were accidents. In the case of Leavitt, no such rationalization was possible, and I belatedly recognized West for the ruthless, reckless fanatic he truly was

Yet seeing is one thing, acting another. Leavitt's murder planted the seed of betrayal, but after my years of subservience, that seed took time to flower. It was only after West and I relocated from the mill town of Bolton to Boston that I resolved to put an end to his crimes.

Unfortunately, I couldn't do so by reporting them to the authorities. The police would have arrested me, too, and much as I deserved it, I didn't want to spend the rest of my life in prison.

That left only murder as a remedy. The question was how to accomplish it.

At first glance, the answer seemed obvious. No one would hear gunshots sounding from West's basement laboratory, and the acid tank would dissolve his body as thoroughly as it dissolved the flesh of his experiments.

Yet on further consideration, I decided this simple plan wouldn't do. By then, West was one of the city's more prominent surgical specialists. If he simply disappeared, he would be missed, and the police might suspect his closest associate of foul play. They might search our home thoroughly enough to discover the gruesome secrets concealed in the cellar.

It would be safer if West was found dead well away from the house, in circumstances that deflected suspicion from me and appeared to render a painstaking search of his domicile superfluous. And I believed I knew how to manage that.

At the start of his investigations, West relied on the chemicals available to any conventional medical researcher. But as the years passed, and he kept falling short of his goals, he tried adding more exotic ingredients to his reagent.

To procure them, he had somehow established communication with a worldwide smuggling network, and when a strange insectivorous plant, cage full of eyeless bone-white scorpions, or jar of toxic crimson fungus arrived, we ventured to the waterfront late at night with a considerable sum of cash to take delivery. At the time of which I write, the occasion for another such transaction was at hand.

For my purposes, the situation seemed ideal. The note West had received from his contact neither mentioned my name nor specified the nature of the contraband. But it did make it clear that criminals had summoned him to purchase something illicit.

My plan was to ensure West never returned home from that meeting. Instead, sunrise would reveal his lifeless body lying on the docks, and when the police arrived, the most cursory search would discover the incriminating message tucked in his pocket. At which point (I hoped) the authorities would leap to the obvious conclusion.

To wit, the clandestine meeting had gone wrong. The criminals had murdered the small, blond, bespectacled surgeon and absconded with his money while Daniel Cain was home asleep in bed with nary a suspicion that his friend and colleague had gotten involved in anything illegal.

On the night of the rendezvous, the dank air smelled of saltwater and oil, and a thin mist had blown in from the sea. Blurred by the fog and the dark, the shapes of warehouses, cranes, and ships floating at their moorings were vague and ghostly, the lights, mere smears of phosphorescence.

In other words, conditions appeared perfect to shoot a man in the back and then run away without getting caught, and, my pulse ticking in my neck and my palms sweaty, I was eager to get on with it. The hatred I had come to feel for West and my need to be free of him burned in me like a fever, and I could barely keep my hand away from the Colt revolver weighting my overcoat pocket.

But my luck was bad. The hub of trade that is Boston Harbor never really sleeps, and as West and I approached our destination, I kept glimpsing or hearing longshoremen, mariners, and others, close enough that, despite the limited visibility, I hesitated to make my move. Reassuring myself that the right moment would surely present itself after West and I met his suppliers, I followed him on toward the freighter.

Like other vessels in the smugglers' fleet, the ship was a grimy rusted hulk. Barely legible, the painted name *Star of Borneo* was flaking away above the waterline.

Clad in a shabby approximation of an officer's uniform, an Asian man waved for us to come aboard. After my previous encounters with the smugglers, this was as I expected. White faces were rare in their fraternity. All the officers on the ships were Chinese, and the crews, mostly so, with a sprinkling of Arabs, Hindus, Africans, and, for all I knew, hands from Borneo and its environs.

Still mute—it was by no means a certainty that he spoke English—the officer led us across the deck to a hatch and the companionway below. This was not quite as expected but still didn't impress me as cause for alarm. Whatever West was buying, apparently no one had gotten around to bringing it up from the hold.

West and I started down, and the officer dropped the hatch above us. Our steps clanked and echoed. Then I smelled a dry, musky odor, and in the gloom beneath our feet, something hissed like an enormous serpent.

West and I both faltered. Then he said, "Well! I didn't realize…"

"Realize what?" I asked. "What's down there?"

"Come and see," he replied, then hurried down the remaining steps.

I followed more cautiously and caught up with him at the bottom of the companionway. There, he stood peering at the cage that someone had presumably dragged forth from its hiding place amid the stacks of crated mundane cargo.

A full fifteen feet long, the beast inside was reptilian with a set of fearsome jaws and glaring, beady eyes. It stood on four clawed feet, and a long tail depended from its hindquarters. Yet no one could mistake it for some species of alligator or crocodile. The spiny sail rising from its back and protruding through the bars that ran across the top of the cage precluded that.

I was no paleontologist, but I was a scientist and possessed some familiarity with the discoveries of Cope, Marsh, and others like them. Thus I recognized the creature as an animal that ought not to exist in our modern world except as a fossil in the Red Beds of Texas, and I gaped at it with a mix of wonder and wariness, the bars that confined it notwithstanding.

"Remarkable, is she not?" said a cultured baritone voice.

Startled, West and I turned toward the Chinese gentleman who was just emerging from the stacks of crates. He was tall and gaunt, no longer young but not yet elderly, with a high, bald forehead and the most arresting eyes I had ever seen (and I had looked into the eyes of the reanimated dead). Vividly green, they seemed to catch the ambient light like a cat's.

I knew little of life in China, but from the gaunt man's embroidered silk robe, I might have taken him for a scholar, aristocrat, or government official. Certainly, he looked out of place in his current surroundings.

The mandarin, if that was the proper term for him, executed a shallow bow. "Dr. West," he said.

West bowed in return. As did I, although it already seemed clear that the Chinese gentleman had no interest in including me in the conversation.

"Good evening," said West, and then, after a moment's hesitation, "I'm afraid the message I received didn't include your name."

The aristocrat's lips quirked into the briefest and slightest of smiles. "I accumulate names and titles as a dog accumulates fleas. Perhaps it will be simplest if we simply address one another as 'Doctor.'"

"Whatever you want," said West.

The mandarin gestured toward the cage, a motion that provoked another hiss from its prisoner. "What do you think of our friend?"

"I'm astonished, of course," West replied. "The information merely alluded to an uncatalogued tropical reptile, not a creature believed extinct for millions of years. I must know, where did you find it?"

"In the general vicinity of Sumatra," the Chinese doctor said, "but well removed from the sea lanes, is an island with a promontory resembling a skull. The interior abounds in fauna and flora from ages past."

"Amazing," said West. Circling to view the creature from different angles, he stepped closer. The reptile's black little eyes tracked his movements.

"Please," said the man in the silken robe, "be careful not to put your hand between the bars. She bites."

"Amazing," West repeated, turning back toward the mandarin. "Amazing, but a bit of a problem. I was under the impression I was simply buying the eggs, not their source. Please, don't mistake me. I certainly will purchase the animal. But I need time to arrange—"

The Chinese gentleman raised a long-fingered hand. "No need. You are only purchasing the eggs. The reptile herself is on her way to Limehouse to join a collection of rare and useful animals that I maintain there. I simply exhibited her to you in the hope you would find her interesting. A courtesy, or, if you will, a token of respect for the groundbreaking nature of your work."

West frowned. "How can you know anything about my work?"

"I have many duties within my organization. One is overseeing the activities of our smugglers. Thus I know what you have procured from us over the course of the past few years, and in the aggregate, those items tell the story. You aspire to resurrect the dead."

West's mouth tightened, and I eased my hand toward my revolver. Neither of us liked the idea that anyone else, even a fellow criminal, was aware of our experiments.

Yet there was no sign of threat in the Chinese doctor's demeanor. Smiling that subtlest of smiles once more, he simply stood and waited for West and me to recover from our surprise.

After a moment, evidently reassured, West asked, "Is it really that obvious?"

"Probably only to me," our companion said. "As it happens, my own research somewhat parallels your own. I am endeavoring to perfect a longevity drug. I wonder if you have considered such a project."

West shrugged. "Briefly. But a man can't work on everything at once, especially when he has to work in secret. And, with all respect, a longevity treatment won't save the unfortunate who succumbs to cholera or steps in front of a bus. My reagent will. It represents the greater benefit to mankind."

The mandarin inclined his head a fraction. "Perhaps. What is beyond dispute is that it will provide a formidable advantage to the United States and its European allies."

Behind their spectacles, West's blue eyes blinked. "Excuse me?"

"What force could defeat armies whose soldiers fall only to rise again?"

"I'm not working for the government."

"But you are an American, Dr. West, and when the moment comes to proclaim your discovery, you will announce it to your countrymen. Still, I suppose that needn't concern a man such as myself. Outlaws will be outlaws no matter who rules the world. Shall we conclude our business?"

"If you like." West glanced at me. "Bring out the money."

I reached inside my coat, which is to say, away from my revolver. At that instant, a length of cloth whipped around my neck and pulled tight, cutting off my air. Across from me, a man in a turban lunged from behind a pile of crates, took West from behind, and choked him with a noose.

Thrashing, I tried to work my fingertips under the cloth that was strangling me. When that failed, I remembered the Colt. I fumbled it out of my pocket and tried to point it behind me, but someone grabbed it and twisted it out of my hand.

My ears ringing, my vision darkening, I was sure I was about to die. But when I was on the verge of passing out, the pressure constricting my throat abated. The smuggler who had garroted me grabbed one of my forearms, and the man who had taken my gun, the other.

For the moment, they were holding me up more than forestalling any further attempts at resistance. Similarly immobilized, slumped in his captors' grips, West was plainly as weak as I was.

"The legendary Thugs," the Chinese doctor said. "They live up to their reputation, do they not?"

West sucked in a ragged breath. "Why are you doing this?" he wheezed.

"I was being disingenuous before," the mandarin replied. "The truth is, my organization *does* care about the fortunes of the United States, Great Britain, and the other colonial powers. That is because we intend to bring them down. Our smuggling and other seemingly mundane crimes are all in service to that end."

"Why?" asked West. "What do you have against America?"

For a second, the aristocrat's jade eyes seemed to burn brighter. "I surmise that you have never traveled in China, Dr. West, or any other land where white invaders have degraded, enslaved, and slaughtered the inhabitants. Otherwise, you would not need to ask."

West managed a twisted smile. "So, after everything I've done myself, I'm going to die for other people's crimes?"

"No," the mandarin said.

West raised his head. "No?"

"I *was* speaking the truth when I expressed admiration for your intellect and ambitions, and I am loath to remove you from the world. Happily, that will prove unnecessary. You will leave here alive and well with the items you came for, and in the days to come, my organization will continue to meet your needs to the best of its ability. But first, we must make an adjustment."

"Meaning what?"

The gaunt man held out his hand. A Chinese seaman emerged from the shadows and presented him with a syringe. The liquid inside was a murky blue.

"The Azure Whisper," the mandarin said, "dates from the early days of the Xia Dynasty, and the secret of its composition has eluded my every attempt at analysis. There are only a few drops left in all the world, and it is another mark of respect that I choose to use them to preserve your existence."

"What will it do?" West asked. "Paralyze me? Reduce me to an imbecile?"

The leader of the smugglers sighed. "You disappoint me, Doctor. Have I not already promised you will depart unharmed to continue your research? The Azure Whisper renders the effect of certain forms of hypnotic suggestion more permanent and profound. Which is to say, it allows one to tweak the subject's personality, augmenting some traits and suppressing others."

West forced a laugh. "And you really think that will work on me?"

"I do," the gaunt man said, "Men such as ourselves, men of genius and will, often have a streak of cruelty or even perversity in their natures. Consider Tamerlane with his mountains of severed heads and Vlad Dracul with his forests of impaled men. I have every confidence those qualities reside in you, Doctor, and I propose to enhance them. From this day forward, you will care less and less about gracing mankind with immortality and more and more about discovering the most grotesque and macabre results your reagent can produce, without, of course, remembering why or even realizing you are changing. My hope is that in some small way, the fruits of your labors will damage your country and so aid my cause. Now that you understand, shall we begin?"

The mandarin tapped the syringe to bring the bubbles to the top and depressed the plunger sufficiently to expel the gas. He then advanced on West, who wrenched himself back and forth, straining to break free of the two men holding him, but to no avail.

The Chinese scientist slipped the needle into the side of West's neck. His cries echoing from the bulkheads, West screamed and thrashed.

His agony was so palpable that, out of simple instinctive empathy, perhaps, a strange thing happened: I forgot I had come to hate him. For that moment, he was once again my friend, and I was relieved on his behalf when he finally stopped shrieking and went limp. But my relief was short-lived, because there was worse to come.

West appeared unconscious but was evidently still aware on some level. For the Chinese doctor took his head between his hands, lifted it, leaned in close, stared him in the eyes, and started murmuring.

West didn't convulse as he had before. The drug had rendered him incapable of such exertions. But periodically, his muscles clenched and jerked, and his features twitched and twisted. Tears of blood leaked from his eyes. Plainly, he was in at least as much pain as before, only now it was a pain of the mind and spirit.

The master of the smugglers was speaking too softly, too intimately, for me to make out what he was saying. But however he was accomplishing his purpose, there was a sick fascination to watching him warp a man's soul into a new shape, and at first, wracked with pity and horror, I could only stare. Then the Thug who had choked me, and who was currently holding onto my left arm, made a tiny sound that hinted at his own revulsion.

The noise reminded me of his presence and by extension of my own danger, for I certainly didn't imagine that the smugglers intended to deal with me any more kindly than they were dealing with West. Did I have any chance at all?

One, perhaps. If the men restraining me were as intent on their leader's performance as I had been. If it had distracted them from their own task. It felt to me as if their grips had slackened just a little.

I jerked my foot up and stamped on one man's toes. Yanked my arm free of his grasp and jammed my elbow back into his midsection. Twisted and gouged at his partner's eyes.

I continued my frenzied assault until I was free and my erstwhile captors had retreated beyond the reach of my flailing hands to regroup. It was plain from their snarls of rage that it would only take them a moment to do so, and then they'd rush me. I certainly had no hope of evading them and all the other smugglers in the hold and making my way off the ship.

So I scrambled to the reptile's cage.

The latching mechanism was sturdy enough to contain an animal of considerable strength but simple to release. I depressed a handle and swung open the door.

In so doing, I placed myself in a wedge-shaped space between two sets of bars. The living fossil could have circled around and killed me anyway, but I was no longer the easiest target. The two smugglers who were chasing after me were. There was no barrier whatsoever between the reptile and them.

Despite its stubby legs, the creature scuttled forth from its confinement fast as an arrow flying from a bow. The sail on its back rattled against the bar forming the top of the exit.

The reptile snapped and caught my first pursuer—the one in the turban, the Thug—by the leg. It bit down and jerked its head, and its fangs sheared off the limb in a shower of blood. The Thug fell down screaming, and I felt a pang of vicious satisfaction.

His Chinese companion recoiled. Spitting out the severed leg, the reptile lunged after him, bit into his midsection, and tore out loops of intestines. This time, the beast paused to feed, to snap down the lengths of gut and rip out its prey's stomach and liver, the dying man writhing and howling all the while.

By then, other smugglers were crying out. The two who were holding up the semiconscious West dropped him and scurried toward the companionway. One waved for their leader to follow.

The mandarin gave them a sneer and then fixed on the reptile. Raising his voice, he rattled off words in his native language.

Whatever he said, it seemed intended to attract the creature's attention, and that was the result. The reptile left off rooting in the body cavity of its second victim to turn in his direction.

Still speaking, the Chinese scientist paced toward the beast. He slipped the fingers of his right hand into his voluminous left sleeve.

The reptile lunged and bit. The gaunt man twisted aside, avoiding the jagged, bloody fangs as they clashed shut, snatched a folded black kerchief from its hiding place, and lashed it through the air in front of his attacker's nostrils. The whipping action opened the cloth, and the gray dust inside it darkened the air.

The animal froze and then fell down thrashing. As it rolled, its convulsions snapped the spines supporting the sail on its back and reduced that unique appendage to tatters.

Showing no ill effects from inhaling the poison he'd just administered, the master of the smugglers retreated a few steps and waited for the reptile's death agonies to subside. Once they did, he called out something else in his own language, and, shamefaced, the followers who'd fled came slinking back.

Which is to say, they were advancing on me, and, recognizing there was no escaping them, I pushed the cage door back to its original position and stepped away from it. I didn't want to meet my fate like an animal cowering in a hole.

"All right," I said to the mandarin. "Kill me. I've got it coming."

"So you do," he replied, "and after the inconvenience you have just now caused me, I would enjoy dispatching you with all the tools of the torturer's art. But unfortunately, Herbert West would miss his faithful servant. Your absence would nag at him, and, over time, perhaps even undermine my tampering. So I have a syringe of the Azure Whisper for you, too."

A wild impulse took me, and I charged the Chinese gentleman, but his followers interposed themselves between us. At the conclusion of a brief but savage struggle, the surviving Thug choked me into helplessness.

"I infer," the gaunt man said, "that you do not wish to accompany Dr. West on his descent into atrocity."

"Please," I gasped, "I can't take any more. Even before we came here tonight, I meant to put an end to it."

"But now you'll drown in it," the mandarin said, "with never a thought that you could disobey. That will be your punishment."

A Man Called West

Glynn Barrass and Ron Shiflet

I. A Chance Encounter

I had only been working for Dr. West a few days when it became apparent that he lived in great fear of being discovered by someone or something. Our first meeting had been a chance encounter and one very much to his advantage. It had occurred one lonely night on the Falmouth beach as he was being set upon by a young gang of hoodlums.

Having been released from prison only days earlier, my first instinct was to mind my own business. Trouble was the last thing I needed but my blood began to boil as I watched the would-be toughs kick and pummel the smaller figure.

"Well Riley," I said, "here's where you put your foot right in it."

With a sigh of regret, I clenched my fists and went charging down the sandy embankment and into the center of the melee. I hadn't yelled or cried out a warning but instead descended upon them in a storm of fists and well placed kicks. Two of the surprised punks went down bleeding before realizing what was happening. A quick glance at the victim—who I later learned was Dr. West—revealed a stunned look of amazement and gratitude.

"Look out!" He yelled as one of the attackers swung a large piece of driftwood at my head. West's warning saved me a headache as the weapon glanced off my shoulder.

I buried a right fist up to the wrist in the careless fool's belly and grinned as his breath escaped with a loud "Whoosh!" He fell to his knees and a kick to the face finished the job. Three of the attackers were now out of commission and the remaining two backed away warily with their hands in the air.

"We're leaving Mister!" Cried one as he turned to run.

I laughed heartily as the battered youths struggled to their feet and staggered off into the night. Turning to their harried, tow-headed victim, I said, "Looks like they bit off more than they could chew."

The smaller man smiled, wiped sand from his glasses and said, "My name is Dr. West and I'm immensely grateful for your timely intervention."

"A saw-bones huh?" I asked, extending my hand.

"I've been called that and worse," he replied. "I hope you haven't suffered any injuries on my account."

"Nothing that a stiff drink won't fix."

West's looked me over appraisingly and chuckled. "You're a large fellow. In what line of work are you employed?"

I started to lie but there was something about West that caused me to blurt out the truth. "I'm without a job. I just got out of prison."

He seemed completely unfazed by my admission.

"I suppose at one time or another that we've all done things not sanctioned by society."

"Yeah," I agreed. "Let he who is without sin . . ."

"Don't worry Mr. . . . uh?"

"Barnes," I supplied. "Riley Barnes."

"Well Barnes, Herbert West is not one to cast stones."

"Glad to hear it, Dr. West," I said. "Did you get hurt in the ruckus?"

"I'll live," he replied. "Now what say we go someplace and have that stiff drink you mentioned?"

"Lead the way," I happily replied.

If only I had known then what I know now.

West led me to a summer house, vacated for the season by its rightful owner. I didn't know that at the time but it was only one of many things I didn't know about Herbert West back then.

He fixed me that drink—several actually—and before the night was over had offered me a job. It didn't pay too well but it wasn't as if I had any other offers lined up at the time. Most people just aren't too eager to hire a jailbird.

"Barnes," West said, pouring another drink. "You've been honest with me and I think it only fair that I respond in kind."

I nodded and let him continue.

"I'm currently working on medical research that will be a boon to all mankind. However, there are certain members of the medical community who are insanely jealous of my early successes and desire to eliminate me at all costs."

"Rub you out?" I asked incredulously.

"Yes, I know how unbelievable that sounds," West replied. "But, success breeds many bitter enemies and there are just as many unscrupulous crooks in my field as in yours . . . which was what again?"

I laughed. "Dock-worker, boxer, leg breaker, take your pick."

"Well, maybe almost as many in my field," he chuckled. "Still, you're just the type of man I can use. You're strong, not a stranger to violence, and can obviously take care of yourself judging from what I observed back there on the beach."

"They were just kids," I said modestly.

"Five very large kids," West answered. "So, I'll get to the point. I need someone to act as bodyguard and to run occasional errands for me since it's imperative that I keep a low profile. In return, I can offer you room and board and a small check each month. Your acceptance of my offer will allow me to work unfettered on the important research I mentioned earlier. So what do you say Mr. Barnes?"

"Hell, I don't even have to think about it," I answered. "I'll take it!"

My first week in West's employment was a piece of cake. I didn't do a hell of a lot and spent the majority of my time listening to the radio or reading pulp magazines. West insisted that I take periodic walks around the windswept dunes and be on the lookout for any suspicious characters. I often got a laugh out of this last request since we were the only suspicious characters in the area.

These outside jaunts were always welcome since it gave me the chance to escape the noxious fumes that frequently drifted downstairs from West's upstairs laboratory. He hadn't given me a tour of that part of the house and had rebuffed my hints to have a look at it.

"It's really pretty mundane," he told me. "But once things progress, I'll be glad to show you."

I couldn't say if things were progressing or not but loud thuds and bumping sounds often emanated from the lab and his answers to my questioning was "Lab animals." Maybe so, but I wondered what type of lab animals would cause my employer to cry out in alarm and fire off three rounds from a .38 revolver. I meant to ask him about that but what I learned after a trip into Falmouth for supplies caused the subject to be dropped.

While purchasing some grub at the area grocer's, I saw a bad character named Trevor Towers who I had once fought to a bloody fifteen round draw in the prize ring. I remained obscured behind some canned goods as I heard him question the clerk.

"Do you know of a Herbert West who might be living around Falmouth?"

II. Stalking West

I'd been working the guy over for quite a while, concentrating all my punches on his skinny, ugly face. The problem is though, that once you've pounded a guy's nose and eyes to mush (well, only one eye this time, as I needed him to see what I was going to do next) and then bashed in his mouth and teeth, all you're eventually doing is bruising the knuckles beneath your leather gloves and whacking against numbed muscle and weeping flesh. The guy had even peed his pants around halfway through my interrogation, which I thought was a good sign, a sign that he was ready to talk, but nothing but the stink of urine was forthcoming from that gibbering little mess I'd been working over.

All said and done, the human face can really take a lot of damage, and what you see on the movies about some guy knocking a bozo out with one punch is all bullshit. But when you see some poor drunken bum in the street with his face smashed up from a bar fight but still conscious and wandering round? That's the truth of it really. Beating up on a guy till his face is a pulpy mess will only get you so far, if you want to get the right answers off of him that is.

That's why I'd brought along the pruning shears.

Anyway, before I get too ahead of myself I'd maybe better explain why I was in that tiny room in that roach-pit hotel almost torturing a guy to death I'd met less than an hour before.

My name is Trevor Towers, I'm an ex-marine with too many medals to mention and an ex-wife I don't like to think about, and since I left the army I've been making my bread by hiring myself out as a bodyguard, manhunter and general heavy handed thug when the cash is right.

Now the man I'd been hired to track down had been leading me on a merry chase for just over three months, ever since he'd disappeared without a trace from a little town called Arkham near the Massachusetts coast. But, like all scumbags with a secret to hide this fella didn't stay hidden for long, and a month after he'd disappeared he resurfaced in Boston, and after picking up his trail I managed to track his wanderings all through the coastal cities of New England till I finally got ahold of his assistant in a sunny little town called Falmouth on the edge of Nantucket Sound. Not the best of leads, but a lot better than the ghosts I'd been chasing for so long.

Now don't feel too sorry for the guy when I describe what I did to him after beating him to a pulp. Trust me, if you knew even half of the awful things he'd done with his boss you'd be egging me on to get a bit rougher with the dope.

As it was, I was a bit pissed at him anyway, mainly due to the fact that after I'd snuck into his hotel room, one of those cheap two room affairs with a bed and a kitchen in one room and a shower in the other, he'd jumped me from behind and tried wrapping his high grade silk paisley tie around my neck. Why the idiot thought I'd just stand there letting him strangle me instead of shoving my elbow halfway into his gut I have no idea. He went down with his face all red and surprised, I turned round to snarl at the silly little twerp, and after closing the door behind me we both got down to a little quiet conversation.

My would be assassin soon gave up struggling after I'd booted him in the chest a couple of times, and getting the wretch up into an arm chair and tied up using his pretty silk tie was accomplished quicker than I can say it.

Anyway, the reason I was wailing on this guy was because he had information my employer was very desperate to find out, and I was going to use any means necessary to get that information from him.

That's why I'd brought along the pruning shears.

I'd already stuffed a sock in his mouth, not only to curb his screams but also to make sure he didn't bite through his tongue from the pain I was about to inflict. I indicated mind you, mimed if you will, what I was going to do to him before I did it. I'm not a totally heartless torturer and I wanted to give him the chance of getting out of there in one piece. But when my chopping motions evinced no change in his resigned demeanor I got right down to business.

Trouble and torture is my business.

Holding his left hand down against the chair arm I then proceeded to dig into his pinky finger with the cheap hedge clippers I'd bought from a hardware store. He squirmed like hell as I cut through to the bone, and me being a bit out of practice with this type of coercion I made the mistake of slowing down as I finished getting through the flesh. I succeeded in snapping through the metacarpal bone, just above the knuckle, but because I hadn't made a clean cut the bone splintered, inflicting far more pain than I'd intended to. The guy passed out on me and good God do I hate the stink of raw bone marrow.

Now nothing worse hinders an interrogation than your victim blacking out on you, an unconscious man being as much use as a dead one. With this problem in mind I wiped the blood off of my gloves and onto his jacket, and after stuffing a tissue onto his hand to stifle the blood flow I walked over to the dirty little kitchenette to get a mug of water to splash in his face.

Pissed at being unable to find a clean cup (I'm funny like that), I grabbed a dirty one from the dishes piled up in the sink, filling it to the brim before heading back to my prisoner with the intention of chucking it over his blood-soaked head.

This attempt to resuscitate him did nothing but wash away the blood dribbling from his cheeks and chin, and I was about to go boil up a pan of water to see if that'd work better when the guy finally awoke.

Soon after his one good eye had blinked open and as I'd set to work removing his ring finger, the fella started spluttering behind his gag, finally looking like he wanted to talk to me. Shears still in hand I pulled the rag down from his mouth letting him spit out the bloody white sock stuffed up there, it slipped down his shirt accompanied by a couple of shards of cracked yellow teeth. They reminded me of almond slivers.

While he slavered and panted I pulled his head up by his greasy brylcreemed hair, waving the clippers threateningly before his one unswollen eye. Before he had the opportunity to winge or beg for mercy I again asked him the question I'd been torturing him with during that bloodstained hour:

"Tell me where can I find Herbert West!"

III. Rude Awakening

Doctor West's reaction to my news of a man inquiring about him was a bit of a shock. His already pale pallor became whiter and his eyes bulged to an alarming degree. I knew of his concern but honestly believed it to be overblown. I mean people in medicine just don't go around offing the competition. It would play hell with the Hippocratic Oath if nothing else.

"Did that dolt at the grocer's tell your Trevor Towers anything?"

West's tone irked me and I snapped back at him. "He ain't my Trevor Towers. Let's get that straight at the outset. You're the one he's looking for and no I don't think he learned anything."

"Are you certain?" West asked, his fists clenched tightly.

"As sure as a man can be hiding out behind the canned goods."

"Where did he go when he left there?" West continued.

"He got into his car and left," I answered.

"And you don't know where he went?"

I looked at West in dismay. "With no car, he was sort of hard for me to track."

"Yes, a car," West replied, crestfallen. "We'll need to do something about that. There's a serviceable one in the garage but I only drive it occasionally."

"And I don't have a license if this state requires one."

"I don't think it's a problem," West replied.

"There is something I've been wondering about," I said.

"Yes?" West asked warily.

"Before I arrived, how did you run errands without the locals being wise to your presence?"

"Oh that," he answered, looking uncomfortable.

"Yes that," I replied.

His face took on a far away expression as he paused for several moments. It gave me the creeps in a strange sort of way.

"There was an assistant before you," West said. "He even assisted me in the laboratory and was damn near indispensable at times. But due to unfortunate events he left shortly before your arrival."

"What kind of unfortunate events?" I pressed. "I need to know what I'm involved in here."

"God man!" he exclaimed. "It was nothing illegal if you're concerned about that."

"Then ease my mind," I replied.

West sighed. "Well, I guess you should know." He dabbed at his eye with a hanky but as an actor he stunk on ice.

"Your predecessor was injured rather severely in a lab accident," West said. "He suffered extensive injuries and was sent out west so his family could be near him during the recuperative period. So, you can certainly understand my prior reluctance to give you a tour of my laboratory in light of this tragedy."

"Sure, I can see your point," I answered, though I felt he was giving me a load of crap. Still, I let it drop and decided to go along with him. "So what would you like me to do next?"

"We'll continue as before for the present," he answered. "Keep your eyes and ears open. Perhaps nothing will come of this."

"Maybe," I agreed though I had my doubts if Trevor Towers was involved.

The following day I was introduced to Doctor West's "serviceable" automobile. After taking a gander at it, I could understand why it was kept out of sight. To say that it might attract attention would be an understatement. West's vehicle was a hearse! That's right, a slightly used 1920 Lorraine Twelve-Column carved panel job.

"What do you think?" West asked as I walked around the meat wagon.

"It's a hearse," I said, stating the obvious.

West frowned and said, "I can see you know your automobiles."

"Sorry Doc," I replied. "It just wasn't what I expected."

"It runs superbly," West beamed. "I inherited it from a dear friend."

"Some friend," I muttered beneath my breath. "You drive around in this and you're damn sure going to attract attention."

"I don't believe anyone in Falmouth has seen it yet."

I walked around the macabre object and suddenly stopped. "There's a goddamn coffin in the back!"

"Calm yourself," West chuckled. "It's presently empty."

"Inherited as well?" I asked.

He nodded and I clammed up about it.

"It's a stroke of genius really," West stated. "If someone ever stops you, just show them the coffin and tell them you're running late!"

"I guess that might work," I replied doubtfully.

"I just wanted you to see it," West said. "I may well take it out for a drive late tonight. I do that from time to time . . . one of my little eccentricities."

"Will you be needing me to come along?" I asked.

"No," he replied. "I would prefer you to remain at the house, especially in light of Mr. Tower's recent appearance in town."

"Whatever you say Doctor West."

West left the house around eleven 'o clock that evening. It was a moonless night and I thought the entire thing was pretty screwy but hey, it was his eccentricity. I sprawled out on the downstairs sofa and listened to a music program from New York. That and a couple of beers made me pretty drowsy and before long I was sleeping soundly.

Something woke me about three and a half hours later. I looked at the clock and saw it was three-thirty. West was still gone but I had the unsettling feeling that I wasn't alone. I sat upright and alert with the hairs rising on the back of my neck.

"Get a grip Riley," I mumbled. "Probably just had a nightmare."

I settled on this explanation and was feeling better when a loud thud came from upstairs.

Without making a sound, I hurried to the fireplace and grabbed the poker. I hefted it in my arm and crept toward the stairs. I'm usually a light sleeper and it unnerved me to think that someone went past me and upstairs without waking me.

On a hunch I walked to the front door and checked it. It was still locked. No one had gotten past me unless they had locked the door behind them which didn't make sense. Another thud came from above rapidly followed by more. The hairs on my neck were standing again and I regretted not having the .38 that West kept in his possession. Deciding that I'd have to make do with the poker, I hurried up the stairs trying to make as little noise as possible. I reached the top landing and held my breath. The silence was ominous as I stood in the dimly lit area.

I finally exhaled and that was when the thuds started again. Someone was pounding on something to beat the band and I determined that the noise was coming from West's laboratory. Racing to the door, I stopped, realizing that the room was locked and only West had a key.

"Shit," I muttered, glaring at the wooden door. Having few options, I stepped away from the door and readied myself for what was to come.

After a running start, my shoulder crashed into the wooden obstacle and sent it crashing inward. I staggered after it, nearly losing my balance but managed to grab onto a steel table and steady myself.

And then someone grabbed me.

I yelled in surprise, instinctively pulling away from the icy grip on my wrist. Still half blinded by the laboratory's bright lights, I blinked my eyes and tried to get my bearings. A huge fist was pounding on the cold steel slab and it took a few seconds for me to realize what I was seeing.

A large naked man was restrained on the table, his face and upper body terribly scarred from what appeared to be chemical burns. It was a stretch to refer to what he possessed as a face but I don't have other words to describe it. Saliva foamed from the parts of his mouth that hadn't been fused together and an eye socket was completely covered with shiny scar tissue. The pathetic wretch's nose looked like a smashed lump of clay with only ragged slits to function as nostrils.

"Holy Christ!" I raged. "What is West up to?"

The thing kept pounding on the slab, causing my ears to ring. I spied the loose wrist restraint and decided to reapply it. The pounding alone was driving me crazy and that's not taking into account what was doing the pounding. I grabbed the figure's cold arm and gagged as a layer of putrid skin sloughed off in my hands. Trying to ignore the horror, I finally managed to secure the offending arm after a hell of a struggle.

I turned from the slab and found West smiling coldly at me. "You've done well," he offered. "I now expect that you would like an explanation."

I started to charge the little bastard but quickly noticed the .38 he was pointing. In his left arm he clutched a cloth wrapped object against his chest and shoulder. I stared closely at the bundle and then lost my supper.

Clutched in West's hellish embrace was a dead child surely no more than four or five months of age at the time of death!

IV. The Hellbound Heart

Have you ever loved someone so much it physically hurts when you think of them? Such an awful aching of the heart and mind that you freeze up in the agony of lost love? That's how I feel about her. Every time I see a woman who resembles her even slightly my heart aches for the love I once had. And trying to form a relationship with another woman has been impossible with her as the yardstick to compare it to.

We were high school sweethearts, and were engaged and married soon after our graduation. Then the war came along, and I joined up to do my bit like all the other dumb, loyal Americans. After two awful years of blood and mud and death I found upon coming home that things just weren't the same between us. I wasn't the same, the war and the things I'd seen having changed me into a different man from the one she'd married. There was just something inside of me, something bad that her love and tenderness just couldn't exorcise. Six months after my return we separated for good and after six more months the divorce went through.

Such is life.

Now I know I said I didn't like talking about her, but this is relevant to the rest of my story so stay patient.

That love I was telling you about? I still feel it now and have done ever since we separated. I went off the rails when she left me, losing myself in blood and violence wherever and whenever I could find it. What's made it worse is that every night, without fail, my dreams are filled with our lovemaking, our holding hands, and all the rest of that soppy stuff I don't have time for anymore. It's like she's haunting me see? And as a man who likes to be in control of every facet of his life it's a real curse to have to suffer these nightly confrontations of what can never be.

I didn't mention she was dead did I?

When she died, it was the fifth time I lost her. The first being when I joined up to go to war, the second and third being when we separated and got divorced. Her marrying her rich bozo of a boyfriend was the fourth, and her dying in a car crash a year later was the fifth. I guess you could say there were no happy endings destined for us.

Fuck destiny, my life is my own.

That relevance I was telling you about? Well it was six times in total that she was taken from me, for soon after her internment some sick evil scumbag stole her from her tomb. Do I need to tell you what his name was?

Doctor Herbert West MD.

Her husband was horrified of course, possibly even more so than me. And with a lot more money than I could make in a lifetime and a chip on his shoulder nearing the size of mine (poor little rich boy didn't like his toys taken away from him), he had enough cash to fling around to find out who'd taken her corpse and enough rage to want the guy stone dead.

To add insult to injury he contacted me to find that grave robbing son of a bitch. He'd heard rumors I was a man that could get things done. What can I say, shed loads of cash from the man that stole my woman and a chance to get even with the sleazy pervert that robbed her from her grave? I signed up, lock stock, and smoking barrel.

Now there's something to be said for a man that'd rather die than give you the information you want, something more to be said for the one who could invoke such fear in another human being.

Herbert West's assistant (and my unwilling playmate), felt that kind of fear towards his former boss and mentor. He'd given me a hell of a time getting West's whereabouts out of him, and by the time I'd finished, he was happy for me to end his miserable life with a bullet through the skull.

Happy to die without the fear of Herbert West coming after him.

I wish in retrospect I'd tortured that grave robbing scumbag for a little bit longer, but being a professional of sorts I had a job to do and no time for distractions.

What he told me before I used a lead slug to end his pitiful existence was that West had been lying low for a while helping out in a church mission somewhere up in Boston. The name and address of this new place was a good enough start for me, and would you believe that before he died he begged me to burn his body after I'd done the deed? Having never witnessed such a pleading expression in another man's face I gladly obliged him, setting the room alight before leaving quietly and hitting the fire alarm on my way out.

I still have some morals left in me after all.

I began my drive to Boston that same night, and not many hours later found myself driving through the city's early morning grayness and coasting along its streets in search of my destination. The place I was looking for was a dump called the 'Gill Street Mission of The Resurrected Father', quite a mouthful I know. After driving round for an hour or so I eventually located it through the directions of a newspaper seller setting up shop for the day.

And hell, the mission itself, which looked like a closed down clothing store enclosed in big, flyspecked windows with a glass door labelled with the notice 'free soup' hung loosely above it, already had a row of bum's queuing up outside. Bums that probably had a sprinkling of war veterans like me filling their ranks, like me if my life had turned a little worse anyway.

Leaving my Ford parked down a nearby side street I shoved past the bundles of rags answering for humanity to step inside the soup kitchen to find the people running the joint.

The inside of the place was your typical haven for down and outs, filled with cheap metal tables and old wooden church pews for chairs. As I walked in the stink of boiled cabbage and sweat wafted to my nostrils, a sour commingling of odors that smelled like loss and despair. A few of the bums were already lined up at a bench set up as a soup stand, adding their mingled stenches of piss and misery to the room's already foisty atmosphere.

Pushing past these derelicts, receiving some half-hearted threats and pokes for my trouble, I asked the fella behind the bench where I could find who ran the place.

I discovered that I wasn't going to have much luck in that respect.

The guy behind the counter, standing rigid while he mechanically poured thin, greenish soup into a chipped bowl, was the biggest fella I've ever seen in my life. He was black, at least six foot nine, and towered over me and the other little people lurking in the soup kitchen. As well as being tall he was also big and ugly, his dull expressioned face showing two awesome scars resembling nothing more than bullet holes. One of these lay embedded across his left eye and stitched in such a manner that the upper eyelid was permanently pulled down over the lower lid. The other scar existed as a gouge at the center of his dark forehead. How anyone could survive such injuries and function was completely beyond me.

His arms, each as wide as my head and as muscle-bound as a prize-fighters looked like huge knotted tree trunks. As he ladled soup into a fresh bowl I could tell by the knuckles on his huge scarred hands that he'd been a boxer at some point in his past.

My questions as to who ran the place and if he'd ever even heard of West evinced no response from his big expressionless face, and whether he was deaf or just a bit backwards I had no idea. It was the third bum he served while I'd been stood there like a moron that actually paid enough attention to my plight to think to help me.

This guy, pockmarked and dirty faced, tapped me on the shoulder with a black-gloved hand, speaking in a mellow Irish accent.

"It's the Fadder you want", his smile was filled with brown teeth, "Fadder Murphy up the stairs"

This polite but disheveled Irishman then pointed towards a wide staircase at the back of the room, a staircase that'd probably looked regal once upon a time, before the dust and the cobwebs took over. I left the soup stand thanking him, seeing as I climbed the staircase that the place was steadily filling up with more bums of all creeds, colors and sexes. There was no discrimination or prejudice within that little offshoot of society.

As I'd suspected, the building had been a clothing store during a more prosperous past, for the cavernous upstairs room was filled with empty clothing racks, naked mannequins and other miscellaneous trash.

"Hello… Father Murphy" I said, clearing my throat in the congealed air of dust and decrepitude. Silence greeted me from the maze of junk and plastic bodies arrayed before me, and after twiddling my thumbs for a minute I was about to turn back to the stairs when a noise on my right caused me to repeat my greeting, and this time, getting a reply.

"Over here" the voice said, a strong Texas accent betraying the small-framed man hopping towards me. This man, quite obviously Father Murphy due to his black outfit and white collar, came forward holding a crutch beneath his right arm. He was hopping due to the fact that his right leg was missing.

So this Father Murphy, a small, thin, gray-haired man, unshaven and with bright blue, intelligent eyes, approached me with a smile on his face and joviality in his voice.

"Sorry young man, I was just in the john, I have a bit of trouble sometimes." He indicated this trouble by loudly banging the base of his crutch onto the floor before questioning me cheerfully.

"So what can I do for someone this fine morning so obviously not in the need of soup?"

It was true, despite my crumpled suit and my being in need of a shave I was far removed from the other clientele downstairs.

"I'm here about a doctor that used to work here, a Doctor West, do you know him?"

As soon as I'd said this, the Father hobbled closer, raising dust from the floorboards as he heavily slamming his crutch down twice, the sounds of it vibrating through the floor. When he got closer I noticed an awful smell about him, an odor like mold and something I couldn't quite put my finger on.

"Oh you're looking for the good doctor are you?" he said, nodding his head in smiling contemplation, "a fine man and a great aid in the Lord's work"

"I was told if I came here I might be able to find out where he is?" I was starting to feel a little creeped by the way he was looking at me.

"You should be careful what you wish for my son" the Father replied, backing away from me without elaborating on his crypticism.

He'd backed away because a second later I found a pair of huge, thick-fingered hands wrapping themselves around my throat before bodily picking me up, causing my feet to dangle about a foot over the floor. And it didn't take a genius to realize that the Father had been using his crutch to signal the prizefighter downstairs.

But me, I was too dumb to realize that until I felt his big brown paws throttling me from behind. Hanging there choking, trying futilely to free myself from that iron grip, the last thing I saw was the holy man limping off through the mannequins, noticing as he did that the back of his head was cleanly shaved and badly dented as if from massive blunt force trauma. Then everything went black.

I don't need to tell you the woman I dreamt of whilst unconscious.

V. The Errand

I stared into the deadly barrel of West's revolver and realized that I had been duped. West was not at all what he claimed to be and I should've known that his job offer had been too good to be true. Now I was a part of God knows what.

"So do you shoot me now?" I asked, trying to remain as calm as possible.

"You could help me dead," he answered. "But, you're much more valuable alive."

I frowned. "What makes you think I'll help you?"

"Fear of death," West chuckled, gesturing toward the figure strapped to the steel slab. "Do you wish to end up like him?"

I stared in horror at the pathetic creature and then turned to West. "Is that your previous assistant?"

He nodded his head and smiled. "The one before this poor fellow got a little squeamish and disappeared, I'll find him though."

"What about the dead kid, you sick bastard?"

"Raw materials," he answered. "You'll need to accustom yourself to such things."

I glared at West in silence, trying to find a way out of this nightmare. Nothing feasible came to mind at the time.

"This is quite a shock to you," West said. "You're currently at a loss as how to proceed but soon you'll begin to get ideas. If anything should happen to me, I've made arrangements with an associate to release certain papers of mine. These papers implicate you in my endeavors and will result in you incarceration. So, it is in your best interest to ensure that nothing unfortunate happens to me."

I spit on the floor. "I can't say that blackmail comes as a shock after everything else. Just remember West that every dog has his day."

"Spare me the clichés," West replied. "Just be certain that you understand your situation."

"Oh, I understand all right," I answered. "But cliché or not, just remember that this dog's day is coming."

"Not for a long time," said West, lowering the pistol. "Now get over here and take this loathsome child off my hands. In the corner you'll find a refrigeration tank. Undress her, drop her in and lower the lid."

I felt sick at my stomach but did as West demanded. For all my threats, I was really over the barrel and had little choice but to follow orders until I could somehow gain the upper hand.

I woke from a series of gruesome nightmares and kicked the sweat-stained sheet off me. Relieved that it was only a bad dream, my stomach clenched up when I remembered that nightmares were the least of my problems.

West had laid out the facts to me the night before and had given me my marching orders. I was to follow his instructions without question and if things went well he would release me from his service within a few months. I found his assurances hard to swallow, thinking of his former assistant and what had become of him. I longed to strangle the perverted little bastard but needed to protect myself in the process. I only half believed that a West associate was prepared to implicate me if something happened to the good doctor but wasn't prepared to take any chances.

After getting dressed, I went to the kitchen and made coffee. West wasn't around—apparently still in bed after the late night—but I still didn't have much of an appetite. Still, I needed the caffeine for the task ahead. West had a big job for me. A job that I dreaded.

It seems that West, from one of his mysterious associates, had received word that Trevor Towers was in the Boston area asking questions about West's whereabouts. My job was to find Towers, subdue him and bring him to West. That would be easier said than done. I wasn't afraid of Towers but knew him to be a formidable foe. I would have to become as ruthless as him if West's plan had any hope for success.

Taking a sip of coffee, I sighed and mentally reviewed my plan of action. I was to drive the Lorraine to Boston and go to an address West had given me. A man named Father Murphy would then provide me with any leads on the location of my quarry. I had really been a dope to get involved with West and hoped like hell to be free of him at the earliest possible moment. Maybe I could stumble across some useful information on my trip to Boston. God I hoped so.

My drive to Boston was uneventful and I found the address West had given to me with little difficulty. I was stunned to discover that Towers was already in the clutches of West's associates and all that remained was for me to transport him back to Falmouth. Towers was unconscious when I saw him and looking pretty much the worse for wear. I wasn't surprised in the least considering the unsavory appearance of the two men who accompanied Towers with me on the return trip.

I had managed to get myself in a hell of a predicament but it seemed a minor matter compared to what was probably in store for Towers. I was damned glad to not be in his shoes. My only plan was to keep my fingers crossed and hope that an opportunity would arise for me to help him before worse came to worse. I had no doubt that things would definitely get worse.

VI. Ties That Bind

There's no more clichéd a scene than a man in my line of work waking up in the clutches of the guy he's been hired to catch. But when I awoke, minutes, hours or days after the nap the black man and his one-legged friend had sent me to, that was the scenario and like hell could I do anything about it.

I'd been through worse and lived through it though; and at least this time, tied to a chair in an unknown room, there was no car battery wired up to my testicles. Seeing the pure look of evil in the eyes of the man sat across from me muted that factor making it not much of a consolation.

Small, thin and blonde haired, I recognized the man facing me as none other than Herbert West, blue shirted and wearing a slim black tie, dressed in a white, blood spattered lab coat. He stared at me with the look of a predator from behind the large, thick lenses of his spectacles. He would've almost looked like a real doctor, holding a clipboard between his slim-fingered hands with a stethoscope wrapped round his neck. Would've done if not for the red smears on his coat and the disgusting state of the lab behind him.

Me? I was tied to a chair, him slouched facing me from another, the whitewashed walls around us were coated in anatomical diagrams pinned alongside yellowing page fragments covered in writing that looked like Arabic. Below these were shelves full of test tubes and beakers, strewn together chaotically with orange rubber hoses. Specimen jars dotted these shelves with abandon, the one closest to me containing a pair of pale, dainty feet flaking apart in some clear fluid. Another held dozens of human eyeballs, bunched together like varicolored grapes.

Two metal tables, located roughly at the center of the room, lay behind West's seat, their contents hidden by stained brown sheets. Of all the things it could or should've smelled of, the room was filled of the stench of overdone bacon. I mustn't forget my other two companions either. Because the one-legged padre and his big black friend were also present, flanking the only door out of the room and standing there like dead-eyed automatons. Whatever pretense of normality they'd put forward at the mission was gone now in the presence of their boss, and I wondered briefly whether the winos were missing their soup.

As West had obviously been watching me for some time I forwent any kind of subterfuge about still being asleep and began tugging at my bonds. For my trouble all I discovered was that my chair was bolted to the floor and the ropes binding me were tied tighter than a mosquito's ass. From the expression covering his nasty little face it looked like West was enjoying my predicament so I stopped struggling to settle on pouring a tirade of verbal abuse his way.

"You dirty little tow-headed dick sandwich," was the best insult I could think of on the fly, followed by various nasty slurs and innuendos about his lineage.

Taking this verbal maltreatment without so much as a blink, West sat as he was before clearing his throat to begin reading from his clipboard.

"Mr. Trevor Towers" he said in his quiet, mellow voice, "ex-husband to Mrs. Jayne Towers… or should that be Mrs. Jayne Smith since she got re-married?" He grinned from a mouth full of tiny white teeth as he said this before covering his mouth to snigger while I turned purple with rage.

"You're as much a doctor as a monkey's ass you creepy little toad," this spat out with more anger and venom than I'd used in many a year.

West finally rewarded me with a reaction, smacking me violently across the face with his clipboard. Feeling a tooth loosen and my mouth fill up with blood was worth it to know I'd actually riled the little freak.

"You don't like what I said?" this was sputtered with blood dripping from my lips, "what else do you call a grave robbing little monster?"

Steeling myself for another clipboard slap I was surprised when all he did was stand up from his chair smiling. He then turned towards the metal bench before addressing me again.

"I can understand why an illiterate snoop would think that, especially where the woman from his failed marriage is concerned."

I took a slow deep breath at this attempt to rile me, one of many as I murdered him with my eyes while he reached over to open a small metal case at the edge of the bench.

"Would you believe she was one of my greatest successes?" He said this while removing a none too clean syringe from the case, checking its needle in the light fixture above. "Far more successful than these associates of mine that captured you," he indicated the two guarding the door, as blank faced and unmoving as when I'd first awoken. "They do as I say because they think I'm their god."

At hearing this claim I spat out a short laugh, eliciting a grin from him as he continued.

"I brought her back to life and you think I'm a monster? She's out there living because of me."

Breaking off from my metal image of flicking his head off like a fly, I told him what I thought of his statement.

"You really are one delusional turd," I sneered.

Leaving the bench to approach my chair, West halted just a foot away, rolling up his sleeve to reveal a pale skinny arm dotted with needle marks.

"I used to have to make my elixir of life in a test tube you know."

Then he jammed the needle into his arm, filling it with blood from one of his broken veins. The colour of that fluid disgusted me, it looked more black than red. West then withdrew the needle, waving it in my face and pleased at the way I pulled away in disgust. He said, "but the times have changed and so have I."

Crazy little Doctor West then spun round on his heels, his sleeve slipping down as he strode towards the metal bench, tearing away its brown burlap sheet with a theatrical flourish. What he revealed from beneath that dirty sheet was a half-immolated corpse as crisp and black as an overdone sausage. At least I knew where the smell of smoked pork was coming from.

The worst thing though, was that from the burned features on the dead man's face it was obvious that it was the guy I'd snuffed while searching for West. I felt like gagging when he reached over to touch the thing.

"You're a war veteran, yes?" he said this whilst picking up the dead man's right leg, one-handedly testing the flexibility of the shriveled limb with the syringe still clasped in the other.

"You've done your homework pecker-head," I replied. I was starting to wonder whether he was going to kill me by force or by the sound of his poncy voice.

"Well I'm a war veteran too," he said, "so I know what death means. But I make death as unnatural as what you did to this man here."

That fiend calling himself a doctor then stabbed the syringe into the corpse's thigh, pressing down on the plunger till he'd emptied the filthy fluid into its poor dead body.

"His name was Dan Kane by the way, a good assistant albeit with too delicate a stomach for our work. He ran away from me but I knew I'd get him back sooner or later. And soon enough we'll have a nice little reunion."

I didn't believe any of his crap-talk about resurrection, but that didn't mean I wasn't going to try and escape his crazy clutches as soon as I was able. So when he began poking around the corpse's chest with his stethoscope I used the distraction to try and free myself from the ropes around my wrists. It was while the doctor was looking for the corpse's heartbeat that I found the small penknife tucked up beneath my watchstrap.

Not knowing or really caring how it'd got there I turned my gaze firmly from the gift horse's mouth and quickly began negotiating the little knife into my fingers. With that accomplished, I then went to work on the ropes binding my wrists.

VII. All Hell Breaks Loose

I had been outside, acting as a lookout but knew I needed to go inside if Towers was to survive his meeting with West. My presence wouldn't guarantee anything but I wasn't going to sit idly by while West violated all laws of decency in his alleged pursuit of knowledge. If my ultimate fate was to be prison, then so be it.

Entering the house, I made my way upstairs and silently entered the lab. I didn't need to be especially quiet to escape notice since one of West's experiments was screaming like a soul in Hell. West and his associates had Towers restrained and a hideously charred figure was on the slab while the other I had seen earlier was covered nearby. I assumed it was the same corpse but with West one could never be certain.

The stench of burnt meat permeated the room and I stifled a gag while watching West inject the human remnants with a vile colored solution he had taken from his own veins.

"Who flunked cooking school?" I asked sarcastically.

"Barnes, you're supposed to be outside!" West barked.

I smiled. "Had to take a leak."

"And you couldn't find a suitable spot outside?"

"Well yeah," I replied. "But that would be so uncivilized. Besides, no one is interested in what's going on out here."

I saw Towers glaring at me and caught the flicker of recognition in his hate-filled eyes. "Hey, I know that bird," I said. "In fact I owe him."

Before West could respond, I walked over to Towers, bent over and backhanded him with a loud slap while mouthing the words, "I'm on your side."

Towers responded to my slap by spitting in my face. I laughed and turned to West. "Somebody did a piss poor job of tying him."

West frowned at Father Murphy but before he could speak I said, "I'll take care of it."

Reaching behind Towers, I discovered the pen knife with which he'd been sawing at his bonds. I clasped it tightly and cut through rope while making a pretense of tightening his restraints.

"There West," I said with satisfaction. "Even a little pipsqueak like you should be able to handle him now."

The charred corpse continued screaming and I yelled, "Can't someone shut that thing up?"

"You're not squeamish are you?" West asked. "Let me remove what remains of his tongue."

"Suit yourself," I replied. "I'm going back outside."

I walked toward the door, turned and pulled my gun. West had allowed me to carry one since he believed his blackmail threat was sufficient to control me. "Time for your nightcap you corpse loving bastard!"

West moved like a flash to the other side of the room. I would've nailed him easily had not the esteemed Father Murphy—acting faster than I thought possible—leaped forward and grabbed my arm as I pulled the trigger. My bullet missed its target but grazed the shoulder of Towers who uttered a series of oaths that would impress Satan himself.

"Son of a bitch!" I screamed, turning my weapon on Murphy. I fired three quick rounds into his chest and a fourth that took off the top of his head and sent him reeling against the wall, leaving gore in his wake. During this melee, West leaped back, reaching for his own gun. Losing his balance, he careened into the metal cylinder in which I had placed the little girl's corpse. It crashed against the floor with a loud clang and the top went rolling across the room. To my horror, I saw the small corpse scuttle out of its prison and make a beeline for West.

"Damn you Barnes!" West railed, struggling to his feet. He finally managed to get a grip on his pistol and was proceeding to turn it on me when the reanimated child threw herself on his back causing him to drop the firearm.

West screamed again as the corpse child tore at his throat with unnaturally developed teeth. Blood sprayed from the wound in West's throat as he struggled with his attacker. I was pleased to see Towers grab the fallen gun and then stunned as he aimed it at me!

"You ungrateful asshole!" I yelled. "What's the big . . ."

My question remained unasked as West's slow-thinking associate—Murphy's hulking black companion—finally entered the fray. He nearly ripped my arm off as he grabbed it and slung me across the room. Thank God for unintentional allies! Towers' shot buried itself in the wall behind where my head had been moments earlier.

I somehow managed to hold on to my own weapon though the impact with the wall had left me reeling on Queer Street. I struggled to gather my wits about me amid the gunfire, screaming and general confusion. I had only one chance of leaving the carnage-filled scene alive. I could only pray that Trevor Towers came to his senses and realized that we must join forces. It was a slim chance at best.

VIII. Things Get Worse

I'd like to say I'd been in worse predicaments by that point, but that'd be a barefaced lie. I knew it, the screeching corpse I'd incinerated a few days earlier knew it, and the rest of the motley crew making up our little war zone probably knew it too. All except for the creepy little zombie creature chowing down on West's throat, she was too intent on trying to tear the bastard's head off to pay attention to anything else going on around her.

Some things about the scene were more than familiar though, including the stink of gunpowder and the sounds of gunfire filling my ears. The only consolation was that the gun I'd nicked from West felt good in my hand, a snub-nose magnum loaded and ready to kill. My shoulder smarted like hell from where West's bozo had shot me, and though he'd claimed to be on my side (he'd sure finished off the hopping mad priest fast enough) I was too confused by all the crap going on around me to know what to think.

So I did what I always do in that kind of situation: shoot first and ask questions later.

My first bullet missed Barnes due to his impromptu tangle with the black feller, and after that beefy monster had tossed him like a rag doll and he'd disappeared behind a table I decided to try and peg West as he danced about with his tiny new friend digging into his throat. The problem was, with him whirling like a crazy dervish and spraying that black shit for blood around the room, making a decent target was harder than shooting a camel in a sandstorm. I noticed briefly that West's surviving guard was kneeling down beside Murphy and shaking him wildly, his huge dark shoulders sticking up like two burial mounds. I hoped he wouldn't be waking the Father up anytime soon, but with West around who could tell? Thank god the ringing in my ears had dampened the noise the burned fella was making, still twisting and turning on the autopsy table.

As the jars of mysterious chemicals that'd been perched on the shelves were now smashed on the floor and mixed with West's blood, securing good footing was becoming difficult. And just as I managed to get a bead on the doctor's skinny chest I banged my knee on something hard and metallic and missed him by a mile. Instead of taking West down I only succeeded in blowing away the creature that would've killed him if I'd have left her to it. Now she was just a splattered memory on the lab wall.

"God, Christ, dammit!" I griped, then reached down to pull out whatever was jabbing my knee. It was something out of West's medical kit, a pair of shiny steel calipers embedded over an inch into my flesh. Tugging the damned things out of my knee I was preparing to aim another shot when I suddenly felt a bullet zip past my ear followed by a loud hiss from behind me. Then I saw Barnes across the room waving and shouting words of apparent warning that my numbed ears just couldn't quite comprehend.

Doctor West was gesturing at me too, laughing giddily as black fluids fell from his lacerated throat. I was about to take my shot when he fell to his knees with a smoking hole in his chest, the wall behind him flowering in black and yellow goo, whatever answered for West's guts and organs joining the mess I'd made of the girl moments earlier.

Seemed like Barnes was a better shot than I was after all.

Realizing finally that West's assistant was on the level came as no solace as something big exploded behind me, peppering my back with white-hot chunks of shrapnel and setting my hair on fire. How my ugly fat body survived that explosion I have no idea but as the wall at my rear became a blazing sheet of fire I again thanked the gift horse and began crawling on my hands and knees towards the exit, surgical scalpels, tools, and West's dark blood surrounding me as I dragged myself away from death and fire.

The room was filling with gagging smoke as I finally reached the door, my journey across the slick floor having taken an age as the flames licked wildly against my escaping ass. Turning round I spied West through the black clouds, still alive and on his knees but juddering like an erratic jack in the box as the fire started surrounding his prone form. At least my hearing had come back in time for me to realize the dead guy on the table had stopped his yammering. I found Murphy was laying next to me as dead as Dillinger, his face and chest burning quietly and adding yet more fumes to the already eye watering smoke. I was about to take aim to finally finish West off when another explosion made him and the room disappear in a sudden fireball of destruction, sending me scurrying away with my clothes on fire like a fleeing rat.

As I tumbled down the stairs patting myself down like crazy I saw my savior Barnes was nowhere to be found, so I had no chance to thank him as I doused the flames burning my head and backside up. God only knows where the big guy with the lovely scars had disappeared to either; maybe he'd gone to buy flowers for Father Murphy's grave. Reaching the ground floor with my best suit a singed mess I hoped sincerely that West himself had departed to whatever hell the likes of him were destined for.

After running from the house, West's thankfully burning and collapsing house, I paused once to look back, wondering whether fire could really cleanse the world of that man's evil deeds, and whether or not the doctor had retired from life for good.

Wishful thinking? If I'd seen him being torn to shreds from a yard away I'd still have my doubts that that evil creep was really dead. When more explosions wracked the top floor and the windows burst asunder I hoped that the greasy black flames billowing up to the sky contained at least a little residue from his disintegrating corpse.

I then wondered, soot-stained, bleeding and burned as I was, where I could find the nearest, cheapest bar. God I needed a beer.

Epilogue 1: The Girl Hunter

I've never claimed to be an optimist, but have always been the kind of dog that's willing to learn new tricks. And two days after the 'incident' involving West I went to visit my employer, informing him that the guy who'd robbed Jayne from her grave was gone and he could finally put his mind to rest. I then tore his check up in his face and broke his jaw for good measure.

I don't think either of us saw that coming.

Just like I'd not foreseen the possibility of my ex-wife coming back from the dead. But what good old Doctor West had done with the corpse in his laboratory had been a real eye opener, and although he may have been full of crap about bringing Jayne back to life if there was a chance of seeing her again I'd take it.

Optimism see, even though I know it'll take a lot more than West's creepy resurrection formula to win her back to me.

So, with my car retrieved from the impound lot in Boston, my hair trimmed down to a buzz-cut to conceal the singes and me wearing a brand new suit, I started my journey with more than enough bullets to deal with any unfortunate incidents that might come my way. Oh, and with a list of Jayne's old acquaintances and next of kin written down in my notebook I'm still hunting for her despite a month of dead ends and false leads.

As long as there's hope I'm going to keep on searching, and woe betide anyone who gets in my way.

Epilogue 2: An Uneasy Reprieve

I regained consciousness and cursed loudly as the pain of a twisted ankle shot through me. I vaguely remembered being nearly overcome with smoke and chemical fumes in West's lab and making a split second decision to exit the premises via the second floor window. Clearing my head, I felt heat and realized that the house was being consumed by fire.

An explosion thundered from inside the house as I struggled to my feet and limped away. I looked over my shoulder but saw no sign of Towers, West or his demented associates. My primary focus was to put as much distance between myself and the scene of carnage. I didn't fancy a return to prison and there was no way I could make anyone believe what had occurred in that house of horror.

I'm now working on the docks of Frisco and say a silent prayer every night that West was lying about implicating me in his sick endeavors. I hope that the bastard is good and truly dead but I saw too many things while in his employ to rest easy on that score. It's hell going through life looking over your shoulder but it's a damn sight better than being dead.

Still, it sort of eats away at me, knowing that he might still be somewhere out there and in a position to blackmail me. That doesn't sit well with me and I know it's only a matter of time until I pull up stakes and go looking for the little bastard. He better hope like Hell that I don't find him because he's got a lot to answer for. I'm usually an easy going sonofabitch but there are things to be said for the Trevor Towers approach to dealing with problems; not necessarily good things but it does tend to be effective.

Herbert West Reanimated

a round robin

I. Charnel Secrets by Robert M. Price

Of my too-long association with Herbert West I can recall nothing good and wish that I might recall nothing whatsoever. When first I made the acquaintance of the young tow-head zealot in our days in medical school little did I suspect the blight that would be cast on the whole of my subsequent life by the meeting. As West began to share with me scraps of his revolutionary theories of organic reanimation of the dead I found myself overcome, at first with scientific fascination, then with misdirected hero-worship, for soon his clandestine experiments, to which I was party, began to win a measure of success. Success or at least results. Years of such Promethe-an endeavours had never yielded a single wholesome resuscitation of a subject into full-orbed rational consciousness, but what grotesque signs of reanimation West managed to achieve lured us both on like the phantom gleam of witchfire. From the locked dissection labs at Miskatonic University to a private practice in nearby Bolton, then to Boston, finally to war-torn Flanders and back home the trail had led, a trail that marked the way to West's increasing decadence and morbidity as well as to my own moral lassitude and complete failure of independent will. Even the prospect of discovery by the authorities and finally of danger at West's own fanatical hands did not cause me to abandon my mad colleague, my master. It was finally West's own diabolical misadventures that did him in one night as the very ground opened to spew forth a stream of West's misshapen, cast-off victims. Before my paralyzed gaze the tomb legion rent poor West to pieces and bore him away into the nighted recesses whence they had come.

Initially I myself was suspected of foul play in my strange friend's disappearance, but then West was well known for unaccounted absences and long periods of secret travel, and in time, with no solid evidence of his demise, the authorities lost interest in the case and in me.

So it rested for two years, my welcome deliverance from Herbert West thus accomplished by other hands. Slowly I set about consolidating the medical practice West and I had shared, all the while considering a move, perhaps to Illinois, to my parents' home which had been left to me, seeing in this plan a real possibility of severance from all that bound me even to the memory of Herbert West.

But now he has reappeared.

It was the very eve of my planned departure. I sat in the living room amid packing cases, interrupted in my preparations by the arrival of an enigmatic, unsigned telegram which bore but a single phrase: RISEN INDEED. As I puzzled over this missive seeking desperately, I now realize, to avoid its inevitable meaning, the door opened at the end of the entrance hall. At first I fancied it to be the delivery boy returned for some reason, perhaps to beg an umbrella against the sudden downpour outside in the winter evening.

But of course it was West. He stood silent and dripping, his slight form unmistakable even in the dim gas-lamp radiance. He remained silent as I approached, slowly, weighted with despair. His grinning face looked no older, wearing its characteristic frozen agelessness, but his hair, no longer yellow, had turned pure white, bleached, as I already suspected but was soon to find confirmed, by the ordeal through which he had passed since that night two years before. Livid, jagged scars on his neck and now-extended hand told their own story in awful hints.

I made no pretense at welcoming him, but dutifully I took his sopping overcoat, indicated my own easy chair before the fireplace, and quickly stirred the embers. Perhaps my shock should have been greater, but it would not be true to say I had expected never to see Herbert West again. In fact I had hoped never to see him, such hope, as all hopes do, containing its opposite fear. West had crossed the Styx in his experiments too often for me to believe it could ever be an effective barrier to him from either side. Now, rubbing his scarred hands before the fire, he began to answer my unspoken questions.

West's nightmarish abduction from our basement by the mob of shambling, reanimated hulks had been directed by the headless yet sentient form of Sir Eric Moreland Clapham-Lee, a colleague of West's during the Great War. Like me, Sir Eric had taken an interest in West's ghastly researches and had even aided him in experiments a time or two. He understood the theory of reanimation, and it is perhaps this fact which accounts for Clapham-Lee being West's first real success. West's new colleague had perished in a battlefield aeroplane crash, only to be scavenged by West who proceeded to impart new life to the corpse, or rather to pieces of it, since the increasingly mad West desired to know whether the nervous system even without the brain might serve to guide a body with consciousness. West was to find that his experiment had succeeded rather too well, for the revived and vengeful torso-thing had managed to bear West away amid the lynch mob of liches that terrible night two years agone.

But it was at this point that West's seemingly final failure had been transformed into his wildest success. The monster's plan had been to take revenge on its enemy by subjecting West himself to the process of reanimation, well understood, you will recall, by West's one-time colleague. Thinking thereby to plunge West into the same nightmare of horror in which he existed, the reanimated Clapham-Lee had somehow contrived to inject West with the reagent solution and sew his sundered members back together in an unanesthetized ordeal of torture.

West, however, was of course the "freshest" body yet, and thus the most complete success! And no man living or dead understood the theory of reanimation better than West, and as the subject's understanding of the process had brought Clapham-Lee himself most of the way back, it now brought West all the way back. Of course he came back with a far greater understanding yet. (How West had at length escaped the clutches of his headless nemesis I did not ask and did not want to know. I only wished that he had not.) Though what he had seen had blasted his sanity and turned his hair white, he had wrestled from the Grim Reaper a deeper glimpse of the grave's mysteries than Dante ever pretended. West, whose eyes fairly glowed with brighter fires of alchemic mania than I had seen in all our years together, proceeded to rattle on semi-coherently of the now-understood truths masked by the allegorical legends of vampires and hauntings. I listened silently, chilled to the soul by the revelations of a science far more terrible than superstition.

The upshot of it all, or at any rate, all I could finally grasp of his rantings, was that a wide vista of new experiments stretched before him—and for them he required my assistance. Weak of will and fearful of the monster before me, I agreed, damning my soul to a deeper circle of hell than that already due me.

The next weeks witnessed our move to new and larger quarters and the equipping of a laboratory with devices the purposes of which I could not easily guess. West evidently planned new crimes against nature as far in advance of our old experiments as these had been from the operations of sane medical science. Of these I will only describe the least hideous.

West went through a phase of experimentation recreating the chimeras of classical mythology, which had captured his imagination in childhood. By secretive torchlight, we now haunted zoos and stockyards as well as our accustomed morgues and cemeteries, finally producing ghastly travesties of wholesome nature. Before us reared up the Minotaur, the Centaur, the Satyr, even the Gorgon, in living flesh! Mercifully none of them lived long.

But even worse was the use of the residue. I shall not describe the ghoulish feasts in which we disposed of what West called the "superfluous portions" both animal and human: how West took damnable delight in injecting with the reagent what lay before him on the dinner platter and devouring it as it squealed and flopped, his face lit by cacodaemoniacal glee.

All these, he said, were but frivolous diversions. His real work, on which he now proposed to commence, was immortality. For as he now knew, even the foxfire life of reanimation was only temporary. And having tasted it, this mere reprieve from death, he must discover a way to cheat it forever.

One moonless night he woke me and summoned me to accompany him to the campus of Miskatonic University. We had never, save for the years of the War, ventured very far from our alma mater, and our recent move had brought us again very close to its ivy-covered walls. As our automobile, traveling dangerously without headlights for secrecy's sake, approached the medical school buildings, I could not but think with revulsion of our earliest crimes here nearly two decades ago. But West moved on further, finally stopping the machine at the curbside of the block containing the University's museum of ancient history! It was a dead body West meant to steal, all right, but an ancient one: he had learned of the recent discovery and display of an Egyptian mummy, that apparently of a hieratic sorcerer of some kind. All this he told me as we made our way clandestinely into the building. He knew me well enough to predict that my nerves would not have proved adequate to the task had I known earlier of its true nature. Now it was too late to back out, and soon we would be done with our mission. How did West and I manage to elude the night watchman and penetrate the locked doors? I will only say that it was a procedure which, given the nature of our exploits, we had long since had to master. Herbert West, to whom the barred door of death was no obstacle, could scarcely be forbidden by more mundane barriers.

Of course, we took only the dessicated, gauze-bound form itself, leaving a remarkable counterfeit, produced from the trunk of West's automobile, in the closed sarcophagus. It was not especially difficult getting the thing back to our laboratory. Once, the police stopped us closer to our own neighborhood. Our lights had been restored and the mummy duly covered, and the dull-witted constable, typically desirous of avoiding trouble rather than resolving it, let us pass, too easily satisfied with West's explanation that he and I, both physicians, had been called out on an emergency to see to a seriously ill patient (indicating the covered form), who alas, had not survived.

Once the dusty burden was carefully laid on our operating table I inquired of West what possible plans he could have for a corpse dead long millennia. He replied impatiently that while "freshness" was indeed of vital importance for the full restoration of life, it was not necessary for what he now had in mind. Indeed full reanimation would be entirely out of the question with a mere shell such as the ritually eviscerated mummy. Ancient embalmers, as is well known, always removed brain, heart, and vitals, preserving only the husk of flesh.

West's mad plan was this. Well he knew from his experiments with severed limbs that more of conscious "brain function" lay in the spinal cord and the webs of ganglia than was suspected by plodding, orthodox neurology. His goal was first to rejuvenate the long-dead neural system, then to transplant his own mad brain into the desiccated form of the mummy, where it would link with the reawakened nervous system. This blasphemous junction, he hoped, would enable him to tap in on the secret knowledge of the ancient necromancer still held in its nervous tissue.

For this I would be necessary. Of course other hands than West's must perform the surgery, though he had provided detailed instructions. Great skill was called for, but you will recall I was long apprenticed to West and in the process had learned unique transplantational skills together with the use of unorthodox instruments and binding tissues devised by West and never disclosed to the medical guild. And in any event West's brain owed its continued life to the serum, not to organic connection with the body. Transplantation posed no greater danger to him now than it did under the hands of the ghoulish Clapham-Lee. Indeed my dread of the whole proceeding was borne not of the fear that it might fail, but rather that it might succeed!

I worked for hours locating, joining, and sealing the proper nerve-endings, stitching severed flesh. Hours passed without my marking them as I performed surgery such as black magicians may have performed but scientists never have. The evening of the next day had commenced before I collapsed, exhausted, into a chair and fell asleep. When at length I awoke it was to see the mummy sitting up and facing me, as if it had simply been propped up and posed as a macabre joke. New horror awoke within me as the flaking, leathery face of the cadaver cracked into intelligent sentience with a grin recognizable even in this alien form as unmistakably that of Herbert West. He croaked, I think, that he would "reward" me, then said no more. I believe I fainted then, back into a troubled sleep.

When I again woke, the wizened form had returned to its supine position. I rose and bent over the thing, and only by a prearranged finger-signal did I know it was time to reverse the procedure. Apparently, West had what he wanted.

Returned to his accustomed form, West recuperated in bed for a week, while he planned his next moves. I was able to return the mummy as easily as we had procured it. Then West ordered me off to secure arrangements for another of his mysterious trips. Only this time, having had to see to the details myself, I knew whither he was bound: Egypt. West had used his connections with the Miskatonic faculty (who of course suspected nothing of the true nature of West's past or present exploits, despite his general reputation for eccentricity) to gain passage into the very archaeological site from which the mummy had been recovered. I suspected that he was now in the position to know where to look for certain treasures the original expedition had overlooked. I also suspected that any such finds would not be making their way into the hands of the University museum!

Once his strength returned, quickly with liberal infusions of the reagent serum, West was packed and off to the Near East. During his absence, some faint semblance of normalcy returned to my life, and I was even emboldened to consider fleeing West, breaking his domination forever. But somehow I lingered and delayed until it was too late, until West wired announcing his imminent return. It was no use. My will was long-vanished. I was bound to West by fetters stronger than the grave. Obediently I picked West up at the station and could not suppress my unholy fascination with what he excitedly disclosed.

The tomb itself was of an odd design never before discovered in Egypt, and the strange, pre-dynastic carvings gave no help in determining the age of the find. It was only with the aid of certain hideously suggestive bas-reliefs that it had been determined that the mummy was that of a magician. None of this mystery had been hinted at in the Miskatonic Review wherein West had first read notice of the discoveries. Likewise, once on the scene, West did not hint to the archaeologists of the truth of the matter as he himself instantly recognized it. The architecture and strange glyph-writing were those of a pre-Egyptian civilization, some elements surviving from a still-earlier prehuman elder race known to West from his early years of unorthodox researches in the Miskatonic University library.

Armed with the stolen memories of the ancient mage, West had had no difficulty locating within a secret niche a nameless scroll written in yet another ancient cipher-alphabet. It was easy to hide this from the others on the site, and in the privacy of his Cairo hotel room West had devoured its exhumed secrets, the secrets of life and death. Much of what it told he had already suspected or guessed, more still he had absorbed from the old mummy's memory. But his own researches, his own experiences, had enabled him to make certain connections, to unravel certain hints that had baffled even the ancient readers of the scroll. Of what precisely these revelations consisted, West would say nothing, contemptuously dismissing my capacity to grasp such secrets. But, he announced with barely controlled fervor, nothing was impossible now. He could "storm the gates of Anubis himself." Much work needed to be done, he said, then added, when I was "ready." Cryptic utterances from West were nothing new, so I gave it no more thought, resolving simply to await his next instructions. As it turned out, I was very soon to grasp the import of West's words.

About a week later I was rudely awakened from a nightmare-haunted sleep by West's cold hand gripping my throat. He uttered some words I did not catch, then fell upon me wielding something that gleamed in the light of the candle he carried in his other hand. Instantly I lost consciousness again, this time undisturbed by dreams. Unless, that is, unless I have not yet awakened and have instead passed through the gates of deeper nightmare since that moment I seemed to awaken, for as I write I finger the terrible scar tissue that runs down my face and neck. I fear that now, having at last tasted of the reagent serum for myself, I am ready to aid my devilish master in his insane and unholy adventures into blacker gulfs than even he has yet plumbed.

II. The Body from the Bog by Peter H. Cannon

You may not be aware of the notorious career of myself and my eponymous friend unless you have read a story by the name of "Herbert West—Reanimator," but no matter. That inartistic hackwork was written down to the herd level by Mr. H. P. Lovecraft, whose sole inducement was the monetary reward. I labor under no such artificial constraints. You must believe that here I intend to lay before the public a full and honest account of the sequel to the case of he who shall surely come to be regarded, if not as the most evil and foolish zealot I have ever known, then as the premier biochemical genius of his or any generation.

Two years after Herbert West's "disappearance" I had resolved to give up my medical practice in Arkham and return to live in the house bequeathed me by my late parents in Illinois, when on the very eve of my planned departure my dubious companion of old appeared on my doorstep. The white hair that had once been yellow, the grinning face frozen into agelessness, the livid, jagged scars upon neck and hands—all mutely testified to the ordeal that West had suffered since his nightmarish dismemberment and abduction from our Boston basement by a mob of shambling, sentient hulks directed by the headless form of his former comrade from the Flanders front, Sir Eric Moreland Clapham-Lee. Weak of will and fearful of the fiend before me, I immediately acceded to his wish that I should once again assist him in his reanimation experiments—which he vowed would open up even wider vistas into the unknown, thanks to his now enhanced understanding of the mysteries of the grave.

After our move to spacious quarters on Crane Street, where we fitted up a new cellar laboratory, we commenced a program of blasphemous surgical procedures that culminated in West's probing the mind of a mummy stolen from the Miskatonic Museum, visiting an Egyptian tomb, and recovering a nameless scroll written in an ancient cipher-alphabet. Soon after my companion had partially deciphered the scroll and claimed to be on the verge of revelations beyond any hitherto granted mortal man into the ultimate nature of life and death, he slipped into my bedroom as I slept and plunged a kitchen knife into my larynx. The next thing I knew I had been reanimated.

At first my impulse was to accompany my satanic mentor on even more lunatic and impious sallies into the abyss, but this time he had gone too far. Since I would in due course have undoubtedly decided voluntarily to join the "undead," I felt upon reflection highly annoyed by this premature and preemptory act. Mincing no words in the aftermath, I pointed out to him that we faced the immediate problem of explaining the hideous scar tissue that now marred my skin as well as his own—plus we would have to take the trouble on a regular basis of preparing twice the amount of reagent serum, and in the long run have to cope with the fact of both of us failing visibly to grow older. Indefinitely setting aside West's original plan to pursue the secrets hinted at in the Egyptian scroll, we determined to leave Arkham and lie low in the one place where a couple of freaks like ourselves would not attract undue attention—New York City!

The sale of my family's property in Illinois was enough to finance the purchase of a shabby brownstone on Perry Street in Greenwich Village, within whose Bohemian precincts we gradually established a practice among the better-off artists and writers while we worked on perfecting the serum essential to our prolonged existence. In our quest for immortality we consulted with a Dr. Muñoz, a gentlemanly recluse with a well-chilled laboratory near us on 11th Street, until his tragic passing under circumstances too loathsome to mention. Later we ventured as far as Providence to confer with a singular individual who gave his name as "Dr. Allen," who promised to teach us miraculous preservation techniques but then abruptly ceased all communication. Undaunted, we eventually developed through our own diligent researches a series of daily injections, rather as diabetics rely on insulin, to stabilize our body chemistry and hold in check the gross physical deterioration that could strike at any time, arousing the suspicions of anyone who might chance to peer at us too closely—or pass within smelling distance.

With the passage of the years we spent more of our leisure in philosophical discussion. West confessed that he was considering modifying his once strictly materialist views, in the light of certain portentous dreams which he was coming more and more to believe represented "past life" experiences. In one persistent dream he saw himself as an aristocratic young Celt of the second or third century B.C. associated with a Druidic cult devoted to the worship of such fearsome deities as Tarainis, Esus, and Teuttates. He could not be sure of the location, but guessed it to be somewhere in northern Europe—Scandinavia or the British Isles. I expressed skepticism at this extraordinary claim of the paranormal, my own nightly excursions into the realm of Morpheus being entirely unexceptional. In answer, West suggested that he was likely to be far more receptive to such phenomena than myself, since the interval between his death and resurrection had been a lengthy one and my own only a matter of seconds. As one inclined to wield Occam's Razor, I was tempted to accuse my companion of "fantasy-prone" behavior but refrained, sensing that this notion that he had been an eminent personage in a bygone era satisfied some deep psychological need which it would do more harm than good to challenge.

Our debate had reached a kind of Mexican stand-off, when one morning at the breakfast table West, with a look of ill-concealed triumph, handed me the science section of that day's newspaper opened to an article headlined "Bog Man' Reveals Story of a Brutal Ritual." A photograph showed the head and torso of a nearly perfectly preserved human body, "Owlind Man" according to the caption, so dubbed for the area outside Anchester, England, where a farmer had unearthed it while excavating a peat bog. Various authorities—forensic pathologists, anthropologists, and ethnohistorians—had estimated that this well-nourished white male, whose uncalloused hands and feet bespoke a gentle upbringing, had been buried in the wet, iron-rich, anaerobic soil for more than 2,000 years. A team of specialists, headed by Dr. Richard Steadman of the British Museum, had begun to submit the corpse to a battery of tests, analyzing the stomach contents for one, in the hope of gleaning a wealth of data—social, cultural, and religious—before exposure to the atmosphere took its inevitable toll.

"I am Owlind Man and Owlind Man is myself!" exclaimed West. "And I don't have to deduce it from any tissue samples like these so-called experts—I can confirm it directly!" That his "former self" had evidently been a sacrificial victim in some Druidic rite did not give my friend pause, though I must admit my sluggish circulation received a jolt when I read of certain wounds from which could be inferred a ghastly and nauseating death. If at first leery of West's proposal to investigate this new subject for reanimation, I found his enthusiasm contagious, my immune system ultimately unable to resist the infection. Indeed, the fires of maniacal thirst for the waters of unholy knowledge rekindled, I agreed to book reservations for the two of us on the next available flight to London.

At the airport security check and later in customs, the bag of syringes and reagent sera we carried with us drew some scrutiny, but fortunately with a minimum of fuss we were able to persuade the officials that we were not trafficking in illicit drugs. I should say that we now appeared more like respectable physicians than we had in ages, since availing ourselves of the latest advances in plastic surgery. Makeup sufficed to give color to our otherwise pale, greenish-tinged complexions.

Breaking into the research wing of the British Museum where the body was kept posed a more formidable obstacle, but late one moonless night we accomplished the feat with a skill that I like to think would have done credit to the most professional of second-story men. Amidst a refrigerated room full of test tubes, beakers, retorts, and other paraphernalia of the modern chemistry lab, we discovered the object of our quest, stretched out on an autopsy table, naked and leathery, stained nut brown from its entombment in the peat. In his excitement West was certain, granted its condition, that the lich bore a definite physical resemblance to himself. As we prepared the familiar tools of our trade, the years seemed to slough off like a shroud and it was as if we were once again medical students at Miskatonic, carefree and idealistic, not yet jaded by decades of decadence.

West injected the serum into the carotid artery, and almost instantly the limbs of the corpse quivered. After two millennia of repose Owlind Man began to wake up. As keenly as Gliddon and Buckingham had anticipated the speech of "Allamistakeo" in "Some Words with a

Mummy," that classic tale by the world's greatest master of the terrible and the bizarre, we awaited his first utterance. It was, in the event, in the ancient Celtic tongue and utterly incomprehensible—a difficulty that we had forgotten to allow for in our eagerness and haste. As is well known, the Celts left no written records by which linguists and philologists could reconstruct their spoken language. "Curse their oral tradition!" muttered West, throwing down the pencil with which he had been planning to make notes on a yellow legal pad.

We were reluctantly coming to the conclusion that I would have to transplant West's brain into the body temporarily, as we had done to good effect with the Egyptian mummy, when fate intervened to spare us from again enduring that cumbrous operation. "Wait, this sudden buzzing in my head," said West, sounding hopeful. "He must be trying to communicate with me telepathically!" My companion seized his pencil from off the table and started to write feverishly, occasionally asking a question or repeating something aloud, while I watched and listened in dread fascination and Owlind Man, now propped up on his elbows, continued his eerie colloquoy:

"He says he was a priest who assumed the sacred name of Trebor in his rapid rise within the secret cult of the Old Bones?—no, sorry, Old Ones," ran West's text as I read it in snatches over his shoulder, "But others in the order were jealous—wary of one so youthful and handsome in such an exalted position—and they started to plot against him. In the heat of being falsely accused of a heinous offense, he was unable to master his congenital stammer and struck a superior down dead, the penalty for such crime among the priesthood being self-annihilation. When he refused to do himself in, they rigged his murder to look like a ritual sacrifice —bashing his skull to appease Tarainis, slashing his throat to placate Esus, shoving his face underwater to delight Teuttates! But what's this now?—he's angry at me—he thinks I'm responsible! Oh no, his final memory before his death has warped his reason. No, I tell you, I am not the filthy high-priest who drugged the burnt bannock cake before your last meal! I am yourself, and you are myself—it's too late to commit suicide now, damn it! Aargh!"

As West scribbled these last words, he had no time to underline them for emphasis, for Owlind Man, or Trebor as I will refer to him hereafter, had leapt up and wrapped his stringy arms around his neck in a choke-hold. My first thought was to assist my friend, but old resentments came rushing to the fore and in the crisis I stood back at a safe distance while he tried furiously to rid himself of the berserk carcass that now clung to him from behind with all the tenacity and hate of the legendary old man of the sea. I could sympathize with Trebor's rage, having once been brutally murdered myself.

In their battle they knocked over priceless scientific instruments, upset rows of noxious chemicals, smashed into shelves of glassware, and scattered manuscripts representing months of raw research into the mess that seemed to be exponentially increasing throughout the laboratory with their every gasp and grunt. Exhausted, the two finally collapsed to the ground, Trebor still fixed like a limpet to West's back but no longer struggling. Too feeble to speak, his old neck scars oozing chartreuse pus, my associate yet had the strength to grope for the pencil and paper conveniently within reach and scrawl another message: "Great God!— he's tugging at my brain—he's not me at all—it was all a trick—he just projected his essence into my dreams in order to get me to reanimate him so he could exchange minds—that's why he pretended he was a previous incarnation of myself—he'd stoop to anything to usurp another's body—though I'll see him in hell first before I let him stick my consciousness in his rotting bulk . . Still, the tugging grows, the tugging, I—" Here the script breaks off, for West had fainted, face down in the viscous brown putrescence flowing like molasses to the floor from the fast dissolving thing sprawled on top of him.

At that moment through the door burst two armed guards, followed by a large, lurching figure in a white gown, wearing a badge identifying him as Richard Steadman, M.D. The chief of the no longer viable Owlind Man research project surveyed the surrounding wreckage as if not wholly surprised by the scene, his immobile features betraying no emotion. Gingerly rolling over the sodden form of my friend with a well-shod toe, he said in a low, vibrationless voice that I could just barely hear: "So, we meet again Herbert West. Couldn't leave well enough alone after you escaped from our protective custody, could we? Well, I daresay we've got you now. Here in the United Kingdom we take a very dim view of the wanton destruction of our national scientific treasures." Then, in louder tones to the two heavies who had been keeping a discreet watch by the door: "Guards, would you please be so kind as to arrest these men."

As we were hauled off, I took a hard look at our captor's visage—which seemed curiously waxen. No, could it be? Yes, it was! After that night of horror in our subterranean Beacon Hill laboratory how could I ever forget? Dr. Richard Steadman was West's old nemesis—Sir Eric Moreland Clapham-Lee!

III. Tombstone Tribunal by Will Murray

I thought I had known horror in my lifetime—I, who as a callow medical student at Miskatonic University had assisted the ingenious but unscrupulous modern Dr. Frankenstein, Herbert West, in his fiendish work as he resuscitated corpse after cooling corpse, with often bizarre results. I was only too happy when West disappeared from my life—even if that disappearance had taken place before my terror-struck eyes as a legion of reanimated dead carried him off in sunders one evil night.

The period of normalcy that followed now seems like some Elysian dream. For West returned, his corn silk hair now shock-white, his blue eyes opaque with a passionless drive I no longer recognised. He told me he had escaped his captor, his fellow delver in death, Sir Eric Clapham-Lee, after having been restored and reanimated by his mortal enemy. And eager to pursue his deferred dreams, West enlisted my aid once more. I was a fool. For West's scientific lusts were now beyond restraint. Not content to wait for fortune to bequeath us fresh meat—as so often happened in the past—West fell upon me and, with one cutting gesture, reduced me to his own terrible state. I was dead—and I remained dead even after West restored me to twitching, dreamless life with a dose of his hellish chemical excitant.

Sentient, but without hope of an afterlife, I followed West to England where we absconded with the peat-stained corpse of the Owlind Man, whom West had believed to be his earlier incarnation. West's efforts were successful—Owlind Man lived again. But through telepathic communication with the resurrected one, we learned that Owlind Man was not West's predecessor, but a predator from the past determined to make West's green-tinged uncorrupted body his own.

West succeeded in putting down Owlind man a second time, but our victory was short-lived. Dr. Richard Steadman, who had discovered Owlind Man, had found us. And as his British Museum guards fettered us for the gaol, we discovered a deeper horror. For Dr. Steadman was in reality the wax-headed Sir Eric Moreland Clapham-Lee!

I knew true horror then. As we were roughly escorted to a waiting car and placed in the rear cushions, Sir Eric convinced the guards to allow him to fit black sacks over our heads to snuff our vision. The rest I can only conjecture. I heard the sounds of a man settling into the driver's seat. The auto started up, and there came the shouting of the guards as Sir Eric drove off, with us as his helpless prisoners. For we recognised his hellish laugh.

Or rather West, who knew him better than I, did. "Where could he be taking us?" I whispered to West.

"How should I know!" West snapped petulantly. "What I would like to understand is how can he drive without a head?"

We soon found out for, after hours of driving through an intermittent rain, the auto coasted to a silent halt. I heard crickets chittering as the door was opened and I was rudely hauled out. I was made to sit on cold damp earth. West plopped down beside me. I sensed a Golem-like presence hovering behind us and then abruptly, the sight-muffling sack was torn from my head.

I blinked into the saucer-shaped headlights of the car that had brought us here. I looked behind me—towering above was the monstrous form of Sir Eric, headless and silent.

I quickly turned away. And as my eyes got used to the glare, I gradually made out the windshield of the car and the horror it framed.

For staring at us with undisguised hatred was the disembodied head of Sir Eric Moreland Clapham-Lee!

"How—!" I began.

"Don't be a fool!" West said. "Obviously he left his head on the dashboard."

West needed to say no more. His past experiments with Sir Eric had proven that residual intelligence remained in the spinal column of a decapitated subject. Obviously, Sir Eric controlled his automaton-like body from afar. It explained our unfathomable ride. But to what end? As if reading my thoughts, the head spoke.

"I have brought you both here for one purpose only," the head said in a dry tendinous voice. "And that is to try you for your crimes against humanity, both dead and not dead. And lest you denigrate the following proceedings with some claptrap about mere revenge on my part West," Sir Eric went on, "I have gone to the extreme trouble of assembling a jury of your peers."

I knew West's egotistical words before he spat them out. "I have no peers."

Suddenly, Sir Eric's hands grasped my hair and twisted my head around. West received identical rude treatment. We found ourselves staring at an illuminated burial ground, ancient and overgrown. And squatting among the darksome tombs were a heterogeneous assemblage. They were the dregs of the tombs-spawn of a thousand accidents, both natural and not. I thought I discerned a shattered, enshadowed visage here and there. Was that Buck Robinson, the "Harlem Smoke," whom West had revived, only to pump six shots into his black chest? And that other one. Was that not Robert Leavitt of St. Louis, whom West had murdered solely to provide fresh meat for his experiments? I turned away when I recognised the subject of our first experiment, the nameless wretch whom we had dug up from a pauper's grave and whose pitiful attempts to return to its cold sanctuary were to no avail.

Then Sir Eric's hollow voice rang out. He launched into an extended summation of West's crimes against the dead, not neglecting my place in that horrid history. Witnesses were called. They were a parade of West's past experiments. They all spoke, damning West for disturbing the natural order of their lives - or should I say, their deaths?. The sole exception was Dr. Allan Halsey, whom we knew to be a gibbering madman. He did not seem to be among the charnel conclave, for which I was relieved, given his past cannibalistic leanings.

When the last witness was done, Sir Eric called for a show of thumbs. Fearfully, I looked back at that squatting legion of jeering jurors. Those with thumbs - and they were by no means the majority - turned them down. Others croaked their judgment.

When the litany of liches subsided, the head of Sir Eric spoke again. "The jury has announced its verdict. As judge, it is my duty to pronounce you guilty and sentence you to . . . death!"

"Do your worst, you quack!" West spat back. "We're already dead."

And Sir Eric laughed as he sent his headless form lurching down the iron door of a tomb and returned with a gnashing, struggling figure in chains. The being was so horrible that the others recoiled sluggishly. As the silent simian monster was brought into the glare of headlights, I heard even the sanguinary West give a gasp of repressed fear. For the being was Dr. Allan Halsey, the late dean of Miskatonic University and the subject of West's second great experiment. And as Sir Eric's laughter rose to an impossible crescendo, West offered a ghoulish remark about this being truly our "last supper."

I never knew exactly what transpired in the frantic moments that followed. The merciful black sack descended over my fright-dazed eyes. Then there came a scream I realized was West's. Not a scream of terror, but one that seemed to combine desperation and triumph in equal measure. I heard sounds of struggle which I attributed to Dr. Halsey being brought within range of his dinner, and the distinct rattle and slip of unshackling chains. A new scream came. It emanated from Sir Eric's incomplete throat.

I remember wondering what Sir Eric had to scream about, being safely perched on the dashboard of his car, when I felt a commanding hand on my shoulder and West's whisper in my ear as he exhorted me to run for all I was worth.

Under the force of West's ungentle shove, I ran without sight, without hope. I was pushed into the back seat of the car. I struggled with my bonds as the machine careened into motion. My hands free, finally I pulled the hood from my head. We were barreling down a rustic forest-guarded road. West was driving. And on the dashboard Dr. Eric Moreland Clapham-Lee bounced and screamed invectives at West's smirking face. I looked through the grimy rear window. A Procrustean horde stumbled after us, comprising most of the tribunal from the tombs—but not by any means all. For on the ground two figures were locked in an unholy communion. Dr. Halsey was on his hands and knees over a flailing body, his teeth sinking into its unprotected neck. And then I knew why Sir Eric had screamed. He - or rather his bifurcated body - was being methodically consumed in the very manner he had schemed to inflict on West and me.

"Who's laughing now?" West taunted the unstable head on the dashboard. Sir Eric's response was pungent. Then, as the auto took a particularly sharp curve, the head tumbled into the seat beside West. West made a gesture as if to brush Sir Eric's head to the floorboards when he let out a scream. The car began to weave wildly as West let go of the wheel. I quickly saw the reason for his anguish—hanging from one of his frantic hands was Sir Eric's head, firmly in place by strong shovel-shaped teeth.

Heeding West's urgent call for assistance, I took the head in both hands and tore it free. West regained control of the car just in time to avoid striking an oak tree. We broadsided it instead, sending the car spinning out of control. When we got our wits about us once more, West bullied the car into motion again. But it was irreparably damaged. It jerked and hesitated with every revolution of its abused tires.

I looked through the rear window, and saw no sign of the shambling horde that sought to wreak its grisly revenge upon us. I heaved a dry sigh of relief. It was at that point that West asked me what I had done with Sir Eric's snapping head. I replied that I had thrown it out the window. At that, a maniacal urge seemed to take possession of Herbert West—that familiar irrational mania of perverted science. He sent the car shuddering in a ragged circle and weaved back the way we had come, unheeding of my cries of concern that we were driving back into the midst of our worst nightmares. I knew that West's avid eyes sought the rain-slick roadside for that last, undigested portion of the man who had troubled his sleep while West lived and continued to pursue him long after normal bodily functions had ceased for both men.

"There!" West cried suddenly. He floored the machine. I had a momentary sense of an object lying in the road. And when the sound that is peculiar to that of a melon being burst came up through the floorboards, I felt acutely sick and would have retched had I eaten food at any time since West had pulled me from the black waters of the Styx.

West had no time to exult in his triumph, for upon rounding a corner, we spied a wall of inhumanity filling the rain-dappled windshield. West applied the brake, but it was too late. We smashed into that erstwhile jury of our peers with all the horsepower that remained in the disabled engine.

The impact was terrific. In my mind's eye I can still see the flying, bloodless limbs, the mushy impacts of bodies striking blacktop and bole. When we at last ground to a halt, I sought egress from the destroyed vehicle. I had no sooner planted my shod foot on the ground when something wrapped itself tenaciously about my ankle. Hastily, I withdrew my foot and saw that a dismembered hand had transfixed my ankle. I kicked it loose with my other foot and screamed to West - for another hand was crawling spider-fashion up the running board. Frantically, I slammed the door on its discolored fingers and depressed the locks all around me.

The auto began to rock with the force of the disconnected limbs and worm-blind torsos striving to crack its metallic shell as if it were a lobster, seeking the delicious meat within—us. Feeling my cold flesh crawl in anticipation of the fate that was foreshadowed by the clacking of unseen teeth, I cried to West that we were trapped. But West was defiant, pointing out that none of our foes had survived the wreck intact. Their ability to harm us was limited. Still I continued to shudder uncontrollably.

It was while we pondered what to do that headlights swept around the bend. A car drew up, and two figures emerged from it. I heard their initial exclamations of shock and horror—and the retching that followed. Finally, one figure approached us with blazing flashlight held high. I made out the towering shape of a constable's helmet. But my hope of rescue turned to ashes when the door was abruptly opened and I was dragged out, along with West.

"Thank God you're here, constable," I gasped.

"God has nothing to do with this," the constable said harshly. "I am placing you bloody villains under arrest!"

"On what charge?" I demanded. But before he could answer Herbert West's acid voice broke in.

"Don't be an imbecile," he sneered. "It is plain why we are being detained. It is for cold-bloodedly running down all these fine citizens whose parts lie scattered about the road."

At that, Herbert West threw back his head and unleashed a cacodaemoniacal laugh—and I wondered if he had finally snapped, or did his bloodless brain simply relish the supreme irony that, having outwitted graveyard retribution, the mundane wheels of earthly justice were about to bring him to task for the murder of the very wretches he had once restored to life?

IV. What Came Up From the Cellar by Donald R. Burleson

Those who read this account will understand, all too well, when I say that there are horrors within horrors. My own life has been to an uncommon degree full of horror due to my acquaintance with the demented Herbert West, with whom I have been through a frightful series of experiences ranging from our early days as medical students at Miskatonic University, to our near- disaster in England, and now beyond that. But now I have witnessed the most soul-sickening outcome of all of West's delving into forbidden matters, and I begin to understand to what depths horror may go.

We were arrested on a lonely country road in England, where we had been attacked by a horde of abortive reanimation experiments led by West's old enemy, Sir Eric Moreland Clapham-Lee, or what was left of him. When the police arrived, they naturally assumed that the charnel mess on the roadway was the result of a mass homicide on our part, and we soon found ourselves on trial for several counts of murder—the number of counts being as uncertain as the number of fragmented bodies.

It would be wearisome to relate all that happened during our many days in court; suffice it to summarise the proceedings as follows. Our defence attorneys (or barristers, as they were called) were quick to argue that the crime of which we stood accused was an official misconstruction, in that forensic evidence made it clear that our driving the auto into the noisome crowd on the road could in no manner have resulted in what the police found at the scene - an indeterminate number of bodies not only dismembered and scattered but, though still feebly animate, showing clear signs of necrosis, as if really long dead. What became of these bodies, or parts of bodies, we never learned, and both sides in court referred to them in tones of reluctance and confusion. The legal outcome was that the crime for which we had been arrested could not be proved against us, and the court ruled that we were dismissed, provided we left England immediately and never returned, a provision with which we were only too happy to comply. Within a short amount of time, we were back in the United States, shaken and exhausted, but free.

Surprisingly, West, whom I had thought wholly friendless, had an acquaintance living in southern New Hampshire, a fellow Miskatonic alumnus named Berle Haisson who lived in the town of Merrimack with his Thibetan wife Mi-Ling. This dubious pair had once been incarcerated in a prison for the criminally insane. I dared not guess why or how West had remained in contact with them. At any rate, the couple had been instrumental in helping West secure a lonely and dilapidated Colonial farmhouse in the nearby town of New Boston. West's acceptance of these lodgings for us surprised me greatly, in light of his usual interests, since the house was a considerable distance from any graveyard, but I soon came to understand that his diseased mind, though still of course obsessed with reanimation, was beginning to run in certain alarming new channels.

For a number of weeks West spoke not at all of his new thoughts, merely muttering incomprehensibly to himself and lapsing into pensive silence when spoken to. I let him be, and was fool enough to begin to imagine that perhaps he was not going to return to his old obsessive fervour. He puttered around the house, and we spent our solitary evenings reading. I noted that he kept a bottle of the most recently updated version of his reanimation serum close at hand, but I tried not to draw any conclusions, hoping that there were none to be drawn.

My hopes were dashed one evening when West, who had bought a rattling and rusty old Oldsmobile, suggested that we break our monotony and drive into the nearby city of Nashua and simply walk the streets and talk. It was the first time in weeks he had indicated any real desire to talk, and I felt nervous already, wondering what the subject of conversation might be, but I went along, and we were soon strolling along Main Street in Nashua, with West beginning in a halting kind of way to relate his recent thinking to me.

"You know how certain it is now," he said, "that even separated parts of bodies retain a species of intelligence."

I swallowed hard and replied, "Yes. Yes."

"Well, I believe that the principle can be carried further. I believe that the real repositories of intelligence in the human body, which we know not to be wholly centred in the brain, are in fact so diffuse and ubiquitous in their cellular presence that they reside even in what one might suppose to be wholly peripheral substance."

I shook my head. "I don't understand. What are you getting at?" I was far from certain that I really wanted to know, but I knew that he would explain. Some new fiendishness was brewing in his brain, and there would be no stopping him.

He smiled. "I'll show you, as soon as I find what I need. It should only take a few minutes."

We walked up to the northern end of Main Street, where the street becomes a level bridge of the river. Stopping at a spot on the bridge, West pointed to the low concrete wall beside us, over which even in the fading light we could see the waters rushing below. At first I could not understand what West was pointing at, but I noticed that he was taking from his jacket pocket a bottle of serum and a hypodermic syringe. Then, with some disgust, I saw what it was that had drawn his interest to the wall. It was a thick, grey wad of phlegm, probably spat there by some wino or street dweller.

"Thus separated from the parent organism," West intoned, filling the syringe with serum, "this peripheral matter is of course dead. But I claim that even such matter as this will contain the cellular code of life, and that that life may be recalled." He stuck the needle into the rubbery mucus on the wall, and injected serum.

"West, if ever I doubted that you are totally insane—"

"Shh." He replaced his materials in the jacket pocket and pointed to the wall. "Wait."

We waited. Nothing, I was relieved to see, was happening.

But suddenly something was happening after all. Involuntarily, I joined West in bending close to the vile liquid on the wall.

Out of the mucus, a sort of bubble was forming, and in the failing light it took me a minute to see that the bubble was in fact a half-formed little human face, which, to the horror I think even of Herbert West, opened its pathetic little mouth and uttered a faint kind of mewling sound before the bubble collapsed back into its source, the face dissolving into undifferentiated phlegm.

It was a moment before I had the courage to look at West's face. The street lamps overhead were coming on, and in their sickly glow I saw an all-too-familiar expression of exultation. But, surprisingly, he said nothing, and we returned home. He did not allude to the event at all, and several days passed uneventfully. In the evenings, West simply buried himself in reading, largely ignoring me.

Then one evening, when my companion had gone down into the cellar, leaving the door from the kitchen to the cellar steps swinging open, I heard something strange from below. It sounded for the world like retching, as if West were down in the cellar regurgitating. I hastened down the rickety wooden steps and found him, in the light of a solitary hanging bulb, standing over a puddle of vomit on the concrete floor. Oddly, he was smiling.

"What-" I began. But West soon made his thoughts abundantly clear. He had in his hand the familiar syringe and bottle of reanimation serum.

"We shall see what we shall see." he said. He filled the syringe with serum and bent over the vomit on the floor, pressing the point of the needle into it. He had already partly depressed the plunger when I strode forward and kicked the needle out of his hand.

"Damned lunatic. Get away from that stuff and come upstairs. What's the matter with you?"

He looked up at me and shrugged. Wordlessly, we climbed the stairs and spent the rest of the evening reading. West seemed to have dismissed the matter from his mind.

That night, at a little past 2 a.m., it happened.

West had gotten up and gone to the kitchen for a drink of water, and, myself restless, I rose from my own bed and followed. We were sipping glasses of water in the light of the open refrigerator door when we heard it.

Faintly but undeniably, there was, behind the closed door to the cellar, a creaking on the stairs. We stood silent, listening. It came again, closer, as if something were climbing up. The quality of the sound was a little different now, as if the feet that pressed upon the boards were wet, making a sort of sloshing. With a deep intake of breath, West reached his hand out and pulled the door open.

Standing in the wan light was something the memory of which I fear can never be wholly expunged from my mind. The thing had a vague sort of shape, an attempt at a head, a diseased suggestion of limbs. But it was semiliquid, yellow, clabbered, dropping pieces of itself off as it slowly oozed its form into the room, bringing a ghastly odour with it. It was vomit, vomit that had gotten up and walked, and its sliding and shifting semblance of a face bore distorted but recognisable features of Herbert West.

Before West could even scream, it was at him, fastening upon him— eating him. I backed away and stood against the far wall, too terrified to move or speak, but oddly unable to resist watching the revolting spectacle occurring across the room. The thing bit and chewed, bit and chewed, ripping flesh off the bone, slurping and sucking with hideous appetite, grinding its unthinkable mouth even on the bones, burying itself in the entrails. It was eating him wholly, and as it swallowed him, it seemed to solidify a little, filling out with more distinct form as the chewed tissue of Herbert West coursed down its gummy and transparent throat. It was becoming Herbert West anew, a stinking parody of Herbert West consuming Herbert West to become a new kind of parody of Herbert West. What was standing there at the end of the process was he, after a fashion. But it sloshed when it turned its head to me to speak, and I fainted.

Now I fear for the future more than ever. What Herbert West has now become continues to move about the house, puttering, humming with a curious sort of gurgle to itself, speaking sometimes to me in a voice that I cannot endure to hear. Despite its repellently liquescent eyes and chunky-looking skin, the thing looks something like my old colleague. The odour, I must say, is truly abominable. He—if I may still say "he"—holds towels about himself at times, when the weather is warm, hugging himself as if to hold himself together, and leaving a strange, sticky, wet little trail across the floorboards when he walks barefoot. As I have said, I fear for the future now more than ever—because even though the creature I share a roof with is clearly failing a little every day, I suspect that even this is not the end.

V. Tears of the Dead by Charles Hoffman

Truly, there is no escaping one's destiny. Whether our fates are written in our stars, our genes, or our subconscious, it makes little difference. The course of one's life's journey is charted before the first steps are taken, and once we embark on a certain path we can never stray very far from it further down the road. It has been my unhappy destiny to be the assistant, apprentice, disciple, and stooge of the mad medical genius, Dr. Herbert West.

Readers of my previous memoirs must have become exasperated indeed to discover how I acquiesced again and again to the mad whims of Herbert West. Given the depraved and ghoulish nature of West's experiments, the only sane reaction to my utter spinelessness must be one of disgust and contempt. While I do not wish to offer excuses for my behavior. I would note only that, unless one has met him, it is impossible to imagine the sheer dynamic presence of Herbert West. Though small in physical stature, the force of his personality is hypnotic. Never a strong-willed person, I found myself in thrall to West's insane ambitions whenever he was present. Never mind that, during his long absence, my suffering soul was wracked by guilt and shame. When he reappeared in my life, I once again came under his spell. Even when West actually murdered me and restored my life with the reagent serum (he doubtless assumed he was doing me a favor), I lacked sufficient independent will to rebel against him. Being now one of the undead, what other company could I seek?

The new series of experiments we undertook were blasphemous and horrible, impossible to excuse as legitimate medical research. West was ever eager to find new and more bizarre uses for the reagent. For where once it was only effective on wholly intact, freshly-deceased specimens, the latest formulas of the serum could actually restore life wherever it once existed . For example, a steak from the butcher could be restored to full independent life as easily as a whole organism. West did in fact reanimate cooked pieces of meat, so as to relish in devouring the seared, writhing flesh. Reanimation could even be effected on a mummy thousands of years old.

It was in search of such an exotic specimen that we were lured to England by West's old nemesis. Sir Eric Moreland Clapham-Lee. As it happened, West and I were able to escape his clutches and destroy him once and for all. Back home, however, West embarked on a new course of research that proved to be pointless and disgusting even for him. He sought to prove his ability to bestow independent life even on organic waste matter. The experiment backfired, however, and with poetic justice West himself was transformed into a monster, a shambling bulk of living offal.

This latest horror proved to be the breaking point as far as I was concerned. At last I found sufficient will to rebel and leave the West-thing to its own devices. In the middle of the night I fled from the New Hampshire farmhouse we had occupied, taking a single valise of clothing and other belongings. It does not speak well of me that I deserted my longtime companion in his hour of greatest need, but given his many crimes against humanity and nature, plus the fact that his condition was entirely his own fault, it was no less a fate than he deserved.

I took the first train south and eventually made my way to Baltimore. There I secured humble quarters in a slum area and offered my services to a Salvation Army clinic tending the ill and infirm among the city's poor. A physician of some renown, I was warmly welcomed into that fold of selfless charity workers. Among them I found a new home and a new life. I toiled for long hours each day on behalf of the needy, receiving little remuneration other than meals and a small room to retire to at the end of the long day's labours. Doubtless I sought to serve some sort of penance for my past misdeeds. I turned my back on scientific research. My sole concern for the next six years was to succor as best I could the pitiful wretches who came to me at the clinic.

It was, however, impossible to immerse myself in my work so completely as to completely forget the past. The reader will recall that I was murdered and restored to artificial life by West. I was in truth a walking cadaver, able to pass for a living person only because of the make-up I applied to my sallow features and my artful mimicry of natural functions such as breathing. I sustained myself through periodic treatments with the reagent serum, which, of course, I knew how to prepare due to my long association with West. Fortunately the ingredients are both fairly inexpensive and easy to obtain. I had access to laboratory facilities thanks to a new-found colleague. Dr. Julius Mapes.

Dr. Mapes was an elderly physician who, despite a thriving general practice, still found time to devote to the clinic. Getting on in years, Dr. Mapes began to find his practice increasingly burdensome, and so made me a generous offer. He wished for me to move into his home and share his practice, thus lightening his work load while permitting each of us still to set aside several days a week for charity work at the clinic. I gladly accepted and delighted in my new role of kindly family doctor.

Another advantage to this new arrangement was that I now had more than periodic access to Dr. Mapes' laboratory. I resolved to devise a formula or serum that would restore me to a more natural form of life. I called upon all that I had learned of reanimation from Herbert West, and then took his theories in entirely new directions. At length I invented a series of treatments that would utilize separate serums to revitalize each of my bodily systems one by one. Over a period of eighteen months I reactivated first my respiratory, and then my cardiovascular, digestive, and endocrine systems.

When the treatments were completed, I stood before the mirror and exulted to find myself completely restored to full, vital, natural life. It seemed as if the sun had never shown brighter than on that day.

Unfortunately, old Dr. Mapes passed away not long afterwards, leaving his practice to me. Great was my sorrow, but try as I might, I found I could not shed tears. My revitalization process had apparently restored all of my bodily functions except for that of the tear ducts. Often, in the darkest hours of those first nights after I left West, I had longed for the catharsis of weeping for shame and guilt over my sordid- past. Now I mused that I was forever to be denied even the dubious comfort of tears as a mark of my eternal ignominy.

Wishing further to distance myself from the past, I spent the next several years devoted to my practice and patients. I delivered new born babes and nursed them through childhood illnesses. I eased the afflictions of the elderly. I went forth at all hours of the day and night to hurry to a patient's bedside. In time the memory of Herbert West began to fade away like a bad dream.

I remember it was spring when Dr. Barbara Bishop came to Baltimore. A fellow New Englander, she was an attractive young woman of about thirty years. I met her at the home of a colleague shortly after she arrived in the city to join the staff of one of the hospitals. She seemed most impressed when introduced to me, for she was familiar with my name from my association with West. West and I had, from time to time, seen fit to publish the results of some of our minor experiments (such as West considered the world was ready for) in the leading medical journals. Dr. Bishop, like the medical community at large, regarded those findings as important steps forward. Had anyone known the true direction of the bulk of our research, West and I would have doubtless been burned at the stake! But Barbara, as I soon grew fond of thinking of her, looked upon me as an esteemed man of medicine.

On the occasion of our first meeting, Barbara and I conversed for several hours, and I had to admit to myself that I was attracted to more than her lively intellect. She was blonde and blue-eyed, with fair skin, a lithe but curvaceous figure, and a dazzling smile. Possessed of an ingratiating wit, she fairly radiated youthful vitality. I was drawn to her from the first.

In the months that followed, I met Barbara again on numerous occasions, usually with other doctors present, but sometimes over dinner in quiet restaurants. I developed warm feelings for her, but dared not dream that she might ever reciprocate. Then, one evening Barbara confessed that she did, indeed, harbor similar feelings for me. I was taken aback somewhat, but overjoyed nonetheless. It was she who boldly suggested that we marry. She pragmatically pointed out that she could share my practice, filling the gap left by Dr. Mapes. She added enthusiastically that we could collaborate on "important medical research." Eleven years after severing my ties with Herbert West, I was ready to embark on a wonderful new life.

I would have wept for sheer joy had I been able to, but I was once again reminded that my tear ducts remained dead and useless. But no matter. Barbara and I were soon married in a simple ceremony before a Justice of the Peace. We shared home and hearth and medical practice, as previously planned.

After settling into a comfortable routine of married life, Barbara and I collaborated on preliminary research towards a method for the replication of cells from preserved tissue samples. We hoped to achieve a viable process for growing various bodily tissues like cultures in the laboratory. Our immediate objective was the growth of dermis and epidermis to be used in skin grafts for burn victims. We soon theorized that it might be possible to grow entire compatible organs for transplantation into patients whose own organs were failing. Indeed, a whole array of possibilities seemed within our grasp. In addition to everything else she had given me, I had my wife to thank for the opportunity to offer the world revolutionary medical techniques that would, when eventually implemented, sustain life in previously hopeless cases. I rejoiced in having come such a long way from the morbid tampering with the dead back in the old days with West.

For months on end I was deliriously happy. Then came the fateful night of September 17, 1939. I had been away all day making house calls during a flu epidemic. When I arrived at home around 11 p.m., I was exhausted and longed to retire to my warm bed. But as I entered the foyer, I heard strange voices from within the house. In the parlour I found Barbara conversing with a couple, both strangers. No, not quite strangers, I realized. I had met them before, long ago. The man was named Berle Haisson and the woman was his Thibetan wife, Mi-Ling. They were friends of Herbert West!

Feelings of shock and confusion and a sudden sense of impending disaster surged over me. My dread was compounded by the realization that these two had briefly been incarcerated in an asylum for the criminally insane. I moved into the room quickly, positioning myself between them and Barbara, and demanded to know what was going on. It was Barbara who spoke:

"Sit down. And do try to calm yourself."

That voice! So unlike Barbara's usual tones and yet . . . uncannily familiar. A premonition heralding some obscene horror about to be revealed was gnawing at the back of my brain. Too stunned to do otherwise, I sat as I had been bidden. A strong drink was thrust into my hand.

My wife turned to me and said, "I'm sorry it was necessary to deceive you, but I had need of your talents."

"Oh ... oh my God," I stammered, beginning to grasp the truth, "Our marriage ... is a lie, a sick joke. All this time . . . you've been working for Herbert West!"

She shook her head as I made my accusation. "Wrong again," she replied, "I am Herbert West!"

I drained the drink in my hand in a single gulp and let the empty glass slip from my fingers. I lapsed into a kind of mute helplessness as he explained.

"You recall of course that I was imprisoned in a rapidly decomposing body when you deserted me. Having no alternative, I summoned Haisson and his wife via telephone, having arranged for their release from the asylum some time previously. It was difficult making myself understood, but I succeeded in bringing them to my aid."

"I was beyond the help of medicine or science. The answer lay in a technique of psychic mind transference perfected by an occultist named Ephraim Waite. That I was able to master the technique in a very short time I attribute to sheer force of will and the desperate urgency of my plight. I was able to transfer my mind into the body of a vagrant abducted for that purpose just hours before the hulk my mind inhabited collapsed into an oozing puddle of stinking filth."

"In due course I transferred my mind into a more agreeable vessel — a twenty-year-old Yale athlete no less, but it had been my intention from the first somehow to restore my original form. I theorized that it was possible to replicate one's entire body from the genetic blueprint furnished by the chromosome material in a single cell. Enough traces of my original tissue remained in what was left of the grotesque form I had just shed to make such a plan feasible. To that end tissue samples were preserved until the technique could be perfected."

Thus concluded Herbert West, for this could be no other. Looking at the beauteous feminine form of my wife, I could now see only West. He had dropped the charming mannerisms of "Barbara" and now the cold, icy inhuman intellect I knew of old seemed to radiate from that form.

"You fiend," I roared, leaping to my feet. "Is there no crime you won't sink to for your own ends? What of the people whose bodies you stole? What of the real Barbara Bishop?"

"Each of the minds displaced by the superior force of my own intellect were forced into the body I had worn previously." West replied tranquilly. "The vagrant perished when my original mutated body fell to pieces—no great loss there. The young athlete whose mind eventually resided in the body of the vagrant was carted off to the madhouse when he attempted to tell the authorities of his predicament. As for the young lady . . . well, I had fully intended to restore her to her rightful form when I had finished with it. But when she suddenly found herself in a man's body, she was seized by a hysterical fit and hurled herself through a large window. The jagged glass cut the body to pieces, killing her."

"And what of me?" I sputtered, choking with rage. "You perpetrated this cruel charade just because you needed my assistance again. You dominated me as a youth. You killed and reanimated me to make me more like you. Now you've stolen my life again!" I was shouting now. "Because whatever the cost, nothing must stop the research of Dr. Herbert West! Well, what about me. Dr.—"

"Oh, spare me the histrionics," West broke in. "After all, you can't say I haven't made an effort to be a more agreeable companion." A numbing feeling of gloom and utter defeat settled over me and I fell silent as West continued talking, explaining his plans for our future. "You've already been of much more help than you know, old man. You see, I'm . . . expecting! With your aid and that of my assistants here, I believe certain modifications can be made prenatally to prepare the zygote to function as a new and fitting host body. The male Herbert West will shortly be reborn !"

In nine months' time I would be witness to the grotesque spectacle of Herbert West giving birth to Herbert West.

With the help of myself, Haisson, and Mi-Ling, West's perverse plans proceeded.

As for myself, I have long since ceased to struggle against my fate. I have even given up trying to dodge or ward off whatever blows fate sees fit to punish me with. My body lives on, but my spirit has died. As a doctor, I tend to my patients all day. Then I return home to my wife—Herbert West—and my son—Herbert West.

Incidentally, I've also made one minor discovery of a personal nature. My tear ducts are working again, and working very well at that.

VI. The Corpse Spawn by Robert M. Price

There are some nightmares, it seems, from which there is no awaking. Such a nightmare has clasped me in its throes, struggle vainly as I will, since the ill-omened day I met Herbert West: man of science, medical genius, ghoul from Tartarus. Twice I imagined I had escaped him, only to find myself back under his nauseous spell more helplessly than ever, each seeming liberation only a tantalizing respite that made eventual reenslavement all the more unbearable. The reader will recall the hideous web into which West had lately drawn me: through arcane means he had supplanted the very soul of my beloved companion Barbara, possessing her beautiful form like some unclean spirit of biblical days. In that form he had in secret mockery received my every conjugal caress in a charade unutterably perverse and soul-upheaving to contemplate.

No less mind-shattering was the news that by his own methods he had so arranged the conception of his? . . . her? . . . our! . . . child that it should be prepared as a new host body to house his vampiric intellect. And in this way Herbert West would cross for once and all that barrier from his half-world of reanimated death into the light of genuine organic life.

With the passage of months the unwholesome delivery had come to fruition. Perhaps it was only tortured imagination that told me I heard in the distance the faint baying of hounds at the hour of birth. With the help of West's furtive factotum Haisson and the latter's sinister Thibetan wife Mi-Ling, West promptly placed the newborn creature in a curious incubator-like device. Outwardly, at least, the babe was radiant and healthy, and though he was my own flesh and blood, I could in no way regard the infant as my own son. Thus it was with detached and listless curiosity that I wondered after the purpose of the incubator.

In the coming weeks and months I was to find out more than I wished of West's designs for the child. The incubator occupied the center of a large room whose various platforms, tanks, jars, and tables held an assortment of bubbling specimens of animate or nearly animate tissue, some distinctly reptilian in character. It seemed that through a blasphemous series of grafts, surgical supplements, and infusions of certain unknown hormonal extracts, West planned to accelerate the growth of the child to a fantastic degree. If successful, the resultant creature would be but a physical shell, having neither time nor opportunity to develop any maturity or personality of its own. But of course that was precisely West's desire. It was only the physical husk that he needed, intending to replace its still-born soul with his own.

In only two years of these procedures, in which I will admit, to no reader's surprise I am sure, I was an assistant. West's new vehicle was ready. I stood with Haisson and the Thibetan, shuddering at the horrid tittering of the pair, as we watched the two supine forms side by side on identical operating tables: the stolen body of my beloved Barbara and the swathed and sheeted form of West's creation. For a moment both were still as in death, and I dared hope the experiment had failed, consigning West's wandering soul to a limbo from which it would never return.

But then my heart sank as the Barbara-thing gave a last quiver and the West-thing sat bolt-upright. Low laughter came through the muffling bandages. I realized the extent both of West's genius and of his triumph only when he unwound the mummy-like wrappings to reveal — the unlined, precocious, tow- headed face of the young medical student I had met so many years before!

With none of the unsteadiness one might expect of him after such a procedure, West swung easily down off the table, casting the handful of bandages aside. He gave one smirking look to the now-vacant form of Barbara, made for the door and called out to me as an afterthought, "She's yours again! May you be happy together!" West's chuckling assistants followed him out, leaving me alone, tears flowing and teeth clenching, to stand vigil by my wife's side. West did not suspect that even he had finally pushed me too far.

The hour was late that night as I prepared my vengeance. I knew well the habits of the three fiends with whom I had lived these last years and could rely on West's collaborators having retired. West himself would be at work in unwholesome studies above in his garret room. Thus it was without fear of discovery that I slunk into the laboratory where lay the inert but beautiful mannequin of Barbara. With me I brought a syringe of the hellish reagent serum. Of course I knew that I could not waken the woman I loved. Indeed she had perhaps never existed save in my own deluded mind since West had taken her over even before our marriage. Now I wanted only what West and I had considered failure in earlier years: a reanimated hulk motivated only by the dim instinct to kill. I would revive her, then set her on Haisson and the Thibetan. It seemed poetic justice. West I would save for myself.

Moments after the injection a mock sentience flickered into those dead eyes. Briefly I imagined I detected a spark of panic as if the long displaced soul of Barbara had been recalled across the wastelands of death to a condition even more horrifying. No matter: her torment would end soon.

With an arthritic woodenness of limbs, the thing rose and took my hand as I led it slowly through the carpeted halls and up the polished stairs, down the hall of the second floor to the bedroom of West's detestable cronies. The door was unlocked, the lights out. By the moonlight both forms were clearly etched in their characteristic postures, Haisson wasted with drink, his twisted form entangled with stained sheets and more than one empty bottle; the woman squatting, legs crossed, in meditation on the floor. Tearing claws opened the woman's throat, sending her, without waking, from Nirvana to a greater and final extinction. The oblivious Haisson was even shorter and easier work. Her task accomplished, the blood spattered avenger only waited for my next direction. Moments later I quitted the room, discarding a second empty syringe and leaving the bedroom littered with three corpses. I made for the staircase again.

As I knew he would be, West's slender form sat hunched over his desk, flooding moon rays illuminating a pair of crumbling papyrus fragments before him. He still had not become aware of me as I stood there hefting the revolver in my pocket.

"West," I said simply.

He turned now, roused from concentration, but surprisingly not annoyed. The old light of forbidden discovery lit his rejuvenated face.

"It's all here in the Black Rituals of Koth-Serapis and the Papyrus of Nephren-Ka! I knew it would be. And my hunch was correct about having lived before. Clapham-Lee led us a merry chase all right, but at least that much of it was true! Death is nothing! It was a bargain I made long ago . . . millennia ago, I mean!, with Sebek, and Bast, and the Faceless One. That's why I . . . what have you got there . . .? Why, you fool . . .!"

I spoke slowly. "Death may be more of a threat than you think, my old friend. Your lackeys have found that out downstairs."

"Bah! That pair of fools had outlived their usefulness anyway. But listen, old man, there's no reason for this . . . !"

That was West's last enormity. I squeezed the trigger and emptied the revolver. Six shots by moonlight and he was gone. With him had died a strange and terrible knowledge, a knowledge better lost, for with it Herbert West had proven not so much that life could triumph over death, but that death could masquerade as life, that life could become more hideous than death.

Epilogue

Years have now passed, years of freedom, years of aimlessness. An adult lifetime of compromise and servitude has made independent existence too great a burden to bear. All is a void of sorrow; all memory is horror. Thoughts of suicide begin their insistent whispering. With the mentor gone, what has one who has never been aught but a disciple to live for? What attraction can the pure sunlight hold for one long inured to a bat-like existence in the shadow- caves of Sheol? And at last there comes a fumbling at the latches of awareness. A self long-accustomed to yielding finds it easiest to yield again . . . and the triumph is complete! The quest can go on! The depths of hell can be plumbed and charted anew! A new assistant must be recruited, though truly our association is closer than it has ever been! Still I shall miss him!

Yours truly,

Herbert West

Charnel House

Tim Curran

The shocking, the unnatural, the unbelievable horror from the shadows.

- H.P. Lovecraft

There are things the human eye should look upon and others which should remain forever hidden. Grim legacies and dark, unnamable things which can destroy minds and wither souls black with their utter malignancy. And some of these things, yes, they dare to walk like men, though they are scarce fit to crawl through the noisome slime of creation's dankest cellar.

I know of which I speak.

For in the second week of August, 1925, I met one of them. And never, ever have I been the same. In all the intervening years since, there has been no true peace for me. An unknown shape seen skulking by moonlight or a tree branch scraping at a midnight window to this day fills me with a manic, irrational sense of horror.

But in 1925, I knew nothing of these things.

I walked tall with a piercing gleam in my eyes, an innate curiosity filling me like a cup.

In those days I was a reporter for the Bolton Chronicle. I had made something of a name for myself investigating the inhuman working conditions at Bolton's textile mills, the political corruption and graft amongst the city's selectmen. The moneyed powers that be despised me for if there was a dusty skeleton hiding in a closet, then I was the man to shake it out. And because of this, my by-line was carried not only in Arkham and Boston, but as far away as New York and Chicago.

Some called me a progressive reformer and others simply called me a radical, a social terrorist.

No matter.

If you are as old as me and few are, I dare say you may recall the trouble at Christchurch Cemetery in Arkham during those dark days. For several months, graves had been opened and horribly rifled, the contents of which were found badly mutilated and strewn about the grounds come morning. At first, this was thought the work of deviants or depraved medical students, but as the facts surfaced, these explanations were abandoned. For the charnel remains found by daylight had all been viciously dismembered and half-eaten. Dogs were blamed originally, given the method of exhumation the graves appeared to have been opened not by shovel and pick, but by a furious and savage digging as of paws but even that was thrown out when the county coroner and pathologists from Miskatonic University Medical School claimed that the marks of dentition on the bones were consistent or near-consistent with those of the human mouth.

All of that, of course, was never released to the public. What with the disturbed graves and plundered tombs, there was already wild speculation concerning body-snatching witches and subterranean corpse-eaters. And this, of course, in the wake of Herbert West, a surgeon of morbid repute who had become something of a local bogeyman among the children and had been labeled as the "Arkham Ghoul" for his involvement in grave-robbing and weird experiments conducted on cadavers in his cellar.

So, as you can imagine, the police were very close to the vest about it, not wishing to fan the flames of hysteria that were already blazing out of control. I hadn't seen such fear and heard such awful stories since the typhoid outbreak of 1905 when I was a boy.

Well, on August 10th of that forbidding year, I was allowed by the police to accompany them on a raid at Christchurch Cemetery. A Poe or Lovecraft could not have imagined a more perfectly macabre place than Christchurch by wan moonlight. There were twenty of us there in that bleak and misting tomb yard, the police carried pistols and electric torches. I could barely carry myself through those sepulchral fields of lichen-encrusted marble. To all sides ancient headstones thrust from noxious vegetation, leaning crosses and high stone crypts were garlanded in dead ivy. We passed down twisting lanes blown by the previous autumn's leaves and hopped over broken slabs webbed with creeping fungi.

Detective-sergeant Hayes of the Bolton force said to me, "Here... see that? He's already picked up the scent of that devil!"

He was speaking of the hound we had brought with us. He was called Derby and he was large and sleek-muscled, his nose pressed forever to the yellow grasses and tangled weeds, sniffing out the trail of the thing that robbed graves. Derby led us on a wild chase through legions of tombstones and sullen monuments, some of which had been there two centuries or more. Now and again, he would pause, casting for scent, and we would stand there, shivering and stiff with tension. The wind was blowing and those great denuded oaks overhead creaked, dappled moonlight filtering through their gnarled boughs. Dead leaves scratched at vault doors and a fetid mist seeped from the moldering ground. One could almost imagine the ghost of Herbert West still plying its grisly trade.

After about twenty minutes in which it seemed Derby had led us in circles, he directed us to the wrought-iron, rusting door of a gray and weathered family mausoleum. And here he paused, howling and chasing his own tail, snapping at his handler and anyone that got near him. Something about that place was driving the animal mad...he was slavering and yipping, growling and whining.

Finally, he had to be led off, his mournful howling vanishing in the distance.

Animals, it has been said, are sensitive to things man cannot feel. But I think we were all feeling it at that moment—a gnawing and inexplicable sense of terror. For as we formed up our lines, the iron door to that leaf-blown tomb swung wide and something stepped into view.

What? you ask.

Even now, I barely have the nerve to tell you. It was almost a man and it was almost something else. An amorphous, twisted shadow that stank of black earth and fungi-draped caskets. It did not walk like a man nor like an animal exactly, but almost like some weird and lumbering insect. The police put their lights on it and it screamed with a squeaking, scratching voice like dozens of roofing nails dragged across a blackboard.

Nothing human, nothing sane, could make a sound like that.

It was a corpse. I say to you now it was an animate corpse. As it shambled down the crumbling steps of that centuried tomb, I think I cried out. It walked almost pigeon-toed, with its rawboned knees knocking together. Its upper torso was twisted sideways as if its back was contorted. It was hunched and broken, the entire left side of its body withered and blackened, burnt nearly to the skeleton beneath as if it had been in some terrible fire. Its flesh was gray and worm-holed, flapping on the bones beneath in that cemetery wind, the left side of its face cremated down to the skull. But the right side…here the flesh was swollen and putrefying, bulging with gases, a single deranged yellow eye staring out at us from beneath locks of greasy black hair.

One of the men passed clean out and an older detective suffered a heart attack at the sight of that thing. Three or four younger men ran off screaming. I did not blame them; I would have run myself if I had not been frozen with fear.

A nocturnal burrower, it did not like the light.

I believe it had been a man once, but now it was little better than an animal…a clawing, hissing ghoul with gouts of drool hanging from its seamed and puckered mouth. The smell that came off of it made me nauseous…a black, evil stink of spoiled meat. With the lights in its grimacing, rotting face, I saw white things squirming in its hair, the entire scalp undulating from the larva at work in there.

It came on with a strident mewling sound, reaching out to us with those grotesque and fleshless hands.

"For the life of Christ, shoot!" Hayes shouted to the men. "Put that damn thing down!"

The men needed no coaxing. Pistols were barking in trembling fists and the graveyard echoed with gunfire, the smell of cordite and burned powder displacing that other and worse odor.

Riddled with bullets, the thing fell over at our feet, twitching and bleeding a vile dark sap that was not blood as we understood it. It writhed there on the ground, completely insane and malevolent. There was no humanity left in it. I believe it would have disemboweled us with its bare hands had it reached us, that it would have yanked our entrails out in steaming coils and fed upon them with those narrow, crooked teeth. Finally, that single yellow eye glazed over and the thing went still.

For a moment, then two.

A final, shuddering convulsion and it vomited out its stomach contents like a dying fish. A miasmic pool of steaming filth spilled from its mouth and in the lights of the torches, we all saw what was in it: human remains. Globs and half-digested things, but five or six decayed human fingers as well.

The tiny fingers of a recently-interred child.

There is no need recounting the terror and revulsion we felt. Nor is there any reason to tell you how we burned that carcass to ash in a pit in the woods. You know now what I saw, the grisly horror that stalked Christchurch Cemetery, that thing from a grave.

I never spoke to another living soul about the events at Christchurch, save those in my confidence that were there that terrible night. And then only in the most guarded of whispers. None of it ever made it into my column in even the most truncated version. I was privy to the most ghastly of secrets and for once, I agreed with the town fathers that no mention of that atrocity should ever be made.

And I kept my word. Until now.

But I would be lying if I said to you that none of it excited my curiosity. For it had. The thing was dead, perhaps for the second time, and there would be no third resurrection. But that was hardly enough for me. Perhaps I should have turned away from that madness, wisely shut it away in the darkest corner of my mind, but my curiosity would not allow it. That thing was a walking cadaver and I had to know how and why.

With that in mind, it was only a matter of time before I started giving some serious thought to Herbert West, M.D, one of the most notorious and shadowy figures of old, witch-haunted Arkham. A town with more spooks in its past than Woolworth had nickels.

If you're not entirely familiar with West, let me briefly recount the local legends that even five years after his disappearance and presumed death were still circulating through the streets. West, a particularly cold and ruthless individual, was a graduate of Miskatonic's Medical School, where he came out in the top five percent of his class. By all accounts he was brilliant and dedicated, though somewhat ostracized in the collegiate community for his radical and aberrant views concerning the nature of death and his theories that it could be overcome artificially. West claimed that life was essentially mechanistic, and via the application of certain chemicals and arcane scientific methods, that this organic machinery could be re-activated.

In other words, West's private research was concerned, so they said, with the reanimation of dead bodies.

Although he did indeed become a celebrated surgeon in Boston and one of no-little skill, it was in the shadows that he carried on his research which required a number of fresh corpses. He and a colleague robbed graves, bribed mortuary attendants, and, yes, even supposedly resorted to murder to gain the raw materials they so desperately needed. West even went so far as to join the Canadian Medical Corps during the Great War so that he could be assured a steady supply of corpses.

Those are the basic facts concerning Dr. Herbert West.

The tales and wild rumors take off from there. Did West actually succeed in reanimating dead tissue? In restoring life to cadavers? Depends on who you ask and what stories you listen to. It was said that he did. That he raised a number of corpses in and around Arkham and Bolton from the dead. That he achieved the same results in Flanders during the war with not only complete remains, but parts thereof. And it was one of these monstrosities that led a legion of the reanimated dead into West's laboratory in Boston in 1921, carrying off the doctor in pieces. An interesting footnote is this: in 1905, Dr. Allan Halsey, the dean of Miskatonic's Medical School, perished during the outbreak of typhoid that swept the city. It was said that West and his unknown colleague stole the body and reanimated it via West's serum. But what they reanimated was a hideous monstrosity that was no longer human, a cannibalistic monster that went on a violent murder spree through the city. The beast whether Halsey or not was captured and confined to the criminally insane ward at Sefton Asylum. Some sixteen years later, Halsey escaped with the aid, it was said, of the very ghouls that would later carry off West himself. You can easily dismiss this as lurid folk myth, but there's no getting around one fact: the gray-faced, demented thing at Sefton bore an uncanny resemblance to Halsey and his body was never located.

I, as much as anyone, wanted to dismiss all of it. But in Bolton and Arkham, belief was absolute. Even Hayes and some of the other detectives whose trust I had gained told me frankly that there was more fact than fantasy in the tales of Herbert West.

And now I will admit to you my personal interest in Dr. West. You see, in 1920, in Christchurch Cemetery, the body of my sister disappeared from the family mausoleum. She had died during childbirth along with her infant son. It was a tragedy for my family and the apparent snatching of her corpse turned a tragedy into an atrocity.

You see, knowing what I knew of West, it was always my greatest fear that he had taken her body. That perhaps he had brought her back from beyond the veil of death, working a change upon her cold clay. And that perhaps in the dead of night, she might come knocking at my door.

For many years, the identity of Herbert West's colleague has been a closely-kept secret of the authorities. But let me say to you now that this mysterious other was a man named Thomas Hamilton. West and he were students at Miskatonic and Hamilton participated actively with West from the very beginning to the very ending. And it was Hamilton whom the police questioned fiercely following the disappearance of West.

In the end, Dr. Hamilton was released from custody.

But, as charges of grave robbing and desecration of the dead had been levied at him, his medical license was revoked.

Making use of my police contacts and swearing an oath to never reveal pertinents of the case itself, I was allowed to visit him in his room at Sefton Asylum.

You see, Hamilton suffered a nervous collapse in the months after the bizarre vanishing of Herbert West. And if even half of what was said about West is true, it's a wonder the man was even coherent.

But he was.

I was left alone with him in his room at Sefton and immediately I felt sorry for him. He was well-spoken, well-groomed, intelligent and kind. He didn't seem to belong there at all. His committal had been voluntary, I was told, and he had been there some four years at that time. The only thing that gave his condition away was the slight tremble to his hands, that fixed and glassy look in his eyes.

After introducing myself, I got right to it. "You're probably tired of this question, Dr. Hamilton, but I'm afraid I have to ask it: Did any of that really happen?"

Hamilton studied his hands, clutched them together as a tremor passed through them. "Did Herbert West reanimate the dead? Yes, he did. Any many times."

Well, that was straight-forward enough. "What...what his ultimate goal? Was it just to see if he could or—"

"At first, yes. And why not? West wanted to beat death, to prove that life was merely a machine like any other, a base process that could be halted or commenced chemically. And he succeeded, didn't he? He succeeded too well, I'm afraid." Hamilton wetted his lips, turning his face from me so perhaps I wouldn't see the tick in the corner of his eye. "Certainly it was an experiment at first, a line of research West had been pursuing for years. But later? Then he became obsessed with raising a cadaver with its faculties intact. But, for the most part, he was not successful. The corpses were never fresh enough and when they were, well, many of them collapsed from shock or fright when they... woke up."

The idea of it was appalling, but I did not doubt what the man said. After what I had seen at Christchurch Cemetery, I believed absolutely. "What sort of man was West?"

"Brilliant," Hamilton said. "Never doubt that. Perhaps he applied himself in the wrong direction, but he was brilliant. A thinking machine. By his second year of medical school, he was constantly frustrating his professors with his vastly superior knowledge of anatomy, physiology, biochemistry, pathology...yes, Herbert West was brilliant. I fully believe that if he had followed a less morbid path of investigation, he would have gone down as one of the greats in science."

Hamilton's haunted eyes sparkled as he spoke at length of West. There was no disguising the admiration, the respect, the awe Hamilton had for the man and his techniques which were so entirely revolutionary that Hamilton fully believed that, one day, West would have toppled the entire medical establishment, left those "charlatans" (his word) groping in the dark like medieval healers with their leeches and cauterizing irons.

But as much as he worshipped at West's shrine, he was also terrified of the man, I thought. Particularly after he discovered that West was not above murder to acquire bodies of undeniable freshness. "So fresh, they were still warm," as Hamilton put it. But as ghoulish and criminal as that business was, West descended into even more lurid practices in Flanders during the Great War. He believed that groups of cells and detached body parts in particular were capable of independent physiological existence from the body…at least for a time. That, perhaps, even consciousness and reason, could survive without the brain or that separated anatomies might have some ethereal connection invisible to the eye.

Wild, fantastic stuff.

But West, once again, triumphed. At least this is what Hamilton claimed. West was able to keep a vat filled with reptilian embryonic cell matter alive indefinitely. Not only was it living and nourished, but it continued to grow at an incredible, almost diabolical rate. West also managed to reanimate severed human limbs as well as a headless trunk and even a head. But of these matters, Hamilton refused to speak in any depth, except to say that West was given a barn to be used as his laboratory, that bodies were shipped to him from the front…some whole, others shattered, and still others completely dismembered, brought to him in buckets.

"It was hideous, obscene, that workshop of West's," Hamilton told me, his face pinched and bloodless, eyes staring and wet. "You can't imagine it, you can't possibly imagine that awful place. Like a dissection room…only the specimens were all horridly alive. Eyes swimming in brine, watching you. Organs pumping and muscles flexing. Legs kicking and hands grasping in jars of amniotic fluid. And, yes, lording over it all, that headless thing in the corner rubbing its hands together and stumbling stiffly about…its decapitated head watching you from its tank, screaming at you, saying the most vile and sinister things. And West, dear God, West laughing about it all, amused by that slaughterhouse of resurrected anatomy."

That's all he would say and, frankly, I was glad. But what he told me next was equally as perverse and horrifying.

"West came out of the war disturbed. His experiments became increasingly gruesome, his morals, his sense of ethics were completely gone." Hamilton was re-living it, sweating and shaking and rambling on in a dry, cracking voice. "At the hospital, a suicide had been brought in, I remember. She wasn't even cold yet, just a girl of perhaps seventeen or eighteen that had laid her wrists open with a razor. West injected her and she woke…her eyes rolled open, a look of utter terror in them. Her face contorted into a scream and she leaped off the table, making slashing motions across her wrist. She had been deranged at the moment of death and that's all that was left…utter, debilitating insanity. She lived maybe ten minutes, screeching and drooling and tearing at her own flesh. And if that was a horror, what came next was a nightmare. West reanimated an accident victim…a young boy that was grotesquely mutilated…just to see if he indeed could. I will never forget that shrieking, contorting mass of human wreckage, attempting to walk with its bones thrust out and its head cleaved open, gray matter spilling down its agonized face."

Hamilton had to breathe for a while after that.

Finally, he said, "You see? That's what had become of that brilliant man. He was reanimating dead things just to prove that he indeed could."

I tried to get Hamilton to tell me about my sister. To see if he could remember snatching any women from Christchurch around the time of her tomb being robbed, but he would not answer any more questions. He was trembling and sobbing, speaking to people that were not there, watching the shadows in the corners very carefully.

As maybe they watched him.

I would like to say that this grisly little narrative is at an end, but I am not finished. I hoped, I think we all hoped, that Herbert West's dark legacy was over, but there was one last harrowing chapter to be played out. God help us, but there was.

It was Detective Hayes that brought it to my attention.

Though he did not need to. Bolton had been set by a series of strange, inexplicable disappearances in the past year or so. And being that it was essentially a mill town populated by the lowest rungs of the working class, a class which generally did not trust the police, I had no doubt that these abductions had been going on far longer than that. Something which Hayes admitted to be true.

But of late, this fiend that was snatching people off the street, had been growing more bold. And in its wake, it had been leaving cannibalized human remains. Sometimes entire bodies chewed and mutilated to an extreme degree and sometimes just scraps from its meals. And the most unnerving thing was that very often these remains were found on rooftops. There had even been a few witnesses and they all agreed on one thing: the killer was small and agile and it displayed almost apelike characteristics…escaping right up walls or into trees.

A single footprint had been pressed into garden soil at the home of an abducted child and that foot was small and deformed, not that of a monkey, but more like that of some misshapen dwarf.

Derby was called in once again and that determined hound led us on a merry chase through the city, finally leading us into the dirty and decaying streets of Easttown. If you know Easttown only by its high-rises, townhouses, and thriving artistic community, then you would not have recognized the absolute slum it was in the 1920's. The streets were unlit, mostly just dirt with rotting timbers shorn beneath, though there were a few colonial and brick thoroughfares. The entire area was filthy and claustrophobic, a collection of shuttered federal houses, abandoned farm buildings, leaning warehouses, and blocks of 18th century row houses. Everything there was ancient and crumbling, a crazy-quilt of mossy gambrel roofs and narrow alleys and crowded avenues. There was no electricity or gas, water had to be fetched from public wells. Outbreaks of typhoid and influenza were fairly common.

But what do I remember best about the area?

The smell: a dank, pestiferous odor that seemed to saturate every dwelling and by-way as if that section of Bolton was putrefying. All of it was bulldozed down long ago and for this we can be thankful.

Anyway, this is where Derby led us, amongst the squalor and tenements, the Georgian monstrosities broken up into flats. He brought us to a gate encircling an overgrown yard. Above us stood a weathered high house with shattered lattice windows. Even in that neighborhood, it was a place of evil-repute.

I stood there on the grimy street with ten policemen, feeling the place and smelling it and not liking it one bit. Hayes ordered two men to break the door open and they did so with little trouble. Even where we were standing, you could smell the hot, seething miasma of putrefaction oozing out.

Hayes and his men led the way in and after our experiences at Christchurch, we expected the very worst and were not in the least bit disappointed. The house had obviously been abandoned for decades, if not much longer. There was no furniture. The wallpaper hung in strips, the wainscoting was chewed to sawdust by mice. The walls were bowed, the floors uneven. Everything creaked and groaned as we entered.

The first thing I really noticed was the atmosphere of the place… festering and rotten, a dank pall in the air that made the flesh crawl at my spine. It felt like what I would imagine a plague ship would feel like, utterly noxious and suffocating. You could almost sense the horror that place had known, the madness and despair and spiritual corruption. It oozed from the walls and bled from the air in mephitic vapors.

"You can feel it, can't you?" one of the uniformed policemen said. "In your belly, your throat...enough to make you gag."

He was right. It not only made you want to wretch, it made you feel like a noose was slowly being tightened around your throat.

"Christ, that stink," was all Detective Hayes would say.

And, yes, it was bad. The atmosphere was something you sensed with your brain, your spine, your belly, but the smell of that moldered house was simply repellent. A seething effluvium of dust and damp, rot and mildew. But it was more than that, because you could smell death there, old death and new death. Organic putrefaction and a more recent odor, one that was violent and raw: the stink of fresh blood, gristle, and well-marbled meat.

"Well," Hayes said, his voice cracking, "let's do what we came to do."

We searched the upper stories and found nothing but dirt and rotting plaster, a trunk filled with ancient clothes. Yet, we knew something was there. We could hear it moving in the shadows and scratching in the walls, always keeping just out of sight. Downstairs, towards the rear of the house, we began to find human remains. Bones and scraps of meat, a few yellowed skulls splattered with brown stains. Like a path, they led us to the cellar door which was missing.

I personally could feel something building in the air, something that made me go white inside. The others were feeling it, too, and we soon realized why.

From that warped square of darkness leading into the cellar, there were a set of huge glistening eyes watching us. They shone like wet chrome.

"Jesus," somebody said. "Do you see them? Do you see those eyes—"

There was a rush of motion, a spoiled stink, and then something jumped out at us. Something with claws and teeth and a shaggy hide, something howling and hissing. Men cried out and others just gasped. It was like fighting a leopard in the darkness. Every time the men tried to get their guns on it, it darted away, scratching faces and biting hands as it went. It jumped and hopped, writhed and slashed. Our torches were spinning about and men were crying out and just about the time it seemed it would gore all of us, a burly sergeant named Trowbridge screamed and all the lights went on him instantly.

The thing was on him.

It was hanging off him like an ape, tearing at his throat, slashing him to ribbons with those claws. But he was a brave men and he held it, refusing to let it slip away. The thing was angry, growling and squealing.

I saw it with the others, but I wasn't exactly sure what it was. It looked, if anything, like some immense albino spider. But it was no spider...it had a head and four limbs and that was about all I saw until Trowbridge managed to toss it to the floor and pistols instantly began discharging. The thing took about ten or fifteen rounds. It jumped and screeched, spraying loops of vile-smelling blood, but finally, wounded, it lay there breathing with a wet, bubbling sound.

And that's when we got our first real good look at it.

Human?

Even now, I cannot be sure. Its body was squat and thick, oddly bulbous and covered in a tight mesh of white flesh that was smooth and shiny like poured rubber. You could see the jutting architecture of bones beneath as it gasped in its death throes. Though its torso wasn't really any larger than, say, a five-year old boy's, its limbs were completely out of proportion—the arms equally as long as the legs. And its face...quasi-human, at best. Its head was large and ill-shaped, the jaws vulpine and exaggerated and set with fine, sharp teeth. But it was the eyes I noticed most, for they were huge and unblinking, set with a grayish membrane like a slick of jelly.

"Kill it," one of the men said. "Jesus, it's disgusting."

But we didn't kill it.

We didn't need to, for it was dying just fine on its own. As it lay there, tangled in those elongated limbs like white whips, glaring up at us with saturnine eyes filled with a flat malevolence, it made a rasping, barking sort of sound, great gouts of blackish blood gushing from its mouth like drool. It was bleeding from a dozen holes, its viscous life pooling around it. Its hands made half-hearted attempts to scare us off, the fingers like jointed knitting needles, each a good ten or twelve inches in length.

It was revolting, yet oddly fascinating and maybe even a bit pathetic. What intrigued me about it was the bleached whiteness of its flesh, completely lacking pigment like something from a cave, something born to darkness. It had a shaggy mane of hair and it, too, was colorless.

Finally, those attenuated, bony fingers began to click madly, scraping at the floor. The thing jerked and shuddered and went still.

It was dead.

Next we went down into the cellar. Five of the men with us had been horribly bitten and clawed and Trowbridge was dead. The rest of us went down into that blackness. But the stairs were missing, so we had to fetch a fireman's ladder to descend.

And to this day, I wish we had not.

For down there, in that stygian murk and rancid stink, we found a perfectly circular pit cut into the earth. The sides were made of brick and we supposed it to be an abandoned well. When we put our lights down its mouth, something perhaps twenty feet below shrieked up at us.

We all saw what it was.

But perhaps I saw more clearly than the others.

There was a thing down there all right, something hissing and chattering its teeth. Something pallid-faced like a woman in a sloshing, fungous pit of bones and decomposed scraps and rags. Its flesh hung loose and billowing like canvas and seemed to be about the same texture. Its scalp was nearly hairless, just a few strands of greasy gray hair falling over the cadaverous, pocked face.

It had no eyes, just lewd sockets filled with worms.

It had but one fleshless arm and most of the skin had been chewed from its breasts and belly and that's how I knew it had been feeding on itself. It tried to pull itself up at us and we saw that its legs had been worried to bony nubs, victims, like its missing arm, of its ghoulish hunger. Auto-cannibalism, I suppose would be the correct term.

It raged and splashed and spit tangles of slime up at us and I knew if one of us had fallen down there, she would have stripped us to the bone in minutes.

Yes, a blasphemy and a horror.

Yet, I knew it was a woman.

And this is what made me stagger from that necrotic, steaming, charnel pit. I barely got away from it before that awful cellar pitched this way and that and I passed clean out.

I don't remember Hayes and his men taking me out of there. But I remember what I saw and I remember what it did to me. Hayes said they dumped kerosene into the pit and roasted that nightmare alive. The other spidery thing joined it for the cremation. He said the house was being torn down and that pit would be filled with cement.

All and good.

But what haunts me to this day was that spidery, dwarfish thing and the woman in the pit. Even so many decades later, it fills me with a shivering terror, an almost lunatic horror. Those things, yes, they were the final legacy of Herbert West and his profane experiments. I had no doubt of it then and I have no doubt of it now.

I recognized the woman, of course.

She was my sister who had died in childbirth. Even though Hamilton would not admit to it, West indeed stole her corpse from its coffin and reanimated her cold graveyard husk. And that unspeakable, starving monstrosity in the pit was what was left of her.

And the spidery thing?

Dear God, that was her child...born post-mortem. My nephew... or niece.

The Crypt in Key West

David Bernard

Ten years ago, in 1931, I was rebuilding my life, relishing each moment of exquisite obscurity, free from the yoke of association with the deranged Herbert West. The last time I had seen Herbert, he was a rapidly deteriorating doppelgänger of bilious emesis. I had not heard from my former partner since that night in New Hampshire, and found great comfort in knowing he could not possibly have survived.

In those days, even the thought of being drawn again into his blasphemous web of experiments terrified me, so much so that the remotest of chances that Herbert West had survived was enough to send me racing to investigate with murder in my heart and a Webley in my pocket. If Herbert had inexplicably survived New Boston, one of us would not survive the reunion.

That is how, on that fateful day back in June of 1931, I found myself standing on Duval Street in front of a faded yellow building that the taxi driver claimed was the La Concha, the grande dame of Key West hospitality. I stepped into an elegant lobby, mercifully cooler than outside, and waited patiently behind a lanky gentleman clutching a battered valise. As he haggled over the room price with the desk clerk, I still wondered if this entire trip was a fool's errand.

The haggler stepped away; the thin smile on his prognathous face indicated his pleasure with the negotiations. I stepped up the desk and gave the clerk a moment to regroup. "My name is Daniel Cain. I cabled ahead for a room?"

The clerk shuffled through a pile of papers. "Ah yes," he said triumphantly. "Dr. Cain from Baltimore. What brings you to Key West?"

"It's been dreadfully rainy in Baltimore, so I have decided a little sun and ocean air would be a marvelous respite," I lied. I was not about to confess I was here on the remote chance that I needed to kill a man who had killed me had himself died on several previous occasions.

I tipped the bellboy and stepped into my room. I drew the curtains, unpacked my medical bag, and began arranging equipment. I would need an injection of reagent soon. A stray piece of paper fluttered from my bag. It was the newspaper clipping that had triggered my journey.

Key West – *German Count Carl von Cosel, a physician at the U.S. Marine Hospital in Key West, was convinced his treatments would cure his patient of consumption. When the young woman died, he remained so convinced that the treatment would revive her postmortem that he paid to have a telephone installed in the crypt to expedite her release after resurrection occurred. It did however take several days for the telephone company to find an installer willing to brave the occupied mausoleum. Count von Cosel, undeterred, visits the crypt regularly to converse with the corpse and has been known to serenade the dead on a small organ he installed in the tomb.*

I'm sure the newspaper editor published it as humor, but presuming success in reanimating corpses and talking to the dead required both unmitigated hubris and questionable sanity, a combination that immediately brought Herbert West to mind. The fact that the American Medical Society directory had no member listing for a Carl von Cosel, told me that the Count was either an alias or had no license to practice medicine. Either scenario also matched Herbert West.

I quickly prepared several syringes of reanimation serum. While in Haiti tracking down voodoo-reanimated corpses, Herbert and I had learned the hard way that animated flesh broke faster in tropical heat and humidity. I placed the syringes in my medical bag and proceeded to the lobby.

According to the front desk, the Marine Hospital was only a five minute walk. I decided to risk the June heat and headed west. The area quickly changed from tourist-friendly shops to blue collar homes and marine business storefronts. The hospital was a small brick building overlooking an industrial dock. The corner stone claimed it was built in 1845 but I would have guessed even older, based on the battered condition of the structure.

I approached the front desk and introduced myself to a rather vacuous-looking blonde receptionist. I suspected her primary skill set had more to do with how her uniform fit than her receptionist skills. Still, I suppose an expansive décolleté did help lift morale.

She looked at me blankly when I asked to see Dr. von Cosel. "I'm sorry, Dr. Cain, but we have no Dr. Castle here."

I felt the start of a headache, and I was certain it was not the reagent wearing off. "No, my dear, his name is Carl von Cosel."

Suddenly she paled. "Oh, you mean Count Dracula! He's not a doctor."

I waited as she pressed a button on the phone and spoke to someone in hushed tones. She hung up the phone and sat quietly, keeping a wary eye on me.

Moments later, a harried looking man came briskly down the corridor.

"Dr. Cain?" he asked, "I'm Peter Kilwar, the hospital director. I understand you're asking about one of our X-ray technicians, Mr. von Cosel. May I ask why?" My arrival had spooked him; there was more than a hint of concern in his voice.

I sensed that whatever was going on with von Cosel, the newspaper clipping had already made several egregious errors, the least of which was his medical degree. I may have stepped into a situation more complicated than expected. That by itself was not uncommon after working with Herbert West for so many years. I decided to use one of West's maneuvers and lie my way in the administrator's good graces.

"May we speak in private?" I looked around the lobby, feigning suspicion. Knowing managers loved secrets, I was not surprised when he ushered me into his office. The room was humid, probably due to a gaping hole in one wall, where an exposed rusted pipe dripped foetid water into a grimy bucket.

He saw me looking at the pipe. "Please excuse the mess. The county has decided that my office is the easiest point to access the main feed to test the water quality. The neighboring shipyard had a fuel spill and they are concerned about contaminants in the hospital's water."

I decided to cut to the chase. "Mr. Kilwar, I fear I may be violating patient-doctor trust, but it's for greater good." It never ceased to amaze me how easily the lies were accepted when egos were being stroked.

He indicated a chair and we sat down. "Dr. Cain, I assure what is said in this office will stay in this office."

I smiled as if relieved, knowing full well that his lie was nothing compared to the one I was concocting. I handed him the newspaper clipping that had propelled me to Key West. He looked at it and frowned.

"I am aware of this nonsense. I sent the newspaper syndicate a tersely worded admonition."

"The man you know as Carl von Cosel was a patient of mine in Baltimore at a private hospital," I said. "He was struck by a falling chimney. When he awoke, he thought he was a German Count. Otherwise, he appeared fully rational. I released him and lost track of his whereabouts. When I saw this article, I feared he had suffered a relapse."

Kilwar's forehead beaded with sweat in a manner exclusive to a career bureaucrat imagining their career about to end on a spectacularly sour note. "That would explain the nonsense about vitality rays."

That revelation concerned me. Our experiments at Chateau d'Erlette during the Great War had convinced us that energy beams only damaged dead tissue and hindered reanimation. We had left the chateau under less than optimal circumstances; it was possible that some of our equipment had fallen into the Kaiser's hands. I needed to assess the German technician and evaluate the situation before Key West was awash in anthropophagous walking corpses.

"Mr. Kilwar, I assure you, that if the delusions have returned, I will take him back to Baltimore for treatment." Of course, by "treatment" I meant "feed him to the Key West shark population" but I wasn't going to quibble.

He looked relieved and gave me directions to the radiography lab. As I left his office, he handed me a lapel badge. I assumed it was visitor's pass, but he shook his head.

"It's a dosimeter," he said. "It measures exposure to x-rays."

My expression must have begged the next question, for he continued.

"Carl is a radiography technician. He only works with late stage consumption cases, and has been known to modify the x-ray coils." He looked embarrassed.

"We've warned him about it, but competent radiology technicians are hard to come by. He's actually quite good at taking x-rays, but he's convinced x-rays can also provide therapeutic treatment. Some of his coil modifications may have, in theory, inadvertently exposed patients to doses of radiation that would possibly be fatal, if they weren't already dying."

I walked slowly down the corridor, wracking my brains to recall anyone who had been experimenting with x-rays for reanimation. I had heard rumors of the Australians dabbling during the Great War but nothing ever came of it. A few moments later, I stood before a metal door warning of x-ray radiation. I stepped into the radiology lab.

The room was empty except for a floor-mounted x-ray machine. I immediately noticed the air felt different, like after a thunderstorm. Ionized air meant von Cosel had been using high voltage electrical currents. I looked up and as I suspected, the ceiling had a circular pattern of small scorch marks. I had seen that pattern before, when Herbert West began a brief but ultimately messy collaboration with Nicholas Tesla. The marks told me that von Cosel had, at some point, used a modified Tesla coil. A door in the back of the room opened and an older man in a lab coat stepped into the room.

"Can I help you?" The man spoke with a slight trace of a German accent.

"Carl von Cosel?" I studied the man as he nodded his assent. He was short and probably in his early sixties. With his bearing, white hair, and carefully groomed goatee, I could see how a journalist might mistake him for a doctor.

"My name is Daniel Cain. I am a physician in Baltimore. I recently read an article on your work."

The old man stiffened and a momentary look of dismay passed over his face. "Yes, Herr Doctor. I am the crazy von Cosel."

"You don't understand. I'm not here to mock you. I'm here to exchange notes."

A look of relief washed over his face, followed by suspicion. "Really? How do I know you are who you say you are?"

I sighed to myself and pointed to the ceiling. "That scorch pattern is evidence of a Tesla coil. Such high voltage would be needed if you were using violet rays or a similar electrotherapy. The pattern is from repeated disruptive coil discharge, caused by the interrupter device needed to apply high voltage, high frequency, low current electrotherapy. It is questionably useful as therapy on healthy patients, tends to trigger hyperkalemic rhabdomyolysis in consumption patients, and exacerbates skeletal muscle deterioration in corpses." I paused to let the old man process the information.

"Herr Doctor, I apologize."

"No apology necessary, Mr. von Cosel."

The little man stood straight. "Count, please, not Mister. I am Reichsgraf Georg Carl Tanzler von Cosel, a direct descendant of Anna Constantia von Brockdorff , the Imperial Countess of Cosel."

"My apologies, Count. I am sorry to have troubled you. I'll leave you to you work." I turned to go. The Count's experimentation with low current electrotherapy was a dead end, literally and figuratively. He was a rank amateur in the science of reanimation. He was not a protégé of Herbert West or following any path that would lead to a breakthrough. I would return to Baltimore with a lighter heart.

"Herr Doctor, Have I offended you?" The old man looked on the verge of tears.

"My dear Count," I said with a twinge of remorse, "Of course not. It's simply that I can tell you are a busy man. I came to Key West in hopes that the report of your work was that of an old friend continuing his research under an alias." I had not referred to Herbert West as a friend since our days at Miskatonic University and the lie burned as I said it.

"Herr Doctor, I always have time to confer with a colleague. Would you like to meet my beloved?"

I nodded, unable to determine how to extricate myself without raising a fuss. Fusses brought attention and I was concerned that the hospital administrator would make inquiries and discover I had no background in psychiatry. I was also getting the impression von Cosel was not the most stable resident of Key West.

We walked through the hospital and onto the street. The little German continuously rambled on about ghostly visions and his beloved's arrival being prophesized, I was no stranger to endless chatter of the insane and nodded just often enough to make him think I was still listening. I wasn't sure where we going, but I was not expecting the cemetery. We stopped before an obviously new tomb, reflecting angry red in the setting sun. An oversized tablet told me it was the resting place of Elena Milagro Hoyos. Von Cosel pulled out a key and unlocked the tomb.

He pulled the door out and announced into the stygian depths "Helen, meine liebe, wir haben einen besucher."

I didn't have to understand German to realize that von Cosel was well beyond the level of delusion that accompanied reanimation sciences. I followed him into the darkness.

My eyes adjusted to the dark and I was stunned. Having been in more tombs than anyone could imagine still left me unprepared. The tomb was nothing short of cozy. Curtains draped the walls and a small oil lamp sat on a shelf, casting flickering shadows over a rocking chair next to a small pipe organ. A radio sat in the corner, softly playing a Cuban station. And of course, a diesel generator ran electrical wires to a Tesla coil, with a violet ray poised and ready to "treat the patient."

The body was an entirely different matter. The young woman in the open coffin may have been pretty in life but death and von Cosel's "treatments" had left the corpse a pulpy mass of sloughing skin and rotting flesh. The abundance of maggots and the violet ray dosages were breaking down connective tissue faster than normal decomposition. I knew from harsh experience that the only things keeping the body's appearance vaguely human at this point were the coffin walls.

I started to say something but noticed my fingernails were turning blue in the lamplight. My reagent was wearing off in the Florida heat and humidity. I needed to inject a syringe immediately or I'd be in no better shape than von Cosel's beloved. I placed my medical bag on the organ bench and while von Cosel fussed over the corpse's hair, I slipped a syringe into my coat pocket.

"Count von Cosel, I must beg your indulgence. I'm afraid I'm a little claustrophobic. I'm going to step outside for a breath of fresh air."

The old German looked up. I think he had forgotten I was still there. "Certainly, my friend. Please accept my apologies for Helen's behavior. She is shy around strangers."

I forced a smile to my face and stepped out of the lunatic's love nest into the twilight. A quick glance showed the cemetery was now deserted. I quickly injected the reagent. The glowing green fluid illuminated the vein as it traveled toward my heart and through what passed as my circulatory system. A moment later, I felt better. I would need to pay closer attention in this heat.

The green glow subsided as the reagent integrated itself into my reanimated tissue. I reentered the tomb. Von Cosel was sitting in the rocking chair next to the corpse, brushing her hair and carefully collecting the clumps that fell out and placing them in a small wooden chest. I wondered what other parts would soon join the hair in the collection of human detritus. I cleared my throat to make him aware I had returned.

He looked up with an oddly serene look on his face. "Doctor Cain, I have kept you too long. Please forgive me. Helen and I thank you for your time and hope to see you again. Auf wiedersehen"

I nodded, grabbed my bag, and slipped out into the night with the distinct impression I had just been dismissed. Perhaps the misguided radiographer had realized there was nothing I could do to resurrect his Helen. I suspected von Cosel would end up in a local sanitarium if his cadaverous affections were made public. And the suspicions placed in the mind of a certain hospital administrator made me believe it would be sooner than later.

Back at the hotel, I decided to leave a syringe out on the table near my medical bag. Having nearly forgotten my injection today, I decided it would be prudent to leave a glowing green reminder in plain view for the morning. There were still two in the bag, glowing with the ominous yet comforting green aura. As I placed a syringe carefully by the bag, it occurred to me that I thought I had prepared four injections upon entering the hotel room. I used one in the cemetery, and two were here now. I had not opened the bag in between the hotel and the crypt. I decided it was just my mind playing tricks. The same exhaustion from train travel that made me forget to inject earlier was probably causing me to misremember.

The next morning, I sat alone in the hotel dining room, debating whether to depart on the early or late train. Then I saw the morning newspaper. The headline screamed of a series of horrific murders overnight. With trembling hands, I read how a hobo was found in the cemetery, "clawed to death in a manner not only too hideous for description" in the newspaper, but so savagely butchered that first assumptions were that somehow, a Florida panther had reached Key West. That proved to be optimistic, for within hours, someone or thing entered a house near the cemetery and slaughtered a family of four, leaving human teeth marks in the dismembered bodies. Body parts were missing from the crime scene, leading to additional lurid speculation.

Immediately, I knew. The description was almost identical to that hellish night when the revived corpse of Allan Halsey began its mindless rampage of terror through Arkham in 1905. Then I remembered the missing syringe. I had left my bag unattended in the tomb while I was outside.

I rushed to the tomb. The door was ajar and inside, von Cosel lay unconscious on the floor. I revived him with spirits of ammonia. When he was conscious, I moved him to the rocking chair and stood there. The old man was in shock. I stared at him as long as I could bear it.

"Do you have any idea what you have done?"

Von Cosel looked up at me, eyes brimming with tears. He looked away and began sobbing. "I know what I have done. How can I save my beloved?"

I looked at him in disbelief. "Save her? You've revived a corpse that had been dead far too long to reanimate. You have a released a mindless zombie on Key West, motivated only by a primal instinct to kill."

Von Cosel dropped to his knees, weeping inconsolably. "Please, we must save my Helen!"

I looked at him, distaste becoming bile in my throat. I lied, "Very well, we shall save her."

I helped the old man back into the rocking chair and handed him the newspaper. With tears streaming down his cheeks, he read the gory details in the newspaper. He reached the part about the family of four. "1018 Grinnell Street? That was where Helen lived after her marriage!"

"Think man, tell me where else she might go?" I barked. If the murderous corpse had enough instincts to seek out familiar havens, we could second guess where the horror would strike next and circumvent any further deaths.

Von Cosel concentrated. This was taking too long. Sharply, I asked "What about the hospital? Would she go back there?"

The German shook his head. "No. She hated the hospital. She'd go to her childhood home on—mein Gott in Himmel, nein!" The old man physically sagged. He looked up at me. "Helen's childhood home was on United Street, quite near here. But..." Von Cosel's eyes were wide with terror. "Several years ago, they tore down the house. It's now an elementary school!"

My experience with Herbert's mistakes told me these mindless husks shunned the light of day. It would roam again tonight, and after killing its fill, it might seek refuge and instinctively go to the empty school. When classes resumed the next morning and disturbed the monstosity, the casualties would be horrific. I could not allow a school be turned into an abattoir. The carnage would dwarf that of Halsey's rampage in Arkham.

Von Cosel would cause a scene if I attempted to killed the mockery of a woman and it would draw the police immediately in a city already on edge. If we could subdue her and put her in restraints, we could return her to the crypt. Another day and the reagent would wear off and the cadaver would again be von Cosel's twisted but decidedly dead infatuation.

Then it came to me. "Von Cosel, that pipe organ – did you play it often for Helen?"

He glanced at the instrument quizzically, "The organ? Yes, I played in her hospital room and then brought it here."

It wasn't a great plan, but surely some Divine figure that had forsaken me long ago would at least allow me to save innocent children. "The music may draw her here. We need to prepare. I'm going visit the local apothecary and prepare a syringe to immobilize her. You must attach some restraints to the bier to confine her in the coffin until my reagent wears off."

"Wears off?" The old man was persistent if nothing else.

"Yes," I stated flatly. "Your electrotherapy treatments and my chemical components are incompatible. Once the reagent breaks down, you can continue your procedures without this adverse reaction." Of course, this was utter nonsense; once the reagent wore off, the corpse would return to an inanimate mass of decomposing flesh. Right now, my concern was preventing a school house from turning into a charnel house.

I slipped out into the noon sun, making sure to carry my bag with me this time. Over the years, Herbert West and I encountered far too many experiments that had gone homicidally wrong. After the incident with Buck Robinson in Bolton, we had discussed ways to prevent another "problem" like the Harlem Smoke's deadly rampage. The difficulty was that Herbert wanted to vivisect the failed experiments to see what went wrong. We found incapacitating something that was already dead was a far more difficult challenge than simply killing it again.

We had experimented with neurotoxins to shut down the nervous systems of the corpses and the research was showing some success when the Great War disrupted our plans. Time was my enemy now. Key West was too small to have the obscure pharmaceuticals needed to recreate our complex chemical formula nor did I have time to synthesize those chemicals in a makeshift laboratory. My plan was for something faster and available locally. I headed to the commercial docks.

After attending college in a port town such as Arkham, I knew commercial fishing vessels accidentally netted fish that no one wanted. Those fish would be tossed overboard to feed the gulls. With any luck, the Key West dock's collection of trash fish would include a pufferfish or two, allowing me to distill sufficient tetrodotoxin to bring down the unthinking killing machine.

The docks were empty; it was still too early for the returning fleet. I carefully worked my way below the wharves onto a shore littered with dead marine life. Twenty unpleasant minutes later, I returned to the street, clutching three pufferfish that didn't appear too badly decomposed. I pulled a scalpel from my bag and performed a necropsy on the edge of the dock. The greatest concentration of toxin would be in the liver. I quickly removed those organs from the fish and discarded the rest.

I had passed several apothecaries on the way to the docks. The one nearest had the earmarks of a business on the verge of failure. That was my next stop. A sad little man listened as I explained I was a visiting physician in need of a chemistry lab to create a medicinal reduction. The twenty dollar bill bought his cooperation and I was ushered into the back room. Two hours later, the fish livers had been distilled down to fill a syringe. It was enough concentrated neurotoxin to kill a dozen men. I hoped it was enough to at least slow down Elena Hoyos.

It was late afternoon by the time I returned to the cemetery. The streets were rapidly emptying. The residents were wisely choosing to lock themselves in for the night in the futile hope it would save them from the mad killer on the loose. Soon, the creatures of the night and a creation of the damned would walk the silent streets of a fearful Key West.

Von Cosel was waiting when I returned to the crypt. Fresh bolts had been driven into the stone bier, securing thick leather straps. The German had done nice work. It appeared the coffin itself was also reinforced. He looked up at me.

"I'm ready." I pulled the syringe out of my pocket to show him. I didn't mention my Webley tucked safely in my pocket. One way or another, Elena Hoyos's reign of terror would not last a second night.

I pointed to the organ bench. "Start playing. Play her favorite song. Perhaps we can draw her back here before there are any more killings."

The Count nodded and sat on the bench. He began playing a melody that in the hands of a skilled musician would have been recognizable. All I could detect was a Latin beat. I opened the crypt door. The sun had begun to set and a light fog was rolling in. The streets were silent; even the insects seemed to sense that a minion of Hell walked the land. The organ music eerily echoed through the cemetery and into the streets as the wisps of fog coalesced.

I felt her presence before I saw it, a white shape staggering through the fog-shrouded tombs, hunched over and shuffling like a malformed ape. I stepped inside and quietly said "Keep playing. She's coming."

Von Cosel nodded but I noticed a fresh sheen of sweat on his ashen face. He had already witnessed Elena Hoyos's mindless wrath. I stepped behind the door with the syringe in my hand. I had one chance. One mistake and we both would be added to the list of Elena's fatalities.

The abomination lurched into the room and turned toward von Cosel. I stepped behind her and plunged the syringe into the base of her neck. She wheeled around, far more quickly than I would have suspected for a corpse in such a state of decay. She lunged and I threw my arm up to fend off the attack. She effortlessly swatted my arm away and I heard the bone crack before the pain registered. I stepped back. The crypt was small and I was already running out of space.

The beast shook her head as if trying to clear it. The neurotoxins may have finally been starting to kick in. Looking for a way to avoid being cornered, I didn't notice von Cosel had crept up behind her.

"Helen, mein kätzchen, es wird alles gut warden," he whispered reassuring. The walking corpse merely shoved the old German backward.

I had hurt her, so I was the object of her attention. She paused, momentarily confused. This was bad. The neurotoxin should have rendered her completely immobile. Instead it was making her groggy. And apparently being groggy made her angry. Then I smelled the ozone. I looked away for a moment; at some point, von Cosel had turned on the Tesla coil.

I looked more closely at the monstrosity and noted the faint pulsing of green fluorescence. Could von Cosel's radiation therapy be over stimulating the reagent? I looked at my good hand. I too was fluorescing. The radiation was acting like a catalyst with reagent and overwhelming the toxin's effects.

I looked too long. The moldering corpse of Maria Elena Milagro Hoyos Mesa charged, slamming me into the wall of her crypt. I felt the wall shift from the impact. Neither the tomb nor my ribs were designed for this sort of violence. Fending off her slavering jaws with my good arm, I screamed at von Cosel to shut down the Tesla coil, but the old fool stood riveted in place at the horror he had wrought in the crypt. With my strength failing, I put my last effort into pushing the slavering mockery of the woman backwards. The putrid obscenity fell backward, tripping over the rocking chair and smashing into the pipe organ.

The destruction of his beloved pipe organ finally snapped von Cosel out of his immobility and he ran to the generator and killed the power. With the power gone, the decaying corpse collapsed like a puppet with cut strings. I saw her fall, but it was it was as if I watching through a tunnel. Then the darkness gathered and I too slumped to the floor.

I woke up in my room in the La Concha Hotel. Von Cosel sat quietly in the corner as the sun streamed in the window. I gingerly sat up and tried the arm that his "beloved Helen" had snapped while attempting to eviscerate me. It was tender, but the reagent that kept me alive also offered tremendous healing properties. In a few hours the residents of Key West would never suspect I had just fought for survival against the mindless homicidal corpse that had slaughtered five residents. Herbert had always considered it wildly amusing that humans were so easy to kill yet so difficult to kill a second time. I never found it particularly funny, considering how much death that trailed our path, like a necrotic wake on a sea of suffering.

I looked at the old German sitting in the corner, deep in thoughts. He appeared to have been weeping. I would probably join him, were weeping something I could still do. While he wept for what he had done to his beloved Helen and the murder spree it wrought, I would have wept for what I had become and how my travels had led me to become the unwitting catalyst for yet more needless deaths.

I returned with the subdued von Cosel to the crypt. The horror was strapped into her coffin, snarling and snapping her spittle flecked teeth at anything in her line of vision. There was no sign of deterioration; the reagent was not wearing off.

I looked at von Cosel. "The formula should have worn off before the neurotoxin. It has to be the electrotherapy; her irradiated cells are reacting differently."

Von Cosel looked at a loss. "What can I do now?"

I shook my head. "I don't know. This is a completely unknown combination. There's no telling how long she may remain reanimated. It could be hours, or days."

Von Cosel looked as the mindless ghoul struggling against the restraints. "Then I wait. I shall continue to visit my beloved and trust in the fates to restore her to me."

I had already given up on explaining she would never be "restored" to him. He would never understand that she would not ever recover; she would simply deanimate and return to a mass of decomposing flesh, regardless of von Cosel's mad experiments.

I shook his hand, wished him well, and returned to the hotel to gather my things and return to Baltimore. I never looked back...

Two years later, in 1933, I received a letter from Count von Cosel letting me know that his Helen had "died again." I shuddered at the thought of that poor crazy man faithfully visiting the mindless husk for all that time. Even more horrific was his postscript. He had moved the body to his cottage, where he had more room to build a larger Tesla coil. Obviously he needed more power to revive his wife. I burned the letter...

In 1940, the newspapers across the country salaciously reported the strange case in Key West of a German radiologist who had stolen a young girl's corpse and lived with it for ten years, reattaching parts as they fell off with piano wire and replacing her skin with satin. The story went international a few weeks later when he was released because the statute of limitations had run out on charges of desecrating a corpse. I barely noticed any of it. The ghoulish Herbert West had returned to destroy my carefully constructed world, and he had exceeded the worst of his previous cruel machinations. My own life had become a far greater hell than anything von Cosel had witnessed or could imagine. I had no desire to live, let alone offer solace to an insane radiologist.

Yet, here I was again, April 16, 1941, stepping off the train at Key West station. Back in 1931, I had come to Key West to assure myself that Herbert West was dead. Instead, I created a horror unseen since the days of West's early experiments. Now, in 1941, I returned, a broken shadow of a man, attempting to right just one of the myriad of wrongs from my past.

I had two hours before the afternoon train departed northward. Two hours to undo the damage done by another broken shell of a man seeking answers best left alone. Two hours to right a wrong and then return to the living hell that was my tainted mockery of a life.

In spite of the heat, I walked to the cemetery. If something went wrong, a taxi driver could be a potential eyewitness to my presence. As I attempted to stroll nonchalantly into town, I arrived at my destination all too soon: the Key West Cemetery. I walked through the cemetery as if leisurely enjoying the landscaping, carefully locating and avoiding each potential witness. I passed my destination, appearing to avoid it like any other pedestrian in the cemetery, but even without the massive plaque announcing her name, birth date and death date, I recognized Elena's tomb. I think von Cosel was aiming for a minimalist version the Taj Mahal, but the tomb just ended up looking like someone had built a small Quonset hut with a pillared dome on top.

"Typical of the Count," I thought. "Aiming for greatness but ending in sorrow."

The crypt had not aged well after a decade in the tropics. The whitewashed walls were spotted with mold; the flower sconces had long fallen from the wall, leaving rust stains on either side of the door that made the building appear to be weeping blood. I glanced backwards at the far wall of the empty crypt. The wall had bulged outward, causing the stucco to flake off and exposing a jagged crack in the brick work. Most passersby would think it was a settlement crack from poor upkeep. I on the other hand knew what caused the damage.

I slipped the letter from von Cosel out of my pocket. His tear-stained letter had sadly updated me on the affair in Key West. He had lost his job and they had taken his beloved away, put her on public display in a funeral home and buried her in a secret place. His home had been destroyed by an angry mob. Now he was being driven from Key West and had been given until April 16 to leave town of his own volition.

A train whistle shrieked in the distance. If I had timed this correctly, that would be the steam engine taking von Cosel into obscurity. I pulled the key from the envelope. Von Cosel had begged me for a favor. Before his house had been destroyed, he had been able to hide his notes, journals, and equipment in the one place everyone avoided: the empty tomb. As the only one who truly understood his research, he asked if I would pack up his materials and ship them to his new address. I had a different idea in mind.

I stepped into the crypt and carefully removed the dynamite from my medical bag. I waited, carefully timing the next step. As departure time neared for the next train, I lit a slow burning fuse and relocked the tomb. I reached the train station just before the explosion rocked the afternoon stillness. As the town rushed to the cemetery, I slipped unobtrusively onto the train as it slowly departed Key West. I glanced back at a billowing plume of smoke that grew smaller as we sped away. No one would recreate von Cosel's experiments, including the little German himself.

I felt elated. For once, a cursed facet of reanimation had been purged from history. Now as the train gathered speed, so too I gathered resolve. I would return to Baltimore with a new mandate. Herbert West must die again, this time once and for all.

Herbert West - Reincarnated

a round robin

I. Colluding Cosmos by Rod Heather

Subservience is not among the desirable vocations of men. Especially so when that subservience is worn like a yoke and it is a ghoul called Herbert West who sits atop the plow thrashing his long whisker at your backside, mercilessly driving you on deeper and deeper into a repulsive abyss of unthinkable blasphemy. Such had been my Stygian association with the tow-headed maniac for well over two long and nightmarish decades.

I had nearly seen the welcome end to this unholy association three times over these regrettable years. Each time the fleeting Elysian serenity of disassociation was shattered by West's damnable, and I have now come to believe inexorable, return.

Thinking I had seen the last of him that first time so many years ago in Boston, I had packed and nearly escaped to Illinois only to see him grinning at the doorstep on the very eve of my planned departure. I had seen him rent to pieces and borne away at the hands of a silent mob of vengeful, shuffling cadavers. I never learned how he managed to cheat his due fate and return, himself reanimated, a walking patchwork quilt of flesh. But, in retrospect, I should not have been surprised. Indeed, knowing West how could I not have known it was inevitable he should return? And it was equally foreordained that he should again conscript me as his soulless henchman.

I, myself, first decided to discontinue the association over a decade ago. No sooner had we discovered that even the crudest excremental matter could be reanimated to some semblance of independent sentience than West set about animating a puddle of his own vomit. What came from that was too much for even my blasted sensibilities! The matter, upon receiving the reagent, had transformed into a shambling bipedal abomination of living putrescence which directly set about devouring West, piece by piece, before my unblinking eyes. And with each glistening morsel that passed over the thing's stinking maw, it slowly metamorphosed into the very man who had given it life. As the constantly shifting West-thing laboured to hold itself together I saw my chance to escape.

I dashed headlong to Baltimore, where I took up practice as a family doctor with a kindly and humane gentleman named Dr. Julius Mapes. It was during my fondly remembered acquaintance with Mapes that I was able to utilize his laboratory to restore my own bodily functions. My erstwhile comrade, you see, had dealt me the mercy of smashing my skull some time before, thrusting me over the threshold I had long skirted but never had the courage to cross by suicide. For this I could be grateful. I blame him not for my murder, but for my subsequent recall, by unhallowed methods, to a life which had already become a loathsome blight and has since, somehow, only grown more hideous. And so, for a time, I foolishly seized on that most desperate and delusive evil left at the bottom of Pandora's box: hope.

It was also during this short-lived period of ignorant bliss that I met and married the beautiful Dr. Barbara Bishop. At the time, it had been nearly a dozen years since I left West to his grotesque demise, and I existed happily, occasionally even able to forget my charnel past. But West had not yet ceased to plague me. He had become a veritable ghost of flesh to haunt me with ever new horrors. Using a technique of psychic mind-transference learned from an occultist colleague named Ephraim Waite, he had projected his mind from that loping vomit-beast in New Boston just before it had fallen apart, and into the body of a vital Yale medical student named Barbara Bishop! It had been West all along! Once again, tranquility was snatched from me like sweets from a babe and replaced with bitterest gall.

In the same breath with which West had admitted his deception to me, he also announced his pregnancy-with my own seed! His vile plans branded me like acid thrown in my face as he explained he meant to transfer his mind out of the body of Barbara Bishop, leaving her dead and soulless clay, and into the fresh body of my...our...son.

I stood fixed with a sense of detached unreality as I witnessed him give birth to my child, and then shortly thereafter impose alchemically aberrant means to grow the body, the homunculus, beyond its natural years. When the body had grown to an adult state in just a few short months, he abandoned the once-beloved form of Barbara and usurped that of my son...who, by genetic manipulation, had become a steel-eyed, blond-haired duplicate of West. The shell of my one-time mate was now occupied by the rudimentary mind of an infant who could do little more than stare and shriek. Understandably, madness nipped and chewed at my own mind. I conspired to avenge my child... my wife.... my very soul as West rose from the table in his new body laughing triumphantly and called out to me flatly, "She's yours again! May you be happy together!"

I can recall with little effort, as he and I planned to steal an ancient mummy from Miskatonic University, that West proclaimed his intention to "storm the gates of Anubis himself!" That was nearly two decades ago. And now, wiser and more decadent through years of astonishing advances, the madman not only stormed those formidable gates, but had reduced them to splinters. Many a night I would dream of that Jackal headed god bowing in supplication to the madman as he would nightly ransack that rich necropolis beyond time again and again. His intention now, it was clear to me, was to replace that infernal shepherd altogether!

Under the cover of darkness, I silently made my way through the house bent on stopping West's insane designs once and for all. I moved to the cellar laboratory, injected my ceraceous Barbara with the damnable reagent and then set her on West's sleeping henchmen, Burle Haisson and his Thibetan wife, Mi-Ling. Of the horrid rending the two suffered at the claws of that fleshy automation, I can bring myself to describe nothing. Only that they were dispatched with savage precision.

I next sought to deal with West, and found him pouring, as he did obsessively, over his beloved ancient manuscripts in the study. As he told me of his most recent profound findings and lunatic vagaries I fired fully six shots into his body by the light of an approving moon. He stared at my grim silhouette in shock for an instant, shuddered and collapsed. Poetic justice. The house was silent; as disturbingly silent as that tomb-legion in the Boston cellar had been on a similarly poignant night long before. The stillness lasted for only a moment before my triumphant cackling shook the house to its foundations... for only another moment before I blacked out.

I woke to find myself tied to my four-poster bed with thick hempen rope. The contorted corpses of Haisson and Mi-Ling stood as best they could at the foot of my bed staring blankly upon my predicament. I realized what had transpired even before West entered the room, gloating impetuously, to explain. As I commenced to empty my revolver into him, he had used those same techniques he had used on Barbara to hurl himself into my own body before he had succumbed. Once he had seized my mind he found it easy to suppress my consciousness-when, after all, had I not cowered before his intimidating glare?-and he set about repairing his bleeding husk with the very hands that had sought its destruction only moments before. Next he revived his henchmen, whose remains were certainly "fresh" enough to ensure at least partial success. He carefully posed his body in the corner of my room, and then ordered the two reanimates to tie my own form to the bed before returning to his body. Once again, West had defeated me.

"And now," he said, standing over my wide eyes, ringing his hands feverishly, "I require the indoctrinated prowess of my one true and able assistant to bring me further toward supreme immortality. I've considered finding someone else, old boy, but who is better-suited for what I now set out to do? We have such marvels to share." Cryptic to the very last, he extinguished the light and left me tied up in the dark with the two unnerving golems. There was no escape—I was meant to be at West's side, and he was created to command me.

Morning once again found West at my bedside, grinning widely. His left eye had taken on a nervous twitch since the night I shot him to death, and he waited for me to come fully to my senses before he spoke.

"Tomorrow morning we shall entertain some very special guests. An old friend of that fine gentleman Dr. Allen, with whom, you'll recall, we'd had some brief correspondence before he quite suddenly vanished. Our friend has gone through great pains to locate us, and is coming all the way from Europe to meet with us. His name is Mr. Orne. Do be polite." With that, West left me again, his lackeys shuffling stiffly in tow. I waited helplessly till he should need me, like an instrument in his bag; reanimated corpses tie better knots than at first one might expect.

The hours till evening went slowly by. My only respite was in staring at the impassive face of the grandfather clock which stood in my room, and puzzling over the strange shuffling noises and heavy thumping which emanated from the story below. Then at 4 o'clock the next morning, as I at last began to doze, a clamour came from outside—the closing of automobile doors—and soon thereafter, I could distinctly discern voices downstairs.

I jumped as West burst through the door, his left eye twitching, that hideously wide grin etched into his face. From the pocket of his smoking jacket he produced a gleaming scalpel and stalked closer. "Our guests have arrived, old man. I'm expecting your best behaviour. No more nonsense with gunplay." He cut my ropes and left.

'Ah! And this must be your factotum, Herbert." The man who rose to take my hand as I walked dazedly from the foot of the stairs set the hairs on the back of my neck trembling. He was an essentially salty, Mephistophelean-looking fellow with a thick, ink -black beard, and his shifty eyes contained an all-too-familiar formaldehyde rheume I'd seen before only in the eyes of Herbert West and some of our more outlandish test subjects. "I am Simon Orne. It's a pleasure to make your acquaintance, sir."

Two other gentlemen had arrived with Mr. Orne, both strapping Nordic types. Orne introduced them, "This is Captain Josef von Manstein of the Sicherheitsdienst." He indicated the younger of the two who, until proffering his hand and acknowledging me with a stiff "Herr Doktor" had been peeking suspiciously out a window into the night. "And this," Orne indicted the older man, who wore a ridiculously monocle, "is Dr. Sievers of ye Reich Institute for Military Research."

"Herr Doktor."

No one seemed to give the rope burns that scarred my wrists a second look. Von Manstein returned to the window, while Sievers joined West and Orne on the couch to continue their conversation. I sat across from them to listen. Listen and watch a prophetic witchfire waver in the fireplace. Apparently, in Orne's eyes, I was party to whatever was transpiring already as he spoke freely and without hesitation.

"Even as you see, Herbert," resumed Orne, "we are alike, you and I. We seek ye same thing, we do. Many years ago I was compelled to flee my own laboratory by ye torches and pitchforks of ignorant peasants. Ye wretches set fire to my home and left me for dead, so I fled to Ye Continent. It was only once I arrived in Munich that I providentially encountered men of a distinctly higher grade, those who understand ye importance of scientific work such as ours. I lost contact with Dr. Allen at about ye same time." Orne's speech was affected by only the slightest German accent, but was nonetheless somehow alien, stilted in some peculiar manner hard to define. "From what Allen told me about you, I knew you at once for a kindred spirit. Just ye sort my associates now seek to recruit."

Sievers interrupted. "Think of it, Doktor Vest. An inexhaustible supply of test subjects, der relic vee hev discussed as payment . . . all der riches of der greatest power in der vorld at your disposal. Romel's Afrika Korp is now poised in Egypt mit Der Valley of Kings in sight. Und, in a few months, our Panzer divisions vill bring Russia to its knees in der East ven vee take Stalingrad. Vith der, um . . . "frisch" troops you could supply us vitt, vee vill vin this var!"

A familiar visionary look had overtaken West's eyes, and without a word I knew it was time to pack. I had learned by that time how futile escape would be. Inevitably, no matter how I tried, I would end up at his side again. With our guests waiting downstairs and ghastly visions of the Flanders front dancing in my head, we hastily packed all we could carry.

Our new friends assisted us in loading our belongings and research materials, along with West's treasured mouldering manuscripts into a car that waited outside, and even to set fire to that Baltimore house wherein Haisson and Mi-Ling remained. The two burned to ashes without a sound.

As we drove away from the bright light of another spent laboratory, I asked West about this relic Sievers had mentioned as payment for services rendered,

"I'll tell you this: if it's the genuine article and our good friend Mr. Orne assures me it is, you may have occasion to meet the one individual in all history who could surprise you more than I, old boy." An aeroplane awaited us on a runway only a few miles away, its whirling props faced toward Switzerland, and our conversation was momentarily interrupted as we made to board. "And, perhaps," West yelled to me above the engines, eye twitching excitedly, "we'll learn a bit from this individual about the principles of carpentry during the time of Tiberius along the way."

The implications of this cryptic answer dawned on me only as our plane lifted off the tarmac just before the first light of morning. The frightening scenes that came to mind nearly made me retch, but for fear that West would inject my regurgitation with reagent. The summer of '42 was to be the weirdest yet!

II. The Horror From The Holy Land by Brian McNaughton

Even before his death, Herbert West was never a cheerful man. His moods alternated between sullen abstraction and, when some especially complex problem gripped the full force of his intellect, demoniacal energy. In either mood, an innocent sally of wit or even the casual pleasantries of normal human intercourse could provoke him to a scathing response.

These moods were exaggerated by the resurrection of his mortal remains, brought about by the formulae and procedures that were the fruit of his lifelong study. In the re-animated West, sullenness deepened to the gloom of the grave; intensity was heightened to a pitch beyond madness. He could smile, yes, when skewering some poor fool who had advanced the inoffensive proposition that it was a nice day, but his smile was a sardonic grimace that might have given pause to Satan himself. Anyone seeking warmth or good cheer from Herbert West would have been better advised to seek them from a shark or a squid.

Imagine, then, my consternation when this morose genius positively blossomed in the hothouse atmosphere of wartime Berlin. The barbaric spectacles, the frenzied crowds, the strutting soldiers and posturing politicians spoke to some need in his formerly reclusive nature. He cheered at rallies, he glittered at parties, he waltzed at balls. He was positively transfigured with joy when he awoke me quite late one night with the news that Herr Hitler himself had shaken him by the hand and praised his work.

"A race is nothing without a sense of purpose, don't you see?" he positively bubbled. "And the Fuhrer has provided one for bonafide Aryans of every nationality. Can't you hear it humming all around you, a hive of industry where no worker is idle, no youth is delinquent, no artist or philosopher is alienated, not if they know what's good for them? Crime, perversion and discontent have been eliminated by the obvious solution of shipping all the criminals, perverts and malcontents to firmly supervised camps. There is food on every table, and the happy workers have splendid roads on which to drive their inexpensive machines. I may have reanimated a few corpses, but that seems contemptible beside the achievement of the Fuhrer, who has reanimated an entire people."

Thus torn from a sound sleep, I was uncharacteristically candid in my reply to this rhapsody: "A sense of purpose? Their only purpose is war, West. Your fine new friends have plunged the world into an abyss of barbarism from which it may never emerge."

"An abyss of barbarism?" He laughed wildly. "Barbarism is the natural, unsullied state of the Nordic hero, and war is the breath of life to him. The abyss of civilization, rather, a corrupt pit crawling with oriental decadence, where the standard of morality is that of the usurer and the whoremonger, where the goal of politics is the tyranny of equality, where the desire of an effete population is fixed upon the phantom of pusillanimous peace: it is from this abyss that the Fuhrer has led us into the sunlight of a new Golden Age. The manly clash of arms has once again risen to wake the gods from their long slumber among the cobwebs of Valhalla."

"You seem to have forgotten the lessons that the veriest dunce could have memorized from the Great War," I grumbled. "And if the gods in Valhalla are awake, it's because not even they can sleep through the pandemonium unleashed on us every night by Mr. Churchill's bombers."

Had some stranger happened upon this scene in the elegant bed room suite at the Grand Hotel, he would have made the woefully inaccurate observation that West and I were young men of an approximate age. But fifteen years before, we both had been dragged screaming through the furnace of the Great War, an experience horrific enough to age any man long before his time.

Even before that, we had been young together at Miskatonic University in Arkham, Massachusetts, where West's dazzling brilliance and his even more dazzling sense of mission had enslaved me as his assistant and accomplice. His goal was simple, and it was deceptively praiseworthy: to restore life to the dead. It was the very promise extended by no less a Personage than our blessed Savior. It seemed to me that West intended to redeem this promise, which had fallen somewhat short of universal expectation, with the methods of modern science. In my most deluded transports of hero-worship, I had confused this madman with Jesus Christ.

But the reality soon grew horrible, and horror was heaped upon horror until the word lost all meaning and the emotion all power to move. With my high ideals and good intentions I was buried in a pit from which a descent into hell would have seemed a holiday outing.

Why, you ask, did I not rebel? I can only reply that man is a despicable worm who can get used to anything, that horror can become a habit, that slavery can bring freedom from the unbearable burden of free will, and that I was no more than a man.

I was a man, I say, but after West tried to ensure my loyalty even further by murdering me and bringing me back to life with his methods, I became something different, something not unlike the mad West himself. With nothing more to lose, I did at last rebel, whereupon I learned that I had not even ventured beyond the outermost anteroom of true horror.

I killed West, and nothing in my life or in my subsequent life-in-death ever gave me such undiluted joy. I was glad I killed him. I was free! I was a fool . . .

I created what I believed was a new beginning for a new life with a beautiful young woman who consented to become my bride. We were sublimely happy together, and no happier than when she told me that she was with child. With the same breath, however, she revealed a secret so terrible that I must leave off writing for a moment to scream aloud with shame and loathing.

There. It brought me no relief.

The abominable West, the unspeakable West had studied the discipline of mind-transference under the tutelage of certain depraved and scarcely-human mentors. Killing him had done no good, for his fiendish intellect had skipped blithely into the body of Barbara Bishop, the woman I had loved. The most intimate and precious moments of our life together had been a sham. The form I embraced so avidly held the soul of the monster, inwardly mocking and snickering at my protestations of love and proofs of desire.

The child, my own son, was rushed to an unholy semblance of maturity by West's scientific skills; whereupon the madman effected another leap, this time into the body of the boy to whom he, while posing as my dear wife, had given birth.

So that this was no pair of ordinary young men that our hypothetical observer would have seen conversing in the Berlin hotel room. West was my son. He had been his own mother. And we were both dead. No writer of pulp fiction, however crazed by drink or drugs, could have hallucinated a tentacled monster more different from the creatures of the sane, natural world than we were. God Himself would have been hard put to find a name for us.

Not even West's piquant social life had prevented us from fulfilling the purpose for which we had been transported to Germany. We had reanimated whole battalions of dead soldiers for service on the Eastern Front. Signally deficient in Teutonic discipline, these resurrected heroes had to be conveyed to the east in sealed and heavily guarded freight-cars. Herded into crude formations, they were shoved into the vanguard for the principal purpose of stopping bullets that might otherwise have found their marks in living men.

At first the walking walls of dead meat had a profoundly demoralizing effect on the ignorant peasants who comprised the bulk of the Red Army, but it was not long before even the brutish Slavs perceived the limitations of our handiwork and overcame their superstitious fears. The dead soldiers seldom had the sense to use their weapons, preferring teeth and claws for hand-to-hand combat. Their formations could be reduced to wriggling heaps of harmless scraps by a skilled machine-gunner; they could be even more easily dispatched with flame-throwers and incendiary shells. I believe most of them were simply immobilized by the fearful cold, since no thickness of winter clothing can keep a corpse from freezing solid.

The ordinary German soldiers liked their new comrades even less than the Russians did, with the exception of the SS troops, whose appetite for nihilism was immoderate. In fact our greatest success was with a private named Werner Spitzbart, who served with such flair that he was rapidly promoted to oberstermbannfuhrer in the crack Totenkopf Division. In line for a Knight's Cross after repulsing an armored attack by calling in repeated air-strikes on his own position, he was instead transported to a labor camp in Poland when it was discovered that he had been a Jew in his former life. My attempts to learn the subsequent fate of our protégé were brusquely rebuffed.

I found myself thinking of Werner the next morning as we were chauffeured to the Reich Institute for Military Research in an elegant touring-car with snapping Nazi flags, for West was ranting on and on about the Jews. He was expounding on the theories of his newest admirer, Reichsfuhrer Himmler, whose views on even the most commonplace subjects seemed bizarre, even to a dead man.

"Christianity is a plot, you see, concocted by the Jews to emasculate their superiors," West said. "They never could have got a stranglehold on so many areas of human endeavor—business, banking, the arts, medicine—if they hadn't spun an elaborate fairy-tale designed to convince their Aryan masters that they should turn the other cheek and love their enemies. The glorious message of the Man who proclaimed that He had brought us not peace, but a sword, was twisted into an unspeakable perversion by the so-called Saint Paul and his co-conspirators, Semites of the lowest type, who promulgated the fiction that this purely mortal Uber- mensch had risen from the grave. "The whole sorry history of Christianity began with a slip of a Greek scribe's pen," he continued, "whereby parthenos, or virgin, was substituted for pontheros, or panther. Christ was no son of a virgin—" here he paused to snicker in his ghoulish way—"but the son of a Roman centurion known as the Panther. Since folkish tradition is our only infallible source of truth, all the traditional paintings of Christ as a blond, blue-eyed, Nordic hero must reflect the reality of his appearance. His father was recruited into the Roman army from beyond the Rhine—where, incidentally, the true Jews of the Ten Lost Tribes, God's Chosen People, had previously made their home after wily Semitic intruders betrayed them to the Assyrians."

"You don't deny that Christ's mother was a Jew," I interjected. "As in the case of poor Werner Spitzbart, that makes Him unquestionably Jewish, whoever His father may have been."

"I have come to expect such captious quibbles from you. Under the Jewish way of reckoning, of course He was, but that way is designed to humiliate the warrior-male and enslave him to women, his natural inferiors. In the Aryan tradition, the father's line is paramount."

"How do you account for the fact that you haven't taken at all after your father?" I said somewhat waspishly.

"Next time, by God, you'll be my wife, and I promise you won't like it one little bit," he snarled.

Our hosts were such masters of efficiency and organization that we had little to do with the mass reanimation of soldiers anymore. Most of this daily drudgery went on at a factory in East Prussia, performed by volunteers from a nearby labor- camp. At our laboratory in the Institute for Military Research, West and I worked on improving our formulae and procedures in a clean and sterile atmosphere of pure Science. It was a far cry from the bloody labors of our earlier years, when we had often toiled under conditions reminiscent at once of a butcher-shop and a lunatic-asylum.

Our main goal was to perfect West's amply-proven theory that even a single cell from a once-living organism contains a blueprint for the entire creature, and that anything that once lived can be made to live again. If you discount the unfortunate Rudolf Hess, reanimated by our standard methods after his secret execution for treason and dispatched to sow confusion among the English, the so-called Loch Ness Monster was our greatest triumph; although, like all our triumphs, it fell short of our intentions. The Cretaceous monster that our hosts had hoped would rampage through the north of Britain proved to be a passive creature that devoted all its energy to avoiding notice. The only serious havoc it wreaked was at a fish-market in Bremerhaven on its way to the docks, requiring Herr Goebbels to broadcast a tirade against the RAF for the cowardly raid that had killed so many harmless civilians.

I had no reason to doubt the sincerity of my master's threat, and its horrific implications so distracted me that I failed at first to notice that we were not taking the elevator to our laboratory, but descending a disconnected set of stairways into the ever-more dank and cavernous bowels of the Institute. We passed through two separate sets of steel doors that would have done credit to the most orgulous bank on Wall Street, each of them guarded by steely-eyed SS men—not the store- window manikins one normally sees modeling their grim finery in the capital, but camouflage-clad warriors from the Das Reich Division, armed with Schmeissers that they clearly knew how to use. They scrutinized our documents and our faces so sedulously that I very nearly apologized aloud for Mr. Roosevelt's ill-considered slurs against these champions in the forefront of the struggle against atheistic communism.

All these precautions had been designed to guard a dripping dungeon of mediaeval origin whose mouldy horrors were glaringly revealed by a battery of bare electric bulbs that West activated as we descended the last stairway. I longed to be back in our clean laboratory, but I knew that had been merely a temporary respite from immersion in the natural element of my master, whose heart was gladdened by the ghastly, who gloated on the ghoulish, who gloried in the Gothic.

Ancient bones and instruments of torture had been tumbled aside at one end of the cellar to make room for a workplace. Among the racks of chemicals and electrical equipment I noted a table where a disconnected skeleton had been laid out, along with a drum of the plasma that had lately been shipped to us by a certain Dr. Mengele, whose experiments with volunteers recruited from Russian prisoners-of-war had kindled uncharacteristic transports of admiration in West. "He's my kind of doctor!" he had exclaimed more than once while savoring the letters of this dedicated man of science.

I observed certain anomalies in the makeshift laboratory as we approached. Planks and tools suggestive of a carpentry-shop had been assembled to one side of the table, while theatrical costumes hung near at hand. West quickly dressed himself in the gown and miter of an ancient Roman pontifex and indicated that I should change into the bronze-and-leather gear of a soldier from the same era.

"Really, West, what on earth—?" But I needed no explanation. The Nazis had lured West into their service with the promise of a very special relic recovered by their agents in Palestine, and he had sardonically observed that this relic might teach us something about carpentry in the era of Tiberius. The implications of these hints had been so horrendous that I had pushed them firmly to the back of my mind all this while, but now they burst forth upon my consciousness like a black and putrid wave from a subterranean sea clogged with drowned demons.

"Yes, my friend, we want to make our very special Guest feel at home when he returns from His long sleep," West said as I goggled at the ancient bones on the table with a horror and loathing that was strangely not unmixed with awe and, yes, reverence. He continued, "We shall prove, for once and all, the absolute correctness of the Reichsfuhrer's views on the nature and origin of Rabbi Yeshua ben Joseph, known to all the world as Jesus Christ!"

"No, West! This isn't merely wrong, this isn't merely wicked, this is a sacrilege beside whose magnitude the most depraved and wanton blasphemies of the Marquis de Sade would seem no more than boyish pranks!"

"Put up that absurd sword and stop your blithering," he said as he smeared the ineffably sacred relics with the latest transmutation of his reagent. "I had deluded myself that an infantile intelligence might be mewling somewhere inside your empty head, but obviously I was wrong."

"But, West ... the Lamb of God . . ."

"Indeed," he sneered. "Pass the leg."

He had uncovered the drum of Mengele's plasma, releasing an odor that defied description. The foetor was so noisome that I feared I might lose consciousness, but West seemed oblivious to it as he dropped the bones he had treated into the drum. Its black, oily contents began to bubble thickly.

And then they stopped. The surface of the liquid was still.

I had anticipated—I don't know what, a bolt of lightning, an angelic manifestation, the sudden entrance of the Four Horsemen of the Apocalypse. None of these could have been more unnerving than the absolute absence of observable phenomena that in fact prevailed. Even West grew nervous, and he stepped toward the drum with unwonted trepidation.

In the next instant he fell back with a scream as a Shape burst upward from the still surface of the vile potion, mouthing and gibbering as it splashed the liquid on our theatrical costumes. My own reaction was an unseemly peal of laughter, for this Person gave the lie to West and Himmler, and probably to the preconceptions of most devout Christians, as well.

What we had re-animated was a thoroughly unremarkable Man, nearing forty, balding, somewhat paunchy, whose limbs and chest were covered with an almost apish growth of black hair. The style of his hair and beard and his general cast of features would have aroused no comment at all among the importunate pushcart-peddlers of New York City's Delancy Street. In fact the only remarkable thing about Him was His height, scarcely four inches over five feet. So much for the tall, blond, blue-eyed, Nordic Obermensch of all those ludicrous paintings!

But I had no doubt at all of His identity. His brow was cruelly lacerated, right down to the bone, as if by a crown of thorns, and His body had been torn as if by a remorseless flogging. Not on the hands, as all those deluded stigmatics believe, but between the radius and ulna of the wrists were ragged holes where iron nails ran in. As His struggles upended the vat and He tumbled onto the floor in a flood of foul liquid, I saw that His ankles had been similarly pierced. The wound in His left side, presumably made by a Roman spear, gaped large and jagged, as if the final executioner had twisted the blade for the best effect.

"Good God, West! Stay clear!" I screamed, for I observed something he apparently had not as he approached our latest and most spectacular failure. It was obvious from the blank, mad eyes of our subject that His intellect, or perhaps His soul, had not accompanied the body in its transit from beyond the tomb. This thing was as dangerous as any of our earliest subjects.

"Those fools!" West snarled. "They obviously recovered the wrong—"

In the next instant, our subject gripped West by the throat, dragged his head down and began gnawing on his chin, mouthing and mumbling in some foreign tongue all the while.

"No! It's not possible!" West cried. "It can't be!"

"What? What is it?"

"He's speaking in Aramaic, which I learned in preparation for this experiment," my master explained, his words somewhat disjointed by his struggles. "He said, 'Take this and eat, for this is My body!" Almost as an afterthought, he added, "For Christ's sake, man, help me!"

It would have been poetic justice, surely, to let the Redeemer of All Mankind devour my monstrous mentor, but some unextinguished glimmer of feeling for a fellow-creature impelled me to seize one of the wounded wrists and tear it from West's neck.

"'Because thou art neither hot nor cold, but lukewarm, I shall spew thee from my mouth,'" West said, his scholarly instincts compelling him to provide a translation even in this extremity; and then, perhaps not translating, he screamed: "This is my blood!"

As all our subjects tended to be, this creature was preternaturally strong, and it was all I could do to hold one of His hands down. But a plank came to hand from the carpentry supplies West had assembled to make Him feel at home. It was the work of a moment to seize a hammer and nail and pin His hand securely to the board. When I had torn the other hand from West's throat and dealt with it similarly, I was appalled to see the unthinking parody I had created of one of the most momentous events in all the history of the world: the Son of Man lay nailed to a crossbeam at my feet.

"What's He saying now?" I asked.

"'Verily, I say unto thee, today thou shalt be with me in paradise,'" West snarled, and added: "It doesn't know what it's saying, you fool! It's just so much worthless meat."

Before I could protest—and I'm not entirely sure that I would have—West seized the Roman sword from my belt and began hacking our subject in manageable pieces, which would still have to be dissolved in acid. At the very end it cried out words that even I understood: "Eloi, Eloi, lama sabachthani?"

As the separate pieces writhed and humped and scampered about the cellar, I became suddenly aware that we were not alone. Unnoticed in the confusion, the Reichsfuhrer himself had entered the room with his menacing entourage and stood pondering the scene. A look of utter loathing crossed his rather prissy face as he stared at the severed, still-mouthing head of the Light of the World, but the reason for his loathing startled me as he spat: "A Chew'. He vass not'ingk but a Chew all along."

West was for once at a total loss for words as he stood fixed in the glitter of Himmler's little, round spectacles. That was for the best, as the Reichsfuhrer astounded us both by declaring, "You haff done vell. Vest! Dis vass not'ingk but a a man, if a Chew can be so designated. Christianity vass all a plot, as I knew, a plot to distract us from the true vorship of Votan."

"Heil Hitler!" West at last remembered to say.

"As your reward, I am sending you both to Auschwitz — " here the Reichsfuhrer skipped a beat, perhaps giving the lie to those who have averred that he was totally devoid of humor—"to oversee and guide Dr. Mengele in his endeavors. His experiments haff lately taken a decidedly odd turn, and I feel you are the only man to evaluate them and report to me confidentially."

III. In The Devil's Garden by Joseph S. Pulver, Sr.

Long had I toiled, damping my own light, both with and for this man—now monster and, if the gruesome truth of it be revealed, far more—but every man fettered and tethered, must come, after the hardships and foul slights of unceasing chafing, to that border where necessity demands quick, hard decisions. I had been to and passed mine many times, once as far as putting six bullets into the horror that was once Herbert West, and now stood, fully consumed by my inmost intention, at the selfsame crossroads anew.

How could I, never West's equal as visionary or master of unnatural blasphemies, forever quiet this unwholesome demon that paraded as a man? And why in the name of all logic and reason had I saved this affront to life men called Herbert West from the death-grip of the resurrected Christ? But save it I did and now regretted that strand of humanity that resided within me as I stood upon the train platform in Berlin alongside West—at that moment almost the picture of dandyism—as he brightly whistled a buoyant beer garden melody he had become quite taken with.

The morning of our departure was bright and warm, mirroring another decade before when West and I had traveled by crack train to examine the bodies of a western Massachusetts family that had died in their sleep while their home burned around them. Now we were about to board a different train to meet a quite different doctor. Unlike the thousands upon thousands of utterly damned souls- spending as many as five or six days and nights upon the rails without food or water or hope—who arrived like so much tightly-packed beef to the slaughter, Herbert West and I were transported to the Nazi KZ camp Auschwitz not as "freight," but as royal guests on a hellhound train of shimmering opulence. For what grim and outrageous purpose, West had yet to share, or perhaps I should more rightly say, torture me with; for West had spent a lifetime and more finding increasingly more hellish ways to brutalize my ravaged soul.

Upon our arrival at the death camp, we were met by a scar-faced Oberschaarfuhrer named Von Strucker and a quartet of his Aryan-pure guards. Behind the rigid and grim jackbooted automatons and Herbert West, I followed like a dog on a tight leash into the gloomy warren of the butcher. There, like a flesh-regaling ghoulmaster upon his throne of bones, perched one far more worthy than myself to converse with Anubis. The Angel of Death, Dr. Josef Mengele, sat behind whorls of tobacco smoke nearly as thick as the clouds that flung themselves skyward from the Devil's chimneys.

As if West were Hitler himself, Mengele rose, smartly clicked his heels, and greeted him. I was quite thankfully not noticed by the living Saint of the Pit as he and West excitedly conversed. After a rustling of precisely-scripted reports and charts and a round of Ah's and Yes's by the impeccably attired beasts, Mengele, in a voice full with pride, offered West the grand tour of "der Fuhrer's facility for cleansing and investigation."

West was quick to accept.

We were escorted by Mengele himself through the camp; his coolly detached and intricately detailed commentary informing us about each iron-handed brutality. From nightmare-infested barracks to the drainage channels below dissecting tables to hellish pyre to the devil's chimneys, life upon life was cast into oblivion as the Angel of

Death, cold as any grim-toothed statue, sentenced entire carloads of the exhausted, hopeless, and wretched to death via the gas chambers.

Hunger and disease lay everywhere. I had thought I had looked upon the quintessential expression of horror before, but the sight of these skin-encased skeletons who refused to lay down their hope was a blister of burning acid to the eye and spirit of my remaining, if slight, humanity.

Perhaps three hours passed as the villains I followed examined and exchanged, with great energy and enthusiasm, favorite techniques and blasphemous hypotheses, all the while callously laughing at the suffering that labored all around us. Filled with the sickness of tragedy and certain I could bear no more of this godforsaken misery, I passed with them through a heavily guarded opening in the thick bramble of barbed wire and came to the bowels of the death factory—Mengele's theater of experimentation.

The Angel of Death's laboratory of black science was nothing less than an asylum fortified against decency and the bright philosophies of priests and poets. Whereas West's endeavors utilized the corpses of the dead as raw materials, Mengele conscripted the flesh of the living for his foulsome delvings.

From room to room to room I was led past disquieting experiments performed upon blasted-eyed women and children—many twins—that made the rack and the cross seem the mildest of inhumanities. Human beings, once in possession of lives brimming with untasted hope, were kept in small pens and miniature labyrinths designed, one must suppose, to produce and sustain unthinkable contortions of limb and spine. Once or twice I cried out involuntarily at the odiousness of their plight, but West, whose new convictions on Jewry saw the damned as nothing other than inconsequential rats to be discarded after each procedure, harshly commanded me to silence. Like a shrinking dog beaten too many times by the hand of its master, I acquiesced.

Upon finishing my spiritually enervating trek through the devil's garden, my outrage ate at me like the searing ravages of the most virulent cancer. For after suffering the horrors of Mengele's visually-augmented dissertations, and hearing West's congratulatory and admiring comments, images of my dearly beloved Barbara, my son, and the Christ himself, all of which I had watched West tear from the world, rose up before me. I, who once was a man in full possession of softer dreams and desires, vowed to swim in West's blood as repentance.

Herbert West and I were established In fairly gleaming, ultra-modern labs next to Mengele's loathsome zoo to facilitate co-operation and, should some breakthrough become apparent or quick need rear up, skilled aid.

West's laboratory lay behind a sign which read:

ENTRANCE IS STRICTLY FORBIDDEN
TO ALL THOSE WHO HAVE NO BUSINESS HERE,
INCLUDING SS PERSONNEL
NOT ASSIGNED TO THIS COMMAND.

Inside high noon-lit walls lay vats of West's hellish reanimating fluid and two long rows of dissecting tables. Man-sized cages lined the two long walls of the research theater, for West would no longer be limited to experimenting with only dead specimens. For the disastrous inadequacies of the zombie divisions sent as cannon-fodder against the entrenched Russians, had shaken West, still maddeningly perplexed that of all his experimental subjects, only he and I had not horribly failed. With his unholy zeal thus redoubled, he entered upon a new course.

At length. West's new soul-mate Mengele hit upon an answer, one that West was willing to pursue for the moment. And now West, slightly redirected his hitherto-vain struggles to achieve immortality. Through a mixture of cellular cloning and West's fluids they would reproduce extensions of the primary's life that would be nearly impossible to kill or harm. Furthermore, both West and Mengele felt sure that by cloning themselves they would, with aid of many multiples of their genius, determine the answers that had thus far eluded even a pair of eldritch geniuses such as themselves.

The Nazis, in their unflinching endeavors, had already sought the formula of Diffel's Oil, the Grail, the Ark of the Covenant, and even to harness the Beyonders of legend with the secrets of the loathsome Necronomicon, and when those delvings failed, they actually made to pursue a pact with Lucifer himself, attempting to obtain and then, they hoped, decode The Book of the Nine Doors to the Kingdom of Darkness. Legend and lore, science or thaumaturgy, no avenue or abyss was left undisturbed in their rabid pursuit of victory. However, since all alike had been failures, none had been allowed to become common knowledge, though Dr. Mengele shared them readily enough with us, his new colleagues. And now with the combined researches of West and Mengele, the Nazis had their rapacious fingers deep in the vital essences of the human body. Days turned into weeks that bloated into months as West and Mengele toiled at their Promethean attempts to replicate themselves. A dozen and a dozen times, their severely handicapped children, upon waking and hobbling and lurching about like much less functional variants of the reanimated monstrosity in James Whale's cinematic release—which West had viewed some years earlier with less than humor—were angrily dismissed to the fiery ravages of the crematorium.

After West's—and Mengele's—unsuccessful experiments were incinerated, they were transported along with the mountains of ashes from the crematoriums to the Vistula, where all traces of the inhumanity were washed away by the river's swift flow. I took some quiet satisfaction in their futility, yet nothing came to quell, or ease, the malice that thunderously beat in my heart. In silent frustration I labored, always hoping to distinguish some flaw, some loophole, that, like the sprig of mistletoe that doomed fair Balder, could be used to slay West. But my own plottings proved as sterile as West's and Mengele's. I detected nothing, though I oft times dreamt of the rages and ravages that incinerating fire and acid might perform upon his inhuman form.

Bound and limited by the gloomy mummy-bands of disheartenment, my hatred festered like some foul and wholly unchecked pestilence. And how could it not, for a man may not thrive without some light and the song of an occasional smile? More and more I found my thoughts turning to images of my precious wife, Barbara, whom this mocking monster had so hideously ripped from my grasp. And whose once captivating body now lay as cold and desiccated as the charnel fruits we had so often labored over. Yet, as fully animated by wrath and hope of vengeance as by West's chemical agent, I continued.

It was at this time that a series of real and rumored attempts on Hitler's life forced a pressing new concern on Mengele. So for a time, nervously fearing a successful attempt that would bring about the collapse of the Reich, West and death's doctor poured their efforts into cloning Hitler himself.

Co-mingling West's reanimation and Mengele's genetic delvings did little other than produce another series of rapidly-developing freaks and monsters. Countless dozens of Hitlers were actualized. Each, horridly mirroring all past attempts, hobbled and shuffled about, gibbering and babbling incomprehensible nonsense before being silenced in the pyres.

Mengele became increasingly more distraught at each failure. He well understood the plight that befell each glory-hungry knowledge seeker who had failed the Nazis, and so he began to envision his own torturous downfall. All his energies poured into heavy fears, and his demeanor toward West became as cold as the bullets absorbing lives on the Russian theater. He and West began to argue almost continually, and I sought every opportunity to quietly stir their chafing.

One evening after nearly a dozen hours of riotous failures, Mengele stormed out of West's lab bitterly promising the wrath of Berlin would cascade over West—who he flatly stated was solely responsible for their persistent failures. After launching a curt expletive at the slammed door, West soon sat absorbed in a sheaf of comparative charts. I asked him two questions regarding the remains of the poor creature upon the dissecting table, but he was too far within himself to hear me.

I spun from the cold wall of his back and returned sullenly to my cleaning chores. And there before me, inches from my grasp, on the blood-grooved butcher's table sat the cleaver we so often used upon our failures. I turned and looked upon the span of his back and the clean line of flesh above his sharply ironed collar, then turned to consider the blade again. I saw the prospect for release from my master's never-ending yoke of debauched impossibilities, the long- desired journey's end of my mission, and took it.

Without pause the blade of justice was in my committed hand.

Four short steps brought me to my distant master. With the savagery of a barbaric Pict I fell upon that which had poisoned the entirety of my existence with the razor- sharp instrument—immediately discorporating head from torso. His eyes were wide with shock and anger. And I laughed. Like a Parisian executioner, holding the fruit of the guillotine before an esurient sea of onlookers, I beheld the wide-eyed head before me and began raining a litany that bore the full of my pained years upon the slack- jawed monster who had methodically cut off all dear ties I had to humanity. When the bodiless head failed to answer the heat of my inquisition, I, fully consumed in the hard ardor of complete, mindless rage, cast West's head at the wall. Following the dull crack of impact, it bounced and fell, rolling onto a smooth-surfaced table before sliding off and into a nearby vat of reanimating fluid.

I then attacked the headless chicken dance of his chemically- empowered body, hacking, and quickly tossing the bloody pieces into a sepulchre-sized container of acid. But before I could remove his head from the noisome vat of percolating fluid and send it to join its recent mount in the acid, three of the Angel of Death's SS butchers, responding to the noise my attack had made, burst in and, seeing the stains of riotous carnage, hauled me away to face the wrath of Mengele.

Harshly bound and pushed forward—to meet my certain death, I was convinced—I cared little as we trod the hallways to Mengele's office, for I had, with boundless satisfaction, forever removed the cancerous stain of Herbert West's presence from the world.

Mengele's outraged and aptly vivid performance lasted only as long as it took the SS officers to handcuff me to a chair, tersely deliver their report, and depart. Then he laughed. But the moment died quickly as he realized that now, he and he alone would bear all responsibilities for the mounting failures of the black research being conducted within the wire borders of Auschwitz.

With the sharpest of bellows he summoned the guards and hurriedly led me back to West's lab. Inside, overrun by his raging fear, Mengele was the very image of a bristling madman as he gathered samples of West's blood with sterile cloth swatches and rushed to a trio of vats of reanimating fluid, hopeful that one swatch would bear enough of West's genetic essence to-recreate him.

I fought, but the steel grip of the guards held me immobile.

For a span of time I cannot define Mengele stood above the triple vat. His rage-taut face, like some worrisome overseer fearing an impending deadline, jerking to observe the bubbling surface of each tank, then quickly moving on to the next. His hands were clenched fists at his sides and occasionally he would turn and mutter some blistering utterance at me.

Then just as Mengele's sloping shoulders signalled that he feared he was too late, West's leering countenance, hoisted on the pinkish neck of a perfectly regenerated body, erupted from the viscous fluid.

West laughed at me and instantly ordered the guards to remove me. Chained more by the weight of my defeat than by the bindings that held me, I sat tied to a chair for hours as I considered my fate. But my death was not forthcoming, for West, always enjoying the infamy he heaped upon my tormented soul, had me locked in a tight room with naught but my failure for companion. Perhaps death itself had become so commonplace a thing to him, and nothing to fear, that he could not even hold attempted murder, actual murder, against me as an unforgivable crime!

The days gathered. The months passed. I was amply fed, and occasionally granted short periods of exercise in a small area of dense barb wire in view of West's lab. During my confinement I was never visited by West, nor sent any communications, but on three occasions —which seemed to me very evenly spaced—when I was out in my barren yard. West stepped from his lab and paused to briefly look in my direction and smile.

The war nearing cessation, the American and Russian forces delivered their crushing might upon the Reich. The shaved and starved and tattooed living dead were freed from the lice-ridden pens of the devil's garden by American soldiers with outrage and revulsion in their moist, blasted eyes.

I was also freed. Yet, within hours, I found myself shackled anew by more adamantine bonds as West stepped to my side and nodded. I thought to free myself with some statement to the authorities, but West had worn me to a point where I firmly believed his tether was utterly inescapable. And so I stood under the open sky without voice.

I watched one American boy openly weep as a hideously-withered Polish woman, using the last of her breaths to thank him, collapsed and died in his arms. Less than ten paces from the camp's most diabolic assassin, Oberschaarfuerer Molle, the youthful corporal withdrew his sidearm and walked to Molle, placing the barrel of the .45 firmly at the Nazi's temple. Although his hand shook as his heart thundered, he did not fire—he may have stood in the heart of Hell, but he was not a monster. My heart mirrored the young American's desire as he stood at West's side and looked at his cold, proud profile.

For weeks in the hive of Hell the Americans were about their labors. Along with the SS assassins, Mengele, West and I were arrested.

Then in all the hasty mistakes created by the oversights and bumbles of occupation, Mengele was set free and slipped away to South

America to continue his work. A good number of years later I would hear that a large amount of Hitler's genetic material had also found its way to Brazil. West and I found ourselves free, too, but, at West's agreement, aligned with a surreptitious United States Government appendage working with the highest levels of the American armed forces. We were then returned home to America. There—after West and I spent nearly a year involved in "Eyes Only" research in Washington, D. C, and near McLean, Virginia —to be assigned to a classified operation West would only reveal to me as "Project Starchaser."

Certain I was to be chained forever to my abhorrent taskmaster, I along with West, boarded a military train bound for a heavily-fortified government facility in the desert of New Mexico later to be designated Area 51.

IV. The Thing From The Ovens by Robert M. Price

The man caught in the grip of nightmare strains at the bonds of Morpheus to awaken. And when one's waking days are spent amid nightmare, one seeks whatever surcease is available. My new colleagues, and West's, had sought and found their refuge in the simple yet drastic expedient of amputation: the hideous depredations performed by the National Socialist experimenters upon their Jewish victims paled in comparison to the self-mutilation by which the mad doctors of the Auschwitz compound mercilessly excised their own once-human consciences. My guess is that Herbert West was born without that vestigial organ. Mine had been many times anesthetized over the years, yet some glimmer of human feeling remained—only enough, it happened, to punish me for the deeds in which I continued to acquiesce.

But even when I managed to quiet my nagging humanity, it was impossible to escape mindfulness of the inhumane tasks upon which we, like coal-shoveling devils in the Pit of Hell, busied ourselves. If nothing else, the ever-present stench of roasting human flesh, smoking and ashen corpses, tainted the atmosphere in a manner to which no one could ever become inured. I imagine that Mengele and West had grown to relish the terrible reek like a connoisseur appreciates the delicate bouquet of a favorite vintage. I knew that the choking smell of cooked human flesh should sooner rather than later draw West, mouthwatering, to the ovens for experimental fodder. But at first he seemed preoccupied with other matters.

To my surprise, and to the visible distaste of Josef Mengele, West spent lengthy periods questioning some of the older Jewish captives, that is, when he was not blasphemously torturing them. He was seeking some information from them, and a few told him what little they could. As polite as West could be on such occasions, his threat to them was clear, as his office contained several of the horrible lampshades and pieces of furniture upholstered in human flesh, all the rage with the sadists who ran the death camps. Only none could match West's for horror of decor, since he had had whole faces carefully removed in a single piece, tanned, and stitched together. One can imagine the number of victims required to cover an entire sofa in this manner. And then, atrocity upon atrocity, he used to rub a rag saturated with the reagent serum into the human leather. The result was a sea of adjacent eyeless faces whose lips ever moaned in silent agonies. I think West's interview subjects knew quite well where they stood.

As for me, I avoided all conversation with the poor wretches, knowing it would only make things more unbearable when I should have to assist West and Mengele in their experiments on these poor skeletons. But eventually I learned what West had been up to. He had over the many years of our acquaintance amassed a considerable occult erudition, and I now learned that he had become intrigued with the mystical shadow-world of the Jewish Kabbalah. Such lore and legend, it seemed, grew in luxuriance in the very corners of Eastern Europe from which the Auschwitz inmates were drawn. From some of the more worldly of the Jewish prisoners West managed to glean bits and pieces of the traditional lore, but these were mere superficialities such as one might expect from outsiders and unbelievers. He soon realized the real secrets would have to be extracted from certain of the wizened rabbis who had not yet perished in the gas chambers. It goes without saying that of these none would vouchsafe as much as a word to their cruel inquisitor, regardless of any diabolical technique he might employ to wring their hoary secrets from their bearded lips. Many died in this way as martyrs to the Jewish God.

But one afternoon, a furtive Jewish boy approached West with a pilfered book. Somehow one of his people had managed to retain a Kabbalistic text, apparently an inheritance from many generations gone and much the worse for wear. The naive lad must have hoped to obtain some favor of mercy from his bespectacled nemesis by the offer of the book, but in this he was as sadly deluded as in any hope he might have had in the mercy of Heaven.

West had studied some Hebrew in earlier years while perusing the medieval grimoires in the possession of the Miskatonic University Library, but his grasp of the language was insufficient to the task he now sought to undertake. Fortunately for him, help was ready to hand. The Reich maintained a group of university scholars, biblical specialists, ironically, who assisted the Führer's efforts by translating Hebrew and Yiddish documents and communiques. It was a simple matter for West to requisition the assistance of one of these men, and it was not long before he was immersed in the mists and shadows of a world of dybbuks, spirits, sefiroth, and fallen angels. Mengele and others were increasingly distressed at this turn in their new colleague's researches, wondering of what possible use such Jewish myths and fancies might be to the war effort of the master race. But West only smiled and promised that soon they should see for themselves.

A week or so hence I sat cataloguing the results of a series of ghoulish new experiments in which Mengele had sought to determine whether Jewish males, being circumcised, were either more or less resistant to genital torture. It typifies the utter madness of those days that a man could sit calmly tabulating statistics on such matters as if they were no more than the columns of digits in an accounting ledger. I had grown benumbed to my chore when I heard West ordering a pair of burly guards, who plainly did not relish the notion, to take shovels and bags to retrieve for him whatever human detritus they could from the ovens (which, as he later explained, had been operated, at his direction, at lower than their usual infernal temperature). As revolted as I was at what I had overheard, I tried not to imagine what he might now be intending, as it could only be even more nauseous in its implications than the defilement of the dead he had just ordered. But I was hardly to be spared the truth of the matter.

"Good, good!" I heard him muttering, as he directed the delivery of the unholy burden into his lab. He called for my assistance: perhaps none even of the Nazi butchers could be relied upon to have the stomach for what he now planned. But I, to my everlasting discredit, could always be relied upon. Reluctantly entering West's lair of abominations, I could see that he had prepared a large amount of the reptilian proto-tissue he had used for years as a kind of organic modeling clay.

He had affixed to the walls several large charts which I first mistook for anatomy diagrams (though of course he could not have any use for such, familiar as he was with every contour of the human form through countless invasions and indignities inflicted upon it in a wicked career). Then I noticed that the captions and legends on the maps of the human forms were all in the square letters of the Hebrew alphabet.

As the guards, with manifest distaste, obeyed West's directions and deposited on the floor the various carcass-fragments, some already crumbling into oozing heaps of gelatinous, ashy foulness, he began examining the human remains with the practiced eye of a housewife squeezing melons in a market stall. Some he rejected, others he rearranged almost like a mason choosing fieldstones for a wall. These he arranged upon a life-size outline of the human form, again surrounded with Kabbalistic sigils. Then he rolled up his sleeves, put on surgical gloves, and began scooping up heaps of the greenish, bubbling reptile-flesh. He was using it as mortar to keep his organic bricks in place. When he grew tired, I took over the ghastly work. Finally he called an end to it, insisting on putting the finishing touches on it himself. I left the room but stayed nearby, knowing that my role in the affair could not really be over.

When he called me in again, he gestured with an artist's pride at an indistinguishable heap of semi-human matter that he had somehow contrived to have standing without visible support in the middle of the floor, to a height of some seven feet. It had roughly human outlines, of that I am certain, but it gave the appearance of a statue still draped in a concealing tarpaulin. And yet it was not draped.

"It is called a homunculus," West announced, "and in the manner of the savants of old, I am about to grant it life!" Here he retrieved the familiar syringe of phosphorescent reagent fluid. Yes, he had managed to devise yet another use to which to put the damnable liquid. And it would be my penance to witness the result. West injected what might have been an arm, and stepped back. Word must have spread about Dr. West's suspicious endeavours, because at this point, the door swung open and the room was quickly filled with rifle-bearing German guards. At first I assumed they had arrived too late to stop West, but it soon became evident that they were there only for the sake of precaution. The men circled the mountain of ashen flesh, which began to quiver just slightly as they did. Only West was unaffected.

The seven-foot thing began to move—not, however, from its place of rest, but to change shape! It seemed to settle, to become more defined, almost as if a mist that had cloaked it was dispersing. Or as if clay were being swiftly sculpted by unseen hands. My eyes were drawn first to the head. It had a vaguely triangular outline, and this was due to there being portions of three distinct crania combined, one almost intact, another skeletal, the third a skinless, fleshy portion of cheek, blind eye and forehead. The two principal arms were mismatched, one being much more thin and gaunt than the other, while the legs seemed almost elephantine, hardly defined at all, suggesting tree trunks more than anything else. Groans began to emerge from unseen orifices, and eyes rolled without mutual coordination. I will not specify how many or precisely where these were located. The thing began to thrust forth its various limbs, as full of alarm and incredulity, by the looks of it, as the still-human onlookers were.

Of these, two of the most vicious guards, whom one would have thought long since hardened to any imaginable horror, fainted dead away, something West found uproariously funny, while others took aim at the shambling heap before them. West sharply forbade them to fire. And to the hulking creature he had fathered he spoke almost tenderly. Looking into its eyes he said softly, "You are the Golem. And I, Herbert West, am your benefactor."

The great shape paused, looking neither at West nor at itself, but perhaps nonetheless assessing itself and its position. And for the briefest moment, rudimentary sentience seemed to flash into conscious recognition. I thought it must attack West in bitter hatred for his cruel usurpation of its, or their, afterlife. But it ignored this most obvious target and bore in on the Germans, clumsily but effectively bludgeoning them with its flailing club-like limbs heedless of the wild gunshots that now and then struck it with greater or lesser effect. Before many moments had passed, West and I standing paralyzed in amazement, all the German soldiers had been reduced to a ring of trampled gore in which one corpse could not be distinguished from another. In truth, the scene was by no means dissimilar to the earlier spectacle of West stepping around among the human oven-remains.

The thing, having gained a modicum of muscular coordination in the last few minutes of its short pseudo-life, then braced itself on widespread feet and lifted a two-fingered half-hand to its forehead and groped blindly. My attention drawn thereto, I hastened to focus my eyes and I saw what I had not seen before. West had carved or branded into the flesh above the eyes a single Hebrew glyph. Later he explained that it was Hebrew for "life." Now the questing talons of the silent Golem, finding the imprint they had sought, proceeded to tear away its own flesh, to be rid of the sigil. Blood spurted in a kind of mist, and the thing collapsed .

West's Kabbalistic researches were over. He picked his way through the heaps of carcases and left to wash up and change clothes. For all I know, it never even occurred to him to wonder how he had been spared the wrath of the thing from the ovens he had conjured. But I have my suspicions. It may be that the Golem he had created did in fact understand that despite himself. West was indeed its benefactor, for had he not unwittingly offered the outraged Jews whose remains he had briefly reanimated to gain a terrible revenge upon their Nazi persecutors? But if his experiments afforded a brief moment of justice in a universe otherwise as dark as his own heart, Herbert West seemed utterly oblivious of the fact.

V. The Fear in Waiting by C.J. Henderson

REPORT OF MEDICAL OFFICER
MAJOR ERNEST T. WHITTAKER

OPENING STATEMENT:

I do not quite know where to begin. As any who read this report and whom also know me or my work will attest, this is not a usual state of affairs. But, of course, as the select few who will read these pages already know, there is nothing usual about what I have been asked to analyze here.

When I was first assigned the examination of this report's subject, various facts were withheld from me. I am not yet certain as to whether or not I should look on this as a disservice or not. Surely, if I had been told everything that was known of the madness into which I was being sent before I had entered, I would have been better prepared for all I was to be told. However, would I have been less receptive, more curious, cautious enough to wear perhaps a more skeptical layer of armor? And even if I had done any of these, could they have helped?

I cannot answer. Nor, maybe, should I even attempt to. My orders were quite simple. With the death of Dr. Herbert West, I was to discover all I could from one of the only survivors of the disaster known as Project Starchaser, his assistant, Dr. Daniel Cain--not to whine on inordinately about how such orders affected me. Dozens of people are dead. Scores more are missing. Damages totalling in the hundreds of millions have been estimated, with the more pragmatic of the ledger keepers predicting that the final total will be over a billion dollars. A billion dollars. Even in the heavy inflation of the late forties, still the thought of a billion dollars' worth of damage, all of it incurred in a matter of minutes...

I stopped where I did and began once more because I was losing my train of thought as well as my perspective. A dangerous admission, I suppose, when the psychiatrist begins to rant and ramble. I reveal this, not to make the case for sloppy emotionalism, or to suggest that my need to assess my own stake in this matter outweighs your own need for precise, uncluttered information, but as a means of supplying you a subtler type of intelligence that you yourselves might assess without my putting any kind of favorable "spin" on things.

I will admit to you now that this is the fourth draft of this report which I have begun. When I found myself rambling in earlier versions--hands shaking, mind wandering—I destroyed the copies and began anew, fearing that you might find me in need of more help than my own patient. But, I have decided after a long night of soul-searching that to get my thoughts down and then to revise them until they are pure and safe and reflective only of terror voiced from other throats would be a disservice to you, my superiors, and to our country as a whole.

It is my decision in the final analysis that you need to feel what I have felt, the horror, the disbelief, the agony and pain, and ultimately, the hysterical fear that has left me trembling and doubting and no longer in any way certain that the world is what I once thought it to be. Cold ink on bright white paper will not suffice. To understand what you have charged me to explain, then you must touch the mantle of chaos as I have, as I did when I walked into the cell of Dr. Daniel Cain and stared into his eyes and learned the terrible truth that, for at least one man in this cosmos, there is no God.

BACKGROUND:

July 8th, 1947, First Lieutenant Walter G. Haut, the Public Information Officer out of the Roswell Army Air Base released what has already become known as "The Roswell Statement." This is the document in which he announced to the world that the military had recovered the remains of a flying saucer.

This report was almost instantly dismissed in favor of a new release which claimed the supposed "UFO" was actually an experimental weather tracking satellite.

At the same time, two captured war criminals, Doctors Herbert West and Daniel Cain, Americans who had been working with the Nazis in the death camps, were sent to New Mexico, specifically, to U.S. Army Restricted Area 51, to spearhead a hastily put together covert project known only as Operation Starchaser.

West and Cain, unbelievable as it might sound, were supposedly experts in, and at this point I quote from General Order #25-A-892, "the highly experimental field of reanimation—that being the resurrection of dead tissues to a once more living state."

So simply said, so casual a statement—isn't it? Such deceptively calm words. I would imagine the scientists working on the Manhattan Project spoke in such pleasant euphemisms. Pleased to meet you, Dr. West. You're the creator of the reanimation process everyone is talking about, aren't you? Didn't I read something about you in the latest journal? No, I remember, I heard it from your colleague, Dr. Cain. Something about the ashes of concentration camp victims being molded into a living, humanoid monster, and about the resurrected body of our Holy Lord chewing on your chin. And what's all that about you transferring the essence of your consciousness from your mind to that of a young woman so that you might secretly become your assistant's lover, then his son...

Again, I stop.

But, do not mistake this for some simple pause to reflect, a moment's rest so that I might compose a sentence in my head. The above was not simply some clever bandy to help convey my disgust for this assignment. Actually, I am at present trying to keep from screaming. My hands are shaking so badly, they are so covered with the slime of my own perspiration that I can barely make contact with my typewriter without my fingers slipping across the keys. My brain is afire with the sins Cain has outlined for me, a hundred disgusting, abominable tales that have left me morose and fearful.

Suffice it to say that my patient claims to be close to sixty years in age, despite the fact he appears to be only in his late twenties. He claims to have died and been resurrected by West. He claims to have killed West more than once to try and halt his horrible experiments, only to have failed time and again. In short, Cain claims many things, each of them more repugnant than the next, and Heaven help me, I believe every word he said to me to be true. With what I have seen, how can I not?

I met Cain in a darkened room. I was told that due to his condition the patient himself had requested that no one be able to see him. He was fed only by intravenous drip, the tube extending from its bottle to his arm through the heavy curtains drawn around his bed.

Cain did not leave his bed throughout our conversation. I saw nothing unnatural in this at the time. Such a number of people had been injured in the New Mexico tragedy that I merely assumed him to have suffered some crippling wound, like so many of the others I saw in the same ward. I would later discover that I was correct. Hideously, monstrously correct.

Enough.

I have hinted at Cain's past, and that shall suffice us for now. This report was to concentrate on Cain and West's activities at Project Starchaser only. From here on in, it would probably be best if I were to allow Dr. Cain to speak for himself.

THE INTERVIEW:

"I think you should leave, Dr. Whittaker. For your own good, I think you should leave this room now."

These were the first words spoken to me by Dr. Cain. He did not sound tired or sedated. Nor either did he sound deranged or lacking of the proper facilities to respond to the questions I needed to ask. Still, he insisted,

"You don't understand. I think something is going to ... I mean there is a danger ... something is ..."

And then, the most peculiar thing occurred. Cain suddenly broke off his attempt to get me to flee his chambers and began talking to himself. It was a mad buzzing noise of hisses and snaps. I could make out few of the words clearly, my patient's none-too-internal debate muffled by the curtain around his bed. Finally however, he spoke to me once more.

"You think I'm crazy, don't you? It's all right. I am crazy, you know. Crazy to have allowed all that has happen to me to occur, crazy not to have killed West decades ago. But, but ... of course, I did, didn't I? I killed him. And then I killed him. And I think I may have killed him again somewhere in there. I'm not certain anymore, you know."

The man rambled for some time after that, telling me in great and horrid detail the abominable tales I have but hinted at in the preceding pages. After several hours I attempted to get my assignment under way by abruptly changing the subject. Without warning, when my patient paused for a breath, I said, "Tell me about what happened at Project Starchaser."

"What do you want to know?"

"Tell me what you saw, what you did, what you were brought there to do. Tell me what went wrong."

There was a long pause at this point. Cain made small gurgling noises for a while; interrupted with disturbing, dry whistles. I must admit, despite my many years of medical service it was a noise I had never quite before heard. Finally, however, he managed to begin to answer my question.

"West."

"What about Dr. West?"

"You asked what went wrong. It was West. He is what was wrong. What went wrong. What is wrong. What is wrong with the world, with the human mind, with existence itself!"

"Why do you say this, Dr. Cain? What makes you feel this way?"

"What makes me feel this way? Are you an idiot? Have you heard nothing I've said? What more does the monster have to do?"

"Yes, I understand that you believe Dr. West responsible for a great many horrors over the years you've been with him. But, even if I accept everything you say as true—all of it without any critical reflection—still, I need to report to my superiors exactly what occurred in New Mexico. There are considerations of national security."

No response was made to that statement, merely the same dry whistling noise slithering outward from between the weighty curtains surrounding the darkened bed. I despaired for a moment. Normally I would want to work with a patient such as Dr. Cain for months before tackling the root center of his problem. But, I had not the luxury of time. My assignment was to get answers as quickly as possible—through whatever methods possible.

God help me, I did as I was ordered.

"There were reports of a flying saucer recovered by the Army Air Corp. The rumor is that this was what lies at the heart of Operation Starchaser. Can you tell me about that?"

"There was no saucer."

I expected more, but again, the air was filled with only the rasping whistle. I was about to question this further, when Cain suddenly snapped fiercely.

"Am I an engineer? A physicist? Is West? We're doctors, you fool. Reanimators! We were not taken to New Mexico to examine a space ship. Think, you idiot. What would they take us there for? What possible reason could your masters have to bundle us off to their desert prison?"

"My assumption had been that you were taken there to examine, and possibly revive whatever bodies might have been recovered from the wreckage."

"Oh, we went to revive a body all right, but there was no wreckage. Well, not from any unidentifiable flying objects."

And then, at that point, my patient began to chortle. It was a thin, drooling sound, as if the notes were being strained through a thick gauze heavy with blood. After fifteen years of working in various mental wards, the laughter of the hopeless and the frightened is nothing new to me. I have waited by patiently while murderers and rapists have laughed themselves into stupors without so much as blinking. But this, this was different.

Cain's gaiety was an inhuman thing, the noises of howling dogs and shrieking crows mixed with the various sounds one hears around wood-cutting machinery. It was shrill and piercing, yet somehow mournful. At the same time my brain held both contempt and yet pity for the creature which could produce such a noise. Finally, however, Cain broke off his wild cackling. The dry whistling returned, a grating irritant so unnerving I almost wished for the laughter instead. Then suddenly, the terrible noise ceased and Cain's voice began speaking to me once more.

"I'm sorry, Dr. Whittaker. I'm sure you're only here to help. You're doing your duty, but still, you think it somewhere within your powers as a healer to rescue me. I suppose you deserve a decent chance at both. I will tell you about Project Starchaser."

I waited in silence. Something puzzled me about Cain's voice. The trembling in it, the hatred, had somehow become subdued. But, they had been replaced by a snide authority, a type of mocking piety I found most troubling. It was a tone I am quite familiar with, the range of vocal pitch used by the worst psychopaths when they are attempting to beguile.

It did not make sense to me, though. Unless Cain were harboring multiple personalities ...

Enough. There is little to be gained by reviewing my inability to perceive what was happening then. All shall be revealed to you as it was to me.

Continuing, I should add that by that time my eyes had become quite used to the darkness in the room. From the thin lines of light leaking in around the door, I could make out a tiny bit of the bed before me. I tried greatly to see through the curtains, begging providence for even an outline, a bit of shadowy reflection on which I might build some sort of picture of the man to whom I was speaking.

But, even as my eyes adjusted to the near pitch dark gloom, I found the barrier to be complete and unyielding. Embarrassed by my insensitive curiosity, I directed my attention to my recording equipment as much as I could. From then on my patient gave me a great deal to record.

"Yes," he said, "New Mexico released news of a cosmic mishap, then sent out another story insisting that it was a weather balloon that had crashed. Tell me, doctor, could you believe me if I told you that both stories were true?"

Cain chuckled again, then explained himself.

"You see, Dr. Whittaker, there actually was a weather balloon, some new, larger type of experiment, capable of reaching much greater heights. It had been sent up with mannequins inside it to record some sort of reactions—not much beyond that was ever made clear to myself ... or West." My patient chuckled briefly, then continued. "But there was a weather balloon, a massive affair of rubber and wire and aluminum, and that was what the beast crashed into."

"The beast?"

"Yes, the thing from space. Oh, it was an incredible sight. Of course, we were not the first to see such a being. Similar creatures were first reported back in the thirties." When I but stared blankly, Cain continued.

"You must remember the news stories, the Miskatonic Expedition to the Antarctic continent. Pabodie, Lake, Atwood—their wild radio reports—none of them returned? The expedition that followed found their land point and their encampment, but the mountain ranges and caverns they claimed to discover had collapsed upon themselves, wiping out all traces of the tool-using prehistoric civilization they reported finding."

When I showed no memory of the event, Cain confided, "The officer in charge of Starchaser said that some small evidence of the underground cities they reported had indeed been uncovered over the past two decades, but excavations at the bottom of the world are slow things. Still, why dig for corpses when they deliver themselves to you so neatly, eh?"

"But, Dr. Cain," I said, more than slightly confused and somewhat convinced that his stories was mere lies, "what are you trying to tell me? Cities under the Antarctic, monsters flying in the stratosphere ... what does all of this have to do with Project Starchaser?"

And then, the dry whistling returned, and in the ensuing silence, somehow my brain filled with a dread combination of leaps, a horrible epiphany of wild connections that allowed me access to Cain's incredible tale.

Decades in the past an expedition discovers traces of an ancient city beneath the southern polar region. An intricate, advanced metropolis created before humanity had found fire or the wheel. Now, a monster similar to those discovered then is found in the upper atmosphere. It crashes into a weather balloon and falls to Earth. It's otherworldly appearance, combined with the wreckage of the balloon, is mistaken for a flying saucer. But, I thought, that would mean ...

"Yes," agreed Cain with an eerie precision, almost as if he could hear my thoughts, "creatures that can transverse the ether of the galaxy the way fish do the ocean. Magnificent things they were ... ten feet tall, dark grey, infinitely dense. The one we were taken to within the brightly lit confines of Hanger 18 was an extraordinary specimen. Nine foot membranous wings, flexible and yet impervious to torch or saw, and its magnificent, five-pointed head ... the wonders within it ..."

Cain stopped talking for a moment at that point. Or at least, he ceased talking to me. Despite several attempts by myself to coax a response from him, my patient engaged in an internal dialogue, yammering under his breath to himself for nearly a minute. Then, the dry whistling returned, slicing keenly through my nerves, followed again by my patient speaking to me once more.

He begged my apology, again in the suspiciously mocking tone I had noted earlier. I bade him continue without mentioning anything. Chuckling as he spoke, he told me,

"Anyway, the beast. That magnificent specimen, fantastically, it was a thing almost completely preserved. Our guess was that the creature, capable of transversing the flowpaths of space itself, had managed to glide most of the way to the planet's surface and thus avoided being severely damaged."

"But, it was dead, correct?"

"Oh, yes," agreed Cain. "As some fabrics can turn or blunt a bullet and yet still be slit through by a knife blade, so was this wondrous beast slain. An almost humorous irony, its skin, capable of turning meteors, had been pierced by one of the recording struts of the weather balloon. The more the great Old One struggled, the more entangled it became, the more it drove the broken strut into its vitals."

The sudden cheerful edge Cain's voice had taken on disturbed me greatly, although I could offer myself no reason for the uneasy feeling. In fact, I suddenly became aware that everything about the interview was beginning to disturb me. I felt that the darkness was closing in on me. I felt myself growing suspicious of the strange noises that interrupted Cain's monologue, and the bizarre—what could I call them—arguments, perhaps, that my patient lapsed into from time to time.

I even found part of my brain listening to Cain's tone and the rhythm of his speech, positive that his voice had changed significantly since the beginning of the interview. Reminding my paranoia that differing emotions can cause fluctuations in the pitch and meter of human voices, I snarled at the runaway edginess slithering through my body, trying to get myself back under control.

And yet, as Cain described the procedures he and West used to examine the great star creature, I could not shake the violent conviction rooting itself throughout the soil of my consciousness that something was dreadfully, terribly wrong. I cursed my unexplainable lack of nerve. There was nothing so unusual, so bizarre to require me to respond in such a fashion, I told myself. Yes, certainly the subject matter being discussed grew more fantastical by the minute, but since when was a psychiatrist supposed to be disturbed by the rantings of one of their patients?

In many ways I was simply furious with myself. So I was sitting in the dark. So Cain's voice had taken on an almost sinister tone. So he wove tales of nightmare and horror. So what? I could not believe the reaction the situation was inducing within me. But, no matter what I could believe, the reaction was real and growing.

I felt an unease I had not known since I had found myself sitting in the back of an Army medical vehicle on the German front only a few short years ago. I was supposedly safe, safe enough. And yet, you always found yourself thinking, all it might take was an errant shell, an off-course bomber, a land mine ... maybe this was the day, any minute, something could go wrong—just one misstep, one tiny error ...

My hands were slick with a cold, yet sticky sweat that I seemed incapable of wiping away no matter how hard I tried. My bones ached, my muscles knotted, my nerves were inflamed. Insanely, I closed my eyes against the darkness, grinding my teeth together to keep them from chattering.

At that point it took the rigid summoning of all my will power to keep myself from fleeing the room. And why—why, I did not know. I begged myself for an answer, but none revealed itself. Why was Cain's voice so frightening to me? What could possibly be so terrifying about a man so withdrawn from the world that he insisted on living in darkness, surrounded by a double layer of windowless walls? What it was, I did not know. I could only think that something in the air of the room had chilled me so utterly that I no longer felt I could control my actions.

My arms began shaking uncontrollably at that point, my fingers trembling. As I wrapped them around myself, hugging myself, pressing my chin to my chest, doubling over, forcing my feet flat against the floor, I could feel tears forcing themselves through my tight clamped eyes, could taste the bile and mucus clustering in my throat.

"Are you listening to me, doctor?"

Terror and confusion blasted through my mind as I sought to answer Cain's smirking question. When later I played back the tape, I realized my patient had talked for almost fifteen minutes without my hearing a word. He had gone through the complete checklist of his examination of the creature, as well as the application of West's potions to the deceased alien.

Knowing from Cain's condescending tone that he knew the truth about my inattention, still I pretended otherwise at that moment, asking him to continue. With a damning snicker, he went on with his story.

"Actually, there isn't much more to tell, Dr. Whittaker. At that point it was only a matter of moments until the creature began to stir. It was, of course, West's greatest moment of triumph. No matter what happened from that moment forward, he had proved himself, had carved for himself a place in the annals of medicine for all time. For, he had not merely reanimated simple human tissue this time. No, finally he had proved that his formulas were not just tied to the basic molecules of human life, but to the firmament of all life—to the very building blocks of the universe itself!"

Cain fell into another sudden bout of strangled whispers. This one was quite prolonged, accompanied by sounds which could mean nothing else save that my patient was slapping himself. In the thin silver coming from under the door, I watched his intravenous bottle shaking on its hanger, but I did nothing. I did not call out, I did not go to him. I simply waited for the unknown inevitability which I knew with sickening certainty was racing toward me.

"It sat up on the table, staring at us, at everyone in the room, the five points of its star shaped head taking in the entire chamber. I thrilled to see it various membranes, the delicate gills and pores of it, testing themselves, instantly deciding what kind of atmosphere it was in, involuntary reactions reasserting their independence. The creature stood up on the table, its wings half-folded, staring about itself. For a brief moment, it was like a utopian vision, the wise and advanced stranger staring down on its lesser brothers, grateful for its life, ready to share the bounties of the universe with us." There came a cold laugh from behind the curtains, after which my patient added,

"And then, reality came crashing down upon us all."

At that point if I had possessed the strength—any strength, any of my own will—I would have fled the room. I no longer cared about this report, about my patient or my country or anything but escaping the vile and odious sound of the belittling voice oozing toward me from behind the curtains. Helpless I had been, though, and helpless I remained.

"Amazingly, from within a fold of its own skin, the creature removed a marvelously intricate device. It was delicate in both size and design, fashioned from some alloy that shone with a blue-green radiance. Despite its appearance, however, the instrument's function was decidedly not delicate. Before any of us could sense the device's purpose, the creature aimed it at the largest knot of men within the hanger and released a shimmering ray utilizing some principle of energy unknown to this world."

"What happened?" I choked.

"Men died," said my patient simply. "By the dozens, possibly by the hundreds. Their clothing and skin exploded into flame, blood boiling, erupting through their flesh, hair afire, nails and teeth melting, bones burning, eyes sizzling, popping—fluid bursting from their bodies, steaming away to mist as it arced away from each ruined host."

"And yet," I somehow found the strength to say—to accuse, really, "You survived."

"Of course I survived, Dr. Whittaker," came the voice from beyond the curtain once more. "I always survive."

I knew the truth then. Actually, I'd known it far earlier. I'd simply refused to believe it until that moment. As I forced myself to my feet, a hand grabbed at the curtains.

"The beast took maybe only a half dozen rounds from the bewildered, frightened troops surrounding it. Peanuts hurled at an elephant. It shrugged off their attack and murdered them all. I had shoved Cain out of the line of fire, knowing that the alien would first slaughter those who seemed an immediate threat."

"How?" I demanded, knowing the answer. "How did you know?"

A second hand grabbed at the curtains beyond.

"Because I had transferred my mind into the alien's brain, of course. Do you think I would let such an opportunity pass me by? Do you think me such a fool?"

Another hand grabbed the edge of the curtain, and then another, and finally, the walls of cloth began to part.

"I felt my body being cut down, but it did not matter. Housing myself within the mind of the great Old One—to be given a chance to raid its storehouse of otherworldly secrets—was ample reward for something so trivial as a sack of oh-so-easily replaced flesh and blood and bone."

I staggered up out of my chair. In doing so I inadvertently kicked over my recording machine. Thus, I have no audible record of what happened from that point on, but it does not matter, for I will never forget any aspect of what happened next. Hearing the curtains sliding apart, metal rings grating against metal piping, I felt my fingers gliding along the wall near the door.

Part of me was searching for the exit knob, but another, braver, far more insane part of me was fumbling for the light switch. Cursedly, curiosity won out. I heard the multiple thud of bare feet striking the floor. My fingers found the light switch. The room was flooded with brilliance. I was blinded for a moment, and then I was damned.

"Now, Dr. Whittaker," came the mocking voice once more, "be a good boy and take off your clothes."

I stared numbly, my fingers moving to do West's bidding. My mouth hung open, saliva dripping. My eyes bulged, unblinking. Before me stood Cain, exactly as he looked in the photographs I had been shown previous to entering his room. And, there next to him, growing out of his side, was a newly born Herbert West.

Suddenly, all made sense. The insistence on extreme privacy, the continuous intravenous drips, the strange noises and bizarre arguments. And, other things as well.

"You entered my mind as well, didn't you?"

"Of course, doctor. I really didn't have the time to wait for you to reach all those conclusions by yourself. In fact, I'm there right now, exerting enough pressure to ensure your cooperation. Now, you will give me your clothing and then you will climb into the bed here and there you will remain until someone finds you. What you do after that, Dr. Whittaker, frankly, I don't care. The entirety of the world is within my reach now. Nothing you do or say is going to change that ... is it, Daniel?"

The pitifully drooped and defeated head of West's assistant shook itself sadly from side to side. And then, West jerked his new body savagely, ripping away the already drying umbilical membrane that had been connecting them together. There was a horrid ripping, a splash of congealing fluids, and a gurgling laughter which promised horrors I could only guess at.

Shamefully, I confess I fainted at that point, my brain overloaded to the point of insanity. But, even in abject defeat, I could not escape the monster's grasp. Much as I wanted to simply surrender to unconsciousness and crumple to the floor, since that did not fit West's plans, I did not fall.

At the madman's mental direction, my body continued to undress itself even as I sat back in a hysterical dither, silently screaming within the confines of my skull. Before I knew it, West was wearing my suit and smock. With Cain in tow he left the room without another word, even as I obediently climbed into the bed they had just vacated. Without hesitation I slid into the pool of sticky purple staining the sheet. And there I stayed until found by an orderly several hours later.

Exactly as West had ordered.

From here on in, you know the rest. No trace of either West or Cain has yet to be found. Intelligence has declared that they both have disappeared without a trace, and there is nothing I can add to that report. What next will come from the fevered mind of this monster, I have no idea. And, I must admit, I believe I am glad of that fact, for already my brain can not hold the amount of foul baggage unloaded there by my brief contact with West's mind.

CONCLUSION:

I have thought on this long and hard. There is nothing more I can add. You have the tapes of the session. What happened to the great Star-Headed Old One, West did not reveal. Where either of them has gone, or what they are planning, I can not say. I can not even guess.

But, I can tell you one thing. For some time during my interview with my patient, I was somewhat hostile to Dr. Cain. I thought, if the stories he told about West were actual, if even half of them were true, then I thought Cain contemptible for not finding some way to rid the world of such a monster.

Now, however, I have felt the beast within my brain, and I know such a thing can not be done. There is no defiance possible. He is Herbert West, and we are but men. There is no resisting him. There will only be the fear in the waiting to see what it is he will do next. I am sorry to say I do not have the courage to face that moment of discovery with the rest of you.

My will is attached to these papers. I believe the place I have picked to leave them will make them easy to discover, and yet keep them safe from any splatter or ruin. I apologize to you all. I'm sorry. So sorry, I can not say.

Do not worry about me, however. You do not have the time to waste. Not as long as Herbert West remains alive. Again, I'm sorry. I'm just so sorry.

VI. The Chaos into Time by Michael Cisco

I know my eyes are open. My eyes are surely open now. Wherever I sit, though I may be a head on a table, it was forever my task to sit and tell, what West had shown me. Again and again, through death and death, I chronicled our experiments. I chronicled those experiments of which I was the innocent subject.

There is no soul left in me. My pseudonyms dropped away one after another, the plainest names, the most innocent and drab names, and now I have no name. Don't look past these lines, or in between - or look as you wish, drink your fill of nothing. I am less than a voice - this body of mine is a prosthetic limb, and the ghost pain for the original, pure, unviolated, (you'll excuse my laughter, if you can here it) body of my innocence is long numbed and the nerves tell me to tell you the last fable of our master Herbert West.

Mirthless laughter is an involuntary matter, excuse my tittering if indeed it is audible... and Herbert West was ever my rapist, he was my bride, my child, he made his latest debut parting the curtains of my own flesh and taking their substance, my master, my devourer, who leadeth me through the valley of the shadow, the substance, the unrelenting scourge of death, the stench and million lacerations of death and steeped me and scalded me in death, gave me death and birthed death in me - his needle and his serum deprive me of all comfort, he laid me down in a reeking grave and made a world of it for me, his will shall be done, yes in heaven too. He has baptized me in the earth, put me in my grave and brought me out, though from that moment on I am a child of the charnel kingdom of Death, and I walked in the lackluster sunlight with a grey heart choked with ashes, a withered brain like an aged leech in the dry pit of my skull, a body stretched on the rack of a blasphemous parody of life without vitality. My endless life is only an expression of my slavery, a salt of shame to massage into my parched and bloodless wounds - but West's, his life could only be the tool of a will so monstrous, so towering, that it could brook no humanity, no contingency, no obstacle. West's will was a black lighthouse, a darkhouse, flaring its beams of life-sapping lustre across the threshold of death, into the leaden, still seas of irretrievable silence and peace, and dragging therefrom, in violation of all that is natural, the mutilated remains, shivering and outraged, cast into the blazing crucible of West's insane will to be infamously transmuted by his supraSatanic alchemy into the living forms of the diseased abortions of his spirit. West admitted no limit, spared nothing. In the infernal economy of his experiments, nothing could go to waste, for West and Hell both feed on their own excrements. And to West's eyes everything was excrementa, material, mere matter to be assaulted, helpless and bleeding beneath the hammer of his impossibly inexhaustible fund of will.

What I did? What is there to tell? Herbert West used me again, of course, he tore himself from me, he used my very flesh again. We escaped that hospital, that poor fool sent to ease my mind (excuse my laughter again), and then I neither know nor care what transpired. I went with him, he pulled me, I went. I was with him, and then I was not with him. I remained where I was. There may be some reason to think that I remained there a long time. I have no particular impressions. I know there were no people with me, that there was nothing around me, that the sun came and went in the sky, and I seem to remember lying on the ground, watching the tree that raised its branches over my head growing. I saw its limbs stretch and grow, with no interest, a budding new mortality, only.

When I rose, and for what reason I have no answer, I had to pull myself out of the ground. What is there to say about what I saw - streets and buildings, sooner or later. I wandered the streets of that city, and sat by the side of the road. People would toss change at the ground around me, and I would sit and look at it, I would rise and leave it behind. My appearance in the cold and polished glass of the storefronts caused me no shock. I have always looked the same.

I know what to expect, and I was not wrong to expect it. I suddenly felt my pace grow brisk along the street, I walked purposefully, with my eyes fixed forward, all the intensity of my gaze directed ahead of me, because I did not need to look to know that West walked with me. His blue eyes were hooded and he wore a strange smile, and without words he directed me to follow him. A plain house, as I expected, cool inside and lightly salted with a stench in the shadowy air, a basement door swung wide. Had I the merest shred of humanity left, had I been a person at all, I would have felt a clawing terror at the prospect of descending into the black basement, the slobbering demonic maw of a familiar Hell whose clutches I had elucidated only for a moment.

"How fortuitous to have found you again," he said. "But then, I have always been lucky." He moved around the depths of his fathomless basement, turning on one light after another, none of them adequate, so that there grew up around him a feeble constellation of leprous, flickering bulbs, that shone on the grisly relics so devastatingly familiar to me, an revealed too, clusters of half-imaginary objects, shocking detritus whose uncanny contours were so abysmally suggestive, weirdly familiar machines of lewd designing, the obscene pudenda of a cancerous lich proffered from out of putrescent dimensions where the very darkness itself stank with rot.

"Recognize these, have you?" West glittered at me from the other side of a long table littered with these machines, and I did know them.

"They seem very much like the weapon of that star beast," my voice was a perforated tissue of corroded sound.

"I touched its mind!" West said triumphantly, still only a vague form behind the table. The time that had passed since then had done little to dampen his bottomless enthusiasm. "I learned its secrets - in a haze, like a child almost, I glimpsed such cosmic principles in that ancient mind, and since then I have been hard at work! I assure you, the weapon you mention was a plaything - a tool, if such a word may be applied to it, as elementary to that beast as a toothpick is to you. What I have been blazing in that mind is the crystal lens of universal form, of the synthesis of dimensions . . . and my discovery, my newest works, are my greatest yet, though not the greatest to come . . ."

West had come around the table to my side: the expression on his face was the foulest possible distillation of gloating demonism, of an unholy avidity crawling in the wallows to the egress of an infernal intestine. He now gestured to a wall nearby. I blinked at the darkness, and he turned one of the battered desk-lamps on the table toward the wall - there I saw a teetering set of shelves, a salvaged sideboard with scarred cupboards and black shelves listing against the wall. and on those shelves, tucked into those cupboards, each with its own bleakly jovial name-tag, were human brains in seething jars, bristling with cruel electrodes and simmering in the reagent.

West made a theatrical sweep of his hand, "I've had the best minds at work on the problem."

With the rustle of a death-rattle in my constricted throat I read the lionized names of prominent physicists, lionized specialists, cosmologists of the first water, some were not even reported dead, hanging before the swollen congeries of tortured, blistering neurons in those jars. Morbidly over stimulated by electricity and mammoth doses of reagents, kept awake and staring and remorselessly agitated, their agony seemed audible through the glass.

"They have made possible the greatest economy of time," he said with a peculiar intonation. "Their assistance, though not indispensable, has accelerated matters considerably; even taking into account the necessity of replacing a few of the still-living originals with doubles of my design . . . Now, what do you make of this?"

West showed me a barrel-shaped assemblage of some greenish metal, that gave off a mildly acidic odor. I noticed, too a transparent cylinder partially housed in the barrel, emerging from its nether side, and glowing with the phosphorescent gas it contained, which, by its color, could only be vaporized - and apparently highly volatilized - reagent.

I am sure I stared with utter vapidity, but West reacted as if I had evinced great curiosity.

"Observe!" he said, operating a small remote control, made of oddly filigreed metal.

There was a brief whine, which accompanied the appearance of a long and very fine needle from the front of the barrel.

"Mystified?" West asked with dismal glee.

"Of course," was my reply. Flat as was my affect, I felt a long unfamiliar fluttering of dread.

"Allow me to show you . . .the other half of this puzzle!" This other half was another device, a nauseous green metal case large enough to hold a man, and into whose "nose," for want of a better word, the barrel assembly he had shown me earlier was fitted, its needle flickering dangerously, pointing out front like the nosecone of a V2 rocket. The Stygian darkness within the case's compartment seemed to suck coldly on the air, and I glimpsed inside a glistening web of mucilaginous threads and membranes whose arrangement so offended my eyes and smarted on my brain that I recoiled involuntarily, much to West's amusement.

"You mere little man, do you know what this is? I won't toy with you - it is what simple minds could call a time machine."

I was brought up short - not so much on West's claim, which I did not doubt for a moment, but by the thought of the reagent gas in the barrel, and the long and incredibly fine needle whose point seemed to taper to infinity.

"... Perhaps all those years with you were not entirely wasted - if in fact you begin to grasp my purpose ..." West mused.

"I am not sure ..." then, as my faltering intelligence groped in squamous oblivion toward a conclusion, a realization barely without the reach of my grasp, I battered or blundered through the crazy-quilt of my deranged thoughts and emerged with a question, whose implications and whose answer I anticipated without clarity - but again and again the words shouted within the maggot-scoured hollows of my temples and chattered from my ruined mouth -

"... but why, why this why everything, West? Your mission - your goal, to cheat death? What was your goal, West?"

His eyes kindled coldly, but his candid face bore an unusual look, unusual for him, as he gazed eagerly back at me.

"My goal? My why? I will tell you - did I hate death, and look upon it as an enemy? Yes! And why? Because death is the same, it is ignominiously the same, inevitable, and regular. I saw, from the very first, that life is chaos, that it is the free and ruthless experimentation of nature itself, but just when it's most arresting, it's most interesting, prodigies emerge into the light of the microscope and the vivisector's blade, up again bounds that hateful limit of death! Do you believe that I was seriously troubled by the failure of our first experiments, the mad beasts that rose from our tables, that had once been peaceful corpses of once rational men?! Those were no failures! It was my intention all along to sow chaos, to uproot the regular and orderly progress of this unimaginative and simplistic life, to redress the insult of life's plainness, its tedious balances, its boring frankness and predictability! To deprive it of death's limit, so that life may not merely expand or diversify, but turn freak, turn mad, turn riot in flesh! ... But this world, this universe, is unworthy of madness, even reasoned madness! I have studied the structure of the cosmos, mastered the eldritch wisdom of our colleague from the stars whose tissues animate this capsule - and found that even it, the very universe, cycles through the blind turmoils of life and death, bursting into its full dimensioned infinity, only to dwindle down to a single subatomic point again, a dead cosmic egg, awaiting the inevitable, natural revitalization. And what was my reagent, if not the ecstatic eruption of wild, rapacious energies alien to both life and death - a wild ferocity, a telluric force to shake the pediments of the heavens, pure chaos!"

Then I briefly, passingly, caught sight of the basis of West's limitless will, which had overwhelmed all in its path, like a patient conflagration; the white-hot hate that burned in West, and eternal god-like hate.

"I have mocked," West ranted, his voice building to crescendo, "the empty miracle of birth, I have trampled death, conquered and razed death to the ground, I have wrestled with the cheap and slipshod biology whose curse you and the rest of mankind have so patiently and submissively borne, and I have bested it, degraded it, time and again!"

" . . . and that still wasn't enough . . ." his tone dropped to a murmur, the rage slid off his face, and he grew calm, and a little grin that shook even me, was there on his clamy, foaming lips.

" . . . that still wasn't enough . . . I had won - but only the battles. I had bested this nemesis time and time again, but I was the victor only in skirmishes. The war raged on, on and on, as smug and complacent in its false security as could be -"

"West - what is the time machine for?" I blurted, in numb shock.

West gave me an indulgent smile, guessing my thought. "Do you honestly think I would be satisfied with that, with the mere undoing of life on this planet? I have touched in dreams the elder genesis of aeons past - how should I trouble myself about this or that primordial shore, when I could have it all?"

"I brought you here . . . how should I say, certainly not to share my triumph, but to witness it, as you have witnessed so many of these steps that brought me to this moment, and - release you! Shall I grant your fondest wish? I set you free - from this day, from this very room, I shall vanish from your life, from life, forever, altogether! Paltry life, paltry room! I shall ride with the viewless wings of madness, of a madness on a level of matter itself! My reagent brings the dead back infected with the madness of that chaos greater than mere life and death, and into the hands of that madness I shall consign myself, its master, its God! The purest, the vastest, the supreme of all possible Gods, in a universe of my own making, and in my own image! And when I am gone, shall you come or go, stand there forever in your cosmic nullity? To your own devices then, and the vacuous, narrow existence you've selected for yourself - you never were up to the challenge, and were it possible for one of my stature to pity such a mite as you, I would."

He stepped into the time machine - which I now understood was orientated toward the future, and not the past, as I had thought at first. The hatch swung shut on its shrieking pneumatic hinges, swallowing for the last time, in any universe we know, the face of Herbert West - but his voice came shadowed out to me through the closing aperture in the side of the metal device, with its mysterious barrel-shaped assembly, a proboscis with a needle dwindling down to a subatomic point, designed - as I saw in a rush of revelation that battered to pieces the flimsy tissue of my mind - to pierce a subatomic, cosmic egg - attached to a reservoir of plasmified reagent, that universal solvent of all sanities - his voice, which would shake a cosmos, spoke, before he vanished forever - with a last supercilious grin no doubt, he said, "I go to watch the Universe itself die . . . and when it does, I intend to re-animate it!"

Cruel Heaven

Rick Lai

I was overshadowed by the Afghan guards armed with machine guns. These fanatical Black Tigers had all sworn an oath of loyalty to the personage they accepted as Genghis Khan's legitimate successor. Those solemn vows were their last words. Their tongues had been torn out as a precaution against revealing secrets.

A muscular Mongol with a shaven head guided a prisoner towards me and my two companions.

"Remove the blindfold, Ilchedai," commanded the hollow voice. "Dr. Cain, I apologize for the abduction, but your recruitment needed to be discreet. Since Roswell, the CIA have searched for you worldwide."

Adjusting to the light cast by the torches from the wall brackets, Daniel Cain's eyes searched for the source of the remarks. Shiwana was seated on the right side of the throne just as I was on the left. We must have made an intriguing contrast to the handsome American. Garbed in golden breastplates and a silken girdle, Shiwana brazenly flaunted her beauty. Since my body was wrapped in a robe with a thick veil, only my black eyes were visible. A squat man brooded on the ebony throne. Garbed in a black robe, his mouth was covered by a yellow scarf emblazoned with a black star. His skull was as closely shaved as Ilchedai's.

"Who are you?" demanded Cain.

"I am the Demon Khan, the living avatar of the Ruler of All That Was. My bloodline can be traced back to Genghis Khan. The Sons of Erlik, the Black Tigers and the Golden Horde all recognize me as their ordained Emperor. The Sacred Scarf of the Dark Star denotes my status as the Viceroy of Erlik, the Omnipotent Rebel."

"I knew a Tibetan woman who lived in California during 1933. She once worked for a Demon Khan in the infamous River Street district."

"You speak of Mi-Ling, Herbert West's servant. What did she say of me?"

"That an Afghan impaled you. After your alleged death, Mi-Ling sought employment with West."

"Mi-Ling was then unaware that I had partaken of the Purple Sacrament. It makes a man almost impossible to kill by enhancing his recuperative powers. Where is Herbert West?"

"I haven't seen him since 1950. For the last eight years, West hasn't contacted me."

"That confirms the information given by Mi-Ling under torture," interjected Shiwana stroking the sack in her lap..

"What does Mi-Ling have to do with all this?" asked Daniel.

"Months ago, she and her husband, Burle Haisson, were hired to perform a task," replied Shiwana. "They failed miserably. My Lord realized that only three men could be capable of performing the required task. The first is Stuart Hartwell."

Daniel laughed. "You won't have any luck in recruiting him."

"The second is Herbert West. Under torture, Mi-Ling and Burle asserted that West had departed for an unknown destination. Yet he assured them of his inevitable return. In the interim, the Haissons were instructed to monitor your movements. They told us that you were living in Calcutta under an assumed name. You, Daniel Cain, are the third man."

"Where am I?"

"You have been transported across mountain caravan routes to the Chinese province of Sinkiang. This is the hidden citadel built by Kublai Khan. This is Tsan Chanyu."

"Xanadu?" said Cain skeptically. "The ruins of Xanadu reside in Inner Mongolia."

"You are repeating the same mistake that many have made. Tsan Chanyu has been confused with the more famous Xanadu."

"You mentioned the Haissons. May I see them?"

Rising from her chair, Shiwana emptied the sack's contents at Daniel's feet.

"Are you pleased with Shiwana's gifts, Dr. Cain?" questioned the shadowy despot of Tsan-Chanyu.

"Quite. What happened to the carcasses?"

"Shiwana fed them to the rats infesting the Temple of Xangi."

"Please have these two items incinerated."

"Why? Do you not relish keeping them as trophies?"

"I mean no offense, Demon Khan, but my experiences with Herbert West prove decapitation doesn't always eliminate an enemy."

"Consign these heads to Om's ovens immediately, Shiwana, and then join me in the Shrine of Silence. Ilchedai, show Dr. Cain the stakes for which he shall be playing."

Ilchedai Khan opened a small chest. "The Seven Rubies of Bolopore, procured during the turmoil of the Indian partition. If you perform the allotted task, the Demon Khan will allow you to leave with them. Our guest has supped on both vengeance and avarice today. Let us give him a sumptuous desert."

"Well said, Ilchedai. We should all quench our appetites with lust."

"A superb suggestion, Almighty Demon Khan. A versatile Circassian awaits in my bedchamber. Do I have your permission to leave?"

"Yes, my loyal kinsman. Let the rest of the evening be filled with carnal delight. Dr. Cain, tomorrow I shall divulge your task. Slave, step forth." I advanced towards the handsome American. "This is Mina Struan. She shall be your bedmate. If she fails to please you, Mina shall suffer the Haissons' fate. Guards, escort Dr. Cain and the slave to their quarters. See that they are not disturbed."

The mute Black Tigers stood outside our chambers as I disrobed.

"My appearance surprises you, Doctor. My mother was from India."

"Your surname suggests your father is a Scotsman."

"He is actually Eurasian. My paternal grandfather was Scottish. My grandmother belonged to a noble house of Manchuria."

"There is an Eurasian branch of my own family. My great-grandfather took a Chinese woman for his second wife. In those days, my family spelt our surname with an extra vowel."

"Time alters many names."

"That mark between your breasts. A tattoo?"

"No, a birthmark. It resembles Yrimid, the Dark Star of Erlik. The Disposer of Souls has branded me. My destiny is to forever serve his Viceroy, the Demon Khan."

As we made love that night, I reflected on Daniel's past. He has the appearance of a man in his twenties, but he had to be around seventy. He had betrayed Herbert West many times in the past. Would Daniel Cain betray me as well?

Daniel's hands gently rubbed my back. "What are these scars?"

"Lash marks. Shiwana beats me."

"Why?"

"Jealousy. Shiwana is the Khanbikeh. I was the Demon Khan's concubine before his marriage. His bride does not want me attracting the Khan's eyes. I must be always veiled in her presence. "

"And these needle marks on your arm?"

"The Demon Khan has enslaved me through a drug more potent than opium."

"What is it? The Black Lotus?"

"Something far rarer. I must not speak of it."

The next morning, Daniel found me kneeling in prayer before a silver helmet.

"Is that helmet the symbol of a god?"

"No, it was worn by the Winged Rider, a brigand of the seventeenth century."

"An identical helmet hangs over the entrance to the throne room."

"That is an imitation constructed by Suleiman Ishak of Ispahan. Mine is genuine."

"Why do you revere it?"

"The Winged Rider was a woman deserted by her one true love. I pray to her spirit not to be similarly abandoned."

"Only a fool would ever abandon you."

The Black Tigers accompanied Daniel and me into the throne room. Shiwana was already there. Her green eyes flashed flirtingly at Daniel. I took my place on the other side of the throne.

Accompanied by his personal bodyguards, the man known as the Demon Khan entered the room and took his customary seat. "Behold the Oracle from the Sea."

A stone sarcophagus was on the floor. Daniel examined the tall mummy inside. The naked body was covered by a tight layer of flesh. The face gave the impression of a grinning skull.

"Who is this cadaver, Demon Khan?"

"The Seven Cryptical Books of Hsan call him Khutulus. Those sacred writings foretell that the discovery of his remains shall result in a mighty empire conquering the world. A similar prophecy can be found in the Upas-Purãnas and Les Chroniques de Nemedea. Khutulus was a sorcerer of the land dubbed Atlantis by Plato. In 1923, a

German savant found the wizard's casket floating off the Senegalese coast. Murdering the scholar, my agents stole the cadaver. The illusion was created that a resurrected mummy had slain its discoverer.

"I instigated a grand conspiracy to exploit the ancient prophecies. The monks in my Mongolian sanctuary of Yahlgan have advanced plastic surgery to great heights. They sculpted the face of an Egyptian hypnotist into a living duplicate of the mummy. I send this false Khutulus to North Africa to gain the allegiance of the Hoggar cults. In 1927, my bogus Messiah perished in an explosion. Three years later, I was able to create another spurious Khutulus. Alas, the second impostor also died. I recently decided to once more manipulate the Khutulus prophecies. You shall provide the means to resurrect the genuine mage, Dr. Cain."

"I need time to create the proper serum."

"How much time?"

"Before making any promises, I must inspect your laboratory facilities. It would also be advantageous to know more about the subject's background."

"Shiwana, show Dr. Cain our scientific laboratory. Mina shall accompany you. Once you are finished, allow Dr. Cain to retire to his quarters with Hsan's fourth volume. While he enjoys the pleasure of reading, you and Mina will return here."

In the laboratory, Shiwana introduced Daniel to his the attractive brunette in charge. "This is the exceptional Dr. Omega Stark. She graduated from Miskatonic University Medical School in 1955 at the top of her class."

"Shiwana, you compliment me too much. Dr. Cain, it's a pleasure to meet a fellow alumnus. Everybody calls me Om."

"Omega is a very unusual first name. Are you of Greek descent?'

"No, my first name is a joke by my mother. She long wanted a daughter. When I was born, she named me Omega because she felt a sense of completion. I've long had an interest in your work with Dr. West. In fact, rumors of those experiments led me to apply to Miskatonic."

During the tour through the laboratory, Shiwana demonstrated general affection for Om. Upon meeting Om in Yahlgan, Shiwana was impressed by the raven-haired savant's intellect and sophistication. Despite being six years younger, the Khanbikeh came to view

Om as her closest confidant. I envied Om's good fortune. For years, I had desired Shiwana to look at me with favor.

After the tour concluded, Shiwana briefed her husband. "Dr. Cain believes that he should have a reanimation serum available in a week."

As those words were uttered, Daniel was reading the following section from Hsan's book:

None suspected that Khutulus, the acclaimed Lemurian philosopher, was the son of the skull-faced Thoolsah. The necromancer from underground Kuen-Yuin had given his son a name indicating subservience to Khalkuru, the Sleeping Kraken of R'ylethee. In the Ceremony of the Red Offering, the young infant had been baptized in the blood of his flayed Lemurian mother.

Khutulus authored an elaborate stratagem against King Cual of Valooze. An Ulthar cat from the Dreamlands was presented to the monarch by Lady Djelcurdes, the philosopher's secret lover. Posing as a slave, Khutulus wore a heavy veil to disguise his lip movements. Through the art of voice-throwing, Khutulus engineered the illusion that the cat spoke wisdom. Pretending to speak as the cat, Khutulus lured Cual into a lake inhabited by monsters. When Cual escaped the trap, Khutulus orchestrated the charade that he had been impersonated by Thoolsah. Believing this lie, Cual made Khutulus a trusted advisor.

Further unsuccessful assaults were launched against Cual by Khutulus and his father. The philosopher tricked Cual into fighting a Silent Servitor of Zushakon. Thoolsah attacked Cual with an enchanted sword, but the necromancer fatally fell victim to his own blade.

Thoolsah's powers stemmed from the Torch Fire of Nug. In order to store the Torch Fire, Thoolsah had transformed himself into an undead Zuyembi. Only the desiccated eyes of a Zuyembi can contain the Torch Fire. Being half-Zuyembi, Khutulus inherited his father's eternal drought of tears.

Retrieving Thoolsah's sword, Khutulus concluded that the bewitched blade had absorbed the Torch Fire. Djelcurdes pointed Thoolsah's blade at her lover's eyes as he recited The Black Litany. The Torch Fire was unleashed from the sword into the philosopher. The Skull Mark of Nug burnt into his features as his orbs became cauldrons of flame. Djelcurdes surrendered Thoolsah's sword to her lover who promptly beheaded her. If this Red Offering had not been performed immediately after the mouth-

ing of The Black Litany, mastery over the Torch Fire would have been deferred for an unknown interval ranging from days to millennia.

Khutulus settled in the continent of Alanhati. There he began a centuries-long quest to successfully unearth the Invocation of Darkness. Khutulus recruited a Circle of Adepts to perform this arcane ritual that awakens Khalkuru from his underwater crypt. The utterance of the Invocation was nullified by a counter-spell of the unholy Neureus-Kai priesthood. The cosmic clash of competing incantations caused the Great Cataclysm which sank Alanhati and Lemuria.

Fatally wounded by the psychic backlash stemming from the blockade of the Invocation, Khutulus and his Adepts entombed themselves in the belief that their cadavers were destined for a future resurrection.

Since I was a lowly slave in his eyes, Ilchedai Khan ignored me as he bade farewell to Shiwana and her husband. Ilchedai supervised the large criminal empire that Shiwana inherited from her father.

"Cousin Ilchedai, do not feel slighted that your Golden Horde guards were replaced here," assured Shiwana. "This is simply a matter of tradition. The Black Tigers were the original bodyguards of Genghis Khan. They should protect his heirs following the recent merger of Tsan Chanyu and Yahlgan. You shall be compensated with the honor of guarding the Temple of Erlik in Yian."

Shiwana accompanied me to retrieve the volume of Hsan's writings.

"This book was published in 1875," noted Daniel. "The translator was Derrick Struan. A relative of yours, Mina?"

"He is my direct forebear."

"Yes, our direct forebear," mockingly replied Shiwana exiting with the book.

"You and Shiwana are related?"

"Her great-grandfather was Derrick Struan."

In our bed that night, Daniel indicated an unusual concern for his own mortality.

"If I die tomorrow, Mina, would you shed a tear"

"I would be lost in sorrow, but why do you brood? You are not like other men. You never grow old."

"I died decades ago. Herbert West reanimated me. A side effect of West's serum was that I ceased aging."

"Everyone wants to live forever, but we are slaves to yin-yang li."

"Who? Yiang Li?"

"Yin-yang li, the Chinese calendar. It metaphorically represents time."

The following day, Daniel stood defiantly in before the ebony throne.

"I can't perform this reanimation, Demon Khan. If Khutulus of Lemuria is revitalized, he will invoke the Black Gods of R'ylethee to feast on humanity."

"You are naive, Dr. Cain. An accommodation can be reached with Khutulus. All power flows from the Old Ones. My ancestor, Genghis Khan, owed his empire to a pact made with the Lurker of the Fourth Axis."

"I've been responsible for many horrors during my servitude to Herbert West, but I refuse to cooperate in humanity's downfall."

"You are inviting death, Dr. Cain."

"Death doesn't frighten a man who has already tasted it."

"Guards, take this stubborn fool back to his quarters."

As I stood by her spouse's side, Shiwana made a proposal.

"Cain can easily be pressured into obedience. Notice how he looks at Mina. He is desperately in love with her. Her periodic injection is due within two hours. Use that fact."

"You go too far!" I protested.

"Silence, Mina! Shiwana is my Khanbikeh. You are a lowly thrall. Your life is of no consequence."'

More than an hour later, the Black Tigers brought Daniel back. His arms were tied behind his back. The guards forced him to kneel before the throne.

The seated figure nodded towards his wife. "Since this was your idea, Shiwana, act as my surrogate. I intend to quietly savor these proceeding. Show Dr. Cain the price of defiance."

Shiwana strutted arrogantly towards me. "Strip!"

Shedding my robe and veil, I stood completely naked.

"You must have noticed Mina's needle marks," stated Shiwana removing a syringe from a small case. "An unusual drug binds her to the Khan's service. Watch the consequences of Mina missing an injection."

Within minutes, excruciating tremors overwhelmed me. My screams filled the chamber.

"Observe closely. Dr. Cain," sneered Shiwana. "See her wrinkled skin and her white hair. You imagine Mina to be in her early thirties. She was born in 1881. I chuckled when she called Derrick Struan her forebear. He is actually her father. In fact, Mina is my grandmother."

Daniel was visibly unnerved by Shiwana's revelations.

"My great-grandfather arranged Mina's marriage to a Mongol chieftain in Sinkiang, After giving birth to my father, Mina fled to Kashmir where she bigamously wedded a native prince. Discovering that his new wife was still married to another man, the prince ordered her to be beaten to death with a slipper. Fleeing for her life, Mina stumbled upon a remote Afghan colony of Erlik worshippers. Due to her star-shaped birthmark, the priests proclaimed her to be one of the Nine Phantom Daughters sired by the Lord of Yrimid. In Afghanistan, she learned of Yahlgan. Fascinated by tales of its medical marvels, Mina went to Mongolia. There my grandmother fell under the domination of the Demon Khan. She married the Khan's chief lieutenant, an American outcast. When her third husband was fatally shot, Mina became the Khan's concubine."

Shiwana raised the syringe. "This contains a serum extracted from the rare Sung orchids of Burma. It is the Elixir of Life that Cagliostro vainly sought. With Mina's help, the Demon Khan stole a supply of orchids from a hated rival's laboratory in 1930. For the last few decades, the Elixir of Life has rejuvenated her."

I fell to my knees before Shiwana's husband. Turning my face away from my sadistic granddaughter, I made a passionate plea. "Please, Demon Khan, let me cover up my aged flesh. I cannot bear to have Daniel see me like this."

"You may," decreed the supreme authority in Tsan Chanyu.

I quickly veiled my face. As I was donning my robe, Shiwana gloated.

"What a sniveling coward! One can hardly imagine that the blood of Genghis Khan flows in her veins. Like the Mogul Emperors, her Indian ancestors were descended from the Great Conqueror."

"Dr. Cain," emphasized the ghostly voice of Tsan Chanyu's ruler, "have you been feigning affection for my Khanbikeh's grandmother? Your face portrays great anguish, but I don't see any tears in your eyes."

"I'm incapable of shedding tears."

"Ah, now I remember. The Haissons mentioned your inability. It resulted from your reanimation by Herbert West. Did it not?"

"Enough taunting, Demon Khan. You made your point. I'll reanimate your Lemurian Khutulus on certain conditions. First, the restoration of Mina's youth. Second, her body bears the mark of Shiwana's whip. Forbid your Khanbikeh from physically abusing Mina."

"That is a presumptuous request!" interrupted Shiwana. "You are in no position to dictate limitations on my diversions!"

"Silence, Shiwana! I am the Demon Khan, not you! I agree to the terms."

"One last condition. Your Purple Sacrament accelerates healing. If Mina drank this portion, would the scars on her back vanish?"

"They would indeed. Mina shall have access to the Purple Sacrament. Shiwana, give Mina her injection."

Once the Elixir of Life was infused into my veins, my youth was restored.

"I, the Demon Khan, have kept my word. Mina, briefly unveil to show Dr. Cain the serum's effects."

Seeing my face, Daniel breathed a sigh of relief. Once I restored my veil, the tyrant of Tsan Chanyu issued further decrees.

"Guards, unbind Dr. Cain. Shiwana, you and I will celebrate the covenant reached with our guest. Await my arrival in the Shrine of Silence. Doctor, you doubtlessly want to celebrate with Mina. Despite your earlier insubordination, my offer of the Seven Rubies still stands."

After the Black Tigers left us alone in our quarters, I implored Daniel's forgiveness.

"There is much about my past unknown to you. My life is paved with degradation."

"There is no need for further exposition. In the service of Hebert West, I committed diabolical acts. Forget the past, let us enjoy the present!"

As our lips touched, I knew that Daniel would never betray me.

The following day, Daniel worked ceaselessly in the laboratory. Shortly after his return, our quarters were visited by Shiwana holding a golden chalice, Two jade inlays decorated opposite sides of the cup. One image was a falcon, and the other a dove.

"The Demon Khan instructed me to bring the Purple Sacrament. You recognize the Choking Chalice, Grandmother. Remember to drink from the hawk side."

"Otherwise, a poison needle will pierce your lips if they press on the dove," said Daniel. "I'm familiar with an identical cup."

Shiwana grinned slyly. "I was only two years old when my father perished in a New York fire. Upon my recent twenty-first birthday, I was proclaimed the reigning Khanbikeh of Tsan Chanyu. The Demon Khan summoned me to Yahlgan to forge an alliance. When I first met my grandmother, she was his concubine. Revealing our familial bond, Mina sought my help to assassinate the Demon Khan. With his death, she could gain his subjects' subservience through her descent from Genghis Khan."

"My motives weren't entirely selfish!" I insisted. "I wanted to scuttle this mad scheme to resurrect Khutulus!"

"My grandmother hired Suleiman Ishak to copy a real goblet owned by Genghis Khan. During a toast to peaceful relations between the citadels of Yahlgan and Tsan Chanyu, I would offer this Choking Chalice to the Demon Khan. Obligated to drink from the dove side in recognition of peace, the Demon Khan would be poisoned. After I exposed my grandmother's treachery, she was no longer the Demon Khan's concubine. I became his wife. Drink, Grandmother, drink! My husband awaits in the Shrine of Silence!"

I emptied the cup. Impatiently seizing it, Shiwana left us.

"What is this Shrine of Silence?"

"I will show you, Daniel. Unbeknownst to Shiwana, I discovered the lost architectural plans of Tsan Chanyu. Kublai Khan had secret passageways constructed throughout his palace. The hidden corridors allowed Kublai to spy on every room. I regret not telling you earlier, but this is my most closely guarded secret."

A wall illustration depicted a jade idol of Yun being serenaded by the howling ape-men of the Gobi. Pressing the idol's stomach opened a section of the wall. Holding a lit candle, I conducted my lover through the passage.

"The Shrine of Silence is the Demon Khan's bedroom, Daniel. He will not allow any words spoken during sexual intercourse. In addition to Erlik, the Demon Khan worships Zushakon, the Dark Silent One. The god's devotees mate in total silence. The Khan is obsessed with Khutulus because he knows the spells to release Zushakon and his Silent Servitors."

We reached a glass wall.

"This two-way mirror covers an entire wall in the Shrine of Silence. The occupants of the room only see their own reflection, but it is a window to anyone inside this corridor."

"But two-way mirrors didn't exist in Kublai Khan's era."

"Shiwana's father must have installed the mirror. My son's untimely death prevented him from telling Shiwana about these corridors."

Though the glass, Daniel observed the married couple. Shiwana's husband was totally nude except for the Sacred Scarf. Encircling his neck, it no longer obscured his lower face. His tongue slavishly licked Shiwana's feet.

"So the Demon Khan is finally unmasked," said Daniel.

"You recognize him?"

"He's my cousin. His full name is William Chung Kang Cain, but he calls himself Kang. He's altered his cultured voice considerably to sound ominous. Kang hasn't aged in twenty years. He must be consuming the Elixir of Life."

"Did you suspect that Kang was the Demon Khan?"

"Only when I saw that goblet. Your plot to kill Kang never would have worked. He knows about the poison needle. My cousin used the genuine Choking Chalice to kill a man in San Francisco during 1936. Kang had some crazy idea that his mother was related to Genghis Khan. After his arrest, he escaped from jail. I told the Haissons about my Eurasian cousin and his Mongolian mother during the 1920's. They must have sought out Kang when was posing as the Demon Khan in River Street."

"If your cousin and I are both related to Genghis Khan, then I could even be considered be of your relatives, Daniel."

"The same logic would apply to Shiwana. This is just one big family reunion, Mina. Do these corridors access the throne room as well?"

"Yes. You've seen the wall carving of Erlik next to Kang's throne. A small panel on a hinge can remove the image's eyes and enable a secret watcher to spy on the throne room."

I took Daniel to the appropriate corridor. Viewing the throne room through the eyeholes, he pointed to a lower hinged panel. "This opens Erlik's mouth?"

"Sometimes Kublai Khan had a minion create the illusion that the God of Death was speaking."

"You must use this chamber to spy on the Demon Khan and Shiwana."

"Yes, my love. Their bargain with you will be kept. You will be allowed to leave with the jewels."

"I won't be leaving. Life without you is unimaginable."

Within a few days, my lash marks disappeared due to the Purple Sacrament. While Daniel toiled in the laboratory, I hid in the passage to observe Shiwana. She was pleading with her husband. Wearing his scarf and robes, Kang majestically resided on his throne.

"Husband, I see no need for Cain's continued existence. Om has monitored him closely. Duplicating his serum, Om has reanimated dead rats."

"Vermin are simple creatures compared to a Lemurian. Cain lives for now."

"But I don't trust him! We should kill him and rely on Om! Her loyalty is unquestioned! She loves me like a sister!"

"Your affection clouds your judgment! I am retiring to the Shrine of Silence. Come there once you have purged these childish notions."

My expectation was that Shiwana would pursue her absent husband. Instead, she prostrated herself before Erlik's image.

"O Lord of the Dead, the legends claim that you spoke in this very room to Kublai Khan. If this be true, hear my plea. I fear my husband is misguided. Should I secretly poison Daniel Cain?"

A corrupt priest of Erlik taught me a trick in Afghanistan. In order to feign possession by the Omnipotent Rebel, I learned to make my voice frighteningly masculine. This old skill was employed as a retort to my granddaughter's petition.

"I, the Lord of the Dead, shall tell you the truth. Daniel Cain must live to ensure the victory of your Royal Dynasty. I, the Ruler of All That Was, shall say no more."

Immediately upon the conclusion of my words, I shut and bolted both the eyeholes and the mouthpiece in the wall.

The day dawned when Daniel had perfected his serum. Continuing his masquerade as the Demon Khan, Kang wore his usual attire with the addition of a belt containing a sheathed sword. He sat on the ebony throne flanked by myself and Shiwana. Ten Black Tigers were present.

In the center of the room, the sarcophagus stood upright. The carcass inside faced the enthroned Kang. Daniel injected the contents of a syringe into the mummy's heart. Slowly flames started to glow in the eye sockets.

The autocrat of Tsan Chanyu issued a series of commands. "Restrain Dr. Cain! Move him away from the throne!"

"Why do this?" I protested. "My lover has fulfilled your bargain!"

Drawing his sword, Kang rose from the throne and pulled me off my chair. Forced to kneel before the sarcophagus, I felt the blade resting against my neck.

"Have mercy!" I screamed.

Tilting her head backward, Shiwana laughed. "Do you think my Lord has forgotten your clumsy effort to poison him? Khutulus must receive a Red Offering. You, Grandmother, are the Red Offering!"

"No!" yelled Daniel.

I looked into the eye sockets of Khutulus. They were filled with bright fire.

The autocrat of Tsan Chanyu spoke in the Elder Tongue of Kuen-Yuin. "Khutulus, receive your knowledge of this new age."

Khutulus raised his arms. The hands were open.

Kang's blade sliced through the neck of the sacrificial victim. The decapitated carcass fell forward, but Kang's left hand nimbly seized the severed head by the hair before it struck the floor.

"Her name was Shiwana." Kang deposited my granddaughter's head into the beckoning fingers of Khutulus. The skull-faced sorcerer raised the head upward. My granddaughter's sightless eyes stared into the necromancer's blazing orbs. Waves of fire shot forth from the wizard's eyes into Shiwana's. Khutulus was reading her dead brain like a book. Having digested Shiwana's knowledge, the mage dropped her head contemptuously.

When Kang beheaded my granddaughter, he released me. I crawled safely to the side.

Walking out of the sarcophagus, Khutulus finally spoke in English learnt through his scrutiny of the Red Offering. "Bow before the Oracle of Khalkuru."

Kang, the Black Tigers and myself knelt and lowered our heads. Only Daniel wanted to stand courageously, but the mute guards forced him to kneel.

Khutulus addressed the subservient Kang. "Why was your Khanbikeh chosen as the Red Offering instead of her grandmother?"

"Mina Struan is a disgraced concubine. A true Red Offering must be a woman of value such as your own Djelcurdes."

"What of the burial caskets of Than-Kul and my other Adepts?"

"They can easily be retrieved from the Atlantic."

"I will need them for the Invocation of Darkness. You have done well, Demon Khan. Arise to receive a special gift."

Kang stood upright. The extended fingers of the Lemurian's right hand glowed.

"Your gift, Demon Khan, is a swift death."

A beam of light from the conjurer's hand tore into Kang's flesh. A smoldering hole displaced the center of his chest. Kang's corpse fell on his throne. His heart had been completely incinerated. The sword leapt from Kang's dead clutch into the Lemurian's gesturing hand.

"Your Demon Khan planned betrayal. This blade had been interred with me in my sarcophagus. It is the Sword of Thoolsah. If energized by the Words of Fear, it could steal my power. The Khan foolishly gambled on my failure to recognize the sword."

Khutulus shifted his malign gaze towards my precious Daniel. "Release the physician. Come forth, Daniel Cain. Grovel before me."

Daniel strode bravely towards the wizard. "There's nothing you can do to me that would be worse than what Herbert West has already done. I refuse to obey."

"You forget your treasured Mina, physician. Shall she incur my displeasure?"

Daniel dropped to his knees. "Forgive my impudence, Master!"

"You have my clemency for now, physician. The Demon Khan once survived a fatal blow through the Purple Sacrament of Erlik. I am unfamiliar with this beverage. Examine the body to determine if the organs are regenerating."

Daniel removed Kang's scarf to feel the pulse on his neck.

"Physician, what are those marks on the Khan's throat?"

"They're surgical scars! The Khan had no vocal cords!"

Before Khutulus could react, I pulled out the real Sword of Thoolsah sheathed behind my robes. My lips mouthed the Words of Fear. The blade lit with emerald fire. I drove the weapon into the Lemurian's side. Khutulus howled in agony. His hand dropped the imitation sword made by Suleiman Ishak. The flames in the mage's eyes evaporated. His body crumbled into ash.

"Black Tigers, arise! I have vanquished the Oracle of Khalkuru! My faithful Kang sits tonight at a place of honor near Erlik's Black Throne." I lifted my granddaughter's head by the hair. "The soul of the disloyal Shiwana drowns in the Lake of Ghosts." I relinquished the head to a Black Tiger. "Take the corpses to Om immediately. I shall remain alone with Dr. Cain."

Removing the bodies, the Black Tigers exited. A stunned Daniel listened to my revelations.

"I am the true Demon Khan, my love. In the early 1930's, I moved my operations from Mongolia to River Street. Having mute subordinates pose as the Demon Khan, I delivered ominous voice commands from inside hidden chambers.

"You were correct, Daniel, about the Haissons searching for Kang, but their quest to find a descendant of Genghis Khan in California inadvertently led them to me. The Haissons alerted me to your cousin's existence. Following the death of my last River Street surrogate, I retreated to Yahglan. Kang was recruited to be a false Demon Khan in Asia. In exchange for being rescued from impending execution for murder, Kang agreed to have his vocal cords removed. The Sacred Scarf of the Dark Star was a mere contrivance to literally cover up his lack of speech. Over the last two decades, I kept Kang rejuvenated with the Elixir of Life. In order to establish a misleading continuity with my River Street exploits, I fabricated the tale of the Purple Sacrament being responsible for the Demon Khan's continued survival.

"Shiwana had no contact with me during her youth. When my granddaughter came to Yahlgan, I was resolved to test her. Kang pretended to rule Yahlgan, and I manufactured an illusory voice through ventriloquism. Mimicking the tale of the Ulthar cat, I wore a veil to hide my lips. Sometimes I provided the voice from a secret passage. The obscure mating rituals of the Zushakon cult were cited to justify Kang's silence during sex. The scarf hid his surgical scars. The Choking Chalice ruse was done merely to gauge Shiwana's true nature. When my granddaughter failed that test, I had no choice but to cast her in the role of a Red Offering.

"Shiwana's marriage to Kang secured control over Tsan Chanyu. When I moved here, Kublai Khan's secret passages aided my deception, I imported Black Tigers from Afghanistan to replace guards loyal to Shiwana. All the mutes know my secret."

"Befuddling my granddaughter required me to suffer periodic beatings. I stoically endured them since the Purple Sacrament would remove the marks of her whip. My deception necessitated delaying my injection. All this manipulation was necessary to dupe Khutulus through his assimilation of Shiwana's memories. The power of the Lemurian mage shall be the foundation for a mighty empire that will prevent the rise of the Old Ones. Only by uniting all humanity under an efficient empire can Khalkuru's coming be forestalled."

"Shiwana wasn't the only person manipulated, Mina. You blatantly lied to me!"

"Forgive me, my love, but I needed to ascertain your worthiness for the choice that you are about to be given. You can either leave Tsan Chanyu with the rubies, or be the subject of a dangerous experiment."

"An experiment that requires a subject with a steadfast devotion and the tearless eyes of the resurrected. Just as you tested Shiwana's loyalty in Yahlgan, you tested mine in Tsan Chanyu. You want me to be the recipient of the mystical force imprisoned in the sword."

"I can't guarantee the experiment's success. Your bodily functions parallel those of a Zuyembi, but I don't know how closely. Also I only have a French copy of The Black Litany from the Livre d'Ivon. Khutulus would have spoken The Black Litany in the Elder Tongue."

"I gained fluency in French serving in Europe during the First World War. You're neglecting the Skull Mark of Nug."

"My Yahlgan surgeons could restore your facial appearance through skin grafts. Dark glasses could hide the fiery eyes."

"And the Red Offering that secures instant mastery over the Torch Fire?"

"That part of the ceremony will be omitted. The Torch Fire shall slowly fester."

"If I decline, there's no one to replace me."

"Om has perfected a reanimation fluid, and now has a suitable corpse to utilize. Of course, she will have to stitch on the head."

"You're letting Om reanimate Shiwana!"

"Why not? If Shiwana is restored to life, she will believe that her murder was solely her husband's doing. Furthermore, she would owe her resurrection to me, a grandmother who lovingly forgives her prior treason. Her hatred for me would completely dissipate. Lastly, Om was very upset when I told her about Shiwana's scheduled beheading. I only secured my daughter's cooperation by promising the reanimation of her niece."

"Omega Stark is your daughter!"

"She was born in 1931, shortly after I first partook of the Elixir of Life. Her father was my third husband. Although unaware of Om's true parentage, Shiwana's affection for her aunt grew from a sense of the blood bond between them. When Shiwana is reprieved from the Lake of Ghosts, she will be guided by Om towards a path of my own choosing."

"You can't intend Shiwana to be my substitute."

"Originally I did, but Kang's death renders him more suitable. Om shall give him a new heart. His faithful service will be rewarded with a new set of vocal cords."

"There's no need for Kang. I'll be your experimental subject. Kang won't make the right choice if the ceremony succeeds. He doesn't share my strong feelings towards you."

What did Daniel mean? Did he still love me? Or had he grown to hate me for misleading him? My instincts were to gamble that Daniel still loved me.

Reaching inside my robe's left pocket, I pulled out the French transcript of The Black Litany and handed it to Daniel. I pointed my sword's tip at my lover's eyes.

"Recite The Black Litany aloud, my valiant lover."

"O Maîtrise des Feux Noirs Cachés . . ."

When he had concluded reading the incantation, the sword's green radiance turned black. Suddenly the blade exploded, I was send hurtling backwards. Lying on my back, I looked upward and beheld a skeletal countenance. The eye sockets shined with flames.

"Compared to you, Mina, Herbert West was a choir boy."

"I don't know whether you love or hate me, Daniel Cain. If you hate me, slay me quickly. If you must abandon my soul to Erlik's Seven Hells, let it be done with mercy."

Daniel's hands slowly raised me upward.

"Your soul is not destined for Hell's mercy. It will always be overshadowed by Heaven's cruelty. I forgive all your deceptions. As once was said, only a fool would abandon you."

"Daniel . . ."

"Your deviations from the traditional execution of The Black Litany have led to an ironic result. You infused your lover with far more than the Torch Fire of Nug. Daniel Cain is no more. Your lover's soul has been supplanted by my own. I am the son of Thoolsah! Your earlier victory over me was a masterpiece of misdirection! Now you shall reap the reward!"

My scream was cut short as the skull-faced man's hand covered my mouth.

"Do not shriek, Mina. I have no intention of making a Red Offering. Ritual sacrifices bind me to the yoke of the Old Ones. The earlier beheading of Shiwana forced me to speak with the voice of Khalkuru. Now I speak with my own.

"My birth was celebrated with my mother's murder. Submission to the Old Ones has only riddled my soul with despair. Djelcurdes meant more than life itself, but my subservience to the Old Ones compelled me to kill her. No woman ever surpassed her in beauty and intellect until I encountered you. I repudiate the name given by my father! It is the name of a slave, and I shall be a slave no more! I am no longer the Oracle of Khalkuru! I spit in the eye of the Dreaming God of R'ylethee! I roar defiance at Zushakon! Why should I give the world to the Old Ones when I can grant it to the woman of my darkest desires!"

Removing his hand, my suitor's parchment lips pressed firmly against my mouth.

My future was ordained by a single kiss. My legitimacy as Genghis Khan's true heir is unchallenged. My resurrected granddaughter abdicated her position of Khanbikeh to me. Ilchedai Khan was placated when I arranged his marriage to Om, my publicly acknowledged daughter. Completely unrecognizable under his new beard and crop of hair, a reanimated Kang currently commands my Black Tigers in Afghanistan. Given a new face in Yahlgan, my fourth husband has philosophically taken the name of Yin-yang Li to represent his submission to the laws of time. He must slowly master the cosmic force growing inside him. The incubation period may last months, years, or even centuries. I can afford patience. Even eons are rendered irrelevant by the Elixir of Life. My ultimate triumph cannot be averted. The world will be engulfed by a Shadow Empire arising from Tsan Chanyu, and I shall become the Ruler of All That Will Be.

Blood & Guts in Highschool

Edward Morris

During the first week I transferred to Arkham High, Mr. Wargo the English Lit teacher asked our class how heroes are created.

How heroes are created. Ha. Ha. Ha. I can't stop thinking about that. I never raised my hand, and I'm sure not raising it now. I've never seen a hero. But I've seen a few survivors.

Survivors are created by choking down the horrible, sitting with the unchangable and outlasting the intolerable. Afterward, the story of what we outlasted...stays. In our muscles. In our nerves. In our flesh, to be unlocked at the wrong touch, the wrong word, to instant-replay independent of the brain, again.

Again. I see it all happen again.

It's all happening. Only the year ever changes in the Miskatonic Valley and the bedroom-communities of Dunwich and Newburyport and Waite Heights at the convex cusp of north-central Essex County on most maps. In the 'burbs surrounding Arkham, Massachussetts, demon winds shriek around the eaves of cheap housing tracts. Each dawn reveals the unutterably humdrum worse than any Dark Age.

The stink of the mill blankets the whole county in a pall of frozen fog in winter and a miasma in high summer, like something still alive but rotting from the inside out. Not like me. I'm already dead. But who defines true Death?

Not me, not plain old Rowley Peters from Walnut Street in the Fifth Ward. It all seems like someone else's experience, and in a way it was. Is. But nothing could have prepared me for what happened.

The greater the fear, the greater the feeling that we're the first person to have ever experienced it. And there's no greater fear than the unknown. The unknowable..

So we grab extra-fast for what we think is the instant antidote. Weapons, stored in the very dark we fear. Canisters. Fluids. Needles. Damage.

When you stop being afraid of the dark, maybe sometimes the dark stops being afraid of you. Your friends are supposed to be the ones who lead you along the path to being a grown-up, figuring things like that out for yourself.

Your friends aren't supposed to push you backward with their own bad luck and bad timing. The cops are supposed to be able to find your friends. You're not supposed to hope that those poor, poor cops never do. Find. My friend. My friend.

Wait a minute. I'll be okay.

Okay, I guess it's good that this is all coming out.

He was never Edward Robert West, never an obituary or a death-certificate or a funeral card. He was Eddie, Crazy Eddie, Eddie Munster, at school. Until a month or two after I transferred to Arkham High from Our Lady when we moved across town, I never even knew he had a last name.

From the first day I sat at his lunch-table, (the one where everyone sat who didn't sit anywhere else) I followed Eddie around like the guy with the broom in the parade who follows the elephants in old cartoons. Not because I like pushing a broom, but because of the energy. That was my undoing.

The Wests were an old Arkham family, but I never found out why no one would talk about them. Not until I learned by going where I had to go.

Where that ended up, for me, was usually behind Eddie, bringing something from my Dad's own workshop that I had no business putting my hands on, or testing two chemicals that might or might not have been meant to ever mix, or some such godawful thing.

I got electrocuted twice in the Wests' basement workshop, sprained both wrists, and so much else. Eventually, with Eddie and his filthier half I mean assistant, we flat-out cowboyed the Arkham High Chem Lab storeroom, repeatedly. With copies of every key whose lack would have made any of it the tiniest issue. At all times of day. And photocopying every scrap of info for the stuff they didn't have on hand. My God. My God.

My God, why hast Thou Frankensteined me? In Ed, I saw a hundred million comic books I never got to be. I saw a mad scientist, a Boy Detective. I didn't know how many different ways that kind can turn out, if left to their own devices. I do now. I admit my part in what happened, but with him gone...

It was like West was the only thing standing the way of what he was doing. The only thing that could control the experiment. And he could never stop standing in his own light, or get out of his own way.

The only real flaw his type start out with is the childish wonder that makes most people want to punch them in the face. It's Society that twists that kind when it starts locking doors, or slamming them.

I didn't even think about unintended consequences or Murphy's Law or any of that. For the love of God, I was still just trying to be a kid!

Am. It's all still happening.

It's all happening.

I remember the day we met in the cafeteria, the sick green thunderstorm-light outside the long row of plate glass windows. I remember Mr. Jeffries the Chem teacher looking like he was about to pop like a big red mushroom in thick glasses and a Pendleton flannel, bellowing at someone through the microphone that was his by right for monitoring fifth-hour Lunch.

Jeffries smelled like booze sometimes, in the mornings, not so much his breath but the skin around his face, his hands, his sweat. He liked to hit guys who started fights in the caf or outside. Sometimes he hit them pretty hard.

Nobody really liked him. He was especially nasty to girls for some reason. Hot ones. And that one gay kid. I always wondered why.

I remember squat, mostly-neckless Jeffries pacing around with that evil squint, looking for t-shirts with bands he didn't like on them, culling the ranks for the weak and deformed and dissident. I remember the banner over Mr. Jeffries' head, ARKHAM HIGH PURITANS and the shitty drawing of the Witchfinder General that looked like the Undertaker from World Wrestling on TV.

And I remember when the scourge, grinning and lethal, spoke.

The scourge had short-cropped black hair that came to a slight widow's peak, pale skin, very red lips and bright green eyes. You had to be exposed to him a little at a time, not all at once. I can see him now as he was then—and I shiver.

Eddie West was way too thin, a human mine-fire that burned and burned inside. He wore silver wire-rimmed glasses whose lenses and the eyes behind them flashed like endlessly, lazily-spinning pinwheels when he started holding forth about something. When he talked, it was a raspy murmur that forgot it could be a yell when it wanted to.

"My Dad's an undertaker, and a part-time Medical Examiner. Ever seen a fetal pig from Bio get back up and oink?" West announced, as if we were talking about the latest episode of a TV show.

"I don't think anyone's ever said that sentence out loud in English," I tried to say back, but I was laughing too hard. "What is your malfunction?" I asked, when I could.

West's smile revealed very sharp, white crooked teeth. "I can do it at the house. I'd try it tomorrow here, if Security wouldn't eagle-eye me, for a fact, about two of the parts it would take to do it. But could you imagine?"

How could a kid like me not follow a creature like that around? West was more fun than a barrel of space-monkeys. His Dad's house, way up on Adams Avenue by the old Presbyterian graveyard, was so deeply cool I'd been perusing the bookshelves and curio cabinets eyes-first in the foyer and gotten no further, letting him ramble once we got there after school let out. But one thing he said made me pay attention, and come sit where I could listen closely.

"My great-uncle Herbie was kind of like a real-life Victor Frankenstein."

I sipped the latch-key cocoa he'd made for us, lipping my way around the marshmallows until last. "Like how?"

"Oh, the jury's still out, in more ways than one. I only have sketchy intel from the fam. Alcohol often helps." He hid the grin, but not well. "My Dad beat the shit out of me one time for even mentioning his name. Only time Dad's ever laid a hand on me. Usually, we just talk stuff out. But... Like, I was seven. And he beat me like I was grown. I had to find out why."

In that genteel, cinnamon-smelling warm place of carpet and old wood and everything either under glass or carefully laid aside or put away, I had difficulty even apprehending that someone could do any of those things. But they had happened. Clearly.

Eddie leaned forward, done with his own cocoa long ago and chewing on a toothpick. "Dad doesn't really...uhhh, pay attention to what I do in my spare time. Not since Mom died."

I looked around, noticing too much dust and not enough pictures on the walls."Shit, man. I didn't ask. When did she—"

Eddie's mouth twisted more. "Drunk driver. Same year I asked about dear old Great-Uncle Herbie. Later that fall. The drunk's in the pokey. Ma's still dead. And we still hold Great-Uncle Herbie's old place in trust, out in Dunwich. I know where all the farmhouse keys are, but even Dad won't go up there unless there's some kind of upkeep that he can't put off."

My eyes lit up. "Dunwich is one bus away. Like half an hour, dude. Did you..."

"Way ahead of you." Ed looked proud. "You'll see. The house was mostly empty, but I found three old journals. Giant ones, like ledgers or something. Again, the place is mostly empty. But the cellar and the sub-cellar will blow your mind. There's still a lot of stuff left there. Lots of space to work, soon. Some of the rooms you... can't go in. Cool?"

"Cool." Then I inadvertently kicked down the wrong door. "How long have you been going up there?"

"A while," But Eddie mumbled it, and he wouldn't meet my gaze.

I'm thinking a lot about that now, too. Like those were famous last words I barely understood at the time. There were so many more words exchanged, right up to the point when I saw him make one of Mrs. Sexton's Biology sharks swim around in its stinking formaldehyde brine and snap its toothless mouth.

"We ...can't do this," I said at the sight of the latest demo, and the little Beckton-Dickson insulin rig full of what looked like antifreeze, now all but empty and capped with a cork in the Sharps-disposal jar by the cupboard.

I'd shot my gloves into the trash without touching them in the removal, the way he showed me. So I was backing well up. Eddie still wore his.

"I have." He shrugged. His tone was innocuous, but his pinwheeling eyes looked quite the opposite. "The less a body's had the chance to decompose, the more of the brain you can wake back up. If this... stuff... and I still can't figure out what it even smells like, let alone how to analyze it.... But if this stuff were given to someone right after they died..."

The green stuff, the goop, the compound, was some kind of alkaloid. That was all he knew. It came with very specific instructions, but the ingredients themselves hadn't been recorded or encrypted anywhere that Ed could find at either house or in any of the effects.

The whole basement workroom smelled like that goop, oddly sweet, somewhere between plastic and strawberries, there in the arc-lamp light that fell in long stripes across the old steel autopsying-table. Sometimes I wanted to stay down there and work forever.

He sighed. "What are we going to do, with what we have, just being kids? I don't know who to tell about this. The government would just steal it and nobody'd get anything."

But I was off on a different tangent. "Mr. Jeffries says you can train any cell of the body to do anything, if you just have the right cues for it. Maybe if—"

"Jeffries doesn't know his ass from third base. Useless human. And careless. Lotta supplies in that back room. Spare key to copy, too. Did it the first day of class."

I whistled. "You're a fuckin' samurai at this kinda thing, West. Show me what all else you did."

"Yes." Ed beamed, but his eyes just looked tired. "Yes, I think I am. Now, I can get a rat heart to beat on a microscope slide, but even with the goop it's never for very long..."

And so began the thousand and one nights of Rowley Peters. I got nervous in Bio and Chem classes sometimes, when Edward started to hold forth on certain subjects out loud. One time when Jeffries whacked him in the back of the head, not that hard, for falling asleep in class, I saw murder in West's green eyes. Pure murder. But not right away.

Not until close to the end. At first, he worked harder than anyone I'd ever seen, turning the hobbies of Biology and Genealogy (and every other -ology that went into those three old diaries he never let me read,) into something that felt from the first like the biggest thing I'd ever seen anyone try to do.

It was nice to offload some of that onto Kathy from our class, when she finally manifested. But before and after, that intellectual machine carried me with him almost against my will.

Kathy was a different kind of thorn in my side. They went together like nitro and glycerine, those two. She was tall and leggy and platinum-blonde, with a spiky Punk Rock haircut and engineer boots that went the whole way up. I never met a girl that eminently fuckable who looked that much like she could kick my ass at the same time, not at Arkham.

Kathy was so brilliant she made me feel like a babbling idiot in the same room. West held his own just fine, though. They played one off the other like comedians. It was fun to watch.

I remember the day West first texted her an invite to one of our lab sessions in his Dad's basement. The Bride of Frankenstein showed up in a leather jacket and a man's white wifebeater, and jeans that were held together mostly by the fishnets beneath them. Her boot heels reverberated on the basement stairs, and her eyes grew so full of stars as she began to comprehend what she was looking at.

"Wicked," was all Kathy said at first. "Now show me the rest."

West bowed, his eyes twinkling. "I'll show you everything. We'll start with the heart, the one on the slide. Come in the back."

Kathy looked at him archly, still wandering around glancing at every detail in between, "I come where I like, West. Show me your heart."

I think that was the first time I ever saw Edward West change facial expressions, first turning beet-red, as he strode toward the smeary glass and yellow light of the door to the back room, one eyebrow raising, a vein beating.

"Maybe the heart second. How about you come here, then. Comma please."

Kathy couldn't hide the corkscrew smile that did amazing things to her serpentine mouth, and lit up her own inquisitive eyes with something I knew not to stick around for. "Make me," she murmurred back, as I muttered something at my watch and began making my own way upstairs. By the sounds as I was leaving, quite a bit of equipment was about to get broken, and perhaps a few Commandments as well.

The old West farmhouse sits at the edge of a whole township full of no people, way out in the woods. Starry Wisdom Township's unincorporated, Eddie told me, and nobody's lived back there...much... since the natural-gas people messed the groundwater all up and the government relocated everybody with a fat check.

That meant very few interruptions, when we could make it out there. Meanwhile, his Dad was thrilled to death about all the weeding and mowing and such that West was actually getting me to do while he played with his body parts.

In a week, Ed and Kathy were using a long mat of rattlesnake tissue to regrow flakes of dead skin from someone's feet (neither one of the lovebirds would ever say which,) using the green goop in its ever-dwindling supply from those dusty old Ball jars at the Dunwich farmhouse, to tie the whole process together.

It was tense, even after we finally moved everything out to the old place. Flatworms, also from Bio, were the first organisms that Ed fully resurrected from recent death. He had some success with a toad, but it wouldn't leave the refrigerator, or move much, so reactions and brain activity were hard to gauge. The goop never worked the same way twice on anything.

I don't know if Kathy was jealous of me, and I don't think I was jealous of her. But we all snapped at each other when our methods got extracurricular. When Ed first got brave enough to cowboy his Dad's night-job.

I never asked him about that part, or about how much time he spent memorizing the security setup. I saw the notes, the way he story-boarded out the position of every camera in the building. It wasn't hard to guess the rest. Most of it, of course, I didn't need to.

I remember asking him the obvious, one time when Kathy wasn't over. Looking down at the spasming hand before us in its cookie-tin full of dilute goop, Ed winced with distaste.

"Oh, I wouldn't even know where to get a whole cadaver, not one that you could use." The smile fell out the side of his mouth when he looked over at me, but his eyes were horrified.

"Could you imagine?"

It seems funny now. Even when I first saw the old Herbert West place outside Dunwich, it looked like Ed had cleared it out and been coming there for a long time. A lot longer than he even let on.

Some of the smaller skulls in his shadowboxes full of specimens were falling apart with age. I found an English paper from sixth grade with his name on it, holding down the inside of a drawer full of hemostats and clamps. The blood on the paper looked faded. Some of the other stuff wasn't exactly blood.

When he let stuff slip, just like everything else he did, West went full-bore. "My Dad got real drunk one night," he said, as if reading my very thoughts, when I came back in the room that afternoon. "Told me that Great-Uncle Herbie figured out how to raise the dead. Which was why they killed him and rode him out of town on a rail, or whatever really happened."

One of the dishes of undifferentiated snake tissue had gone over, and the stink was like nothing I'd ever smelled. Ed was making an incinerator-tray of that and several other things from the cooler. "It's not hard to duplicate. He did it in the Twenties, for fuck's sake. He barely had any idea what he was doing, just got lucky and knew who to read..."

And on. I tuned him out a lot, when he was talking in one long sentence like that. I wish I would have tuned Ed out a lot less. But what can you do? What can anyone?

I'm back here now at the old farmhouse. No one's come, long enough for me to chill out and get a little of my head back. These woods are ugly, dark and deep. On the way here, I heard...things... and

I started coming apart out there, on the long nameless road past that big windy old Puritan graveyard where you can see forever, the stones and moss on everything, marching out to the fogline in the trees.

Monumental ruins. Lost in the grass. I had to find the path made of headstones, and the one little baby stone that didn't match, just at the end, the green veins in the sandstone and the way the earth dipped under the dirt.

I had to find all the graves with new scratches, down the steps my legs could barely descend. Every stone in the necropolis was crumbling, and the oldest had lost their very shape.

It felt so easy to fall, though I'd never say out loud how broken I was. The long path of headstones repeated the death.

Everywhere I turned looked like No Way Back, not moving in any direction; just turning, losing the sense of why I'd come.

I had to trudge back out here and look at the Paupers' Field just over the hill, and all the empty houses in the empty whistling woods beyond it. All the trailers that aren't even all the way cleared out, sometimes with stereos and furniture and great big bags of that methamphetamine like ground-up glass sitting on stained counters where the dishes haven't been done from the night before, forever.

I had to remember. In sequence. No matter how I cried. Or screamed.

To remember the old wino who went bad. Who undoubtedly had a name, and relatives somewhere on Earth. The one Kathy found, who died in her arms.

When she drove the wino out to Dunwich in her Mom's Jetta and they injected him, his eyes turned black and he started puking blood clots everywhere. We just left him back out on the street.

He was dying when she found him, and Ed skin-popped him in one arm with the goop, and it was just. Just. It was. We had to go. He fell apart fast.

Fast.

For a short while, we watched the Obituaries, waiting for fresh sample. Ed tuned us into a police scanner frequency to which he wasn't supposed to have laptop access, once more courtesy of Dear Old Absentee Dad. The first time we ever got there before the cops did, the newly/formerly-DOA drunk driver opened his eyes and screamed a midnight confession at both of us before vapor-locking into a petrified shell forever. He'd crashed his Celica in the Baptist graveyard out on Loop Road. Funny.

But Ed was elated. "Almost fresh enough, that time," he observed when we'd caught our breath from running, a few minutes after the bubblegum lights began to finally approach in the distance. The insulin-syringe in Ed's hand was drained dry.

"How much of him was left? You gotta figure that the brain..."

Ed fumed. "Soul's not in the brain, dickweed. There is no soul!" Floodlights on the pinwheels, like West's eyes made their own mad-scientist light, brighter than the lights of the cops on our cold trail. "It's just electrochemical. And I can prove it. I tell you. I've seen it...."

I snorted. "What? You've been dead?"

"No, but..."

And on. The next day at school, there were vague announcements about vandalism, and lectures from certain teachers about the sanctity of public parks and such, and Did You Hear About It On The News, and No Respect For The Dead...

The beginning was the end. That night, when we went down to the school for a bit more potassium cyanide and a fresh slew of glassware, it felt wrong as soon as we disabled the alarm. Ed and Kathy had been hard at 'research' the night before, and he was bleary-eyed and covered in hickeys. He said he had to piss, and to just go on ahead.

And when I opened the storeroom door, I heard a click. A big one. A Ruger, .44 mag. In my nose. A fist, a forearm, looped around the back of my neck. Aqua di Gio cologne, what Kathy called Eau de Chem Lab. A throbbing little hard-on that was the least threatening part of Mr. Jeffries.

"Thieves," he hissed. "You think we don't keep inventory here? Get on your knees." His face was as red as it got during lunch. And at the moment, he was just plain old Drunk As Shit. "I could have the police down here right now and you'd be locked up until the end of time, Peters. Now come here and do as you're told."

I was right there. But I was starting to get the idea. And I saw something else that made me pretend to comply.

"It's all right," I heard myself whisper. "I'll do it. You don't have to force me."

His eyes changed. "Oh. You're like that other kid. Well, then, this is Extra Credit."

The gun went down. His breathing changed, too, and as I dipped and began to kneel, he unbuttoned his pants and the paperweight from his own desk rose behind him in the darkness like a good magic trick, going upside his head with a dull little meaty sound that was probably louder from the inside. Edward dropped it at the top of the swing and it fell in the wastebasket.

Without even thinking, I had my hoodie off and was wrapping it up and wiping the can down before Jeffries' body hit the floor. "You're welcome," Edward West told me flatly. "Now get his legs."

And God help me, I did.

I'm back here now. Back at the old place. Waiting for the boiled-looking, lurching, red-faced thing that smells like shit and old clothes and foul sweat, like somone in a closed room about to rot. Waiting to see its little black eyes, the blood and plant-matter on its skin.

Mr. Jeffries is calling to me now. I hear him out there, in the rain, not in words or pictures. But inside. He says I'm changing too. Like him. It has to hurt at first, and it will always hurt more. But I'll get used to it more, too.

He got inside my head somehow when he showed up at Edward's house with part of Edward's Dad in his hands, and then West disappeared, just ran off somewhere and said nothing.

When I looked at the thing that had been John Jeffries, I understood what he was Becoming, even all the parts where the embalming fluid and the goop were still leaking or the ties didn't quite bind.

When my formerly-living Chem teacher shot me point-blank at center mass, surprise was the furthest thing from my mind, and a full syringe was the closest thing to my hand.

I could feel the vein jumping in my neck. There was one more syringe, also full. One. One for the one who got unceremoniously dumped in the living-room when Mr. Jeffries kicked down the door, earlier. He'd been...at her.

But maybe there could be several kinds of repairs. I wasn't sure if any of it would work. I was ready to walk away. I could hear him almost figuring it out. Almost finding me.

I began to scream as I changed. I couldn't hold still. I wanted to stop hurting. I wanted to eat. And drink. And howl.

But when it came up and touched my cheek, Kathy's hand was warm, and it didn't feel like a vise-grip at all.

"Rrrrrowlllleeyyy...." she slurred in a spacey, groggy voice. Her eyes were like mine now. I helped her to her feet.

"All I can see is light," Kathy whispered. "I was going Home. Why didn't you let me go h—"

"Eddie," I reminded her. She took me in, her expression changing at the sight of my eyes, my pallor, the things my muscles were starting to do. "And there might be others besides..."

"Yeahhhh...." Kathy got it. I shut up, not wanting to tell how many others I'd felt nearby in the long period when the goop was starting to work.

How much more on-call help Edward Robert West had for miles, this whole time. And how long that on-call help had waited. Ridge-runners and stump-jumpers. For miles. This whole time. Those weird Starry Wisdom hillfolk who look like debased Amish and don't talk to anybody....

He called them and they came, and they brought him pieces. All different. I saw some of them in process, you might say. Out in the woods. In between. They talk. I had nothing else to do but listen.

But I never told her what else his minions many and various were discussing outside, on their way through the front forty.

"Go upstairs and wait," I managed. "Get a blanket and curl up. Won't be long." I started looking for weapons, hoping she'd come back down of her own accord when Shit Got Real. Not If. When.

"Okay," Kathy breathed, lurching back upstairs toward the couch.

That was four hours ago. Now pain is the world. I don't have anywhere to run.

Lights flickering, I am so sorry, Kathy. I knew it wouldn't be long. He's here. He's... Well, he was dead. He is here. For he has risen. His hands precede him. All his local hands.

So many, now. Too many. Lights out. Listen. Hear the storm?

Tiny sounds, but sounds. Crawling through these cracks, orphans, lobotomies, who want everything. The silent whitewashed horde are taking apart the front wall, brick by brick—

Out on the walk,

dear God what is out on the front walk—

Coming down the walk

A smile splits the open dark ditches of Edward's face

**

Sacred to the Memory of Kathy Acker

Afterword

Before Lovecraft, before Cthulhu, there was The Reanimator

At least, that's how it was for me.

My first taste of anything Lovecraft happened in my early teens, watching late-night cable TV long after my mother would have approved. It was on HBO so all the good stuff was still intact, a fact I was about to be very grateful for. I stumbled upon this movie during the scene where Herbert West and his hesitant assistant were in the morgue, dealing with a very angry, Arnold Schwarzenegger-sized reanimated corpse, and the sheer audacity of it all, the energy, humor, and over the top gore, sunk their hooks deep into me. I couldn't look away. What followed: the shovel decapitation, the now headless but still talking dead doctor with mind control powers, the exquisitely bad taste of the head giving head scene, the final rampage in the Miskatonic Medical School morgue, and more made sure my eyes stayed glued to the tube. And when it was over, I wanted more.

I immediately jumped to the cable guide to see what it was I had just watched and when it would be on next. I had to know how all the awesome I had just witnessed started, and to see all that amazing, mind-blowing stuff again. And again. And again. I binged on Re-animator, I watched it every time I could. I wanted to be as smart, funny, and cool under fire as Herbert West, and well, I just wanted the blonde bombshell that was actress Barbara Crampton. I must have watched that movie a half dozen times in a month before HBO took it off the rotation.

But I still wanted more.

The first story I read by H.P. Lovecraft was "Herbert West: Reanimator." Three guesses as to why. And while the serialized story had little in common with the movie I had grown to love, and the literary Dr. West was described looking nothing like the Herbert West I had in my head thanks to film, it won me over on its own merits. In many ways, it was far more audacious than the movie. Herbert West, while being a horror movie icon thanks to the excellent acting of Jeffrey Combs, was far more a complete character in the Lovecraft story, not to mention much more frightening in his single-minded obsession. It was a far grander tale, set over years rather than the weeks in the movie, and the action didn't stay confined to good ol' Miskatonic University.

So naturally, after watching the movie and reading the story, I had to get more of this Lovecraft fellow. I mean, if everything he wrote was like "Herbert West: Reanimator" I knew I was going to love the guy.

Well pretty much nothing else he ever did was like "Herbert West: Reanimator." It wasn't one of his stories that would later be grouped together under the title Cthulhu Mythos. It wasn't one of his fanciful dreamlands tales. It wasn't one of his works of Poe-like horror. It might have some kinship with his dark science stories, like "Cool Air," but even then they were third cousins at best. Yet I ended up becoming addicted to the writings of Lovecraft in spite of that and I could not think of a surer testament to the strength of H.P.L.'s voice and vision.

The now decades-long love affair I've had with the cold, cosmic horrors of H.P. Lovecraft started off with a brilliant weirdo looking to conquer death. So when Pete Rawlik approached me with the idea to do this book to not only celebrate one of Lovecraft's most popular characters, but the 30th anniversary of the movie that set me on the path to loving Lovecraft, I jumped at the chance. After all, Herbert West is too cool to be confined to one story – no matter how many parts it had – and three movies. Like the good doctor's experiments, Herbert West has taken on a life of his own and just won't stay dead no matter what happens to him. There is still a lot of life in them old bones yet.

We hope you enjoyed your time with this book and were able to get to know the esteemed Dr. Herbert West a little better. For all involved, The Legacy of the Reanimator was as much a labor of love as anything else. Years in the making, it is a combination of twenty distinct voices, all coming together in a cadaverous chorus to sing the praises of one of H.P. Lovecraft's most beloved characters. Whether it's on the printed page, the silver screen, or now on the stage in a musical, there's just no stopping the Reanimator. His legacy is a long one, and I'm positive this is only the beginning of it.

— Brian M. Sammons